BIG COVER STORY

BIG COVER STORY

JEFF SYKES

Copyright © 2026 by Jeff Sykes
Cover design by Jackie Whitt.
All rights reserved. No part of this book may be reproduced in any manner whatsoever without written permission except in the case of brief quotations embodied in critical articles and reviews. This book is a work of fiction. The characters are imaginary, and any resemblance to actual persons is unintended. First Printing, 2026

For Sharon and Deena. For Eric and the others. I heard you.

Bingham Park, 1972

A kickball, faded red and scuffed to the skin, bobbed at the bottom of the slope, nudged downhill by the crooked geometry of play. The girl, small and narrow-shouldered, followed it at a half-run, her bare feet drumming Bingham Park's grass. Her name floated in the air behind her, rising from the lips of a mother who could no longer see her from the porch.

"Goldie!"

The voice came again, sharper now, like it had to cut through more than just distance. Through time, maybe. Or something harmful. But the girl didn't stop. She moved with the purpose children have. The ball had rolled just past the slope's end, where the grass thinned and the ditch began to yawn open like a split in the earth.

The creek made no sound, not like water ought to. It moved like syrup forgotten in the sun, and its color shifted with the light. Mud brown at the banks, but strange in the middle. A pulse of violet-blue beneath the film, then a pale shimmer, greenish and iridescent, like the belly of a fish turned wrong side up.

The ball drifted in the shallows, caught in a curl of reeds. Goldie crouched at the edge, her knees digging into the wet clay, and leaned forward. The surface rippled around the ball, breaking into silent whorls. The water caught the last amber flicker of day and fractured it. She saw red, gold, something like flame. It was beautiful. Too beautiful.

She reached out but didn't touch the ball. Her fingers hovered above the surface, close enough to feel the heat rise, not warm like summer water, but fevered, like something living underground. The colors danced. It looked like glass melting. It looked like magic.

Behind her, the call came again, sharper this time.

"Goldie. You get away from there, now!"

The girl flinched, her gaze breaking. She stood, sudden and direct, the knees of her jeans soaked dark. The ball slipped its perch and began drifting downstream, caught in a current she hadn't noticed.

She turned and walked back uphill, the grass brushing her ankles. When she reached the crest, she looked back. The water still glowed in the near-dark, holding color long after the sun was gone.

Before it was Bingham Park, it was a scrap of pastureland at the city limit's edge. The ground was sloped. Red clay and full of rocks that wouldn't turn and runoff that drained into a small creek. South of a railroad line that cut the growing city in half. A cemetery took up the level land below a nine-block neighborhood, serene in the early 1920s. In the boomtime of the mid-20s, the city fathers decided to put an incinerator for the city's industrial waste below the cemetery. Perched just before the ground fell away toward the creek, the incinerator fed a 13-acre landfill that stretched to the water's edge. It pumped smoke into the air and toxic waste into the ground until 1955.

More than 300 people gathered at a school house in 1922 to protest the incinerator site. Newspaper articles described the mood as "indignant" and a reporter wrote that "the women are greatly opposed to the council's plans, and resolved to do all they can to have the proposed site changed." In 1953, they laid pipe to drain industrial runoff from the east-side plants into a culvert that ran just beyond the park's property line. The pipe gurgled and steamed and sometimes coughed up a thick black residue that dried into flakes. People stopped letting their kids play too close. They stopped complaining. Complaints had a way of turning into citations.

Despite the garbage and growing toxicity, the neighborhoods around the incinerator site, Cottage Grove, Morningside Homes, grew to become vibrant working class areas for the city's black residents. The landfill sat idle after 1955, but the damage was done. Ash, molten metal, glass and brick formed a substrate beneath whatever grass had the temerity to grow.

Following the turbulence of the late 1960s, city planners decided to build a park atop this toxic swirl of municipal detritus. A single basketball court was poured, crooked and shallow, with no net on the hoop and a permanent puddle in the southwest corner. A swing set came later, the kind that creaked under a child's weight. Grass was seeded once and never reseeded. And still, people came. Children climbed rusted monkey bars toward some possible horizon. Sunday picnics rose up with folding chairs and deviled eggs. Men played cards under the picnic shelter while their grandsons threw rocks in the ditch.

The city named the park after William James Bingham, a slaver from Orange County. No one really knew why. A new sign was erected. A ribbon was cut. A photographer came. And then nothing. The park went back to being what it had always been: a buffer zone between the people who lived too close to the factories and the people who never had to notice.

By the time Goldie was a child in the early seventies, Bingham Park had hardened into a kind of urban ruin. It held what the city refused to see. Beneath the slide, beneath the picnic shelter, beneath the inch-thick patch of kudzu that climbed the fence posts in summer, there were stories laid down like sediment:

kids with rashes that wouldn't clear, coughs that started in spring and stayed through winter, a dog that licked from the creek and died inside a week.

No one mapped it. No one warned them. It was just a park. It was just there. And still Goldie came. Because it was theirs. Because the other parks were miles away and didn't want her kind anyhow. Because even poisoned ground can grow memory. Because her brother had his first kiss behind the jungle gym and her cousin learned to cartwheel beside the busted water fountain and on Sundays, if the breeze was right, you could pretend the smell came from trees and not the waste below.

She knew the ground was strange. But she also knew it remembered her. And when you grow up in a place like that, remembering is half the battle.

Part One

1

Alan Ransome stepped over the jagged rise where the pavement buckled near the old swing set. Beneath his shoes, the surface gave a soft, rubbery yield—remnants of safety poured over poison. Bingham Park had once been padded with promises. Now it blistered in silence. Rusted bolts protruded from the climbing bars, their caps long gone, leaving metal teeth for ghosts to climb. Goldie Hayes was already ahead, her pace clipped, chin tucked down the way people walk when they know they're being watched.

The smell was precise. Decomposed foam, sun-soured plastic, and the mineral scent of something unnatural in the dirt. It was the smell of every neglected playground, but more determined. A child's plastic sandal lay on its side near the edge of the basketball court, cracked at the heel, its strap melted into the concrete. No one had played here in years. Yet the court still held a faint arc of paint along the three-point line, like the memory of motion refusing to fade.

"They cut down the maples," Goldie said. She didn't look at him. "Said the roots were interfering with drainage." She let that sit a moment. "Roots. That's what they said."

Alan pulled the folded map from his coat pocket. The paper had a waxy stiffness, like it was salvaged from a drawer not meant to be opened. The red circle burned through the crease.

Beyond the playground, the creek ran in a narrow artery between two chain-link fences. Someone had tied a stuffed animal—a sun-bleached bear with no arms—to one post. Below it, spray paint flared out in a nervous spiral. Goldie slowed beside the bear and touched its side gently, like it might still feel pain.

"They dumped slag down there in '64. My uncle worked the cleanup crew. Said it glowed sometimes."

Alan could see it clearly, though he hadn't been there. Gloved hands shoveling gravel and ash into the shallow water, laughing, coughing, lighting cigarettes to kill the smell. It always came back to this: men doing jobs too dangerous to question and too poor to refuse.

"I need soil data," he said. "From the creekbed. From the mulch layer here."

Goldie raised an eyebrow but said nothing. She watched a squirrel leap from the broken jungle gym and vanish into the kudzu along the lot line. It was not the kind of silence that needed filling.

Alan moved to the base of the slide, crouched, peeled back a strip of artificial turf. Underneath, the soil was dense and dark. Claylike. Laced with a thread of deep red that ran parallel to the slope, a secret trying to rise to the surface. He didn't touch it. He just looked, and thought of blood held beneath skin, the kind that pools from impact before it bursts.

They were there because no one else would come. Because the city had stopped returning emails and the public hearings had devolved into slide decks and euphemisms, each one smoother than the last. Because Goldie's neighbor's boy, Devin, started coughing blood last fall and the clinic blamed mold, blamed diet, blamed everything except what was buried in the soil his sneakers touched every morning.

They weren't there to reminisce. The past didn't need witnesses. It needed unearthing. Goldie had called him after the third neighborhood kid was diagnosed with anemia. She'd said only this: "You remember the red stuff that seeps when it rains? It's back." So Alan came with his boots and his notebook and a brittle hope that the thing could still be documented, that evidence might still bring consequence.

They were there because Bingham Park had been "closed for improvements" for twelve years, and the only thing that had improved was the city's press kit. Because at the edge of downtown, a mile away, a parcel behind the redevelopment zone had been scrubbed from public brownfield maps and resurfaced with playground renderings that looked like design fiction. Because the red sand at Bingham Park wasn't just showing up again. It was spreading, like a memory refusing to stay buried.

A boy's bicycle tires whipped over the fractured concrete, spokes catching light in slivers as he coasted the street along the park perimeter. He didn't look in, just kept his eyes ahead, as if the instinct had already rooted in him not to stare too long at broken things. His handlebars dipped slightly with the uneven grade, and he stood on the pedals to right himself with the grace of someone who'd learned to move through neglect. Alan watched him pass, the small body upright, determined, carefree in the way children are before they're taught what's heavy.

The gate hung crooked, as if pulled once with intent and then forgotten. A rusted sign dangled from the chain-link: "Closed for Improvements – 2004." The font chosen to inspire confidence. Bold sans-serif, kelly green on white. Now it was freckled with orange bleed and moss at the corners. The coating had peeled, curling upward like a snarl. Wind nudged it against the metal and it clacked as if knocking to see if memory still lived here.

There had been no improvements. Only time, and what twelve years had allowed to fester.

Goldie kicked a splinter of playground bark off her boot and motioned toward the crumbling picnic shelter, its roof warped by the sun.

"They said we'd have shade canopies," she said. "Native plants. Shit for pollinators." She laughed, but the sound had no curve to it. "All we got is a neglected sign."

She folded her arms, fingers tucked into the elbows like she was holding herself back. Her eyes scanned across the broken park, noting what was gone, what had never come, what had been promised in meetings with sign-up sheets and name tags and boxed lunches. Goldie had been at every one. Sat through every slideshow that labeled her neighborhood a "transitional opportunity zone." She'd asked about the chromium then. Got nods. Got a "we'll follow up." Got silence.

"You know what I keep thinking?" she said, turning to Alan. "That they're waiting for the last of us to move or die. Then they don't have to answer no more questions. No more names."

Alan opened his mouth, then didn't. Because what could he say? That she was wrong?

"My grandson used to run through here barefoot," she went on. "Back before we knew better. Before his asthma got so bad we couldn't keep him in school more than three days a week." She didn't soften when she said it. Her voice didn't rise. That wasn't how Goldie worked. She carried her anger like a brick in her palm. Solid, ready, but never thrown.

"I'm not asking for a miracle," she said. "I just want them to admit what they did. Put it in ink. Put it in court if they've got to. But say it out loud."

She crouched then, digging her fingers into a patch of exposed dirt near the monkey bars, the nails of her left hand coming back black. She rubbed the soil between her thumb and first knuckle. Smelled it. Held it up.

"This ain't just dirt, Alan. This is what they think of us."

Alan's tires thumped into the seam where Bingham's side streets met the repaved artery of South English, the patch job clean enough to be cosmetic, asphalt laid down like a fresh coat over bruises. He adjusted the rearview to catch the park fence receding and then it was gone, tucked behind a row of half-renovated bungalows and a Baptist church turned community pantry.

The light at Gate City Boulevard stayed red. He watched a man in a stained tank top push a stroller with no child in it, a pack of toilet paper balanced where a toddler should've been. Next to the curb, a payday loan billboard frayed in the corners: "Solutions Today. Security Tomorrow." Behind it, a mural faded under years of sun—three children holding hands, their outlines cracked open at the wrists.

Downtown appeared with its polish. Boutique signage block by block, each window dressed with modern light and neutral-toned merchandise: a plant store where the auto parts place had been, a kombucha taproom with chalkboard pricing and a tip jar that read "Mutual Aid." The boulevard narrowed near the main intersection at Elm, and Alan let the car idle as pedestrians jogged across in yoga pants and branded lanyards, phones to ears, dogs on leashes.

He looked left to the health corridor anchor site, sanitized former industrial areas cleared and graded and under construction. A "wellness corridor" they called it. The signage read "The South Elm Wellness and Innovation Corridor: A Place for Healing and Art."

Then the street gave way to the outer campus, where the sidewalks widened and the benches were sponsored. The university's banner slogan stretched across a pedestrian bridge: "Ideas That Matter." Alan parked in the faculty lot behind the behavioral sciences building, his pass still swinging from the mirror on a frayed blue lanyard.

Before he turned off the engine, he sat for a moment with the AC running, watching the movement of students along the path—laughing, shoulder-bumping, insulated by the soundproof of headphones and ample time. He reached over to the passenger seat and touched the map without opening it. The paper still held the warmth of the park's sun. He pressed his thumb into the red circle through the paper. It left no dent.

Everything inside his building moved in a predictable choreography. Light from the transom cast a pale strip across the floor, broken by shadows of passing figures. The sound of students rehearsing presentations under their breath, a printer jamming three doors down, the uneven footsteps of a colleague with a bad hip. Through the window at the end of the hallway, sunlight struck the glass at an angle that turned everything behind it vaguely golden—trees, bike racks, students sprawled on the quad with laptops and takeout containers. From up here, it looked like a catalog version of a university. A place built on purpose.

His office, by contrast, was narrow and warm with stale air. The mini fan on the filing cabinet clicked every six seconds, a mechanical stutter he'd grown too tired to fix. The scent of dust mingled with coffee gone cold in an unwashed mug, and the heat from his desktop monitor made the corner nearest the wall feel like a sauna. His inbox overflowed with two missed messages from Facilities, a follow-up from a senior about summer housing insecurity research, three separate grant foundations asking for budget revisions. The day had pressed on without asking how he felt about any of it.

Alan sank into the chair. His lower back objected with a dull complaint. He pulled open the drawer where he kept hard copies of applications, his fingers moving across thick folders, most of them with coded labels: "CP-23, SCSY-PropB, HornMemo." His hands had a practiced rhythm, as if he'd done this enough times to understand the futility and keep going.

It was the same last week when he first saw it. The manila envelope, slightly smaller than the rest, unsealed. It lay beneath a stack of printer paper. The flap not even folded shut.

Inside: a single sheet. A photocopied city planning map, stamped in one corner with the seal from 1994. The grid was familiar—south of downtown, the hospital's wellness corridor project, the adjacent lots once belonging to the rail line. But one parcel near the South Connector was circled in red ink, the line drawn in a way that looked almost thoughtful.

Alan sat back. The fan ticked again behind him. Outside, a lawn mower fired up with a ragged burst. Someone's music thumped through headphones—low bass, wordless.

He held the map at arm's length, as if more distance would help it make sense. But the red ink bled slightly into the paper fibers, and he found himself staring at that spread, like a wound left too long under gauze.

He didn't know what it meant. Only that someone wanted him to see it.

Alan held the paper with both hands, thumbs pressed into the corners like steadying a fragile thing. The map was city-standard: grayscale, plotted in grid units, the kind used in zoning meetings and budget hearings. Parcel numbers ran like veins across the page—little squares of language meant for developers, not people. The red circle disrupted it. Just one loop, precise, as if drawn with a compass-guided hand.

His eyes scanned the surrounding landmarks—Bragg Street, the southern flank of the hospital project, the vertical rail spur long out of use but never decommissioned. And there it was: Parcel

524-B. Circled. Positioned just behind the expansion's new wellness wing, tucked between two properties now merged into the corporate tract. At first glance, nothing about it screamed significance. It was anonymous in the way dangerous things often were.

The stamp in the corner—1994—made his jaw clench. That year had surfaced before. In a memo buried two levels deep in the redevelopment filings, a brief mention of a land transfer to a legacy trust with no employees, no address, no web presence. He'd flagged it and moved on. Too much noise to chase every whisper.

But this wasn't noise. This was placed.

He stood, as if his body had decided before he had, and walked to the window overlooking the quad. From here, the campus looked bright and unfinished, like an architectural rendering, all clean angles and strategic foliage. A group of undergrads tossed a frisbee near the sociology building. Laughter carried, the kind that used to lift him before it started sounding like distance.

Behind the laughter was the timeline of his own work—the lectures, the symposia, the policy white papers—and now, this circle. This piece of archival debris, slipped into his life as if whispered through a crack in the wall. Someone had sent him this. Someone who knew where he sat and what he'd recognize. And someone who understood how maps lie: by omission.

Alan turned back to his desk, laid the sheet flat, and smoothed it with his palm. The red ink flared against the dull paper. He couldn't shake the feeling that this was something he'd been trying not to remember.

For a long time, Alan had believed his life could be charted in concentric circles—education as escape, research as return, justice as geometry. That there was a moral elegance in systems, a kind of symmetry to doing things the right way. He had been the child who filed his father's pay stubs in shoeboxes by date. The teenager who corrected history teachers under his breath. At UNC, he memorized the Clean Water Act like scripture and carried a copy of Pedagogy of the Oppressed in his coat pocket. He thought information could displace injustice. That knowing was the first step toward repair.

He had met Paula in a seminar room with yellow walls and broken blinds, where the professor spoke of Foucault but Paula wrote about women in cages. She had a stillness to her. Alan had never seen anyone think so quietly. They shared photocopies, bitter coffee, a language. He walked her home once after a lecture on redlining, both of them still shaking from what had been said, what hadn't. She'd touched his forearm at the crosswalk and asked if he really believed cities could be healed. He had answered yes too quickly.

He loved her handwriting as much as he loved her laugh. The loops of her lowercase "f" carried something secret in them. In his notebooks, he copied her phrases to remember them. She read Audre Lorde out loud to him once in the dim corners of the student union, voice urgent, careful. When she left the room, her presence stayed like breath fogged on glass.

David Moss, when he arrived, did not move slowly. David made decisions as if time itself bowed to him. He stood straighter. Spoke cleaner. Smiled with self-assurance, as if he'd always been smiled at. He laughed at Alan's books. He called theory "cute." He wore Paula's attention like a tailored suit, nevermind what it covered. When she chose David over Alan, it was not cruel. It was devastating in how reasonable it seemed. As if this was always the shape things took—light bending toward certainty, not truth.

Alan lost whole months to the wound. He forgot deadlines. His body changed shape—took on weight he didn't feel until he tried on last year's shirt and couldn't close the collar. His advisors called it adjustment. He called it displacement. He watched them from across campus, Paula and David, walking in stride with each other through the quad. She never looked unhappy. That was the worst of it. Her stillness remained, just not his to orbit.

In the years that followed, he took jobs that aligned with what he believed and watched those beliefs grow narrower under funding constraints and timelines. He became strategic. He used the word "impact" more than he meant to. He taught classes where students nodded and took notes and left unchanged. At night, he would sometimes take out the old photocopied pages from Pedagogy of the Oppressed, edges curled, notes in Paula's hand—Who gets to decide repair? written in the margin. He never answered it.

Even now, when the wind caught the scent of something burnt and civic—paint thinner, asphalt warmed past tolerance—he thought of her. Of the silence after she left. A redirection. A gradual turn of light.

Alan barely noticed the silence. He had found his people—students who stayed after lectures to argue about housing ordinances, who passed bootleg copies of Adorno and Naomi Klein like contraband, who spoke in the language of change with the desperation of those who needed it. He began volunteering in the east side neighborhoods, attending city council meetings with his notebook open and pen twitching.

He filled his days with policy briefs, late-night research sessions, case studies from cities he'd never visit. He took an unpaid internship with the Greensboro Housing Coalition, commuting by bus every Saturday from Chapel Hill to shadow a field coordinator who spoke in footnotes and carried two sets of keys. They mapped eviction hotspots by hand, made phone calls to landlords who never answered, walked sidewalks with tenants whose leases were written in disappearing ink.

In the spaces where feeling had once lived, Alan built a new architecture: zoning language, census data, parcel histories, floodplain overlays. He became the student who always stayed after class—not to talk, but to work. He ran regression models in the lab late at night, chasing correlations between vacancy rates and asthma clusters, between absentee ownership and code violations.

His advisor noticed. Pushed him toward conference presentations, then co-authored articles, then grants. One thing followed the next, as it always did when grief dressed itself in achievement. By the time he finished his graduate degree, he had already been offered a position back in Greensboro—teaching urban systems, consulting on housing reports, sitting in on municipal subcommittees where decisions were made behind PowerPoint decks.

He moved into a modest apartment off Walker Avenue and bought blackout curtains. He told himself this was the work. That justice required the numbing. That no good came from carrying heartbreak where data belonged.

Only sometimes, in meetings where someone used the word revitalize, or when a tenant cried over the loss of a stove they didn't own, he would feel a slight softening inside. Just memory: of her voice, quiet and precise; of the way she'd once asked if he really believed cities could be healed. He still wanted to say yes. But now, the answer had to pass through codebooks, grant applications, and the weight of accumulated knowing.

So he stayed. In Greensboro. In the same university where he'd once lectured in borrowed rooms and now kept an office with a ticking fan. He stayed out of unfinishedness. Because the problems were local. Tangible. Because the soil still told the truth, even if the funding didn't. Because people like Goldie kept showing up to meetings with manila folders full of names no one had bothered to record. Because truth, when you could find it, still shimmered like a sliver of light through contaminated glass.

But what he wouldn't admit—what he carried in the drag of his posture and the tightness in his jaw—was that he'd begun to feel the edge of it. The entropy of meaning. His lectures still filled seats, but the students came for bullet points and action items. He'd become a curator of disillusionment, charting the failures of urban renewal and environmental neglect like a pathologist. And still, somewhere beneath all of it, he wanted to believe there was a prism buried in the void. That if you held the right angle to the light, you could still see color. Truth fractured into clarity.

He took the map from his coat pocket and spread it on the desk. The red circle pulsed now, as if the ink remembered something. There was a name for this feeling, he thought—the moment when the familiar slips, when a page becomes a portal.

Instead, he folded the paper into quarters and slipped it into the file marked Wellness Corridor – alt zones. As he reached to close the drawer, there was a knock at the door—sharp, apologetic.

"Professor Ransome?"

He turned. Ava, his new graduate assistant, stood in the hallway, backpack half-zipped, a nervous smile already forming.

Alan straightened in his chair and gestured for her to come in, but his mind lingered for one more instant on the corner of the map, the faint bleed of red into the crease.

He didn't yet see the color in the beam. Only the outline of a question he'd yet to ask.

2

The ballroom sparkled. Light traced the molding, gold against cream, catching the crystal of the chandeliers before resting on the glassware, the florals, the lacquered faces leaning in over linen-covered tables. Everything gleamed on purpose. The centerpieces arranged for height and symmetry. Music hovered at the edge of ambient, instrumental and unspecific. Waitstaff glided between huddled circles of donors, their trays balanced with shrimp skewers and champagne flutes that caught the light.

Paula Moss moved through the space as if it had always been. Blue silk shaped her at the waist and fell clean to the floor, her shoulders bare but held without tension. The dress David had chosen—no, suggested—weeks before, casually, while scrolling through photos from their last benefit in Charleston. "You know the one that matched the Delft," he'd said. "That hue does something." And it did. It did exactly what it was supposed to: cooled her, elevated her, polished her into the kind of presence that could be admired without being questioned. Each step drew attention without needing to earn it. Her mouth held a smile made for photographs, her chestnut eyes soft but alert. She carried a glass of still water in one hand now and a program in the other, each balanced without thought. Her presence signaled fluency.

She paused beside the auction table, where a silent bid sheet sat beside a weekend in Asheville and a private tour of the new wellness corridor. A woman in gold sequins leaned in to whisper something about city permits and Paula nodded, attentive, her fingers grazing the rim of her glass with the intimacy of a pianist holding a final note.

Paula's expression didn't falter. Not when a camera flash went off to her left. Not when a board member brushed her shoulder in passing. Not when her own name was mispronounced by a city planner's wife who'd had too much rosé. She existed in these rooms as if born to them—unflinching, exquisitely vague, the perfect convergence of manners and memory.

She hadn't eaten. The wine earlier slid through her steadily, and she welcomed its blur. Her heels were three and a half inches, though she preferred two. The clutch she carried was bone-colored leather, empty except for a lipstick, a folded agenda, and a slip of paper she had not yet thrown away: Alan's most recent op-ed, printed from the Observer, creased at the spine. She had read it that morning in the kitchen, the sunlight growing and impolite. The language was spare. Precise. It hadn't asked for her attention, but it held it anyway.

Someone called her name. She turned, the smile rising again—soft, maternal, almost democratic.

Behind the mask of light and fabric and charm, her thoughts moved business like. The room smelled of overwatered orchids and Mary Kay. The speakers hissed at the upper frequencies. The white lights above the stage flickered briefly, as if about to surrender.

She had been perfect for too long. She knew this. And still, she continued—across the floor, past the tables marked by foundation names, toward David's voice. The color blue held. She moved through it.

She had been seventeen the night of her debutante ball. The Piedmont Club, seed pearls sewn into satin, white gloves so tight they left marks. She'd descended marble stairs with her cousin

James while orchestra music swelled and older women watched with approving eyes. Her mother had said it then, in the car ride home: "It's not about being beautiful. It's about making people believe you belong."

Paula had learned everything that night. How to hold discomfort until it softened. How to stand so still the room bent around her. How to vanish without ever leaving.

In college, that training followed her like a soft hand at her back. She knew how to enter a room already in conversation, how to make a professor lean forward, how to answer with just enough hesitation to seem humbled by it.

Alan Ransome had been different. Earnest in a way she hadn't known was allowed. He asked questions and waited for answers. He made her want to confess things—half-thoughts, quiet doubts. With him, she felt unfinished in a way that thrilled her.

Then David returned. MBA program, new haircut, business cards already printed. He didn't ask questions—he made assessments. He offered placement. And she'd chosen him not in a moment of betrayal, but in a quiet alignment of expectations. The version of herself Alan had seen—hopeful, unfinished—was too fragile for what lay ahead.

Paula paused to greet the director of neurology, kissed the cheek of Councilwoman Lynn Hoffman who smelled of powder and citrus. Her voice adjusted by degrees—warmer here, more clipped there—each conversation ending before it could overstay its welcome. At the silent auction table, she wrote her name next to a framed landscape and didn't read the title.

From the stage, David's voice lifted above the crowd with ease. He spoke about transformation, about public trust, about the future. Laughter followed one of his lines, light jokes laced with policy terms, charisma stretched over a calculus of outcomes. His approval moved across the room with her in the form of silent attention.

She had learned long ago to keep her face still in moments like this. Stillness made people feel safe. Her gaze passed over the crowd, pausing at the back table where the mayor sat with a developer who once called Paula immaculate. Beyond them, a younger man in a borrowed blazer kept adjusting his tie. One of the interns, probably. Already learning how to dress as if lineage could be bought.

David had risen fast through the hospital's nonprofit wing, first as a consultant, then a strategist, now something broader and more abstract—Chief Director of Strategic Equity and Development—a title designed to imply both ethics and vision while tying him to no single accountability. His job was to ensure capital flowed cleanly: from city grants to private donors, from developers to foundations, from promises to renderings. He spoke fluently about access and infrastructure, about the Wellness Corridor, about legacy. Paula had listened to enough of his calls to know that outcomes mattered less than alignment.

Together, they had become a presence in Greensboro's civic landscape. He managed the institutions. She managed the rooms. Paula had grown into a kind of soft power—the woman who chaired the right boards, hosted the right fundraisers, whose thank-you notes arrived on heavy cream stock, whose Instagram featured candlelight galas and morning garden walks with just enough blur to seem unplanned. The city's newspapers called her a vital bridge between community and capital. She knew what that meant. She let them write it.

On this night, they were hosting the annual Hospital Foundation Equity Benefit, a curated event designed to reinforce the narrative of transformation. The wellness corridor was underway—new buildings rising on the old downtown fringe, parks promised, housing incentives announced, partnerships secured. The evening was meant to cement the optics: donors in linen, speeches full of soft verbs, a silent auction featuring weekends in the mountains and hand-thrown pottery made by youth enrichment programs.

Paula's role was orchestration. She had approved the lighting, selected the floral arrangements, vetted the talking points. She would greet the mayor, thank the sponsors, nod through toasts. She would pose for photographs that would be emailed by morning to press and donors alike, the file names already coded: progress, equity, future.

This was what they did now. She knew the rhythm. She could move through it with her eyes closed. Only tonight, something in her posture strained. A tightness in her jaw since she read Alan's article that morning. A question that hadn't stopped swirling since she stepped into the blue dress.

What happens when the future is built on ground you refused to see?

In the far corner of the ballroom, where the light pooled less generously and the orchids on the centerpiece had begun to droop from the energy of deceit, three figures sat at a table marked Community Partners. The two men were dressed in the sort of suits that managed to suggest humility without costing less than a mortgage payment. Their ties were neat, their laughter infrequent but well-deployed. Each wore a superfluous name tag. They knew each other, and the game.

Councilman Lyle Dent pinched the edge of his napkin between two fingers and dabbed the corners of his mouth with exaggerated care. He had been elected seven years ago on a platform of small business incentives and pothole eradication. The potholes remained. The incentives had worked well enough for the donors.

Across from him, Walter Channing, the senior vice president of a regional property firm that specialized in distressed acquisitions, swirled the ice in his glass without looking at it. He had the satisfied expression of a man who had only ever encountered consequence as a theoretical concept. To his right, Andrea Wexler, director of a community non-profit with a name that suggested action and a board that guaranteed discretion, leaned in slightly, her elbow just brushing the white cloth.

"You think Moss can manage it?" Dent asked. "All the way through?"

Channing didn't look up. "He's clean enough. And clean plays well right now."

Wexler tilted her head. "He talks like he believes it, though."

"Even better," Channing said. "The ones who believe are easier to steer. They work twice as hard to keep the performance consistent."

Dent grunted. "The church folks are nervous. That creek near Bingham's still radioactive, metaphorically speaking."

"There's signage," Wexler offered. "That's all they asked for in the last meeting."

"They asked for a soil report too," Dent said.

"Yes," she said, smiling, "but they used the word transparency. That's not a demand. That's a pose."

They all chuckled.

"Anyway," Channing added, "the land for the South Elm wellness anchor's already moved. Title changed hands last fiscal year. Moss's corridor wraps around it now like a ribbon. They're calling it environmental revitalization."

"And we're the bow on top," Wexler said, raising her glass.

"I'll toast to that," Dent said, though he did not raise his own.

Behind them, applause swelled from the main stage. David Moss had just finished his speech. Words like innovation and wellness still hung in the air.

"Doesn't hurt that his wife looks like an endorsement," Channing said. "She makes it all seem inevitable."

Dent leaned back in his chair. "Do we need to do anything else on our end?"

"Just keep the permits moving," Wexler said. "And let him keep talking. Once that playground parcel is built out, the momentum will carry it through."

Outside the circle of candlelight, a waiter stepped toward the table, but they waved him off. Plates were cleared. Another toast began. They sat in the half-shadow, full of strategy and tenderloin, certain of their position in the machinery.

Paula reached her table at last. Once the greetings were complete, a woman with a diamond crucifix whispered a question about the corridor's stormwater permits. The woman leaned in over her salad, her voice muted, the way women spoke when they'd been taught that certain questions, though impolite, were necessary for good stewardship.

"I just want to make sure the South Elm soil issues are really addressed this time," she said, tapping the stem of her wine glass. The diamond cross at her neck caught a shard of chandelier light. "My husband remembers the flooding near Arlington Street. And I'm hearing whispers about old runoff lines near the new playground site."

Paula turned to face her more fully, smile composed, teeth visible but not too white. "Of course," she said. "That's been built into the Phase II infrastructure planning. We're coordinating with the city on basin-level retention. They're calling it the integrated greenwater initiative."

The woman's brows rose, intrigued.

Paula continued. "All new paving on the health corridor's south end will be permeable composite. Stormwater will flow into below-grade filtration tanks, then through bio-retention swales planted with native species. And the units near the community pavilion? Each one will have a rainwater catchment system with municipal integration, so they can contribute back to the grid."

She paused, not because she needed to, but because she'd learned that breathing in the middle of technical language made it seem more authentic.

"The team is also partnering with a climate impact researcher from the university. They're modeling the whole thing to be net positive by year five."

The woman exhaled lightly, as if mollified.

"Well that's impressive," she said. "And what about the environmental screening? The soil tests?"

"They're well within the DEQ thresholds," Paula said, steady. "The South Elm corridor was chosen precisely because of its clean record. Any residual materials are trace and contained. Nothing migratory. The reports are public, if you'd like to see them."

She said it as if of course the reports were available, as if anyone could understand them, as if public meant more than a footnote buried in a link on a grant foundation's website. Or six folders deep in a Department of Environmental Quality database, each document labeled with random numbers.

The woman reached for her napkin, folded it once, smiled. "You're very good at this," she said.

Paula's glass was empty. She lifted it slightly. A server noticed.

"I try to keep things clear," she said, and then turned slightly in her chair, just enough to suggest the conversation had been concluded, just enough to keep the warmth intact.

She let the tines of her fork rest against the rim of the plate, the lettuce touched but uneaten. The conversation had ended. The room eased around her—waitstaff collecting plates, the vibe of collective goodwill softening the air. She allowed her shoulders to settle, just enough to feel the line of the dress across her collarbone.

Across the room, beneath the blush-colored uplighting near the silent auction tables, stood Keith Collins. He had filled out over the years but still carried himself with the same cautious posture, chin lifted just enough to appear self-assured. His hands were clasped loosely in front of him, the way he used to stand during presentations in undergrad, unsure whether he believed what he was saying until Alan Ransome nodded.

Paula had met Keith when Alan was still walking her to class and highlighting her course packets in the margins. Keith had been Alan's roommate, his best friend, maybe his only friend then. She remembered quiet dinners at their off-campus apartment, the two of them eating frozen curry from mismatched bowls, arguing gently about zoning policy while rock videos played on the muted television set. Keith never spoke first, but he always had something stored up. She had liked that about him. Still did, maybe.

She nodded in his direction. He smiled—polite, quick, already fading as he turned to say something to the woman at his side. Allison. Paula knew her, but only vaguely. Theater board. Fundraisers. Well-tailored. Pleasant. Carefully withheld. There was something about Allison she had never managed to understand, a quality beneath the surface that never quite arrived. She watched the way Allison touched Keith's arm as she leaned in, a gesture that read as performance more than affection. But then, Paula reminded herself, she wasn't one to talk.

The lights dimmed slightly. Onstage, someone stepped to the microphone. Paula returned her gaze to her plate and lifted her fork. The leaves had wilted. She chewed without tasting.

Seeing Keith pulled something forward. It wasn't just the face. The way Keith stood beside his wife, careful, practiced, deferential to the moment but slightly out of sync with it. That uneasy blend of privilege and self-awareness, always trying to calibrate itself, never quite landing.

Keith had always been adjacent to conviction. He read the right articles, used the right words, voted the right way. But he never started the conversation. He waited for consensus, and then repeated it back. That had been true even in college, when Alan filled the rooms they shared with idealism that peeled paint from the walls. Keith had been the one passing the chips, checking the time, nodding along. Supportive, but never central.

Seeing him now—older, better dressed, still scanning the room as if for instruction—brought Alan into the present without warning. Alan had never stood like that. Never hesitated when the moment called for force. He argued until it exhausted the room. He showed up when it wasn't convenient. He got himself thrown out of two planning commission meetings before anyone took his name seriously. And he had looked at her, back then, with that belief that people—she included—could be part of something that mattered.

Keith reminded her what she had traded. Fire for comfort. Integrity for ease. Alan would have burned the room down if it demanded silence. Keith would make a spreadsheet to track the damage, sort of like he had done the last three years as secretary of the Guilford Wellness Alliance board, which Paula chaired.

She watched Keith raise his glass, smile at someone passing. A woman leaned in and he nodded, agreeable. Always the best friend. Never the voice. She felt a small pressure in her chest. The kind that comes from remembering a version of yourself you chose to neglect.

She told herself at the time that it wasn't betrayal. That she and Alan had never defined anything. That David could offer something complete. Stability. Access. A life without the roughness of hope. And she had chosen that life. She had performed it well. But sometimes, like now, when Keith's presence cracked the surface, she wondered what would have happened if she'd paused. If she had allowed Alan the space to matter. What kind of woman would she have become alongside him? What rooms would she not have entered. What truths would she have been forced to confront sooner.

She swallowed, the salad thick in her mouth. The applause started again near the stage. Her glass was full. The light above her barely noticeable. She smoothed the napkin in her lap, her fingers steady. It was the right choice. She told herself that again, because it had to be.

Her phone buzzed once inside her clutch. She knew who it was. Her daughter had a monologue to memorize. Paula had helped her with it that morning, the words still echoing beneath the music. Something about memory. About how little time we have.

She excused herself from the table before the next toast began and moved toward the powder room, the water in her glass undisturbed. Her heels struck the marble in even rhythm. Behind her, applause filled the room and passed without sticking. She stepped into the hallway outside the ballroom, her heels silent on the carpet, the noise of the benefit sealed behind the polished doors. The hallway was lined with portraits of donors and former presidents of the foundation, all gazing forward with that same fixed expression of well-fed purpose. She moved past them without looking.

Her phone buzzed again. She answered before the second ring.

Her daughter's voice was immediate, pressed.

"I can't get the line right," she said. "It doesn't sound real when I say it. It just sounds like I'm reading."

Paula leaned against the wall beside the powder room, the phone close to her ear.

"Tell me the line again," she said.

Her daughter recited it. A sentence from Our Town, something about time and how people never notice it while they're living. She rushed the words, stumbled near the end.

"Breathe," Paula said. "Say it like you've thought it, not like you've been told to say it."

There was a pause on the other end.

"I'm trying," her daughter said.

"I know. That's why I'm here. Try it again."

She listened as the words came back, slower this time. Not perfect, but closer. Paula closed her eyes.

"That's better. But stop thinking about how it sounds. Think about what it means. Do you know what it means?"

Her daughter didn't answer right away.

"It means everything moves too fast," the girl said finally. "That people don't pay attention."

"Yes. Good. So say it like someone who noticed."

Another pause. Then the line came again, and this time Paula heard the shape of thought in it. The edge of a girl trying to feel something real.

She felt it in her throat before she could stop it. Pride, yes, but also something sharper. The knowledge that her daughter was already braver than she had been at that age. That she might grow into a woman who didn't have to trade her voice for access.

"You're doing beautifully," she said. "You're getting there."

"Are you still at the thing?"

"I am. But I can talk longer if you want."

"I'm okay now. I just needed you to hear it."

Paula smiled, though no one could see it.

"I always want you to ask the question," she said. "Always."

They said goodbye and she slipped the phone back into her clutch, her fingers slow on the clasp. She took one breath before re-entering the ballroom. The applause had started again. Another speech. Another round of thanks. She stepped back into the light.

David returned to the table with his shoulders squared, face composed, the kind of expression he wore after a speech or panel had gone precisely to plan. He nodded once at the foundation chair, touched the back of Paula's chair briefly, then sat. The smile he gave her was shallow, already fading by the time he reached for his water.

He didn't ask how she was.

She smoothed her napkin and kept her posture still. The table was full of motion—forks rising, laughter coming in small, restrained bursts—but none of it touched her. She watched David butter a piece of bread without looking down, his movements rehearsed, hands clean, watch catching the light. He was already scanning the room again, checking who was looking, who was approaching.

She could still hear her daughter's voice from the call. The thought in it. The risk of saying something out loud.

David said something to the man seated beside him about procurement timelines. Paula nodded once when she caught his eye, but the shape of her face didn't change. The room pulsed with polite society and generational wealth. She placed her hands in her lap and pressed her thumbs together until her knuckles warmed. No one was looking at her now. No one was asking anything.

She was seated in the center of a table that bore her name and yet she felt unremarked upon, necessary but unnoticed. A fixture. A presence merged into the architecture of the evening. She had learned how to inhabit that space without cracking. She had trained for it. Still, something in her skin bristled, just under the surface, where feeling pressed unseen. The night continued. Plates were cleared. Someone new took the microphone.

David placed his hand on the table, fingers drumming once. He leaned toward the man beside him. Paula stared out the window.

3

The office was already warm by the time Keith Collins arrived. The sun hit the western wall in the late morning and turned the glass into a slow kiln, softening the air before the HVAC caught up. He didn't complain. The view made up for it.

From his desk, Keith could see most of downtown. The bank towers, the museum with its oversized glass panels, the flat gray roof of City Hall directly across from him like a lid. Farther west, the hospital's main facility climbed the skyline in clean, rectangular lines. Its newest wing gleamed, the glass tinted to reflect the sky. The building had been rebranded three times in a decade—first a nonprofit, then a partnership, now a "regional health engine," according to the fundraising mailers that occasionally crossed his desk. It was the cleanest structure in the city's story about itself.

East of City Hall, the grid began to fray. The lots tightened, the roads bent. He could see the shape of the east side not as topography but as pattern: smaller rooftops, schoolyards in between duplexes, more traffic at the intersections with fewer lights to manage it. That was the part of the city where numbers didn't stay in line. Income, asthma, graduation—none of it moved the way the models wanted it to.

He had once tried to explain that to a new hire from Chicago. Showed her the housing overlay, the transportation mapping, the poverty index zones. She'd asked if they had plans for intervention.

He said they were working on visibility. That was months ago. She'd left before her contract ended.

Keith turned from the window. His desk was clean, as always. Two monitors, a keyboard, a stack of budget revisions in a red folder. He'd reviewed them last night after Allison fell asleep with the TV on. The numbers worked. They always did. That was the skill. You could make anything align if you gave it enough narrative.

He opened his email. A report from the urban redevelopment firm sat at the top of his inbox. Attached was a spreadsheet, flagged in yellow. One line caught his eye: Parcel 524-B, South Elm Redevelopment Zone – Remediation Infrastructure Pending.

He clicked it open, leaned forward. The line item was familiar. He'd seen variations of it before, but something about the phrasing was different now. Less defined. The language had been softened. "Pending" could mean anything—planned, promised, forgotten. He reached for his pen, tapped it once against the edge of his desk. He looked out the window again, this time toward the east. Then he turned back to the screen and began to scroll.

Keith worked on the twenty-first floor of the White Oak Financial Tower, a clean glass monolith that rose without apology from the heart of downtown Greensboro. It housed the regional headquarters of Edgemark International, a multinational investment firm whose influence stretched from European bonds to southeastern municipal credit markets. Keith was a senior data analyst, which meant that he lived most of his professional life inside spreadsheets, infrastructure reports, and balance sheets filed by public-private partnerships with language that intentionally blurred certainty.

His job was to read beneath what was written. He reviewed the filings of the city's most critical economic machinery—transportation authorities, medical systems, real estate development groups—comparing projected revenue flows against policy risk, population movement, and investment exposure. It wasn't creative work, but it rewarded discipline. The data didn't lie. The people behind it, of course, did all the time.

He had been tracking the proposed expansion by Guilford Health System for months. The new medical corridor—its clinical name was the "South Elm Wellness and Innovation Zone"—had been flagged as a Tier 2 Risk-Backed Opportunity. That meant it had the potential to draw in national investment if the permit structure held and if public subsidy could be paired with measurable health outcomes. David Moss's name had begun showing up more frequently in the filings—first as a project advisor, then in signature blocks, then in board meeting minutes where no votes were recorded but influence clearly peddled.

Keith had known David in college. Not well. David had been part of a different tier, the kind of student who spoke with ease at department mixers and already had a business card sophomore year. Still, they'd crossed paths. More importantly, David had once dated—no, married—Paula, who had once been close to Alan, who had once been Keith's closest friend.

That network didn't matter here. The system didn't care who had fallen in love with whom in 1996. But Keith couldn't ignore the connections when they surfaced in front of him in column D, row 192: Remediation Infrastructure – Parcel 524-B.

The language was new. It hadn't been flagged in earlier filings. He opened the linked document, read the summary twice. There was no cost breakdown. No timeline. No site history. The line was inserted with the kind of ambiguity that was either a placeholder or a deliberate omission.

He minimized the file, sat back, and looked again out the window. City Hall stood steady in the middle of the frame. To the left, the hospital's main wing gleamed behind its rebranding. To the right, the east side stretched, denser and dimmer, just outside the reach of most investment summaries.

He turned back to the screen. The numbers hadn't changed. They never did. But something else had entered the room. Doubt. Curiosity. Keith knew the structure of the deal because he had watched it unfold in filings before it ever appeared in the news.

Last year, the city had announced a joint initiative with Guilford Health System to create a regional anchor on the south edge of downtown—a full-service medical facility positioned as the centerpiece of a broader redevelopment corridor. The pitch had been precise: a mixed-use medical hub that would bring urgent care, specialty clinics, behavioral health services, and small business opportunities to an area long labeled as underutilized.

The land in question sat at one of the most visible intersections in the city, a four-block plot where three main thoroughfares converged beneath a skyline of municipal ambition and deferred maintenance. It had been vacant for nearly two decades, held in limbo through a patchwork of failed redevelopment efforts and temporary zoning overlays.

Under the new agreement, the city would sell the land to Guilford Health for a nominal fee, citing "strategic public benefit." Infrastructure upgrades—sewer, stormwater, road realignment—would be publicly funded through a bond issuance structured around an older tax increment financing model. The mechanism was legal, quiet, and designed to avoid a public referendum.

Because bonds were involved, regulatory filings had been made to state financial databases, most of them buried under the language of asset-backed security and "municipal leverage optimization." But Keith had access to the archives. It was part of his job to know where those documents lived and what they refused to say directly.

He had already traced the funding structure through three subsidiaries, one of which listed a partner address that matched the consulting firm David Moss had briefly joined before being absorbed into Guilford Health's executive team. That kind of overlap wasn't unusual. It didn't mean corruption. It meant fluency.

What stood out now—what caught in his mind more than the lack of a cost breakdown—was the absence of an environmental note. The land had been listed as brownfield-adjacent in a grant application five years prior. It had history. That history had vanished.

He pulled the parcel report again and checked the chain of title. The city had acquired it through forfeiture in the late '90s. Before that, it had passed through several limited holding entities—most now dissolved, some never named beyond initials. The map linked to the report showed the plot in soft green, marked STABILIZATION PENDING.

He sat back and rubbed his chin, then typed a note into his research log. Just a line, nothing flagged:

Cross-reference Parcel 524-B — historic use? Overlay remediation? Public filings match?

Then he minimized the screen again. For now, he didn't want to look directly at what the numbers were beginning to say.

Keith had read Alan's op-ed two nights ago, propped against a cereal box on the kitchen counter while the dishwasher groaned in the next room. He hadn't meant to read the whole thing—just a scan, a glance at the opening paragraph—but the voice pulled him in, steady and unsparing. It was the same tone Alan had used in college when they argued in their apartment kitchen about the public trust doctrine, Alan always drawing some red moral line while Keith hedged in practicalities.

The piece was about Bingham Park, or more precisely, about the city's long-standing refusal to treat it as anything but an inconvenient patch of green. Alan had detailed the contamination—arsenic, lead, old incinerator ash—and the decades of quiet neglect that followed. He listed the children who had grown up next to that soil, the missing signage, the buried assessments, the grant proposals that were written and rewritten and never funded.

Keith had read each sentence with creeping discomfort. He knew the history. Not in detail, not with the texture Alan gave it, but he had seen the parcel on a planning map years ago, flagged in yellow with a note about "legacy municipal use." He had moved past it. There had been no request for review. It hadn't touched any current project. The cost-to-risk ratio didn't register.

But Alan's piece wasn't about risk. It was about consequence. About memory. About the gap between institutional language and the lived air of a neighborhood. Keith had finished the article and closed his laptop without saving the page. He hadn't forwarded it. He hadn't said anything to Allison. He had gone upstairs, brushed his teeth, stared at his reflection, then scrolled through housing market data until the numbers calmed him.

And yet, reading the language around Parcel 524-B this morning, seeing the phrase Remediation Infrastructure Pending, something in him caught. The city had ignored one site for decades. Now it had cleared another, cleaner by omission, and handed it off to Guilford Health System with no public hearing.

He minimized the report again and sat back in his chair, the window behind him throwing light across his desk. Alan would know what to call this. He always did. Keith wasn't sure yet. But the silence in the numbers was beginning to sound familiar.

Keith remembered that about Alan—how he never let things rest. Even when it would've been easier, even when it made him look obsessive, even when the outcomes didn't change. He didn't just care; he couldn't help it. There was no off switch and that was what made it hard to be around sometimes. Alan didn't let people look away.

They hadn't spoken in over a year, maybe longer, but Keith had seen him on the news. A local segment—WFMY, midday. Grainy footage of Alan outside a row of gray brick apartment buildings in Cottage Grove, standing between a reporter and a cluster of tenants holding paperwork in manila folders. Mold spores had been found in the HVAC ducts, and asbestos in some of the old tile work. Children were getting sick. Tenants were being blamed for moisture damage.

Alan had walked the units himself. Had interviewed the tenants, filed a report, and pressured the city into opening an investigation. The segment showed him holding up a sample bag, speaking with the kind of calm that came after anger, after exhaustion, after proof had already been collected and ignored. He had looked older. His voice deeper. No wedding ring.

Keith had watched the clip twice, once at his desk and once again in his car, engine running in the parking garage. He hadn't texted. Hadn't liked the clip or emailed a word of support. But it stayed with him. Alan had always done that—gone all the way to the bottom of a thing. A policy change, a site plan, a buried report. In college, he'd taken apart a campus rezoning document line by line for a student journal no one read. He'd missed two days of class just to track down an unposted variance form.

Keith had admired that, once. Then resented it. Then ignored it.

Now, staring at a spreadsheet that concealed more than it showed, with Alan's voice still fresh in the back of his mind, Keith wasn't sure what he felt. Just that something in the data was wrong. Not proveable. But he knew Alan would dig. He always did. And if he found something, he wouldn't let it go.

Keith closed the spreadsheet, opened a new tab, and typed Parcel 524-B site history + public use permit into the search bar. He hesitated, then hit enter.

The results loaded, a staggered crawl through state databases and municipal records not designed for public navigation. Keith skimmed past the top links—real estate listings, a short article on the hospital expansion, a zoning announcement from last year's council meeting. He clicked deeper, filtering by date, adjusting keywords. After ten minutes, he reached a PDF buried on a state environmental compliance site, last modified six years ago.

Preliminary Environmental Screening – Parcel 524-B (South Elm Redevelopment)

North Carolina Department of Environmental Quality, 2011

Archived. No action recommended pending additional review.

The language was dry but familiar. Parcel 524-B had been flagged during a preliminary screening conducted as part of a broader redevelopment feasibility study. The summary noted residual materials from "historic municipal incineration activities" and recommended additional soil sampling to determine the presence of "persistent contaminants."

There was no follow-up document linked. Keith checked the file properties. The report had been uploaded by a subcontractor for the city. It had never been reissued. No mitigation plan attached. No public notice. He leaned in closer, scrolling to the second page.

A table of field observations listed surface staining, irregular soil coloration, and a notation beside a groundwater flow that read elevated sediment discoloration — further analysis required.

He recognized the phrasing. It was the language of risk deferred. The suggestion that something should have happened next. But no new test results appeared in the state archive. No remediation order. The report simply sat there, suspended in bureaucratic air, its warnings intact and unacted on.

He opened another browser and cross-referenced the property's sale to Guilford Health System. The closing documents made no mention of the 2011 screening. The property had been transferred from the city to a holding entity two years ago, then from the entity to Guilford Health under a redevelopment initiative classified as "environmental opportunity zone." That classification required clean environmental compliance at the time of transfer.

Keith felt a tightening in his chest. A kind of internal arrangement—pieces moving toward a conclusion they hadn't quite reached. He clicked back to the environmental PDF and printed it. The office printer whirred once behind him, the sound too loud for the room.

No one else had looked at this. Or someone had. And chosen not to care.

Keith stood, the chair's wheels sighing across the floor, and crossed the room to the printer. The report slid out in warm sheets. He tapped the edges together, scanned the header again. Six years old. Archived.

He returned to his desk and set the pages down beside his keyboard. The top sheet stared back at him. Parcel 524-B: Sediment discoloration. Municipal incineration.

This wasn't his jurisdiction. He wasn't in compliance, wasn't risk mitigation. His job was exposure. Projection. He worked with current numbers, confirmed filings, visible transactions. Old site reports were outside the boundary. He knew better than to pull the thread. He could stomach history. But once you started reading beneath, once you confirmed that someone else had known and moved forward anyway, you became part of the silence. And silence required maintenance.

He stared at the line again: no further analysis conducted.

The office was quiet. The next cubicle over had been outsourced three months ago and never returned. Across the city, the hospital's wellness corridor was already being built out. The headlines had run. The funding approved. Any push now would read as obstruction.

Keith looked at the time. He minimized the browser. Opened a new email. Typed Alan's name into the address field. Then deleted it. He stood, walked once to the window, pressed a knuckle to the glass. From here, the corridor site was invisible. But he knew the shape of it. Knew how a map could erase a history if no one insisted otherwise.

He sat back down. Closed the folder. Saved nothing. Just left the report sitting there on the desk. Quiet, unfiled, but closer now. Closer than it had ever been.

The house was dark except for the soft light pooling out from the living room. He didn't turn on the overheads. Just closed the door behind him and dropped his keys on the counter. From the living room, the sound of something animated and high-pitched drifted up—his ten-year old son's tablet, probably. The boy didn't look up when Keith passed through the archway. Neither did his twelve-year old daughter, curled into the couch's far corner, headphones on, knees pressed to her chest. They were both wrapped in screens, lit from beneath.

He nodded once toward them, not expecting a response, and walked into the kitchen. The dishwasher hadn't been run. A glass sat in the sink with milk drying inside. He rinsed it, turned it upside down, wiped his hands on a towel. Allison wasn't home. Her coat wasn't on the hook. Her car hadn't been in the garage when he pulled in, but he'd told himself not to make that mean anything. It was Thursday. There was always something.

He opened the fridge, closed it again. Poured a glass of scotch. No ice. He took it into the study and sat down, leaving the door half open so he could hear if the kids fought. They didn't. They stayed quiet. A good, manageable quiet.

He opened his laptop and stared at the desktop. The report from earlier was still sitting there, minimized. He pulled up a search bar and typed in Allison's name. Her social media opened in a separate tab. A photo had been posted an hour ago. She was leaning toward someone at a wine bar in Midtown, her hair down, a glass held mid-laugh.

He stared at it. Then clicked away. Then back. The man in the photo was unfamiliar. Younger. Or maybe just less tired. He closed the laptop. Sat still. Took a slow sip.

The house settled around him. Upstairs, a floorboard gave under shifting steps. He imagined the kids brushing their teeth, getting ready for bed without being asked. He imagined Allison pulling into the driveway without explanation. He sat in the dark, elbows on knees, the empty glass sweating in his hand. No movement upstairs. No footsteps on the porch. The long, stable quiet of a house where everyone had drifted inward.

He hadn't meant to end up here—not exactly. But the path had been so well-laid that choosing it never felt like a choice. His father had called it alignment—that pleasant convergence between talent and tradition. Keith had shown early promise, the kind that drew praise from principals and private school counselors, the kind that made men like his father proud. Not for who he was, but for what he could prove. He learned to move with precision. Never first, never loud, but always right. Always correct. That was the rule.

His intelligence had been a liability only once: when it tried to speak. In high school, he'd written an op-ed for the school paper about legacy admissions and racial inequity. His father read it at the breakfast table, finished his eggs, then told him if he wanted to be taken seriously one day, he should think about who his audience was.

He'd never written anything personal again.

Allison had come into his life the way a merger does—polished, mutual, strategic. They met at a party in Chapel Hill. She laughed gracefully, drank just enough, asked questions she already knew the answers to. She looked good beside him. She knew when to lean in and when to smile. He told himself that mattered. That compatibility was a kind of intimacy.

He never asked if she believed in any of it.

There had been heat, early on. Enough to convince them both. But nothing unstable. Nothing that asked too much. She wanted a life that looked whole from the outside. He wanted quiet. Predictability. Forward motion. Now the house was quiet in all the wrong ways. Especially since his oldest daughter had left for college last fall.

He looked down at the carpet. The lines from the last vacuuming still visible. The order of things preserved. He had everything his father said he should want. A good job, healthy children, a wife with the right kind of smile. A reputation for reason. And still, something had begun to open in him. Slowly, uncomfortably. As if the years had passed and he'd forgotten to ask whether he believed any of it was real.

The guilt didn't arrive all at once. It came in pieces, long after the affair had started. In the beginning, it had felt like oxygen—sharp, necessary, undeserved. Her name was Marissa. She worked two floors down, red hair pulled back, voice excited, eyes that seemed to understand something about the exhaustion he never admitted aloud. She laughed at the right moments, touched his wrist when she handed him documents. The first time had been after drinks, in a hotel near the airport. Afterward, he sat on the edge of the bed and stared at the air vent, certain he would never do it again.

He did. For nearly a year.

It changed him, though not in the ways he expected. He wore his suits with a cleaner line. Meetings ran tighter. He started jogging again in the mornings. He came home late but cheerful, present in a way that passed for affection. Allison noticed. She softened slightly, misreading his new ease as renewed care. For a few months, the quiet between them wasn't so sharp.

Then the receipt.

It had fallen between the car seat and the console. Burlington. A Double Tree, nondescript. He'd told her he was staying overnight in Raleigh for an investor briefing. She'd found it while searching for her keys, which he'd taken by mistake.

The fight happened in the kitchen. She named the date, the lie, the city. She waited for an apology and got an explanation. That was worse. He remembered standing there, hands on the counter, watching her adjust the strap on her purse as if deciding whether to stay. She didn't leave. Neither of them did.

They agreed, after a long weekend of separate silences, to hold the line—for the children. That was the phrase they used. For the children. They rearranged rooms, drew new boundaries. Spoke kindly in public. Coordinated schedules. Maintained the appearance of two adults navigating something mature.

That was three years ago.

Now, the distance had calcified. No more late-night fights. No more pressing questions. Her laughter belonged to other rooms. His remorse had quieted into habit. They still went to fundraisers. Still stood side by side at school events. Still used the word we in emails. In the hallway between their bedroom and the stairs, there still hung a photograph from their wedding. He passed it every morning. Neither of them had taken it down.

The upstairs hallway held a damp warmth, the kind that lingered after showers and slow arguments. Keith stood at the top of the stairs, hand braced on the wall, calling down to the living room.

"Let's go. Screens off. Now, please."

A rustle, a groan. The familiar resistance.

"Five more minutes," his son called back.

"You already had ten."

Footsteps on the stairs. His daughter appeared first, tablet hugged to her chest, hair still damp from the bath she took without being asked. She gave him that half-lidded look of minor betrayal and passed him in silence. His son came slower, mumbling something about finishing a level. Keith didn't respond. They'd had this dance a hundred times.

"Alright, toothbrushes. No negotiations tonight."

His son rolled his eyes but turned toward the bathroom. The hallway settled into motion—doors opening, water running, the muttering of a brother annoyed by hygiene.

Keith leaned against the doorframe of his daughter's room. She sat on the bed, pulling a sweatshirt over her pajamas. He watched the way she tugged at the sleeves, then looked up at him.

"Where's Mom?"

He hesitated.

"She had a meeting," he said. "Late one. She texted. Said she might be home after you're asleep."

"Oh."

She looked down at her lap, picked at a loose thread near the hem of her sleeve. She didn't push. She rarely did.

"Want me to leave the hall light on?"

She nodded. "Yeah. Just a little."

Keith stepped forward, kissed the top of her head, then turned toward the door.

"Night," he said.

"Night."

He pulled the door mostly shut. Left a gap.

Down the hall, the bathroom light clicked off. His son's door closed with a quiet thud. He stood in the hallway for a moment, listening. The house felt balanced again. Stable. For them. But inside, the answer to his daughter's question hadn't settled. He hadn't heard from Allison since morning. No check-in, no call. The wine bar photo still sat in his mind.

He told himself not to assume. That maybe she really had stayed out late with friends. That maybe she needed air. That maybe she'd come home soon, slip into bed without comment. But he also knew the math. The slow accumulation of distance. The signs he'd stopped naming aloud. He went downstairs. Poured another half glass. Sat in the dark and said nothing.

The house was silent now. Upstairs, the doors had stayed closed. Keith sat in the same chair in the study, the second scotch half gone. The room smelled of air freshener and electronics. He opened the laptop again. The screen lit his face, sharp at the cheekbones, tired around the eyes. He hesitated. Then typed her name into the search bar again.

The same account. Still public. A new story posted fifteen minutes ago—a boomerang clip of a wine glass lifted in a toast, table scattered with plates and linen napkins. Motion and mood. The caption was just a white heart.

He clicked back to her main feed. The photos were recent, spaced enough to seem casual: a breakfast croissant half-bitten beside a paperback, a pair of boots arranged artfully on brick, her reflection caught in a boutique mirror. She rarely posted selfies. When she did, her expression was neutral, mouth closed, gaze steady. They weren't meant to invite comments.

He scrolled farther back. A photo from a fundraiser two weeks ago—her smile tight, eyes slightly glazed. He was in that one, just behind her, out of focus. He clicked the screen closed. Opened it again. Typed her name into Instagram this time, then Twitter, though she barely used it. Nothing new. Nothing traceable.

The night was thinning. He looked at the time—close to midnight. No message from her. No read receipt on the last text he'd sent four hours ago. He stared at the cursor blinking in a blank message box. Typed All okay? and deleted it. Typed Still out? and deleted that too.

He leaned back in the chair, let his eyes rest at the ceiling. There was nothing dramatic about the feeling. Just distance. A quiet confirmation. He sat a little longer, then shut the laptop for good.

4

David Moss stepped into the council chambers with his tie already loosened half a notch. Just enough to suggest ease without disrespect. The room was half-full, that awkward hour between staff briefings and the scheduled public agenda, when the temperature hadn't yet caught up with the body heat and the microphones hadn't been turned on.

He paused just past the door, eyes scanning the familiar geometry of chairs, coats, name placards. Councilwoman Hoffman was already seated—navy suit, hair pinned, glancing between two agenda items without reading either. She would ask a procedural question, as she always did, to signal independence. He'd nod. Make room for her language. Let her land the blow if she needed to.

To the left: Halgren from municipal planning, leaning into his assistant's ear, eyes flicking up. David didn't wave. Halgren would prefer not to be acknowledged in public. He liked the illusion of neutrality. Across the aisle: Dent, councilman-at-large, fiddling with a silver pen. David gave him the briefest smile, a twitch at the mouth. Dent nodded. That was enough.

He didn't look for the mayor. That conversation had already happened in a side room. The votes were there. The corridor would move forward. Tonight was for shaping the language.

He walked down the center aisle, unhurried. One woman from the chamber of commerce rose slightly in her seat—subtle deference. He stopped to greet her. Two sentences. Appreciation. Intent. Kept moving. At the front row, he unbuttoned his jacket and took a seat behind the podium's curve. He wouldn't need notes.

He looked out across the room. The citizens who showed up for these meetings were almost always the same: retirees, activists, clergy, a few neighborhood association reps full of questions that had been answered elsewhere. He knew which ones would speak. Knew the cadence of their complaints. What they asked for didn't matter. The plan was moving. It had already moved.

Still, presence mattered. Composure mattered. He took a slow breath. Behind him, the overhead lights dimmed. The meeting would begin soon. He let his face settle into the expression he used when something difficult but necessary was about to be explained. Something closer to concern. It always played better.

Earlier that week, over lunch at the club on Spring Garden—the one with the high windows and the noise softened by carpet and deference—David had met with Dent and Channing to finalize the tone of the upcoming vote. The menu hadn't changed in years. Cobb salad, trout almondine, something called a wellness bowl for appearances. David ordered coffee. Channing went for iced tea, extra lemon. Dent didn't order anything. He preferred to finish meetings before the food arrived.

"So," Dent said, creasing his napkin without putting it in his lap, "we're aligned on the language."

David nodded. "We're using the 'wellness corridor' framework now. 'Innovation zone' is staying, but only in the supplemental materials."

Channing sipped his tea, set it down carefully. "The anchor facility's good. No blowback on the urgent care or the diagnostics wing. But we're still getting questions about the green space."

"From whom?" David asked, already knowing.

"Neighborhood association. Someone on the east side pulled an old land survey. Brought it to the civic roundtable. Said the site's history might 'complicate trust.' Their words."

David didn't blink. "The site's already cleared. Graded. Irrigation lines are in. The playground's been delivered to the holding site in Winston. We're within environmental compliance under the grandfather clause."

Channing raised an eyebrow. "You're calling it a playground now?"

"In the outreach materials, yes," David said. "Health-adjacent youth space, technically. Language is built around generational wellness."

Dent leaned back slightly. "And the soil?"

David didn't smile. "Stabilized. We kept the original overlay from 2009. Engineering signed off on substructure. Anything prior to that was labeled as 'pre-regulatory municipal history.'"

There was a brief silence. Channing tapped the side of his glass.

"Because if anything surfaces," Channing said, "we have to be able to say we were operating in good faith."

David met his eyes. "We are. The city transferred the parcel under the condition of redevelopment. We fulfilled the terms. There's no outstanding mitigation order. No active DEQ flags. And no legal language requiring historical disclosure on non-remediated subsoil unless there's evidence of current exposure risk."

Dent leaned forward again, voice low. "And if someone comes asking?"

"They'll be referred to the public filings," David said. "Which are clean."

Channing nodded once, slow. "And the 2011 report?"

David held his gaze. "It's not linked to the bond. It was never escalated. We've confirmed it's not part of the audit trail."

Channing sat back. "Good."

Dent glanced at his watch. "The vote will pass. You've got six for sure. The rest won't break ranks this late."

David folded his hands on the table. "That's what we need."

Their server approached with a tray. David didn't move. The food arrived quietly. The coffee was hot. Outside the window, the street was full of noon light and constant traffic. The wellness corridor would be approved. The playground would open. The soil would stay where it had always been—beneath the surface, unseen, known by those who had decided it didn't matter.

David crossed his ankle over his knee and placed one hand lightly on the folder he would not open. The lights overhead bumped to their brighter setting as the council members arranged their nameplates, water bottles, and mild expressions of interest. The mayor glanced his way and offered a nod. Her face looked pulled tighter than last month, the result of some recent recalibration. The skin beneath her eyes held a stiffness that made blinking seem deliberate. David returned the nod with measured neutrality. Their agreement didn't require warmth.

The meeting began with procedural muttering: minutes adopted, abstentions logged, budget amendments introduced for later review. He let the rhythm carry past him, his focus drifting toward the gallery of citizens who'd signed up to speak. The same names appeared again and again. A few new ones. Most with folders, printouts, time limits they'd ignore.

The first public speaker launched into a condemnation of recent camp sweeps downtown, demanding a moratorium on police harassment of the unhoused. She held up a photo of a makeshift shelter beside a dumpster behind the train station. The council members listened with the careful, unmoving faces of professionals who knew the outcome had already been decided.

Then Goldie Hayes stood.

She wore a faded blazer the color of wet clay, sleeves pushed past her wrists, a yellow legal pad in one hand. She gave her name, her address, her years of residence. She spoke with certainty. Her voice was clear. Unshaking.

"You stood in this room six years ago and promised a cleanup. That promise went into the minutes. It went into the paper. And then it vanished."

She held up a photo of a drainage ditch behind the closed fence at Bingham Park. The waterline was red, the soil crusted dark around it.

"You said the park was closed for safety. That the city would test, remediate, restore. What's happened since? A few signs? A grant proposal that went nowhere?"

She paused. Let the silence press.

"My grandson lived three blocks from that site. He played there. He died at eleven. Renal failure. You said it wasn't connected. But I've read the records. I've read what you buried."

David felt the words land around him. The gallery leaned in. Councilwoman Hoffman adjusted her water bottle. Channing, seated two rows behind David, exhaled through his nose and looked at his lap.

Goldie continued.

"You're building a new facility downtown. You're calling it innovation. But you've paved over one silence and replaced it with another. Do you think a new playground on South Elm Street will make people forget where their children got sick?"

She let that question hang. Then folded the photo. She walked back to her seat and sat.

David didn't move. The mayor cleared her throat. Another speaker was called.

He kept his hands still. Smiled once for a council aide walking past. Adjusted the file beside him though he would never open it. The plan was already approved. But the room had shifted. Slightly. Enough to notice. He made a note to revisit the outreach language. The story was still intact. But someone else had begun telling it.

The agenda marched forward with the grim steadiness of process. An asphalt resurfacing plan for the west side. A stormwater mitigation upgrade near the botanical gardens. A budget amendment to reclassify three administrative salaries as grant-funded. David tuned most of it out, keeping his posture neutral, his expression open—engaged but not assertive. The pose of a professional who didn't need to interject because the machine was working. Then came the item that mattered.

The clerk read the language into the record with precise cadence: Resolution 2017-118: Approval of the South Elm Wellness and Innovation Corridor Concept Plan and Authorization to Proceed with Anchor Site Construction.

A murmur passed through the gallery. The phrase "anchor site" had not appeared on any city flyer. David recognized it as intentional. The mayor opened the floor. A few comments of support came first—Councilman Ibarra spoke about job creation, Councilwoman Shaw mentioned preventative care access. Neither used the word "playground," but both gestured toward it euphemistically: green space for youth wellness. A term that cost nothing and promised less.

Then Yvonne Hightower leaned toward her mic. She didn't raise her voice, but the tension in her shoulders made her displeasure clear before she spoke a word.

"I don't know how we sit here and greenlight a new medical facility—with all the renderings and ribbon-cutting language—while Bingham Park still sits behind a chain-link fence collecting dust and sickness."

She didn't look at anyone in particular. She looked at all of them.

"I understand the budget constraints. I understand that this project has its own funding stream. But the optics, Madam Mayor, are devastating. We are telling east side residents that we can't build for them, can't clean up after ourselves."

David kept his face still. The words weren't a surprise. Hightower had raised this point before, in subcommittee. But tonight, she was sharper.

"We're trying to build trust on top of buried problems," she said. "That's not innovation. That's narrative."

She glanced at her notes, slid them aside, and sat back. The room settled into a brief quiet before Councilman Dent, as always, found the seam. He cleared his throat and leaned forward with a small, sympathetic gesture.

"No one on this council disagrees with the urgency around Bingham Park. Let's be very clear on that. But what we're facing there is a legacy issue. Environmental remediation at that scale isn't just about willpower—it's about capital. We're talking about decades of municipal neglect, and a price tag deep into the millions. In this economic climate, with our manufacturing base all but gone, that kind of undertaking isn't just hard—it's reckless without a sustainable plan."

He smiled mildly, glanced at the gallery.

"That said, the wellness corridor isn't a distraction," Dent continued. "It's a start. It's forward momentum. We're not ignoring Bingham. We're sequencing our priorities responsibly. This project is shovel-ready. It creates jobs. It connects people to care. It builds trust where we can, even while we work—quietly, carefully, patiently—on sites like Bingham Park."

There were nods from the dais. Not full agreement, but a readiness to move forward.

The mayor thanked him. Called the vote.

One by one, names were called. Voices answered—aye, aye, aye.

Councilwoman Hightower paused before answering no.

The motion passed. Applause followed, brief and scattered. The kind meant to mark completion. David stood as the resolution was affirmed. He shook hands. Nodded at Channing near the door. Gathered his papers, untouched. Behind him, Goldie Hayes sat unmoved. Her arms crossed. Her eyes locked on the projection screen still displaying the corridor map—green space, clinic, playground.

An image superimposed on contaminated ground. But the vote was done. The plan was approved. And the language, as always, had held.

The SUV moved through the city with the fluid indifference of tinted glass. David sat in the back, angled toward the far window as the old mill buildings gave way to newer façades: converted lofts, microbreweries, a coworking space in what used to be a factory.

Cecilia sat beside him, tablet in hand, skimming the draft of the press release. She read quietly, barely audible over the soft traffic and the occasional thump of a manhole under the wheels. The driver said nothing. He wasn't paid to notice the conversation.

"We're leading with the city's unanimous support for regional innovation," Cecilia said. "Then pivoting to the language about the anchor site's potential to catalyze investment and—"

"Unanimous?" David interrupted.

"Six to one. That's effectively—"

"Don't say unanimous. Say overwhelming." He turned to look at her, the edge of his voice calm but sharpened. "We're not writing a transcript. We're writing belief."

Cecilia nodded. Tapped the screen. "We've got the playground mentioned in the third paragraph. I used the language from the outreach materials. Community-centered. Intergenerational wellness hub."

David gave a small nod. Then leaned forward slightly. "And the reference to Parcel 524-B?"

She hesitated. "It's included as part of the green space footprint. I said the site had been—"

"Don't say clean-up," David said, his voice clipped now. "Say stabilization."

She blinked, adjusted her grip on the tablet. "Right. Stabilization."

"Stabilization suggests motion. It suggests action. Clean-up suggests guilt." He leaned back again, straightened his cuff. "And guilt doesn't build trust. It invites oversight."

The SUV turned left, the glass catching a row of streetlights along the complex's edge. The Guilford Health System executive building loomed ahead—four stories of glass and steel, a banner still hanging across the front: Innovation Starts Here.

Cecilia scrolled again. "Do you want to quote the mayor?"

"Only if she mentions resilience. If not, use Dent. He says whatever we give him."

They pulled into the underground lot, the headlights catching the curve of concrete and the pale gleam of a security badge reader. David reached for the door before the vehicle had stopped moving. "Have it to Comms before nine. Framing matters. Not just what we're doing. How it sounds while we do it."

Cecilia nodded. He was already gone. The door shut behind him with a gentle thud, clean as a signature.

Upstairs, the executive floor was dim except for the soft spill of hallway light and the glow from David's monitor. His office faced west, and at this hour the glass reflected more of the room than the city beyond. On the screen: the hospital's internal dashboard. Rolling admissions by district. Outpatient forecasts. Pro forma earnings from the corridor once the anchor site came online. Each metric greenlit. Bars crawling steadily upward. The efficiency of it soothed him.

Messages slid in on the sidebar—board members offering congratulations, a few already repositioning themselves for credit. One note from the legal advisor asking whether the new language around "stabilization" should be added to the quarterly investor packet. He flagged it, didn't respond.

He began typing a response to Halvorsen, the foundation chair. A short note: Resolution passed. We'll need to fold in the donor push for the wellness wing next week. Language still flexible—

His phone buzzed in his hand.

Incoming call. Personal.

He glanced at the name: his daughter.

He hesitated only half a second, then answered.

"Hey, sweetheart."

Her voice was quick, excited. She wanted to show him a painting. Something she'd done at the afterschool program—acrylic on canvas board. Bright colors. A house with a tree and a dog. He could hear the rustling as she held the phone up to the picture, narrating what each part was.

He smiled. Real, if small.

"That's wonderful, he said. I love it. You did such a good job with the colors."

She asked if he'd come see it when he got home.

"Of course," he said. And he meant it. For that moment, he did.

"You're amazing, you know that?"

She laughed, shy but pleased.

"Okay. I'll see you later," she said.

"Okay. I'm proud of you."

He ended the call, held the phone in his hand a moment. Let the screen go dark. Then turned back to the dashboard. The bars kept rising. The earnings held. The future remained stable. He started retyping the note to Halvorsen. The painting already gone from his mind.

The door clicked shut behind him and David stepped out of his shoes, removed the tie that had already been loosened, and walked through the hallway without turning the light on. The house was still except for the faint turn of a page.

Paula sat in the den, legs tucked beneath her on the corner of the couch, a blanket tucked neatly beside her, though she hadn't pulled it over her lap. A book rested open in her hands. Her reading glasses sat untouched on the side table.

He paused in the doorway.

"You're up late," he said.

She didn't look up immediately. Then she did, eyes resting on him without narrowing.

"You're back early," she said.

"The vote passed," he said, walking in.

She nodded once. Then turned the book over in her lap.

"Did the gala help?"

He watched her for a second, the way her hand remained on the book, steady.

"It didn't hurt," he said.

She raised her eyebrows. The gesture of someone waiting to be told something true.

"You were effective," he said. "People noticed. Dent mentioned it in the green room before the vote. The council sees you as neutral. That's valuable."

"Neutral," she repeated. Her voice didn't rise.

He sat then, across from her, hands between his knees.

"You spoke with Wexler," he said. "That was good. She was still on the fence about the playground."

"She was drunk," Paula said. "She asked me if stabilization meant digging or paving."

"What did you tell her?"

"That it depended on who was asking."

He smiled at that. Let the silence pass without chasing it.

"You wore the blue one," he said. "That landed. It photographed well. The lighting worked in your favor."

"I'm aware," she said.

"You held the room," David said. "With ease. That's no small thing."

She looked at him then, directly.

"Is that what you needed from me?"

He didn't flinch.

"It helped," he said. "The room needed the gesture. The project needed continuity."

She nodded once, eyes still on his.

"Good," she said. "I like to be useful."

Then she turned her gaze back to the closed book. The room filled with its old, familiar quiet. David stood and moved to the kitchen, opened the fridge, stared at nothing, then poured a glass of water. He leaned against the counter, the glass untouched in his hand. The light from the refrigerator had already faded, the door long closed, but he still saw her face in the wash of that early blue—Paula, twenty-one, sitting cross-legged on his dorm bed, outlining a chapter from a sociology text he'd never finished. She was wearing his sweater, sleeves rolled, eyes bright with the certainty of people who hadn't yet made concessions.

He remembered the night they skipped a reception to cook pasta in her apartment, candles stubbed down in antique holders, music humming from a laptop speaker. She'd stood behind him at the stove, arms around his waist, reading aloud from a grant proposal she'd edited for him. He hadn't needed the help, but she had done it anyway. That was the way she loved him then—attentively, insistently, without condition.

She'd stood by him when the hospital's board restructured the charity foundation into a "revenue-aligned care delivery system." She had defended the change to friends, smoothed edges at galas, reminded him of the broader good. He had believed her. Or wanted to. It had made the work easier, the compromises cleaner.

The early stages of the wellness corridor had been chaos. Land acquisitions, zoning pushback, activist noise. Paula had kept him focused. She read his talking points when he was too tired. Rehearsed them with him in the mornings. When Dent wavered during the first bond negotiation, she'd invited his wife to a private luncheon. David hadn't asked her to. She just did it. For the project. For him.

He left the glass on the counter.

In the living room, Paula hadn't moved. The book was still closed on her lap, her gaze not fixed on anything in particular. The lamplight caught the side of her face. He sat beside her without asking.

"Thank you," he said.

She let the silence stretch, both of them resting inside it. He waited a moment, measuring her stillness. Then his voice softened, recalibrated to something closer to home.

"How's she getting along?"

Paula looked toward the hallway, as if she might hear footsteps, as if her daughter might emerge and change the shape of the conversation.

"She's fine," she said. "She showed me a painting after school. Acrylic on cardboard. A house with a red roof and a river that curved too sharply to be real. She called it a dream."

David smiled. "That sounds promising. She's always liked bold lines."

"She said it was just a house," Paula said. "But I think it's something else. The roof was too tall. The windows too small."

He leaned forward, his hand reaching across the cushion, resting lightly on her knee. His fingers brushed against the fabric, paused there.

"That's a good sign," he said. "Imagination. We should nurture that."

She didn't respond. Her face didn't shift. Her body gave no permission. He withdrew his hand slowly. Sat back.

"Maybe we need a trip," he said. "Somewhere simple. Just the three of us. Something to shake off the routine."

Still nothing.

He cleared his throat, added a layer of suggestion.

"What if we took her to Spain? Madrid. The Prado. Flamenco in Andalusia. She's old enough now to take it in. Really remember it."

Paula's eyes didn't flicker. But something settled deeper in her expression, as though a fissure beneath the surface had widened—not from the proposal, but from what it revealed. Spain.

The perennial solution. The fantasy destination he returned to whenever he sensed distance. A place far enough away that nothing had to be confronted here.

She reached for her book again, didn't open it.

"Maybe," she said, voice level. "We'll see."

The wound didn't bleed. It just breathed. Something old and unspoken had stirred, and she had chosen to let it remain unnamed. David didn't press. He stood a few minutes later, told her goodnight. She stayed where she was.

The studio lights were cold and clinical, even through the soft haze of powder and broadcast polish. David sat in the guest chair, upright but relaxed, his tie anchored in a perfect Windsor, navy with a diagonal slate stripe. The mug on the table beside him bore the station's logo, though it held only lukewarm water. Across from him, Kara Wills, the city's longest-tenured morning anchor, adjusted her cue cards with the grace of a woman who knew exactly how far she could push without losing access.

"And we're back," she said, turning slightly to the red light on camera two. "Joining us this morning is David Moss, Executive Vice President at Guilford Health System, here to talk about the big news out of City Council last night—the final greenlight for the South Elm Wellness and Innovation Corridor. Congratulations."

David gave the practiced nod. "Thank you, Kara. It's an exciting moment for the city, and for the communities we serve."

Kara leaned forward, her smile just the right size for television. "Let's talk about the anchor site. What does that actually mean for folks waking up this morning wondering how this affects them?"

David folded his hands once, then opened them. Gesture, pause, control.

"The anchor site is the heart of the project. It will house a next-generation urgent care clinic, outpatient diagnostics, and a behavioral health center that's integrated with community-based services. This isn't about building another siloed hospital. It's about creating access."

He watched Kara's expression flicker toward interest. Or she played interest well—it didn't matter which.

"And we're not just talking health care," he continued. "The corridor includes a green space initiative—what we're calling a wellness hub—for families and youth programming. Outdoor classrooms, mobility paths, and yes, a community playground. It's a comprehensive reimagining of how health infrastructure fits into the daily life of a neighborhood."

Kara nodded, carefully impressed. "And the location—right on the south edge of downtown. That area's seen a lot of disinvestment over the years."

"That's exactly why we chose it," David said smoothly. "It's about redirecting energy, resources, and dignity to the parts of the city that have waited longest. This is restorative planning."

Kara raised a brow. "And what do you say to critics who argue that other parts of the city—places like Bingham Park—still haven't seen their share of remediation or investment?"

David didn't blink. "Every city faces legacy challenges. What matters is momentum. We can't fix every injustice overnight, but we can build forward in ways that acknowledge the past without being paralyzed by it. The corridor is a down payment on a better model. It's not the final word. It's the first sentence."

Kara paused. Let the line breathe.

"Well said," she finally replied. "Construction starts when?"

"Preliminary work is under way. Full build-out in eighteen months."

"And what should viewers watch for in the next few weeks?"

David smiled just enough. "Community engagement sessions. We're bringing neighbors into the process—design feedback, program suggestions, local hiring priorities. This isn't being done to a neighborhood. It's being done with them."

Kara gave the closing nod, camera two swung back, and they rolled into weather. David stood after the segment wrapped, shook her hand with firm warmth, and exited through the side door before the next guest arrived. His driver was waiting.

He didn't look at his phone until he was back in the car. Six new messages. Two from Communications. One from Dent. One from his daughter—a photo of the painting she'd decided to hang above her desk. He smiled. Not for the camera this time. Just enough to mean it.

The office was bright with late-morning light, high and thin, filtered through frosted glass. David sat behind his desk, jacket off, sleeves rolled. The room filled with quiet systems: the soft pulse of the server cabinet, the whisper of air through the vents, the subtle click as his index finger scrolled the touchscreen on the wall-mounted dashboard.

Admissions trending upward. Wait times down. Outpatient referrals climbing just ahead of projections. Behavioral health engagement up fourteen percent since the pilot expansion. He tapped to expand the corridor site interface. Permitting complete. Procurement contracts locked. Two-thirds of the local subcontractors already vetted and greenlit. He let the numbers settle around him. Metrics, schedules, supply chains. It was all in motion now. Not a concept, but a structure. A visible proof of execution.

In the last five weeks alone: zoning cleared, council approval sealed, public messaging aligned. The morning show hit had landed just right—earnest but authoritative. The anchors always responded to terms like momentum, restorative planning, care equity. They didn't ask about soil depth. They didn't ask about chain-of-title. They asked how soon the playground would open.

He leaned back in his chair, let his eyes linger on the east wall where a framed rendering of the anchor site hung, slick and photoreal. The grass impossibly green. The sky clean. A child mid-sprint, frozen in simulation. Still, a thought circled. Not panic—he never panicked—but an awareness, thin and steady. The environmental screening from 2011. The file that had been archived but not deleted. Someone had once noted the sediment. The color. The chemical trace.

It was buried in regulatory language. Obscure. He told himself it would stay where it was. That no one would think to dig. He hoped no one would ask. Not the press. Not the foundations. And definitely not Alan Ransome.

The phone buzzed, screen flashing. A board member. David picked it up, voice level.

"Yes. I've got a moment."

He turned in his chair, away from the screen, toward the window where the wellness corridor would soon rise—new lines on old ground.

5

The folding chairs were misaligned and squeaked when moved, and the floor beneath them still smelled of Pine-Sol and old coffee. Goldie Hayes arrived just before six, as she always did, her canvas bag heavy with printouts and a clipboard under her arm. The meeting room in the back of New Bethel Baptist was neither large nor chic—cinderblock walls, a warped bulletin board, fluorescent lighting that made everyone's skin look tired—but it held people who remembered.

Thirty-two chairs, most of them filled. Grandmothers, young mothers, two older men from the block watch, a high schooler who lived across from the fence line at Bingham Park. A pot of decaf brewed in the corner beside a tray of sandwich quarters someone had cut with care. Goldie took her usual seat at the end of the row closest to the door. She never stood first. She listened. She waited.

Tamara Morrow spoke up early, standing while the others murmured. Late twenties, denim jacket, keys looped around her wrist. Her boy had just turned six. First grade at Hampton Elementary. She wasn't there to make a speech—just a mother who hadn't slept.

"My son's been having nosebleeds again," she said. "Three times this week. Says the back of his throat burns when he plays too long. Every time he runs near that ditch, he comes back wheezing."

People shifted in their seats. Someone whispered, *That's the water again.*

Tamara looked around the room. "It smells different. Not just musty. Like chemicals. Sharp. And there's red in the mud now. I seen it. I told the pediatrician and he just shrugged."

Goldie didn't speak. She nodded, writing nothing down. It was already written.

A man in the second row asked if the park was still listed as a closed remediation site. Another woman—old-timer, sharp—said she'd called the city but got put on hold. Again.

At the front of the room, Councilwoman Yvonne Hightower stood with her hands clasped just below her waist. She wore a dark blouse and flat shoes, no jewelry beyond the pin on her collar. She'd been to three of these meetings in the past month. She looked more tired each time. But she showed up.

"I'm pushing every lever I can," she said. "I've raised this in subcommittee, brought it up during capital budgeting, and filed a formal request for environmental reassessment. I'm not getting traction."

Tamara's voice came again, small but hard. "Why not?"

Hightower hesitated—not because she didn't know, but because she couldn't say it plainly.

"It's like... like something's shifting out from under it," she said. "Every time we move toward answers, someone rewrites the map. The reports vanish into other reports. I don't have the language for what's happening, but I feel it."

She looked across the room, let the heft of that admission settle.

"I know when we're being ignored. This is different. It's like they want to act like the harm never happened at all."

That was when Goldie stood. She straightened her spine and cleared her throat.

"That park has buried more than toxins," she said. "It's buried memory. But not all the way. Because we're still here."

She looked at Tamara, then at Hightower.

"So we stop waiting. We get our own soil tested. We start the neighborhood group. We make it formal. Not just mad. Organized. And we keep saying the names."

A quiet fell over the room. Goldie sat back down. And the pens came out.

The kettle clicked off with a hollow tick, and Goldie poured the water over a sachet of black tea in her aged mug—the one with the faded gold text: Dudley High Class of '76. The handle had been cracked for a decade, but she wrapped her fingers around it with the same quiet stubbornness she applied to most things.

Through the kitchen window, the early light hit Bingham Street in slanted pieces—angled across the porch rails, the busted mailbox two doors down, the buckled concrete where tree roots had lifted the sidewalk. She watched a man walk his dog along the park's northern fence, same dog, same coat, every morning since January. Beyond him, the high grass swayed around the chain link. Nothing had changed, except everything had.

She'd lived on this street most of her life. Her mother's house first—a narrow shotgun three blocks west, the smell of fried okra and mothballs stitched into the curtains. She remembered the protests in '68, when her father had stood outside the textile mill with a cardboard sign and a linen suit too warm for spring. She was ten, wearing her Sunday shoes on a Tuesday because her mother said dignity had no schedule.

She moved to this house the year after her second child was born. Back then, the neighborhood was dense with working families—mail carriers, teachers, veterans with back injuries. Before the layoffs. Before the mortgage pyramid that collapsed in on itself. Before the flood of closures and the slow, mean silence from the city.

They remodeled the basketball court at Bingham Park the same year Reagan won his second term, made it look like progress. They upgraded the playground with metal swings, picnic tables sunk into the dirt, trash bins that tipped in the wind. Then came the first leachate—quiet, unacknowledged, oozing from the soil above the creek, layered under topsoil the color of denial.

Her daughter had grown up beside that park. Her youngest grandson had played there until the coughing started. Goldie rinsed her mug, laid it in the sink without sound. She moved with the careful rhythm of a woman who'd learned not to waste energy on what wasn't hers to control. She packed her bag—testimony printouts, a vial of creek sediment double-bagged in plastic, a list of names handwritten last night at the dining room table.

She pulled her coat over her shoulders, locked the door, and stepped onto the porch. The morning was cool. She looked south, toward the chain link fence and the red warning sign still clinging to its bent post. She didn't need it to be fixed yet. She just needed it to be seen.

It hadn't started with rage. That came later. What came first was a kind of confusion—quiet, persistent, difficult to name. Her grandson, Marcus, had always been a sturdy boy, broad-shouldered by six, legs full of run. He spent his afternoons tearing through the yard and into the slope below the park, tossing rocks into the creekbed, coming home with mud caked on his shoes and under his nails.

Then came the wheezing.

At first, it was only at night. Then in the morning. Then even after rest. He'd wake coughing, his pillow damp, nose bleeding without warning. The pediatrician called it seasonal. Then viral. Then maybe something environmental, maybe mold. She scrubbed the house twice over. Pulled up carpet. Bought new filters. Changed the soaps. None of it mattered.

One night she caught him kneeling by the creek, hands sunk wrist-deep in the rust-red mud where the slope dipped behind the fence. The boy said it shimmered. That it looked magic in the late light. He wanted to take some home in a jar. The color sank into her then—not just the mud, but the shape of his lungs, the absence of clarity in every answer she was given.

She'd lived through city promises. Knew what it meant when a report went missing, when the cleanup never got scheduled, when the grant writer stopped returning calls. But this wasn't theoretical anymore. It had a body. It had breath.

She called the city's environmental line. Left voicemails. Asked for documents. Drove to the county building twice and waited in the records room. Found a clerk who remembered the name Bingham but not what it had been built on. Found another who handed her a file with half its pages missing. She began to walk the neighborhood. Asking. Listening. Collecting.

The anger came slowly, but when it did, it was total. No one was coming. No plan was on the way. And she couldn't afford to sit with the quiet knowledge that children were growing up with their bodies mapped by someone else's mistake—someone else's indifference.

She joined the PTA, then the neighborhood committee. She called old friends from her organizing days. Got on the agenda at city meetings. She asked questions. Asked for records. Asked again. And when the answers remained silent, she made a list of everyone who had ever fallen ill within six blocks of the park.

She didn't care if it proved anything. She just needed someone to see. To hear the names spoken aloud. It wouldn't save Marcus.

But it might stop the next shimmer from catching someone else's child.

The lot behind the old duplex on McConnell Road had been used as an illegal dump site for years—busted lawnmowers, broken pallets, old tires half-buried in bramble. But it backed up to the creek, and Goldie had a memory of that space before the rust came—when kids used to chase bottle caps in the runoff and summer evenings still smelled like grass.

She wore gloves, thick and frayed at the fingertips, and dragged a bag of plastic bottles toward the curb. Behind her, Tamara was stooped over a pile of soggy insulation, eyes watering from the effort. Her hoodie was spotted with mud. Her hair tied back in a loose scarf.

"Found a toy truck in there," Tamara said, straightening. "Plastic wheels melted flat. God knows how long it's been under all that."

Goldie pulled off one glove. "Some child had a birthday in the dirt," she said. "That's how it is around here. No party favors. Just rot wrapped in ribbon."

Tamara didn't laugh. Her face tightened. She opened her mouth, hesitated, then spoke with worry.

"Devin was back in the ER last week. Breathing again. They gave me a pamphlet this time. Asthma management for urban families."

Goldie looked up.

"You ask them if they test the soil behind your place?"

"They said it's probably allergies. But they don't ask what he breathes when he plays. They just write another prescription." She exhaled. "He used to love going behind the fence. Now he doesn't run. Just sits and looks. Says the air makes his chest feel hot."

Goldie wiped her hands on her jeans, her eyes narrowing toward the tree line.

"That's how it started with Marcus," she said. "First the wheezing, then the bleeding. They kept saying maybe mold. Or just nerves. But nerves don't make your mouth taste metal."

A rustle in the brush caught their attention. Ava emerged from the path beside the creek, her messenger bag swinging at her hip, lab coat half-zipped over a Howard University sweatshirt. She carried a soil auger and a narrow cooler marked with Alan Ransome's university seal.

"I brought new sample vials," Ava said, stepping onto the cleared patch. "Alan wanted new readings along the north bank. The last batch came back... weird."

Goldie nodded. "The stuff near the water?"

"Chromium levels elevated. Too high for standard runoff. And there's something off with the coloring—like iron, but not. It's binding in ways I've never seen."

Tamara's face paled. "Chromium? Isn't that the stuff in that Erin Brockovich movie?"

"Depends on the valence state," Ava said, crouching beside a patch of disturbed soil. "Could be trivalent—less toxic. But we think it's hexavalent. That's the one that gets in your lungs. Your bones."

Goldie's breath slowed.

"You can tell that from dirt?"

"Not fully," Ava admitted. "I need lab confirmation. The equipment we have isn't perfect. But I know when a sample glows wrong."

Tamara crouched beside her, watching the extraction.

"How does it just sit here? Like this? With kids playing feet away?"

Goldie didn't answer. She stepped closer to the creek, where the water ran slow over stones flecked with red sediment. She watched the current shift around the roots.

"We're not waiting anymore," she said. "Not for the city. Not for a study. We're collecting, cataloging, documenting. We'll make our own record."

Ava sealed the first vial, labeling it in careful black pen.

"And when you have proof?" Tamara asked.

"Then we say it out loud," Goldie said. "To every paper, every camera, every council seat too scared to listen. We hold up the jar and we say: This is where the children got sick. And you knew."

The creek moved on beneath them. But the silence in the lot had changed. Tamara stood, brushing grit from her knees, eyes narrowed toward the skyline barely visible through the trees.

"But why?" she asked. "Why does it stay like this? Why the hell are we the ones always cleaning up what they leave behind? Why's the park still fenced off a decade later like it's waiting for a funeral?"

Goldie straightened, pulled her gloves off finger by finger, and tucked them into her back pocket.

"It's not about the park," she said. "Not really. It's about what the park reminds them of—what they've tried to forget. And what fixing it would mean."

Tamara crossed her arms, the anger starting to settle into something harder.

"So why doesn't Hightower call it out? Why can't she do more?"

Goldie turned toward her, steady.

"Because she's one woman in a machine built to grind that kind of voice into procedural dust. Don't let her calm fool you. She's been fighting. She's asked the questions, called the hearings, pushed for the budget lines. But she can't move when every committee chair cuts her microphone, and every vote gets traded for a sidewalk outside a brewery."

Tamara didn't look convinced. Goldie kept going.

"You know who writes the agendas? Dent. You know where the federal block grants go? Business development zones. You know what gets called a 'community priority'? Bike lanes between the baseball stadium and the vegan bakery."

Ava, crouched nearby, looked up from the cooler.

"We don't even have a damn crosstown bus route," Goldie said. "How you gonna tell people to apply for jobs at the industrial park if they can't get there without two transfers and a walk under the highway?"

Tamara let out a bitter laugh.

Goldie continued, voice quieter now. "They cut the east side out the minute they saw profit in the South Elm corridor. Left us with no grocery store, no pharmacy, no cleanup plan. Only promises. Pretty renderings. Shiny words."

"And the playground," Ava added, closing the cooler. "Don't forget the playground."

Goldie looked past them, down toward the ditch where the creek caught the morning sun and glimmered red.

"They think if they build something sweet on top of the silence, we'll stop talking."

Tamara wiped her palms on her jeans.

"They were wrong," she said.

Goldie nodded once, slow. "They were."

Ava zipped the cooler shut and stood, brushing a line of pine needles from her coat. Her fingers moved quickly—vials secured, clipboard stowed, labels double-checked. She adjusted the strap across her chest and gave a small exhale, not out of fatigue, but as if her mind was already moving ahead to the chain-of-custody form and the lab fridge she'd need to clear out before lunch.

"I'll get these logged by noon," she said. "We'll run initial assays in Dr. Chen's lab, and Alan wants to cross-reference the chromium spikes with a map he pulled from a zoning archive. Something about stormwater runoff patterns from '94. I'll call you as soon as we know more."

Goldie gave her a long, appreciative look. "Thank you for showing up. I know how these places treat students. He's lucky to have you."

Ava smiled but didn't deflect it. "I grew up across the street from a brownfield. Nobody told us what it was. I'm not doing this for a résumé."

Tamara stepped forward and handed Ava a plastic grocery bag, tied and knotted. Inside was a small plastic container—mud from the yard near her boy's playset.

"In case it helps," she said.

Ava took it gently, nodding. "It might."

She turned then, boots crunching across the gravel path. The sun had cleared the rooftops now, casting sharp shadows across the chain-link. Ava stepped over a cluster of glass shards near the curb, paused, and looked back.

"Goldie," she said. "He believes in this. He's not chasing press. He wants the truth."

Goldie nodded, the corners of her mouth pulling into something firmer than a smile. "So do we."

Ava lifted her hand, then was gone, her figure disappearing past the edge of the lot and into the narrow street where the world still moved as if nothing were burning beneath it. Goldie stood for a while after. Tamara beside her. The creek muttered its steady, poisonous lullaby. The red shimmer in the ditch caught the light just once before clouding back over.

Back in her kitchen, Goldie peeled an orange slowly over the sink, the rind curling in one long spiral before it dropped into the basin. The house was quiet except for the radio on the windowsill—classical, something string-heavy and sorrowful. Her thoughts were back in February, when the mailer from Guilford Health had arrived, all white space and careful fonts, declaring the future with a glossy smile: South Elm Wellness and Innovation Corridor—Equity in Action.

She'd stared at it for a long time before setting it beside her coffee cup. Then she'd picked up the phone. Alan had answered on the third ring, voice tight with surprise. They hadn't spoken in over a year.

"You seen this brochure?"

"I've seen the plans," he'd said, quiet. "Didn't know they were already pushing it."

"They're not just pushing it. They're planting it. Right in our faces. Like we ain't shit."

Three days later, he came to see Bingham Park again. Wore the same threadbare field jacket he always had, carrying a leather-bound notebook tucked under his arm. She met him at the south fence, where the slope dipped into the tangle of kudzu and low brush. He climbed the ridge and stood silent a long time, looking down at the run-off crease. The red shimmer was there even then, faint in the mud.

"You remember that hearing in 2009?" Goldie asked. "The one where they promised a full soil remediation plan? Said they were seeking bids?"

"I didn't have tenure yet then," Alan said. "But I pulled the file. They stopped at phase one. No test beyond two meters. They called it cost prohibitive."

"They called it closed," Goldie said. "Left the fence and a sign and said it was safer that way. Safer for who?"

He crouched to pick up a piece of trash—half a rusted toy car. He turned it in his hand like it might still explain something.

"Back then," he said, "we didn't have data sets. Just witness testimony. Now we've got isotope testing. Thermal spectrometry. If we build the right evidence chain, we can put pressure on multiple points—city, county, environmental review. Maybe even the city's insurer."

Goldie had raised an eyebrow. "Pressure doesn't mean cleanup."

"No," he said. "But it means shame. Which, if wielded right, can get results."

She'd looked at him for a long moment, measuring whether he still meant it. Whether his fire had turned academic or stayed lit.

"What do you need from me?" she asked.

He'd answered without hesitation.

"Names. Patterns. Soil access. And time."

She gave him all of it.

And now, as the orange rind filled the sink with its sharp tang, Goldie rinsed her hands and looked out the window toward Bingham Street, where a boy had once knelt by the creek and whispered that the mud looked magic. This time, the lie wouldn't hold. Not with Alan watching. Not with her walking the fence line again.

They came early, as they always did. A Wednesday night ritual in a building that had survived three storms, two break-ins, and one roofing scandal involving a cousin of the deacon's wife. The drywall had been patched, the ceiling fan still ticked overhead, and the heat stuttered on just enough to fight off the spring chill that crept up from the foundation. Goldie slipped in behind Mrs. Forrester, who wore a lavender coat and carried her Bible in a cloth sleeve embroidered with gold thread.

"You still wearing that coat?" Goldie teased.

Mrs. Forrester gave her a look. "Child, when they start burying us with new coats, then I'll get one."

They laughed, and around them the space filled with gentle chatter.

Maya Dennis, who ran the in-home daycare down on Gillespie Street, was talking about her niece getting accepted to A&T—full ride, biology track, said she wanted to be a vet. Leroy Banks had news from his cousin in Fayetteville who got rehired by the post office after two years out. Someone passed around photos of a birthday party in a backyard lined with lawn chairs and foil pans stacked on a picnic table. Children were mentioned—report cards, dental work, football tryouts. Recipes were exchanged, softly, over the wheeze of an old heater: collards with smoked paprika, a cobbler done with frozen peaches when the fresh weren't right.

The meeting hadn't started, but the gathering had already done what it came to do—remind them they were still here. Goldie made her way toward the coffee urn. That was where Miss Bernice sat, as she always had, her coat neatly on her lap, her white hair pinned back in the same twist she'd worn since before Goldie was born.

"You walkin' stiff," Bernice said, without looking up from her tea.

"Creek path's muddy," Goldie replied. "Hard on the knees."

"They've been hard on us for a long time," Bernice murmured.

She looked at Goldie then, and something passed between them.

"You keepin' it all?" Bernice asked. "The stories, the names?"

"I'm trying."

Bernice nodded, slow. "The ones who could tell it clean are going quiet. Clara's forgettin' street names now. Vernon couldn't place his mother's address last Sunday. We don't have much time."

Goldie swallowed. "I've written down what I can."

Bernice's eyes narrowed, kind but unsparing. "It's not just the facts. It's the feelin' in 'em. If you don't pass that down right, they'll think we were grateful. They'll think we agreed."

Goldie nodded. "I know."

"They built this city over our backs," Bernice said. "And now they want to smooth the ground and call it history. You don't let them."

"I won't."

Bernice took a sip of her tea and looked away again, satisfied by the tone. By the resolve. The heater hissed, and the rustle of Bible pages began as someone called the meeting to order. Goldie returned to her seat. She didn't need the scripture to tell her what she already knew: The truth would vanish unless she walked it into the future, one story at a time.

Goldie moved through the house in the quiet of evening, clicking off lamps, checking the back door lock, straightening the shoes by the threshold with one toe. The porch light cast a glow across the front room. The windows were dark now, reflecting her shape back to her—a silhouette that had grown thinner, more still.

In the hallway, she paused by the small table near the coat rack where a photo of Marcus leaned against a vase filled with silk lilies. His second-grade portrait. Wide smile, two front teeth missing, blue polo shirt too bright for the frame. She touched the edge of the photo, just once.

The final weeks had passed like water through cupped hands—impossible to hold, impossible to forget. One day he was running through the back yard, hollering for her to watch his cartwheel. The next, he was waking at midnight with blood on the pillow. Then hospital stays. Inhalers. The small oxygen tank by his bed. He never stopped being sweet, not even when the coughing came in fits that bent him double.

They said the diagnosis was genetic. Said it might've been caught earlier. But Goldie knew better. She'd seen the mud under his nails, the red dust on the soles of his shoes. She'd washed it out of his socks with her own hands, and still, they told her nothing was proven. The rage had arrived like a fire that wouldn't quit burning.

The council meeting that spring was supposed to bring answers. Instead, it brought Dent and his placid voice, reciting phrases written somewhere far from the creekbed. "Pre-regulatory landfill," he'd said. "Limited municipal capacity." Then he'd pivoted—smoothed his hands on the podium and praised the promise of the wellness corridor project. He called it a step forward. Called it healing.

Only Hightower had met her eyes when Goldie stood to speak. Goldie remembered the tilt of Yvonne's head, the way her lips pressed thin. A look that said: Girl, we know. We all know. But knowing wasn't power. Not in that room. Not when the gavel dropped and the vote sailed through. The chairs scraped back, the papers were gathered. No one asked about the child who had stopped breathing before his twelfth birthday. No one named the soil. No one returned her calls after that.

Back in the present, Goldie flicked off the final light. The house settled. She stood in the hallway for a long time, the photo still catching what little light remained. She was tired—yes, her bones told her so every time she bent, every time she stood. But Marcus had trusted her. Had told her, even in the thin days near the end, that she made him feel safe. That she made things make sense.

So she couldn't stop. Not when the city had built a park on a dump site and called it progress. Not when his shoes still sat in the back closet, toes scuffed from running through dirt no child should ever touch. She whispered his name once, as if to remind herself what mattered. Then she turned and walked down the hall, steady, deliberate, as if each step carried him forward too.

The fume hood droned as Ava adjusted the pipette, her gloved hand steady despite the hour. The lab was quiet—just her and the thrum of machinery, glass clinking fragile on glass, the centrifuge warming up in the corner with its usual whine. Mid-afternoon sun filtered through the blinds in dusty shafts, catching the edge of a whiteboard scribbled over with compound chains and half-erased deadlines.

She'd run the soil sample twice already. Once with the colorimetric kit, once with the ion-specific probe. The second result matched the first. Chromium. Elevated. She leaned over the readout again, tracing the peak on the spectrograph, the numbers just outside the range of plausible runoff. Not enough for a regulatory flag. But high enough to say the land was holding more than history.

Alan would want the full breakdown. She could already hear his voice in her head—careful, even, but tight with that edge he carried when something confirmed what he'd feared.

She pulled out the logbook and wrote:

Sample 022 – Bingham perimeter, north slope, 10cm depth. Chromium elevated. Possible incinerator signature. Source unresolved. Further analysis required.

Then, under her breath, just to herself: "It's definitely from the old incinerator..."

But she hesitated. Because she knew what the old reports claimed: that the incinerator waste had been removed, capped, sealed under clay decades ago. She'd read the city's environmental narrative—the sanitized version. The one that never mentioned ash or runoff. The one that listed "pre-regulatory materials" without naming what they were.

She wiped her gloves on a fresh towel, stared down at the third vial still to be tested, and realized she didn't believe the story anymore. Not the official one. Not the engineered silence passed off as public record. This wasn't a residual trace. It was active. Still moving. Still seeping. She labeled the final sample, sealed it in the cooler, and sat for a moment without speaking.

The lab was alive around her. Ava reached for her phone to text Alan.

Prelim looks bad. Will explain in person. Need full panel. She paused. Then added: It's not just ash. Something's alive in this.

She hit send. Then turned back to the table.

Alan arrived at the lab still carrying the pressure of the day. He moved with a kind of internal momentum, a quiet, urgent energy that knew the difference between waiting and wasting time. Ava looked up from her bench as the door clicked shut behind him. She gestured toward the data printouts splayed across the lab counter.

"I ran the quick panels again. Same result. Chromium. Elevated enough to make me sweat a little."

Alan peeled off his coat. He leaned in, tracing the numbers with his index finger.

"How much?"

"Baseline ambient for this region should be around 2 ppm," she said. "We're pushing eight. Ten in the ditch runoff. That's outside normal industrial background levels, even without a live source nearby."

He exhaled. "And they still say the incinerator waste was remediated."

"'Capped and transferred,'" she said, using air quotes. "But no one logged a chain of custody for the waste. The site inventory just... stops."

Alan leaned back, rubbed his temples for a moment. "That neighborhood's waited over a decade for a fence to come down. They've watched their children get sick and been told it's coincidence. If this chromium's tied to the old waste..."

"Then somebody lied," Ava said. "At scale."

She walked to the far end of the bench and pulled a small plastic bag from the cooler. Inside was a sample of red particulate soil—fine, dry, and oddly uniform.

"I didn't run this yet," she said. "It's not from a core. Tamara scooped it up off the top layer near the creekbed. I've seen iron-rich clay before. This isn't that."

She held the bag toward the light. The red wasn't natural. It was too vivid, too stubborn. Not brick dust. Not rust.

"Weird stuff," she said. "Looks like rust, but it isn't. Doesn't oxidize right. Doesn't break down in water. My guess is it's carrying something—maybe chromium in a compound we don't have the tools here to isolate."

Alan took the bag from her, turned it in his hand. "Red sand," he said, almost to himself. "Same color I saw in the runoff last year behind the Hampton school site. But that tested clean."

"Clean doesn't mean safe," Ava said. "Clean means inconclusive unless you're willing to dig deeper."

He was quiet for a long moment. Then: "If they stabilized the site without real remediation—if they capped it and built over it—they might've trapped active material. This runoff could be leaching through whatever barrier they left."

Ava nodded. "Especially with recent rain. That would explain the spike."

Alan placed the bag on the table gently, as if setting down a fragile part of the past.

"This neighborhood deserves answers," he said. "Not placation. Answers. We owe them more than peer-reviewed silence."

Ava's voice dropped, quiet but firm. "Then we need outside testing. Beyond campus. And someone with standing to demand access to the construction data."

Alan's gaze sharpened. "I'll talk to Hightower. She still has committee leverage. Enough to open records without triggering red tape."

"And if the records are buried?" Ava asked.

"Then we make noise," he said.

He picked up the printout again. The numbers were just data—but underneath them was something breathing. Something long hidden. Maybe not just negligence. Maybe a design. The city had moved forward, yes. But it hadn't cleaned up after itself. He looked back at the bag of red sand. What lies get planted under playgrounds, he thought. And how many children run across them before someone decides to look down.

"Let's keep going," he said. "All the way in."

6

Alan gripped the elliptical's handles tight enough to ache at the knuckles, legs driving the motion forward in symbolic violence. The pulse sensor blinked red at intervals that didn't match the music in his headphones, didn't match anything but the sharp rhythm of his breath.

The fitness center was half-full. Students on treadmills scrolled phones without breaking pace. A staffer wiped down benches near the weight rack. Rows of silent TVs played muted morning news loops—headlines of national nothing, B-roll of perp walks and political handshakes.

He watched none of it.

He'd been pushing hard for twenty minutes—too hard for a warmup, not quite hard enough to punish himself. Sweat mired the collar of his shirt and ran down the inside of his arms. His thighs burned. His jaw clenched. And still he pressed forward, one stride after another.

A valve opening. That's how it felt. Every push a release. Every movement a way of keeping panic from hardening into paralysis. The red sand. Ava's report. The map still silent in his desk drawer. He'd slept little the night before. Lay awake thinking about the children who had played in soil marked safe by omission. About the parents who had stopped asking because asking had never been enough. And now, under the lights of the university gym, with the rubber molded rhythm of the elliptical beneath his feet, he allowed himself to drift. Only breath. Only motion.

His muscles pulled harder with each surge, a pace approaching something desperate. His heart thudded like it wanted out. And he let it. For now. He let it all burn. The body had its own way of sorting truth. The body knew before the institutions ever would.

His footfalls never slowed, but his eyes caught the flicker—top-right monitor above the tread row, sound muted, chyron scrolling. The city seal in the background, a brushed steel podium in front, and David Moss's face angled slightly in profile, tie sharp, smile held in a sculpted half-step between sincerity and resolve.

"We're not just breaking ground. We're building trust."

The caption beneath his image crawled past twice before Alan registered it. He tore the headphones from his ears. Not because he wanted to hear—he didn't—but because the sight of David speaking while Alan burned under fluorescent light was suddenly too much to mute. The segment cut to footage of a render: sleek glass walls, a playground bright with synthetic green, benches curving along concrete stamped with the words Community First. The crowd behind David nodded in ceremonial agreement—council members, clergy, a girl in a windbreaker smiling politely for the camera. Someone handed David a shovel. The photo op completed the arc.

Alan's pulse leapt. His hands tightened until the elliptical's plastic grips creaked. It wasn't just the hypocrisy—though that was endless. It was the gall of the gesture. The city, newly invested in a wellness corridor whose very soil was supposedly cleaned, its promises smoothed by budget language and borrowed equity. Moss knew how to stage it. He always had. He knew how to wrap betrayal in civic velvet, how to smile while stepping over the wreckage.

We're advancing opportunity for all, the chyron read.

Alan could still hear the woman at the Bingham meeting—Tamara—describing her boy's nosebleeds, the way his breath caught when the wind turned the wrong way. Could still see the glint in Ava's sample bag. The shimmer in the soil where no shimmer should be. The corridor vote had passed. The permits were issued. The money was flowing. All with a fence still up around Bingham Park and no remediation plan on file.

We're building trust.

Alan wanted to tear the screen off the wall. Instead, he slammed the machine's stop button. The elliptical slowed to stillness. His breath came hard, broken by fury. David had always believed the future belonged to those who could narrate it best. But Alan had walked the dirt. He had tested the water. He had listened to the families when the cameras were gone.

Let them build their corridor, he thought. Let them smile for the ribbon and call it justice. But the ground still held its secrets. And now he did, too.

The hallway to the locker room smelled of chlorine and sweat masked under citrus. Alan clutched his towel in one hand, jaw tight, skin still hot from the elliptical. But the heat in him now wasn't from exertion. It had risen the moment David's face appeared on that screen. And with it, the memory—the one that always arrived without being summoned, the one he could never scrub from the archive of his mind.

She'd said it in the courtyard behind the Wilson Library. Winter light falling through leafless branches, Paula wrapped in a charcoal wool coat, gloves pulled on too tight. He'd thought they were meeting to talk through a fight. Something fixable. Instead, she said it plainly.

"You're a good man, Alan. But this isn't working."

He remembered the way his ears had started ringing, not with sadness—at first—but with confusion.

She kept going, gentle but mechanical.

"You've got so much... intensity. You care so deeply about everything. That's not bad. It's just..." Her eyes drifted. "You need someone more on your level."

That sentence had never left him. What level? What terrain had she decided he no longer shared? Was it about class, polish, ambition? Was it that she had grown tired of the way he read federal housing codes in the evenings while she played Chopin in the next room? Or that he asked too many questions no one wanted to answer?

Later, he would understand that David had already been in the background. That some paths are easier to walk when the path is already laid smooth. But in that moment, all he'd heard was that she was stepping into a world where he didn't belong. He had nodded, he remembered that. A single, hollow nod, and the feeling of his breath going nowhere. She hadn't said goodbye. Just turned and walked, her boots careful on the gravel path.

And he had stood there, stunned. Not heartbroken in the way poets describe. Just... displaced. Like someone had changed the rules of the world and handed him the manual in a foreign language.

Alan threw his towel on the bench and opened his locker. He wasn't done. Not with David. Not with the truth. And not with the woman who had once looked at him and decided he was too far from where she wanted to be.

Alan stepped into the shower stall and turned the handle hard left, no negotiation. The frigid spray slammed against his chest, a sharpness that banished the last threads of sweat and rage. He stood motionless beneath it, jaw clenched, palms against the tiled wall, breath held as long as his lungs would let him. He'd learned this discipline in the dark months—those weeks after Paula ended it, when mornings blurred into afternoons and sleep came only in pieces. Back then, his therapist had taught him how to interrupt spirals. "Come back to the body, Alan. Return to the breath. Say the thing that's real."

Now, beneath the glacial water, he closed his eyes and said it.

"I do the work because it matters. Even if it hurts. Even if I lose."

It was survival—a posture he'd pushed himself into until it became permanent. He let the water beat down another minute, then turned it off with a sharp flick. Toweled himself dry in silence. Dressed slowly in clean clothes, hands steady again.

By the time he stepped out into the hallway and pushed the glass door open onto campus, the wind had softened, the sky sharpening into one of those late afternoons where the light looks dipped in gold and the buildings stand taller just for being seen in it. The quad was half full—students sprawled on the grass, earbuds in, laptops out. Two walked past him debating something about corporate taxes and fair share, their voices bright and hopeful. He walked without hurry, cutting across the lawn toward the humanities building, then past the sculpture garden that always seemed to change shape in shadow.

He wasn't thinking of Paula anymore. But her presence still moved through him, like a trace metal in the bloodstream. Inert. The anger was quieter now. And under it, the work remained.

Goldie's voice came back to him—low and unshakable, from that morning by the creek. "We say the names. We keep asking. We don't stop just because they pretend not to hear."

Alan reached the main path, the campus opening before him. He would keep going. Because someone had to. Because if the city wouldn't answer, he would ask louder. For Marcus. For Devin. For the red sand and the quiet poisons and the mothers who kept their calendars full of doctor's visits and silence.

The air smelled clean in that moment. But Alan knew better. He walked on anyway.

The office was sharpened by the afternoon sun warming the edge of the windowpane. Alan stepped in, let the door close behind him without thought, and slid into the rhythm of small tasks—calendar updates, a faculty memo on an accreditation visit, three student emails answered in clipped but kind sentences.

There was still time before his lecture. Enough to settle. Enough to forget, for a moment, the concern he'd carried all week. But the map remained where he'd left it—half-unfolded at the corner of his desk, as if waiting. He hadn't moved it in days, yet it had taken up more space than it should. He reached for it now, flattened its creases with deliberate care.

The paper was thick, archival. City-issued, stamped in blue ink from 1994. The parcel boundaries etched in neat lines, zoning codes in faded serif. Most of it was unremarkable. But near the bottom edge, between a wastewater easement and a former rail spur, one rectangular plot stood marked in red. A single circle, drawn in firm, steady pen, as if someone had wanted him to notice.

There was no annotation, no cross-reference. The city's current GIS files didn't mention it. Ava hadn't found it in her preliminary overlays either. It didn't show up in any public redevelopment plans, or the corridor documents that had passed through council last week with all their glossy renderings and PR spin.

He leaned closer, finger on the red ring. Someone had wanted this parcel seen. And whoever had sent it—anonymous, deliberate, silent—had known that was all he needed.

The records desk was tucked behind a half-wall of plexiglass and faded signage, quiet but not hushed. The ruffle of paper, the occasional thud of a drawer, and the stale fluorescents overhead giving the beige linoleum a tired glare. Alan stepped up and offered the parcel number, already written on a notecard. The woman behind the counter took it without looking at him, glanced down over the rims of her glasses, and sighed.

"You a lawyer?" she asked, tapping at a dusty keyboard.

"No," Alan said. "University."

She nodded slowly, unimpressed. "Of course you are."

She stood as if her knees gave feedback with each step. Her orthopedic soles stepped softly against the tile as she disappeared behind a row of metal cabinets, muttering something inaudible that might've been about the weather or public salaries or both. Alan leaned on the counter and waited. The city records office always seemed like it had once been set up for speed but was now a labyrinth of slowness.

After a few minutes, she returned with a slim file, rubber band barely holding its corners.

"This is all we've got," she said. "Some of the stuff from that year never made it through the second scanning initiative. Back then they were too busy playing musical chairs with redevelopment titles."

She slid it toward him, then squinted. "Midland parcel?"

"That's right."

She shook her head. "People don't usually come digging for that one. It's been quiet since the early aughts. Some grant consortium tried to buy it once, but they got redirected to stormwater easements and never circled back."

Alan opened the folder slowly. A thin stack—deed transfer, zoning map, a redacted compliance letter dated May 1994.

"Midland Legacy Trust," he read aloud.

"Yeah," she said. "That was a ghost outfit. They handled parcels nobody wanted to name. Real behind-the-curtain type stuff. Shell of a shell. Folded in 2006."

He looked up. "Who owned it before?"

"City," she said, already returning to her seat. "Since the sixties. Before that, it was listed as surplus utility land. Some of the old parks and dumps got labeled that way when they didn't know what else to do with them."

Alan held the compliance letter up to the light. Half the lines blacked out.

"Any environmental documentation?"

She snorted, cracking a mint from the side drawer of her desk.

"Not unless you brought a shovel," she said. "Or a subpoena."

Alan asked for several of the documents to be copied and slid them into his bag and nodded thanks. The woman cracked the mints between her molars. "Don't let that place get under your skin," she said. "Every inch of this city has ghosts. Some just wear suits."

The late afternoon outside was unseasonably warm. The breeze pulled at his coat as he stepped into the street, head still inside the paperwork, his mind layering names and parcels, trying to see the lines where everything had been filed just enough out of sight. Then he heard it.

The rumble of a diesel engine rounding the corner—one of the city's work trucks, gray body dulled by time and usage. It passed slowly, turning toward the municipal yard. The side panel bore the remnants of an earlier era: peeling vinyl, half-scraped lettering that caught the light for only a second.

South End Redevelopment Initiative.

Weathered. Almost erased. Alan stopped walking. Watched it disappear into the noise of the street, then reached into his bag and touched the envelope again. Its presence steadied him. He had what he needed. Not enough for proof. But enough to begin the telling.

Part Two

7

Allison Collins stood in front of the vanity mirror with one earring clipped, the other still resting in her palm. Her face, she thought, had become its own kind of production. A softness at the cheekbones that read as composure. A half-second delay before her smile that people mistook for elegance. It wasn't that she was unhappy. It was that the performance had gone on too long to remember which part of her was unscripted.

She met Keith her junior year at a fraternity mixer she hadn't planned to attend—last-minute dress from Belk, a friend who insisted. Keith, already sharp in a blue sportcoat with buttons too tight across the waist, spilled club soda on her skirt and apologized three times in a row. That, she would later realize, was his charm: excessive remorse masked as politeness. By Christmas they were inseparable. She liked the way Keith paid attention. At the time, she thought it was love. Later, she would understand it was something else—a kind of casting. She played the part well: dinners with his father at the country club, nodding through stories about leverage buyouts. Her own family—small-town, low budget, too much theater and not enough money—had taught her how to hold a room, but not how to belong in one.

By graduation, marrying Keith seemed not only reasonable but inevitable. He offered a future that required no rehearsals: clean apartment, plans articulated in spreadsheets and upward trajectories. She didn't love him, not the way the books promised, but she admired his steadiness. She admired what he seemed to offer—a life arranged in advance. The wedding was held in a converted vineyard outside Charlottesville. Her mother wept during the vows. Keith's father toasted to stability. She wore a backless gown and made it through the night without giving too much away.

In the years that followed, she built a life with precision. Seasonal mantles. Cocktail pairings. Pilates before board meetings. The children arrived on time, followed by the fundraisers, the social calendars, the committee memberships. She became the kind of woman who kept extra chargers in her glove compartment, who could execute a dinner party with two hours notice and leave no damage behind.

But lately, she had begun to feel herself sliding. The facade held. But there were pauses now. Long ones. In the kitchen, at the stoplight, at the edge of a child's recital. Gaps in the choreography. A slowing of breath between one gesture and the next. The performance was intact. But the line between the actress and the role had blurred. And somewhere in the quiet, she had begun to wonder what would happen if she missed her cue and no one took notice.

She clicked in the second earring, stood back from the mirror. The room was still. Her reflection looked polished. Pleasant. Almost real.

She had been looking for her keys. That was all. A Thursday in early spring, too warm, the kind of day when the windows stayed cracked and pollen filmed the cars before noon. She was late for a board meeting—garden club, or maybe PTA finance, they all blurred—and her handbag had been overturned in the rush to find a checkbook the week before. The keys were not on the hook, not in the junk drawer, not wedged between the couch cushions. She went out to the garage barefoot, already irritated, already composing the apology she'd offer when she walked in late but composed. She opened his car door and bent low, reaching beneath the driver's seat.

Her fingers touched paper. She pulled it out, expecting a grocery list, a child's drawing, maybe a takeout menu folded in half. But it was a hotel receipt. Burlington. A DoubleTree. Room 412. One-night stay. The date was two months old, a Tuesday. She remembered it immediately: Keith had said he was in Raleigh overnight for investor meetings, a dinner with someone from the Charlotte office. He'd texted her goodnight at ten-thirty. She had believed him because belief was easier than confrontation.

She sat in the car with the door still open, receipt trembling in her hand, eyes wide but dry. The name on the card matched his. The time stamp for checkout was six forty-five a.m. She had dropped the kids at school that morning and made eggs with too much pepper, thinking about a trip they might take in the summer, a place with water and quiet.

The anger arrived second. Shame came first. Not shame at his betrayal—but at her own dull surprise. The understanding that this had been possible for a long time. That she had enabled it with her detachment, her ease, the very same grace people complimented her on at fundraisers. She had made herself easy to admire, hard to feel.

That night, she didn't mention the receipt. She put it into the back of her journal and kissed him at the door. The confrontation came days later, staged as though the emotion had just surfaced. She cried then, quietly. He admitted it was "a lapse," that it "didn't mean anything," that he "felt disconnected." She had not screamed. She had not threatened to leave.

They agreed—for the children—to work through it. That was three years ago. And every day since, she had worn her life like a necklace too fine to remove. In public, she was luminous. At home, she was invisible. She knew what the receipt had taken from her. The illusion that her performance had meaning. That the act could substitute for love.

Now, each morning, she chose her earrings with care. She filled vases. She baked for school auctions. She answered with a smile when asked how she and Keith were doing. And she never again lost her keys.

The Porsche Macan pulled smoothly into the gravel half-circle outside the Lindley Park arboretum pavilion, tires crunching lightly over the trimmed path lined in daylilies and river stones. Allison paused before getting out—checked her lip gloss in the visor mirror, reapplied without thinking. The jumpsuit was cream linen, tailored at the waist, and fell with a softness she trusted. She had chosen the gold sandals with restraint: enough shimmer to catch the light, not so much as to suggest she was trying.

The fundraiser had been themed by committee—A Midsummer Garden Fête—a name pitched by a retired Shakespeare professor whose own backyard still bore fake cobblestones from a failed Romeo & Juliet immersive experience. But the setting was, as always, beautiful.

Hydrangeas were blooming out of their seasonal rhythm. The table linens were pale rose, and someone had arranged the hors d'oeuvres in a spiral that looked lifted from a wedding magazine. The theater board had brought in high schoolers to wear fairy wings and pass rosé in chilled glasses. Allison slipped in, greeted by a round of air-kisses and soft hands. The shade fell in patterned slices across the lawn.

"Darling," came a voice behind her. She turned. Blythe Carrington—married to the orthodontist on the hospital board—stepped in close. "You absolutely killed it as Titania. I told Bill, if the city still had any taste, you'd be running Triad Stage instead of fundraising for it."

"Careful," Allison smiled. "Say things like that and I might start believing you."

Blythe took her arm in a companionable clasp. "The whole second act—you floated. I wept. Real tears. My sister said the way you turned your head when you dismissed Oberon—it was like Catherine Deneuve with better posture."

Allison gave a modest shrug, her cheeks lifting. She had learned long ago not to disown praise outright. Accept it cleanly, push it inward, let it evaporate on its own. Another woman joined them—Virginia Lassiter, who chaired the theater auxiliary's outreach committee. She wore a floral caftan and carried a champagne flute though it was barely eleven-thirty.

"We were just saying," Virginia said, "the lighting, the costumes, the ambience—it made me remember why we need theater. In a world like this, God, we need something beautiful."

Allison nodded, feeling her cue.

"We try to give people that. A little hour in the dark where something honest might happen."

Virginia laughed lightly. "You make it sound dangerous."

"It is," Allison said. "That's the point."

The two women exchanged a glance, pleased by the sophistication of the sentiment. Blythe squeezed her arm again and wandered off toward the mimosa bar. Allison remained, letting herself scan the lawn, watching the tableau unfold—canvas tents pitched for shade, the mayor's assistant in a pale-blue dress making her rounds, two donors discussing the next season's gala in tones meant to be overheard. The scene was perfect. Everything in place.

And yet, as she moved forward to greet the next circle of patrons, Allison felt the familiar slip beneath her—something inside her body tugging one step out of rhythm, like the floor beneath her feet knew this too was only theater. And that she was both star and prop.

The prosecco was dry, poured too cold, and fizzed too fast, but Allison held the glass with grace. She moved through the garden with ease now, nodding, touching a shoulder here, offering a knowing glance there. Her smile had shape and calibration. Her presence gave the event a kind of legitimacy. One that couldn't be bought, only inherited through years of the right silences.

But the lights were wrong. Too flat near the fountain. Too much yellow in the whites. The garden's depth was being collapsed instead of sculpted, and it made her scalp prickle. She stopped near the stage riser and scanned for Drew, the young lighting tech who'd handled the second act cues on A Midsummer Night's Dream and made a point of complimenting her diction after every rehearsal.

She found him fiddling with the generator beside the hedge wall, crouched like a mechanic over something he'd half-rigged out of borrowed parts.

"Drew," she called, her voice low and directed. He stood quickly, nearly knocked the wrench from his belt.

"Allison... hi," he said. Then caught himself. "Mrs. Collins."

She tilted her head, a small smirk lifting the edge of her mouth. "You can drop the formality. It's a fundraiser, not the Folger."

Drew smiled too wide, pushed his hair behind one ear. "Sorry, I just... didn't expect you to notice the lights."

"I notice everything," she said. "It's a condition."

He laughed, but she didn't. She stepped closer, glass still held delicately between her fingers. "It's flat near the trellis. And the string wash is too close to the canopy line. You're losing the verticals."

He blinked, processing. "I thought... right. Yeah. I did bump it back six inches this morning. The stand kept catching wind. I can re-angle."

She nodded, then let her eyes linger. He had that clean, sun-warmed look. Freckles at the temples, arms just beginning to show their early-spring tone. Younger than she remembered from rehearsal. But not too young.

"I knew you'd get it," she said. "Most people just compliment the table settings and call it art direction."

He flushed, clearly thrilled. "You're not like most people."

She sipped her prosecco slowly. Tilted her chin toward the fountain. "Walk me through your fix?"

He moved beside her, quickly falling into rhythm. "If I reset the gels on the back rig, I can cool the angle. Let the foliage catch shadow. It's kind of what you did with your monologue in Act IV, pulling attention not by volume, but space."

She turned to him with half-lidded eyes. "You actually listened to that?"

"I was in the wings every night."

She let the silence stretch between them, let the heat of the day rest between their bodies. Then she smiled, small and slow.

"You should come by the next read-through. They're doing Twelfth Night. I'm playing Olivia."

His eyebrows rose, unsure whether to believe the invitation.

She touched his forearm lightly.

"Don't let them tell you lighting is background," she said. "Some of us know where the real power is."

She walked off before he could respond, her empty glass swinging gently in her hand, her pulse carrying something unfamiliar in its rhythm.

The clink of glass on silver tray followed her as she crossed back toward the drinks table, but Allison moved slowly now, cooling the flush that had risen under her collar. She didn't look back at Drew. The impression had been made. It would ripple, as these things always did.

She stepped lightly over a cracked stone paver and looked up and there was Paula Moss. Across the lawn. Standing with a small cluster of donors under the shade of the dogwood, hands folded just so, her face composed in that permanent calm that Allison had always found impossible to categorize. A kind of sovereign ease. Radiant, but in a muted register, as if her money had learned to whisper.

Allison slowed, suddenly parched.

She remembered the first time they'd met. It was her first baby shower, hosted by someone from Keith's firm in a sunlit living room with creaking floors and a grand piano no one played. Allison had been seven months along, wearing a long navy dress that clung just a little too much, her ankles already swelling. Paula had arrived late, apologetic but glowing, newly back from her honeymoon in Barcelona. She wore pale linen and carried a bottle of wine that wasn't on the registry. She moved through the room without effort, her voice warm and exact.

They had been introduced quickly. A brush of hands. A compliment on the dress. Allison had smiled and said thank you and then excused herself to the bathroom, where she sat on the edge of the tub and counted her breath in twos. She hadn't disliked Paula. But she had known immediately that she wasn't made of the same fabric. Paula had never performed for love. Love had always been given to her on porcelain plates, with the edges scalloped.

Allison watched her from across the lawn—her posture perfect, her expression composed, her silence more eloquent than Allison's best lines—and something inside her pinched. She accepted another glass from the tray and turned away before their eyes could meet.

The luncheon was plated with silver-rimmed porcelain, each salad arranged with a brush of vinaigrette and microgreens too fragile to serve by accident. Allison lowered herself into her seat at table three, smoothing her linen pants, the stem of her prosecco glass steady in her hand though she could already feel the wine's warmth moving into her chest, a gentle buzz that blurred the hard edges of desire.

The quartet played something baroque, all ornament and grace. She let her eyes drift again to Paula, still poised, now half-turned in conversation with a developer's wife, her hands motionless in her lap. Even seated, Paula's posture suggested a kind of contained knowledge, as though nothing in the room could surprise her. Allison looked away.

Drew was by the stage risers, crouched again near the lightboard, making adjustments that no one else would see. She watched the way his head tilted as he scanned the canopy, how careful he was not to intrude on the tableau. When he turned, their eyes met for only a moment and something in Allison's belly fluttered, sharp and foolish.

Then Prescott Brooks stepped to the microphone with his purple bow tie slightly crooked and endearing. The room quieted. He was the theater director. Prescott always spoke as though the world were made of secrets you could only hear if you truly listened.

"We gather in this garden," he began, "not only for beauty's sake, though God knows beauty is reason enough, but for the sacred labor of theater, which is, at its best, the act of telling a community the truth in disguise."

Allison took a sip of wine. Her name was coming.

"And today I want to thank someone who has, with more grace and stamina than most of us deserve, kept that sacred labor alive even when the ticket receipts ran thin. Allison Collins."

Applause. Light, restrained, the kind reserved for a familiar face in a town with too many luncheons. Still, it came. Even from Paula, who raised two fingers off her glass in a small, almost imperceptible nod. The sound reached Allison in a soft swell. She smiled, nodded. The clapping faded. Prescott continued with the pledge tiers, the matching donations, the sponsor shout-outs. Allison's thoughts drifted again.

She thought of Drew's fingers adjusting the light. The way he'd said "you're not like most people." The way he hadn't tried to charm her. How long had it been since anyone had looked at her like that and meant it? The wine deepened in her blood. The string music returned. The hydrangeas tilted in the breeze like they were listening. And for a moment, she allowed herself to believe—without doubt or defense—that she mattered.

The luncheon thinned, as if the entire affair had been choreographed to unravel gracefully. Chairs pushed back with polite laughter, linen napkins dabbed at corners of lips already retouched with balm or gloss, waiters collecting half-finished salads and untouched rolls. The donors rose in staggered pairs, exchanging brief, luminous compliments— "You looked radiant." "We must do coffee." "So good to see you in person again"—words flung like petals in retreat.

Allison remained seated, her empty plate a quiet excuse. It gave the impression of calm. Of deserved rest. Of a woman receiving what she had earned. Several women passed by to touch her arm or praise her performance again. Lyle Dent's wife murmured something about the fall gala, about how they couldn't imagine it without her. Allison smiled the smile that required no response. She was not performing now. She had simply become the performance—a creature shaped by obligation and etiquette, stitched from approval and faint applause. It had once thrilled her, this visibility, this admired ease. Now it landed lithely on her shoulders, weightless and exhausting. She knew what she looked like in rooms like this: polished, purposeful, complete. But under the table her hands were still. She didn't know when she'd stopped fidgeting in public, only that it had once been a habit and now wasn't.

Then Paula appeared at the edge of the table, envelope in hand. Cream stock, embossed. A private foundation's seal in discreet foil on the corner.

"I meant to give this earlier," Paula said, her voice calm and almost warm. "We're thrilled to support the company again this season."

Allison stood, accepted it with a nod. "Thank you. That means a great deal."

Paula's eyes lingered long enough to read something. She didn't comment on the outfit or the turnout or the wine. Just this: "You looked like you were born in that role."

Allison blinked. "Titania or hostess?"

Paula smiled. "Does it matter?"

For a moment they stood in mutual understanding—not kinship, not animosity, just the recognition of another woman who knew the script. Who knew how it drained.

"I hope we can catch up soon," Paula said, already turning. "Coffee, maybe."

"Yes," Allison said, too fast. "That would be lovely."

Paula moved off, her posture faultless. Allison stood there for another few seconds, the envelope in her hand, the compliment still hovering like smoke that clung. She felt the eyes of the departing crowd brushing past her, felt herself resume the role by instinct. There was no applause this time. No lines to deliver. Only the sound of silverware being collected and the hiss of the generator behind the canopy.

She didn't know how to leave. Not just the luncheon, but the self she inhabited inside it. She smiled at the next person who passed, though she didn't know who they were. And for a moment, just a moment, she imagined what it would be to walk into her own kitchen and find no one there. Just silence. She blinked the thought away.

The lawn was nearly empty now, the orchestra packed away, the tablecloths folded and lifted into catering bins by high school volunteers in matching polos. A breeze moved through the treetops without anyone left to notice it. Only Prescott remained at the edge of the pavilion, hands clasped behind his back, his bowtie now loose at the collar. He stepped toward her with the grace of a man who had once trained in ballet and never fully let the habit go.

"Allison," he said, voice quieter now that the room had emptied. "I wanted to thank you again. Truly. I've worked in cities three times this size, and I've rarely seen a volunteer command a room the way you do. You give us credibility. You give us class."

"I just care about the work," she said. "And about making sure people see what this place is capable of."

Prescott touched her forearm lightly. "You make them believe it's possible."

He turned then, already heading toward his car, the moment evaporating with his steps. She watched him go, the praise settling somewhere near her collarbone, spreading in a slow flush. Not just flattery—influence. She was, if only briefly, the axis of something. The center to which people turned their heads. She breathed in, held it.

And then—behind her, near the gravel path—movement. A flight case snapped shut, its latch clean and final. Drew was lifting a coil of extension cable into the van, a small sweat stain darkening the neck of his black t-shirt. He looked up and their eyes caught. He didn't smile. But he paused.

And in the pause, Allison felt the shimmer of something unsanctioned. The hush after the curtain fell, before the house lights rose. There was nothing in the moment except possibility, and the unbearable lightness of being seen.

He'd slipped through the service gate at the back of the pavilion, the path narrow and half-shaded, a fine layer of pine straw scattered along the edges. She followed, the scent of the garden fading behind her, replaced now by the smell of mulch and lust. The door to the storage room had been left open. Light spilled onto the path in a narrow wedge. She stepped through without speaking. He straightened, startled, her name already forming on his lips.

She stepped inside and closed the door behind her. The latch clicked.

"Allison, I—"

Her finger pressed to his lips, gentle but firm. "Don't."

She felt his breath catch beneath her fingertip, felt the energy—the hesitation becoming possibility, the space narrowing, the script discarded. Then she kissed him. Soft at first, tentative, searching, less an invitation than a confirmation. His lips were still, then not. His hand came halfway up her back before stopping. She pulled him closer.

The second kiss came harder. Her arms wrapped around his shoulders, as if she were gathering something to herself she had not touched in years. Her body pressed into his, anchoring herself in present-tense urgency. She took his hand and guided it upward, precise, until it cupped the shape of her breast. His fingers froze.

"Here," she whispered.

She looked up at him then, saw the flushed hesitation in his face, the pulse just visible at the base of his neck. He looked young, but not naive. Awed, but not blind. The silence she had lived inside for so long began to break apart in the single, undeniable fact of being felt.

For a moment, she closed her eyes. She moved against him again, and this time, he moved too. His body responded now, the barrier between them dissolving as though it had never existed. She reached for his shirt, pulled it up in one clean motion, hands flattening over his chest, mapping him. He exhaled, the hesitation gone, replaced by something else. Their mouths found each other, hungrier, lips open now, breath shared in gasps between deepening touch. His hands settled at her waist. The metal shelves beside them rattled as they moved, clumsy and honest.

What took her over now was deeper than rebellion. Something rooted in all the hours she had spent alone in beautiful rooms, speaking lines she hadn't written, smiling because it was required. Now, there was no audience.

Her hands undid his belt. She knelt. Not to perform. Not to give. To feel power without apology. He gasped. One hand pressed against the wall behind him. She closed her eyes, let herself disappear into the motion, into the fact of her own body being hers again. In that narrow room, under fluorescent light, amid the scent of mulch dust and warm wiring, Allison Collins stopped pretending.

Time thinned to a soft blur. The light in the storage room faded in her awareness, replaced by the pulse behind her chest and the cool press of concrete beneath her shoulder blades. Drew moved inside of her. She was nowhere she had ever been before, and yet she was utterly within herself, more present than in any stage-lit room or fundraising brunch or dimly lit kitchen where love had become a matter of routine logistics.

She breathed deeply, eyes open, focused on nothing. Her body moved, but without choreography. Each sensation arrived as proof. That she was still alive and capable of wanting without asking permission. She felt herself peeled back to something prior to obligation. Beneath the rehearsed domesticity, beneath the smiling diplomacy of school events and gala committees, beneath even the bruised silence of her marriage, was a woman who remembered—briefly, fully—what it meant to be touched.

It wasn't the man but the moment. The audacity of it. The suspension of all her careful calibrations. There had been so many years of keeping herself aligned to the expectations of the room. And now here she was, unlit, unstyled, undone. A noise outside—birds or wind or maybe just the branches settling in the sun—made her eyes flutter open. The room was the same. But she was not. She would dress. She would drive home. The world would resume its polite clockwork. But something had broken in the quiet. And not everything that breaks is loss.

The afternoon light radiated through the windshield as Allison drove with both hands on the wheel. Her fingers trembled from an energy that had nowhere else to go. Her thighs still tingled from pressure and release; her skin held the warmth of desire. The scent of lavender hand lotion and something more intimate hung in the Macan's cabin, mingling with the chemical chill of the air conditioning.

The tears came unannounced, loose and clean, the kind that didn't need explanation. Just a kind of strange, exhausted joy. It was soft, full-bodied, animal.

She blinked and the road held steady beneath her. The Porsche moved toward the quiet neighborhoods west of downtown, the streets lined with crepe myrtle and ambition, where lawns were fed and marriages weren't. She thought of the receipt again. That damned rectangle of paper, crisp at the corners, the typeface so precise it could've been printed just to hurt her. Keith's betrayal hadn't been a rupture—it had been a soft fade-out of something she'd mistaken for love.

But she had kept it. Tucked it into the back of her jewelry drawer, inside a velvet box with a broken clasp, beneath discarded costume earrings. Just to know it existed. Now she understood: she hadn't been saving it. She was it. The proof. The line item, unaccounted for but always there.

And today—her body still alive with sensation, her mouth still tasting of decision—she'd finally cashed it in. Not out of vengeance. But because she had wanted to. Her foot lifted off the accelerator slightly. A child on a scooter darted past a mailbox and vanished into a cul-de-sac. Allison exhaled.

The woman who parked in her driveway ten minutes later would set her keys in the bowl. She would fix her hair in the hallway mirror. She would answer her daughter's question about dinner with a voice perfectly even. But something in her heart had turned over and there would be no putting it back.

8

The conference room had the sterile shine of new money—high-gloss veneer, brushed chrome legs on the table, a panoramic view of downtown Greensboro that flattened the city into a game board of manageable risk. Frosted glass framed the door, engineered for discretion but not soundproofing. A ficus plant in the corner stood too straight, fed by ultraviolet panels programmed to mimic daylight, because even the greenery here had been denied the chaos of reality.

Keith sat in a mesh-backed chair with lumbar support and quietly tried to remember the last time he'd breathed without measuring it first. At the head of the table, Chad Denton—Division Manager, Southeast Growth Strategies—clicked through the final slides of a pitch deck labeled Targeted Public Yield: Civic Liquidity Instruments, FY18–20. The projector glared against the far wall.

"In conclusion," Chad said, adjusting his collar, "we're seeing a once-in-a-decade alignment between municipal infrastructure backlog and federal pass-through stimulus that creates an extremely attractive entry point. Particularly in post-industrial Tier Two metros."

Post-industrial. Tier Two. Keith felt his pulse ticking behind his eyes.

Across the table, a younger analyst nodded vigorously, scribbling nothing onto a pad. Keith stared at the final bullet on the slide: Opportunity Clusters: Health Corridors, Eco-Stabilization Zones, Transportation Innovation Nodes.

They could have been amusement parks. Or war zones. The language no longer distinguished between them.

"This corridor thing in Greensboro?" Chad went on. "Perfect case. A regional health system with latent land, city-bond backing, and political cover from a 'remediation' narrative. It checks all the boxes. They're burying bad dirt with good optics."

There were chuckles. Light, collegiate. One woman said, "God, that's so smart," and Keith wasn't sure if she meant the bond structuring or the cover story.

He looked around the table and saw believers—people who had long since learned how to talk about water quality as a "sentiment driver" and school funding as a "citizen optics concern." They didn't hate the public realm. They just didn't recognize it anymore.

A graph appeared: interest rate trends versus trust in government. The curves mirrored each other—one rising, one falling. It looked like justice being re-priced. Keith shifted in his seat, then stilled.

It hit him as Chad leaned into the closing line: a deep, physical chill, sharp as a wire down the spine. Panic, but measured—like a needle sliding into the meat of his body. He gripped the edge of the table. His tie pulled at his throat. Not because of guilt. That was the old religion. This was something more primal. He was watching the machine talk about his city like a carcass.

The room dimmed as Chad advanced to another slide—interest-rate futures plotted against municipal default histories, a meaningless constellation of blue bars and red lines pretending to carry narrative. The lights overhead adjusted automatically, too slow to be unnoticed. Keith felt the chill sharpen. A cold breath climbing through his ribcage. His skin prickled under his dress shirt.

"This is nothing," he told himself. "Just a moment. Just your blood sugar. The room's too cold. You skipped lunch." But the panic pressed deeper. He looked out across the city through the floor-to-ceiling windows. The skyline beyond the glass offered no comfort—City Hall's bureaucratic bulk, the oblong silhouette of the hospital wing, the sprawling geometry of the east side's subsidized housing, all reduced to gradients of shadow.

He thought of Allison. An image arrived, vivid and unbidden—her body, too still in sleep, curled away from him in their bed. The line of her shoulder bare against the pillow. What if she was in danger? What if something had already happened? He imagined a car crash. A seizure. The phone ringing too late. Then, just as quickly, he dismissed it.

"No. Not that. Not the children either." His breath steadied slightly. He rubbed a knuckle against his thigh beneath the table. Chad was talking now about synthetic bundling, about risk layers in distressed municipal portfolios. "You can't let the sentiment drive the pricing," Chad was saying. "You have to let the narrative sound civic. But underneath it's just paper."

Keith drifted.

It was spring, senior year. He could still feel the press of the auditorium's cheap seat under his legs, the way he had leaned forward, elbows on his knees, watching Allison onstage during the final dress rehearsal of The Seagull. She played Nina with a tenderness that astonished him. Not because she was believable—though she was—but because for the first time he saw her as entirely herself. Unrehearsed in the very act of performance.

The stage had been lit in a pale, bluish wash, like dusk stretched into something operatic. Her costume was little more than gauze—delicate, nearly translucent. And when she stepped into the upstage glow, her silhouette sharpened to something he wasn't prepared for. The curve of her waist, the supple strength in her thighs, the faint outline of her torso beneath the fabric. He had swallowed hard then, heart lurching. He would marry her. He needed to stand close to that light. To hold it before someone else did.

A burst of laughter snapped him back. Chad had made a joke about green bonds being the new "faith-based investments."

Keith's stomach turned. He closed his laptop without a sound. The panic had dulled into a throb. But he knew now it wouldn't leave. The problem wasn't the numbers. It was the architecture of belief. The way everything had been hollowed, dressed back up in moral language, and sold again. And somewhere inside that system—his name. On a spreadsheet. On a filing. Next to something that shouldn't be there. Something he might not be able to look away from anymore.

The chairs scraped back on polished wood, expensive shoes tapping as they slid beneath the table. The projector clicked off with a sigh and the room returned to its full brightness, exposing the vague fatigue on every face. Keith stood, forcing a casual nod to the analysts packing up their laptops with the kind of cheer that came from caffeine and six-figure bonuses. His spine felt like someone had taken it apart and reassembled it wrong.

At the doorway, Roger—one of the mid-levels from compliance, always too eager with a grin—said, "We're laying healthcare over a brownfield," then chuckled at his own brilliance, waiting to be rewarded. Keith smiled, just enough. The line lodged in his chest, splintering outward, thin and sharp. Healthcare over a brownfield. He imagined the still toxic park on Bingham Street. The half-vanished city logos on the side of rusting work trucks. The quiet fact of forgetting capped and covered with metrics. He said nothing.

In the hallway, the carpet was too soft. Everything in this place muted your weight. He passed the break room where someone had left the Keurig open and a mug half-drunk beside it—an office still life of midlevel discontent. His office door was closed, but the light glowed behind the frosted glass, as if waiting. He stepped inside and shut it behind him, the latch clicking into place with an accusatory precision.

The skyline still stretched beyond the window—west to the hospital, east to Bingham Park. He stood there for a long moment, hands on the edge of the desk. The panic hadn't left. The creeping, quiet dread that something had already been lost. Not a file. Not an opportunity. Something older. Something human. He scanned the horizon as if it might name what he'd misplaced. And when it didn't, he sat—back straight, eyes wide—and opened his laptop again.

He hadn't meant to become the kind of man who wore polished shoes to meet with consultants about municipal waterline incentives. That was never the plan. But then again, he'd never had a plan—only a set of permissions, slowly acquired, handed down like heirlooms he hadn't earned.

His father had been the first system he learned to navigate. A man built from pressed shirts and immovable logic, who could flatten any disagreement with a single raised brow and who once told Keith, without irony, that a good reputation was worth more than affection. Love, in the Douglas Collins household, had been a decorative idea, like crystal tumblers displayed in the hutch—visible, unused, always just out of reach. He learned early that compliance was currency. That silence at the right time could get you a pat on the shoulder. That reciting the day's wins—test scores, a second-place debate trophy, the details of a varsity scrimmage—earned peace at dinner.

By the time he got to UNC, he had perfected the art of pleasant self-erasure.

That's how he found himself flanking Alan and David, orbiting their intensity without challenging it. Alan, with his righteous fire, walking out of lectures over university housing policy, quoting Foucault in dining halls. David, already sleek, all posture and polish, who could make a room fall in line without ever raising his voice. Keith stayed between them because it was easier to measure himself in comparison than to stand alone.

It was Alan who first introduced him to Allison. A cast party. Sophomore spring. She wore a green dress that didn't quite fit her shoulders, and she laughed at something Alan said, then touched Keith's arm without seeming to notice. He fell into her orbit fast—stunned, really, by the attention, the ease. She could glide through a room like she'd been trained to do so since birth. In a way, she reminded him of his father—charming in public, impossible to read. She was already fluent in surfaces.

They started dating before finals. He proposed before graduation. They moved into a condo his father helped them buy, had their first child within two years. It was the kind of life you could print on cardstock and send to relatives. And he had told himself, for a long time, that it was enough.

But now, seated in a tower of glass, parsing the language of poisoned parcels and masked incentives, Keith began to feel the full shape of his mistake. Not a dramatic fall. Just a long, unbending drift toward safety. Toward invisibility. He had never made a hard choice. He had only followed the path of least resistance, mistaking it for character. Now, his city was being paved over in pieces. And he'd helped smooth the ground.

Keith leaned back in the chair, the fake leather sighing beneath him, and stared past his own reflection in the glass. The skyline beyond was clipped and silent. Somewhere down there was the park with its rusted swing set and poisoned soil. Somewhere down there were names he'd typed into budget cells, lives he'd anonymized into census tracts and risk indices. He was good at this kind of work—efficient, invisible, comfortably abstract. It was the abstraction that had become the problem.

He had once told a colleague, during a lunch break they both forgot five minutes later, that he considered himself "left of center." It was meant to sound modest and intelligent, politically fluent without the need for commitment. In truth, Keith's politics existed in the browser tabs he opened and never finished reading. He donated to campaigns when prompted by a well-designed email. He added statements of solidarity to his email signature when necessary. He corrected people politely when they confused terms but never raised his voice in a room where it might cost him something.

He had opinions, of course. Thoughtful ones. Sharp enough to deploy over cocktails, dull enough to avoid consequence. And it shamed him—this cowardice—not in the moral sense, but in the private, masculine way he couldn't admit. That even his failings lacked conviction. His marriage was an arrangement now, sexless and brittle. The affairs were occasional, muted—more about forgetting than pleasure. Small eclipses of the life he'd built.

His job, too, had become a mirror of this duplicity. He spent his days building models to simulate economic outcomes, assigning weights to assumptions, reducing whole neighborhoods into actuarial probabilities. He could predict home values five years out to a 2.3 percent margin of error. He could forecast which block would gentrify and which would stall, which parcel to flag for acquisition, which one to bury under euphemism. He trafficked in numbers that described human consequence without ever touching it. He read about environmental justice like it was literature—something to be appreciated. And now, something was pressing at the edge of all this, some unnameable tension between the things he believed in and the life he had allowed to calcify around him. He wasn't brave enough to call it guilt. But it was there. Growing. Pacing the floors of his quietest thoughts. Was he a coward?

He opened the secure database slowly, the way one might return to a photograph that hadn't changed but now seemed to hold something previously missed. He typed the parcel number into the search field without hesitation, though his fingers paused just before he hit enter, as if expecting the system to flinch.

It didn't.

The screen blinked once and there it was: Parcel 524-B, South Elm Wellness and Innovation Zone. The note buried in the bond filing hadn't changed since last week, nor had the invoice from Guilford Health's infrastructure contractor—both hiding in plain sight. He scrolled down to the footnote that had snagged his attention the first time, a line so ordinary it could've been mistaken for an internal memo:

"Remediation Infrastructure (pre-regulatory fill): subsurface stabilization per Phase I ESA, pre-development scope."

He read it again, more slowly. He parsed each word. Remediation. Infrastructure. Pre-regulatory fill. These were not errors. They were camouflage.

"Subsurface stabilization" was the language they used when something couldn't be removed, only buried. And "Phase I ESA" meant there was a record of contamination—acknowledged, documented, but spun into forward-facing language. Environmental

Site Assessment. The phrase sounded protective, scientific. But the filing didn't include the assessment itself. Just the euphemism.

What it meant, when you stripped it of its elegance, was that something toxic had been left in the soil. And the city was building over it. He toggled to the development schedule, the interactive timeline laid out in soft corporate blue. The site had already been prepped for early-stage vertical construction. And—there it was—"playground buildout: Q3 community relations incentive."

The playground was part of the optics. A bright, family-friendly front stitched over compromised ground. It settled in his chest now. The playground was cover. Literally. The note in the bond filing was a nod to liability, carefully coded, indexed just enough to suggest due diligence but obscured from any real scrutiny. Someone had to sign off on that phrasing. Someone had to decide that "pre-regulatory fill" was a more useful truth than chromium or ash or cancer cluster.

Keith leaned back in his chair. His screen still glowed. He understood now what he was looking at. Parcel 524-B wasn't just a clever acquisition. It was a grave. And the city had budgeted the flowers.

He didn't even notice that he'd stopped blinking. The lines of code and filings and PDFs stacked behind tabs like sediment layers in a creekbed—each one waiting to be brushed lightly, interpreted with the right calibration. This was his language, after all. The parsing of systems built to disguise themselves. It was his form of intimacy. A private fluency that let him feel superior without speaking aloud.

He dug.

Midland Legacy Trust. An entity with no website or operating address, only a post office box and a string of annual filings that terminated in 2008. A dead shell, long expired. And yet, at one point, it had held title to Parcel 524-B. The records didn't even appear in the public assessor's site. You had to pull them from state-level rollovers. Transaction sheets recorded in bulk, wrapped in generic transfer language.

Then, in 2011, a paper trail so faint it might as well have been whispered: the parcel reabsorbed by the city under the umbrella of a capital planning vehicle called the South Elm Health Innovation Zone. Not a department. Not a real agency. Just a fund. A name. A story.

He pulled up the S-4 schedule attached to the last general obligation bond issuance. There it was—Parcel 524-B, tagged by grid coordinates. The same ones marked on the invoice last month. The budget line was a low six figures. Just enough for topsoil, signage, synthetic turf.

He sat back, hands hovering above the keys. This was what he did. Find the shapes in the noise. And here, the shape was becoming clear. What struck him, more than the data, was how easy it had been. There was no conspiracy, in the cinematic sense. It was paperwork and euphemism. The lie had never been buried. It had been filed. And the others—his colleagues, the council, the voters—they didn't see it because curiosity had become a kind of liability. No one asked questions unless the answer could be monetized. Isn't that what made him valuable here? That he still looked?

He clicked through the metadata one more time. The signatures. The filing dates. A name jumped out—an old city planning liaison, now on the board of GHS. The circle closed itself, without effort. The story was there. If someone wanted to read it.

He paused at the name, fingers still hovering mid-keystroke.

Charles F. Lanier, Jr.

It looked familiar in the distant way inherited names often did—stamped on placards, engraved into donor walls, attached to the vague beneficence of ribbon-cuttings and press releases. It sat there, unthreatening, in the signature line of a 2012 city redevelopment memo approving the parcel's reclassification as "eligible for transitional health use." A phrase so bloodless it might've referred to a broken sidewalk or a subsidized clinic.

But the name refused to unstick.

Keith opened a new tab and typed it out. Found the LinkedIn profile, dusty but still live. Former VP, Strategic Acquisitions, Guilford Health System. Retired 2010. Still listed as "Board Advisor, Emeritus."

A second window: the tax filings for the Douglas Collins Charitable Trust. His father's pride. A monument to private generosity that never strayed too far from the golf course. Keith scrolled back through the archived PDFs, year by year, columns of names and figures so flat they'd once lulled him to sleep.

Until 2002.

There it was.

Lanier, Charles F. – $25,000 – General Operating Support.

The column read like an old ledger, but now the lines flared with color. Lanier. His father. The wellness corridor. Keith sat back slowly. The room tilted, then settled. That was the year his father had run that media blitz about "civic stewardship"—an ad campaign funded through the foundation but targeted at pushing municipal bonds for the expansion of hospital services west of downtown. There had been controversy, sure—pushback about zoning, environmental due diligence—but it had all washed away in the PR storm. New maps. New mission. New vision for growth.

And Lanier had been there. At the front of the room. Donating. Speaking. Signing. Keith let his eyes close for a moment, the edges of the office softening behind his lids. It wasn't just the city. It wasn't just David. It was lineage. It was legacy.

The corridor plan, the buried reports, the casual remediation of toxins beneath mulch and signage—none of it had emerged from malice. It had emerged from proximity. From dinner conversations and development briefings, from shared logic about value and vision and the greater good. It was belief, passed down like heirloom china.

And now it lived inside him, too. Because he had touched it. Because he had benefited. Because he had never asked where the money came from. Keith leaned forward, elbows on the desk, forehead in his palm. Lanier's name blinked from the screen, passive and absolute. It had always been there. He just hadn't been ready to see it.

The tab clicked shut with a soft, final sound, the browser window collapsing like a drawn shutter. The blue glow dimmed. The spreadsheet vanished beneath it. But the unease stayed behind, pulsing under the surface of Keith's skin, a low electrical current in his gut. He sat motionless for a moment, eyes unfocused, the cursor blinking in an empty search field as though waiting for him to ask the next question. Instead, he turned to the window.

The sky was perfectly indifferent, the kind of spring clarity that people mistook for optimism. Below, the city bent along its long-prepared grids—downtown corners redone with benches no one used, sidewalks that ended in traffic, banners with slogans about innovation and belonging. The old smokestack on the northern edge of downtown loomed in the distance, blackened brick scarred by decades of rain and soot, the remnants of whatever plant it had once anchored long gone.

That smokestack had marked the boundary of the city for as long as Keith could remember. As a kid, he thought it was beautiful in the way dangerous things were—still, tall, unarguable. His father had once called it "an eyesore waiting to be razed." But it had never been razed. Just absorbed. It stood now beside a luxury apartment complex. Keith watched it, still and silent, while inside his chest something began to come unmoored.

There had been a time he thought morality was a structure—taught, agreed upon, maintained. His father had built his version with discipline and donation receipts. At UNC, Alan had carried his direct and declarative. Keith had always thought himself too rational for all that. Morality, to him, had been a mood. A position to be tweaked depending on circumstance. But now, the architecture of his own belief was collapsing. Or maybe it had always been hollow. Maybe he was only now hearing the echo because the web was tightening.

He had been complicit through the comfort of not asking. Through the career built on being the kind of man people trusted with secrets they never spoke aloud. Sweat bloomed under his arms. He couldn't yet name what the guilt was about—was it the parcel? The new playground? Allison? Or was it just the slow erosion of something essential in himself, finally visible in the matrix of these transactions?

He rubbed his palms together slowly, then pressed them flat against his thighs. The smokestack didn't move. Neither did the facts. And yet, the more he stared, the more the city looked like something he had misread—some complicated equation he'd solved for comfort, not truth.

The knock was a tap, light and careless. A sound like punctuation on a thought he hadn't finished.

"Jesus, Keith," Roger said, poking his head through the office door, his blazer slung over one shoulder. "You look like you've seen a ghost."

Keith blinked, slow and dry-eyed. He hadn't realized it had grown dark behind the glass. The smokestack was now a silhouette against the sinking sky, the downtown lights coming on in polite rows. His screen had gone to sleep. He hadn't noticed. He turned from the window. Managed a half-smile. "Just... zoning out."

Roger stepped in, smirking. "Yeah, well, if the ghost's name is David Moss, tell him thanks for the short squeeze on that hospital refi. Numbers came through better than expected. Somebody's getting their bonus early this year."

Keith exhaled something between a chuckle and a cough. "Lucky us."

Roger glanced at his phone, then back. "Couple of us are heading over to Gibb's Hundred. You coming?"

Keith hesitated, the word no half-formed in his mouth. But his body, still half elsewhere, moved on reflex. "Yeah... I might see you there."

Roger grinned, gave a mock salute, and backed out the door. Keith stared at the open space a moment longer. Then turned off his monitor. The glass darkened behind him, now offering his reflection. He loosened his tie. Sat still. And let the silence press down like the first layer of concrete.

The car moved on instinct, as if it knew the way better than he did. Keith sat behind the wheel, elbow balanced on the edge of the door, eyes trailing the tree-lined streets as they curled toward the old neighborhoods north of town. The light had gone soft and slanted—dinner-hour light, golden and obliging. New Irving Park wore it well. The brick colonials with curved porticos, the tulip beds manicured to excess, the hedges squared off like little promises.

This had once been the address. Old Greensboro money lived here until it crept north to Summerfield, where the roads widened and the houses stretched farther apart. Still, there was comfort in this part of town. Legacy comfort. The kind you didn't have to perform.

Keith turned onto his street, let the car coast into the familiar curve of his driveway. The lawn was neatly edged, the kids' bikes leaned near the garage. A pair of blue chalk lines streaked the sidewalk—evidence of some recent, forgotten game.

He put the car in park and sat a moment, hands resting on the wheel. The sun dropped just enough to hit the windows of the second floor, where the guest room curtains swayed from a ceiling fan. This was what he'd built. The home. The status. The insulation.

And yet. The smell of treated soil, the ghost of Lanier's name, the spreadsheet language for burial still floated somewhere behind his eyes. Still, he stepped out. Inside, the house was bright and full of human noise. His son was on the couch, controller in hand, the flicker of digital firelight bouncing off his cheek. His daughter came around the corner with a stuffed llama under one arm and a Popsicle stick in her mouth. She looked up, grinned wide.

"Daddy!"

Her arms wrapped around his waist with a force that caught him off guard. He touched the back of her head, her hair warm and damp from play. Behind her, the dog came trotting in, tail wagging. The TV chattered. Something in the kitchen hissed. It felt—for one long, suspended moment—like clarity. Like grounding.

"Hey," he said, voice softer than he meant. "Hey, you two. You good?"

"Mom said we could stay up late," his son called from the living room, not looking up. "She went to the store."

Keith nodded, unsure if it was true. Unsure if it mattered. He dropped his keys in the bowl by the stairs and glanced at the framed pictures on the hallway wall—vacation shots, school portraits, a blurred photo of the five of them from two Christmases ago, all wrapped in reds and greens, smiling like people who'd never missed a step.

The house smelled like garlic and steam. For now, it was enough. He was still inside it. And they were still his. He went upstairs to change, the ritual movement of buttons and fabric giving him something to do with his hands. In the bedroom, the comforter was still turned down from the morning rush, her side of the bed holding the faint indentation of absence. He peeled off his work clothes, hung his slacks on the valet chair he never used, tugged on a soft t-shirt, jeans, bare feet on the polished wood. He stood a moment before the mirror—not looking for anything, just confirming he still had a shape.

Downstairs, the front windows glowed with the haze of early evening, the kitchen already warmed by the smell of garlic and tomato and heat. The door clicked. He heard the gentle chaos of Allison arriving: the familiar rustle of her purse, the clatter of her keys in the ceramic bowl, the automatic sigh she always made when she stepped out of her shoes.

She came into the kitchen with a brown paper bag tucked under one arm and a breeze of citrus perfume trailing her.

"Ran out for bread," she said, placing the bag beside the cutting board. "You can't do this sauce without a decent loaf."

Keith nodded, stepping beside her, watching her unload the groceries with a composure that didn't quite match the hour. She moved with precision, like reentering a space she knew intimately but didn't trust. As she turned to hang her purse on the back of the chair, a small white rectangle fluttered out—a dry cleaning receipt. She caught it mid-air, smooth and casual, but he saw the lettering, the timestamp. She laid it gently on the counter, like it meant nothing.

"The luncheon went well," she said, opening a drawer for the bread knife. "Raised more than last year, actually. Someone spilled wine down my front, though. Ruined the outfit."

He nodded again. He didn't ask who.

"Had to drop it off on the way home," she added, slicing with calm efficiency. "They said they could probably save it."

The knife clicked against the board. Keith stepped toward the sink, turned on the tap, rinsed his hands. The water rushed and pooled and ran clear. He looked at her with stillness, as if learning to watch what he used to ignore.

9

Paula left the gift bag on the bench by the stairs, the satin ribbon already loosened, the contents rattling as it tipped to one side. Her heels sat splayed on the rug, one upright, one collapsed—an accidental sculpture of exhaustion. She didn't bother changing.

The theater luncheon had gone as expected. A white-linened gesture toward cultural stewardship, flanked by beet foam and undercooked lamb. Someone from the wellness corridor task force gave a speech about art's role in healing communities, and someone else followed with remarks about legacy and storytelling. Paula had clapped at the appropriate times. Her mouth ached from smiling. She hadn't eaten much at the luncheon. The beet mousse was gelatinous, the conversation rehearsed. Someone had made a toast—art as anchor, or art as mirror, she couldn't remember which—and everyone clapped like it mattered. She'd smiled, of course. Smiled until her face felt brittle, until she imagined the expression lifting from her like a mask.

The downtown theatre had always drawn a particular kind of woman to its board—art history minors turned community patrons, women with soft shoulders and precise haircuts, women like herself. They believed in cultural capital the way others believed in recycling or God. That belief had shape, schedule, a logic of paper programs and underwriting footnotes. Paula had loved it, or told herself she had. It gave structure to her days, to the versions of herself she had needed to maintain. You could justify anything in service of a production.

She opened the fridge and stared into the light. Nothing appealed. She closed it again.

On the counter sat the glossy program from today's luncheon. Her name was printed above the fold, bolded. She turned it over. The back page was a rendering of the theatre's upcoming renovation—a new education wing, a glass façade, a "healing arts partnership" with the wellness corridor. It looked like an airport terminal. It looked like erasure. She didn't want to be cynical. She wanted to believe. But belief had started to feel like a polite form of compliance.

In the pantry, placed in the back of the tea tin behind the packet of chamomile she never drank but kept for guests who claimed it calmed them, was the letter. It was creased sharply, growing soft at the edges from handling. Two pages, typed late at night after a fundraising dinner when the speeches had all blurred together and she'd found herself holding a glass of wine she couldn't remember pouring, staring out the window of the event venue at a dumpster surrounded by roses—landscaping meant to conceal, but failing. The irony had clarified something in her, as if the ornamental hedge had parted and shown her the mendacity underneath.

The letter wasn't addressed, not yet. She had wrestled with the mechanics—anonymity versus ownership, clarity versus implication. The voice she used in it wasn't her public one, not the stillness she summoned for boardrooms or donor luncheons. It was stripped of the habitual softeners. It was simply the truth, shaped to fit within the grammar of exposure.

She had written about the wellness corridor project. About parcel 524-B. About David's language in the early meetings—underutilized asset, legacy remediation, public-private integration. About the private conversations, the steering committees, the quiet withdrawals of public funding from East Greensboro initiatives in favor of the new "health anchor" downtown. She had named names—softly, yes, but distinctly. And she had explained how, through layers of delegation and branded equity initiatives, Bingham Park had been left to rot so a playground could rise elsewhere on chosen ground. The letter didn't accuse David directly. But it did everything else.

She hadn't mailed it.

Not because she was unsure of the facts—she knew them now, knew them in her body the way you know a house is burning even before the smoke alarm sounds. It was the pause that came from having lived perpetually inside performance. She had spent years smoothing edges, recasting harm as oversight, aiding and abetting through posture and deflection. She had been fluent in the language of avoidance. And now to switch tongues—it took a kind of inner violence. Even now, part of her wanted to revise the letter one more time, make it sing less sharply, modulate the guilt into a civic suggestion. But she knew that impulse for what it was: complicity with better lighting.

She had come to this point in layers. It began with the grant denial for Goldie's youth arts initiative—Paula had read the email, glanced at the language about "realignment of strategic community priorities," and felt something go cold in her. The phrase had been lifted, nearly word for word, from a memo she'd proofread for David six months earlier. Then came the meeting with the theatre board, where a consultant floated the idea of placing a mural about environmental justice on the side of the new corridor parking garage—as if history could be appeased with paint. Then her daughter's monologue, the op-ed, Alan's voice, unsanctioned and unshaven, speaking a truth she'd once fallen in love with and had spent two decades politely forgetting.

It was cumulative. A slow erosion of compliance.

What held her back, if she was honest, was grief. Grief for the version of herself who had once believed that marrying David was an act of clarity, that she was choosing stability not cowardice. Grief for the way her hands had learned to shape narratives instead of holding truth. Grief, too, for David—not for who he had become, but for the fact that he hadn't become anything. He had always been this, only shinier.

She closed the pantry. The tin stayed where it was, its contents undisturbed. The letter would be mailed. She felt that certainty now. Not righteous. Inevitable. A slow formation under pressure. A truth that would one day arrive in the mail slot, addressed in a hand no one recognized, and there would be no doubt what it meant. She had made the mistake of thinking she needed the perfect words. But clarity had no syntax. It only had timing. And she had waited long enough.

The partnership announcement at the luncheon had earned a murmur of approval—the theatre joining forces with the downtown corridor initiative, bringing "health narratives to the stage," performances designed to "foster intergenerational dialogue around ecological equity." It had the ring of something worthwhile. Or at least harmless. And yet, Paula had smiled too quickly, nodded too often. A part of her wanted to ask: and who gets to write the script?

She got up. Climbed the stairs. The carpet runner muffled each step. In the upstairs hall, her daughter's bedroom door was cracked open. Inside, the girl sat cross-legged on the floor, flipping through the script. She continued down the hall, stopped at her own door, and stood there for a moment with her hand on the knob. She thought of Alan—not the man he'd become, not the articles or the accusations—but the boy in the campus theatre lobby who once said, We perform because truth is unbearable when spoken plainly. She hadn't known then if it was a line from the play or something he meant. She still didn't know.

She changed without thinking, arms moving through soft cotton like she was brushing dust from herself. The dress fell to the bed in a gentle collapse. In its place: old yoga pants with the faint outline of bleach near the thigh, a sweater she no longer wore in public but kept because the neck had stretched to fit her perfectly. She tugged her hair back and left her earrings on. They clicked softly as she walked.

The house held its silence. Upstairs, the hallway filtered gold through the blinds, stripes cast at angles sharp enough to measure. She paused by the linen closet to gather herself, as if stepping into a different motivation required a moment, some preparation.

Downstairs, the sunroom faced west, catching the last bend of light across the neighbor's yard and their unused swing set, warped now from years of stillness. The room had once been marketed in the listing as a conservatory, which Paula had found ridiculous. It was not a place for secrets or longing. It was a square addition with faded terracotta tile and large windows. But it had become hers in a way other rooms weren't. No mirrors or no screens. Plants, mostly, and the quiet work of keeping them alive.

She stepped across the cool tile. The philodendron had begun to vine again, thin tendrils reaching toward the nearest beam, as if reminding her it would never stop trying. The fiddle-leaf fig, stubborn as always, had dropped one leaf near the heater vent. She crouched and picked it up. It had browned at the edges, veins still visible. One of those small domestic deaths she took personally.

The hydrangea had faded from cream to parchment, the blooms stiff and papery now, not quite ready to release. She checked the soil with two fingers, pressed into the earth until the first knuckle disappeared. Still damp. She rotated the pot slightly to angle it toward the light, though it probably didn't matter anymore. Behind her, a house finch darted past the glass, its shadow flashing across the floor.

This was the hour she liked best, when the sunroom turned theatrical. Gold and copper and long shadows thrown across the plants. She often told herself she would sit here more. Read, maybe. Just be. But she rarely did. The room remained a promise she kept forgetting to keep.

A stack of unopened mail sat on the wicker side table, anchored by a small bowl of river stones Paula had arranged years ago and never moved. She sorted through the envelopes absently—catalogs, donation solicitations, a water bill tucked inside a bright graphic of a droplet wearing sunglasses. She tossed it back on the pile and turned her attention to the small orchid by the window.

It had bloomed once—on her birthday, two years ago—and never again. Still, she couldn't bring herself to throw it away. There was something honest about its refusal. A single green shoot had emerged last spring and then stopped, as if reconsidering the effort. She stood there a while, watching the light move down the wall, inching toward the framed photograph of her daughter in second grade, arms raised mid-recital, face frozen in a blur. Paula exhaled slowly. The hours had slid past her while she was looking the other way. She brushed a layer of dust from the sill and stepped back into herself.

Her daughter padded in barefoot, the hems of her leggings curled like tide lines around her ankles, holding a packet of paper to her chest as though it contained something delicate, or radioactive. Paula was still in the sunroom, one hand on the window latch, adjusting for a breeze that never arrived. The girl hovered at the edge of the threshold in that way children do when they aren't sure if they're interrupting something sacred or merely adult.

"Mom?"

Paula turned. "Yes?"

"I need help."

"Come in." She gestured toward the chair beside the shelf of succulents, the one upholstered in a linen pattern so muted it might have once had color. "What kind of help?"

The girl sat down and arranged the packet on her knees. Her fingernails were bitten. There was marker on her wrist. "It's for health class. We're doing these little presentations. Mine's on 'health deserts.'" She did the air quotes with a mix of sarcasm and deference, the linguistic posture of a child raised around the casually politic.

Paula didn't respond immediately. She adjusted a slant in the sheer curtain, then settled into the seat opposite. "What did they give you?"

Her daughter unfolded the packet—loose pages, an article with faded color graphs, and a printout of an op-ed clipped from the Greensboro Observer. Paula saw it and recognized the byline instantly. Alan Ransome. The name flared inside her like a struck match.

"This was in the materials," the girl said, holding it up. "He writes really intense. Like, kind of mad. But smart."

Paula took the page. The photo was old—Alan half-turned, one hand mid-gesture, the kind of picture taken by someone who didn't believe in posed authority. The headline read: "Zoning as Weapon: The Legacy of Divestment in East Greensboro." She skimmed the first paragraph and felt something tighten inside.

Her daughter was watching her.

"He teaches at UNCG," Paula said, keeping her voice steady. "I knew him, a long time ago."

"You dated?"

Paula raised an eyebrow.

The girl grinned. "You totally did."

Paula let the silence stretch just long enough to win. Then: "Let's focus on your assignment."

They sat together in the angled light, papers spread between them like evidence. The girl flipped through a worksheet with fill-in-the-blank questions. One prompt read: List three structural causes of limited healthcare access in low-income neighborhoods.

"Do you know what that means?" Paula asked.

"I think so. Like... no hospitals?"

"Not just that," Paula said. "Doctors don't set up practices where reimbursement rates are low. Pharmacies close when there's not enough foot traffic. Grocery stores move out when property values drop, and then you don't just lose medicine—you lose fresh food, reliable transit, safe sidewalks, schools that aren't falling apart."

Her daughter picked at a corner of the paper. "So it's all connected."

"It's always all connected." Paula hesitated. "Do you remember when we drove across town for that art fair last year? The tent festival near Barber Park?"

"Yeah."

"Remember the part of town before we got there? All the boarded-up houses and weedy lots?"

The girl nodded.

"That's Cottage Grove. A few blocks from there is a park that's been closed since before you were born. There's no sign explaining why. Just a fence and a promise of improvements."

"But they're not fixing it?"

"They say they will. They've said that for twelve years."

Her daughter looked at the article again. "So this guy, Alan—he was writing about that?"

"In part. He was trying to explain that disrepair isn't random. It's designed. Or at least allowed."

"But why?"

Paula studied her daughter's face, the narrowed eyes that made her look older, too much like David when she was concentrating. "Because it's easier to pretend the system is broken than to admit it's functioning exactly as intended."

The girl exhaled. "That's dark."

"Yes," Paula said. "But not untrue."

They sat a moment longer. The house creaked as it cooled.

Her daughter pointed to the last page. "He talks about water access. Like how some houses had brown tap water and no one tested it."

"That happened."

"Here?"

Paula nodded.

The girl's mouth twisted slightly. "Why don't they just sue?"

Paula gave a small laugh, bitter and quiet. "Because they can't afford lawyers. Or time off work. Or the years it takes for people to care."

"That sucks."

"It does."

The girl flipped the article shut and stared at her lap. "Do you think it'll change?"

Paula considered lying. Instead, she said, "Not easily."

The girl stood, gathered her pages with a quick rustle, and pressed them to her chest again. "I still have to make a poster," she said. "Can I use the nice markers?"

"Yes. Just put down paper first."

She turned to go, then paused in the doorway.

"Hey, Mom?"

"Yes?"

"That guy. Alan. He's not just mad. He's right."

Then she was gone, and the room felt dimmer in her absence.

The kitchen was cold in that particular way only late-night kitchens could be, with the kind of stillness that suggested the whole house had recoiled into itself. Paula moved without sound. She'd left the overhead light off, choosing instead the under-cabinet glow that made everything look forgivable. She'd poured a half glass of chardonnay and forgotten it twice before sitting down with it, the edge of the stool pressing into her thigh. The laptop toned as it woke, her password typed automatically, a ritual her fingers remembered better than her mind.

She typed his name without hesitation. Alan Ransome housing equity Greensboro Observer. The article came up first—dated two years ago, just after the road infrastructure and housing bond debates. She remembered the noise around it, vaguely. Something about bond misappropriation. She hadn't read it then. Too busy. Too close.

"We pretend zoning is neutral. That red lines fade with time, that concrete doesn't remember. But neighborhoods tell on us. Look where the clinics aren't. Where the pharmacies used to be. Where the school nurse works three jobs and the closest hospital is twenty minutes away if your car starts."

She paused at that line, one hand at her mouth, not covering a gasp—just touching her own skin to stay oriented. His voice hadn't changed. Still precise, still unafraid of indictment. But there was a new undertow now, something weighted. Frustration, maybe. Or fury that had dried into resolve.

The tone wasn't bitter. It was worse. It was measured. She read further.

"The city will tell you about revitalization. About greenways and infrastructure investments. What they won't tell you is that the money follows whiteness the way water follows slope. You can't reverse erosion by reseeding the ditch."

She whispered the sentence aloud. You can't reverse erosion by reseeding the ditch. A line he might've once said on a walk across campus, hand-rolled cigarette perched on his lip, quoting Baldwin or Baldwin quoting someone else. But this wasn't performance. This wasn't poetry for flirtation. This was a man who had stopped asking to be believed.

The clock on the microwave changed: 12:14. She read on. The article was denser than it should've been—someone at the paper had either liked him or feared the backlash. She wondered if he'd submitted it with that same stubborn cover letter he'd used in college, the one that refused flattery, that always ended with "I only want to be useful."

"When you cap poison with playground mulch, don't call it remediation. Call it deferral. Call it a child's lungs playing against time. Call it what it is: a compromise with forgetting."

She inhaled sharply. She could see his face. Not as it was in the photo, or as it might be now—lines deeper, hair gray. But as he'd been that fall before David arrived, when they'd stayed up in her dorm lobby arguing about whether politics was just moral theater. He'd said yes. She'd said no. He'd changed her mind.

It wasn't just the lines. It was the himness in them. The way he constructed an argument with the precision of a surgeon, each cut made in advance of the next. The refusal to sermonize. The directness that left no place to hide. She used to love that about him. Then she'd married someone who preferred deflection—preferred plausible deniability, even in his own thoughts.

She scrolled to the bottom.

"Accountability doesn't come from awareness. It comes from proximity. Look closer. Look until it hurts."

She let her hand rest on the trackpad, breathing slow through her nose. That last command, quiet and blunt. Look until it hurts.

Behind her, the refrigerator whirred and stilled. Upstairs, David's snore bayed in the register of a man deep in a medicated sleep, or the confident unconsciousness of someone convinced nothing he'd done would catch him. She stared at the screen for another minute, then closed the tab. Not from shame. That wasn't how it lived in her. But something in her posture gave way. A tilt of the head, a softness at the mouth, as if she'd just seen a face across a crowded room that once made her believe everything could be different.

The cursor blinked in the dim kitchen. She had pulled up the old thread without fully meaning to, her fingers navigating through folders named after years—2010, Fall Gala, Personal—until she found it, buried beneath logistics and RSVP confirmations, one subject line that hadn't aged. A line from Gibran. "Half of me is longing, the other half is waiting."

Alan's messages had always arrived late. Not late like inconsiderate—late like considered. One every few months, a few lines at most, full of unguarded thought. A link to an article about school redistricting, a photo of Bingham Park before the gate rusted shut, one single poem she hadn't read since college, sent without comment. The thread had gone quiet after her daughter was born. He had written: "Congratulations! You're doing important work." She hadn't replied.

Now she stared at the old exchange, its typographic stillness, and clicked "Reply". She typed straight into the void.

"You were always right about him."

Her hands hovered. An admission, long overdue. Not a confession. A confirmation. That David had been playing chess while Alan was observing the board. That Alan, in all his too-serious, too-earnest intensity, had seen what the rest of them had chosen to call "complicated" or "nuanced" or "inevitable."

The line sat there in the window, clean and perfect. And then, with one backspace, gone. She closed the draft and shut the laptop. Not because the moment had passed. But because something in her understood: this wasn't a message for sending. It was a sentence she needed to be able to write and erase. A thing said, then unsaid.

In the hallway, she paused beside her daughter's door, one hand resting lightly on the brass handle, fingers curled around the cool metal as if testing its temperature, or her own resolve. The floor creaked beneath her heel, the only sound in the corridor besides the rhythm of the girl's breath behind the door—steady, trusting, unknowing. The room inside was full of fleece blankets and glitter pens and the fragile bits of a self still under construction. A place untouched by the compromises that stained every other square foot of this house.

Back in her study, the lamplight was low, the desk dustless, arranged with the sterile precision of a life meant to feel busy.. She opened the middle drawer—not the locked one, not the one with the receipts and the file labeled "Medical", but the long, shallow one where the fragments of sentiment lived: boarding passes she hadn't thrown away, a keychain from the botanical gardens, a thumb drive with no label.

The map was folded cleanly, its creases crisp. She had mailed a copy, not the original. She remembered standing at the post office window, pressing the envelope flat against the Formica counter, the weight of it insufficient but undeniable. Now, unfolding it again, the red circle drawn around parcel 524-B, the ink slightly smudged where her hand had hesitated that night, not from doubt, but from muscle memory—the same way you pause before pressing send, before saying yes, before leaving.

She studied it a moment. The edges were beginning to yellow. A bureaucratic relic made dangerous only by attention. In the top drawer of the vanity beside her desk was a small velvet jewelry box, once white, now tinged with the patina of whatever collected on soft surfaces in long marriages. She opened it and placed the map inside, tucking it beneath a photograph—black-and-white, slightly blurred—of her and Alan at a protest in college, their faces angled toward the camera. She was holding a sign about transit access, he had his mouth open mid-sentence, gesturing to someone just out of frame. They looked like people who thought truth was a thing you could deliver by chant.

She closed the box slowly. The click of the clasp was soft but complete. David had gone too far. She saw that now with the kind of clarity that didn't allow for deflection or excuse. Not just in what he'd permitted, but in what he'd engineered. The manipulation was no longer strategic. It was feral. The lie had outgrown its host.

She was certain. About the parcel's soil. About the red ooze leaking from rivulet seams in the fill. About what the city knew and when. About Alan's anger and its shape, the slow-burn moral architecture he'd spent years constructing while she smoothed linens and tempered donors and adjusted narrative to fit the room. She sat for a moment longer, back straight, hands in her lap, the map tucked away like a lit fuse in velvet. Alive in a way that felt startling. The power of a secret wasn't in its silence. It was in its inevitability.

The house breathed into morning with its usual choreography. Light sifted through the kitchen window. Paula stood at the counter arranging her daughter's school items into a bag: a reusable water bottle with a chipped anime sticker, a folder labeled "Science – Unit 3", a zippered pouch with markers that barely capped. The ritual was mundane, automatic, but precise in its own way. These were the acts she had learned to perform without applause.

David was already seated at the kitchen table, a bowl of dry cereal pushed to the edge of his placemat and the Wall Street Journal opened before him. He scrolled his phone with his left hand, pausing occasionally to sip black coffee. The screen reflected in his glasses. Headlines about housing starts, bond yields, a paragraph circled in red about new opportunity zones. His expression didn't change. He had learned to consume the news without absorbing it, like one might stare into the sun from behind polarized shades.

Their daughter came in last, half-dressed but somehow radiant, trailing the scent of vanilla shampoo and the unmistakable anxiety of a 12-year old trying to remember if today was a test or a free period. She reached for toast without asking, crunched noisily, one foot tapping out a rhythm under the table.

"Do you have your permission slip for the field trip?" Paula asked.

The girl froze. "It's in my room. I think."

"Before shoes," Paula said, without looking up.

David folded the newspaper cleanly in half, set it aside. "I'm heading to the site today," he said, voice smooth with professional detachment. "Want to see how far along they are on the anchor project. Ground crews moved fast this week—weather's holding."

Paula nodded. "Take your boots," she said. "It was muddy last time."

He smiled faintly, leaned in, and kissed her cheek. It was the same kiss he'd given her for years—dry, precise, calculated to appear affectionate without disarranging anything. She received it as one might receive a monogrammed envelope—impersonal, but fine.

He lingered a moment, watching the girl shove notebooks into a backpack already swollen with neglect. "You ready?" he asked her.

"Sort of."

Paula watched him move through the back hall, keys already out. The door clicked behind him, and the house reshaped itself around his absence. She stood still, one hand on the table edge. In the afterimage of his presence, she felt it, that tinge. The ache of recognizing a choice you've already made. The envelope had been sent. The map folded just so. Her silence broken in the only way she could live with.

She had helped him, once, craft the narrative. Helped launder the language, soften the edges of his ambition so that it looked like stewardship. She had sat on panels and smiled through ribbon cuttings and fundraisers where the hors d'oeuvres were more carefully sourced than the building materials. She had convinced herself that harm diluted over distance. That intention insulated guilt. That silence, maintained properly, was a form of grace.

But the house was full of cracks. She could see them now—not in the walls, but in the calibration of their days, the careful way they moved around each other. The glances that contained too little, the space between touches too exact. There was rot beneath the silk. And she had helped stitch the fabric.

The girl bounded in, shoes half-tied, face flushed.

"Can you sign this?"

Paula reached for the pen, signed without comment, and handed it back. The girl grinned and vanished, all motion and breath. She stood alone in the kitchen, the sunlight now sharper, the air tinged with citrus and brewed coffee. She wasn't waiting for absolution. She wasn't expecting anything at all. But she would remember this moment.

10

It began, as these things do, in a conference room with too much glass and very little memory. David Moss sat at the head of the reclaimed wood table flanked by an economic development advisor from Chapel Hill and a former nonprofit executive whose recent title upgrade to "Chief Strategy Officer" had endowed her with the peculiar dialect of someone learning to think in branded tiers.

The Guilford Health System was three months into its post-privatization rebrand, and no one quite knew what it was anymore. The name had changed, the board had changed, and the language around care had undergone a full renovation. Health was now wellness, patients were stakeholders. The hospital, now ringed by glass pavilions, was no longer a place for the sick, but a destination for the proactively engaged. They needed a win. Something that photographed well but also read as structurally sound.

David leaned back in his chair, one ankle crossed over his knee, as if unbothered by urgency. "We need a project that resonates," he said. "It can't just be a facelift. It needs to transform the system."

It was the fourth meeting in as many weeks. Ideas had been flung like spaghetti against drywall. A mobile diagnostics van for rural triage. A public nutrition partnership with the community college. A grant-funded health literacy initiative focused on "underserved populations," a phrase so broad it included both the uninsured and anyone who hadn't mastered deductibles.

"We need a place," David continued, his tone almost offhand, which in David's universe meant prepare to write this down. "Something people can stand on, walk through, name in conversation. Not another app. Not another task force."

Across the table, the strategist nodded with the reverent enthusiasm of someone hoping to be quoted in a press release. "A center?"

"A corridor," David said, before the word had fully formed in his mind. It felt structural. Directional. Purposeful. The room tilted toward him, as rooms often did.

A junior consultant—the one with the folders always color-coded—pulled up a GIS map. "We've been tracking this parcel cluster south of downtown," she said. "Four city-owned lots, unused for two decades. It's already zoned mixed-use. The bones are there. Just no spine."

David walked to the monitor. The lots stared back—grey voids on a bright field of parcel lines. Officially: underdeveloped. Locally: forgotten. The corner lot had once been a dry cleaner, the building razed in 2002. Another had housed a charter school experiment that failed before its second cohort graduated. The other two were rumored to have bad soil, though no one could locate a test result. The entire site had become a kind of civic shrug—an inherited disappointment, too boring to protest but too expensive to fix.

"People will push back," someone offered. "That area's had failed plans before. The baseball stadium. The grocery store."

"That's the point," David said. "It's been vacant long enough to be neutral. There's no active stakeholder memory. And it's close to the downtown core. Optics are ideal."

"But the site—" the consultant began, and then didn't finish.

David had already moved to the next slide, a rendering they'd used before: gentle landscaping, open green space, a childcare wing shaped like a honeycomb. The image never changed. Just the labels.

"We're not talking about gentrification," he said, as if to preempt something no one had yet said aloud. "We're talking about wellness equity."

He let the phrase land.

"Walkability, green space, access to nutrition and preventive care. A new model. Something that says we're not the old hospital anymore. We're Guilford Health System."

At some point in the discussion someone said "health desert," and someone else said "civic activation," and the idea hardened. One lot became the anchor project, and the anchor project became the new language for public-private renewal, which meant no one had to say displacement or contamination or what used to be there. By the end of the meeting, a task force was appointed and a press packet outlined. The city would be brought in later, ideally after the local partners had been named and the outcomes drafted. You had to show momentum, David always said, before you showed need.

In the car afterward, he dictated three notes into his phone. One about stormwater mitigation grants—low-hanging fruit. One about framing the project through community health gaps. And one to himself: Get Paula on board early. Tie it to the arts. Use theater. People trust the arts.

That night, he watched his daughter draw on the back of a takeout menu while he fielded a call from the board chair about a potential naming sponsor. A banking family with old land money and a new social conscience. He told them yes, it had legs. Real ground-up potential. No, not another tower. This was better. More human-scale.

Afterward, Paula brought him a glass of wine and mentioned a Bingham Park grant Goldie Hayes had applied for that had fallen through again. He nodded. Made a mental note to route the discussion elsewhere next time. He slept well that night. He always did after decisions. Especially the ones no one noticed until the shovel hit dirt.

It arrived in a bulleted PDF, quietly attached to an interdepartmental memo labeled Preliminary Site Environmental Review – South Elm Redevelopment Parcel Group. No cover letter. David opened it on a Wednesday, in the middle of a Zoom about "branding alignments" for the corridor concept, while half-listening to a man from Durham explain how an amphitheater could double as a mobile testing site with the right LED installation.

He clicked the document, expecting the usual box-checking language—terms like trace presence, legacy compound, within tolerance—the bureaucratic incense burned before any real estate offering. What he found was older, less esoteric. A 2006 report from a defunct environmental firm, resurfaced during due diligence. The phrasing was blunt. Elevated levels of hexavalent chromium consistent with ash runoff. Source likely municipal incineration between 1946 and 1961. Soil disturbance not advised without full mitigation.

David read the paragraphs three times, his mouth drying in slow increments. The name hexavalent chromium rang with that specific toxicity of something once used in industry and later banned everywhere respectable. He remembered Erin Brockovich in a loose sense—not the case, not the science, but the contagion that could derail a project. One word, whispered at the wrong gala, and a year's worth of renderings turned radioactive.

He paused the Zoom. Faked a dropped connection. Opened his private browser and searched chromium Greensboro contamination. A few dead-end articles from the Triad environmental blogs, one archived protest flyer from a defunct community group. The term Bingham Park came up. So did Legacy Redevelopment Initiative—a name he recognized. One of the old shell entities used in the nineties to offload liability into philanthropic assets. The more he clicked, the more it calcified: the soil was bad. Had been bad for decades. And, crucially, the city had known.

He called the project's legal liaison, a woman with a litigation background who'd spent a career softening the edges of negligence. She wasn't surprised.

"They buried it," she said. "First figuratively, then literally. Cap-and-cover became the default mitigation strategy after '02. It's common."

"And legally?"

"We're fine, as long as we frame it correctly. We aren't disturbing the known plume. We're building adjacent. Plus the city indemnified all post-sale entities under the Brownfield Protection Act. Language is your friend here."

Language had always been David's friend. He knew how to make a sentence say one thing and imply its opposite. His real talent wasn't administration or development—it was sequencing. Knowing what came first in a sentence, what to subordinate, what to hide inside prepositions. He'd built a career turning cause into correlation, liability into leverage. He closed the PDF and stared out the window at the scaffolding wrapping the new oncology pavilion.

Later that day, in the standing meeting with Facilities and Civic Partnership, he framed it cleanly: "There's historical contamination. Known, not active. We'll be emphasizing stabilization, not remediation. That distinction is critical. We're not fixing damage. We're transforming the site's narrative."

No one blinked. The project moved forward. The contamination became a footnote. Then pre-regulatory. Then a design opportunity—bioswales and native plantings and educational signage about "healing landscapes." The rot, properly narrated, had become a feature.

That night, at home, Paula asked how the corridor meeting had gone. He said it was promising. "Some hiccups," he allowed, pouring himself a drink. "But manageable." He didn't mention the chromium. Didn't mention the buried report or the firm that no longer existed or the quiet erasure of the phrase full remediation from the next press release. There would be a playground. And a mural. And somewhere beneath the synthetic mulch and imported topsoil, the past would remain, still chemical, still toxic.

He began with the easiest lie: omission by sequence. In the next round of board presentations, David moved the soil report to the appendix, renaming it Pre-regulatory Findings. The document itself hadn't changed, but its narrative position had—tucked behind cost estimates and images of a walking path bisecting a wildflower meadow. The flower beds, of course, did not yet exist. But their imagined presence softened the room. By the time someone reached the fine print, their eyes had already gone slack with optimism.

The memo to the city was crafted more deliberately. He asked Legal to revise the correspondence with the language of "ongoing compliance review" and "collaborative stabilization strategy." The city's Director of Environmental Oversight, a man who'd been promoted three years too late and knew he'd never catch up, signed off on it within the week. No one wanted to be the person who stalled Guilford Health's banner initiative. Not in this climate. Not with grants pending. David offered a partnership on a future asthma awareness campaign—symbolic, low-cost, a press-friendly fig leaf—and the matter evaporated.

The original environmental report, the one from 2006 with the blunt phrasing and the bad data, was harder. It lived in three places: the firm's defunct archive, a scanned version in the city's outdated database, and a paper copy held by an urban historian who had used it in a lecture series called "Toxic Legacies: Greensboro's Hidden Brownfields." David couldn't delete the history, but he could redirect the inquiry. The scanned version was replaced with a link to a newer study commissioned by a private consultant. The firm—three engineers and a drone—had produced cleaner numbers, lower readings, promising projections. David's team circulated that version broadly, always with the note: For latest data, refer to this report.

The historian, he decided, didn't matter. Those who taught adjunct rarely had the stamina for sustained resistance. And in any case, the public had little interest in lectures about the city's past misdeeds when future renderings were so charming, so inclusive. The corridor would be built with light, with motion. With color-coded benches and free Wi-Fi and a farmer's market on alternating Sundays. Soil didn't photograph well. Playgrounds did.

Internally, he made another move—he reframed remediation as activation. This required careful scripting. The site would not be "cleaned." It would be "transformed." The term remediation suggested culpability, even crime. Activation was gentler. It evoked potential. The communications team took to it instantly. The term appeared in the next board memo, the next grant proposal, the next round of donor materials. By the end of the quarter, it was doctrine.

There were, of course, voices of dissent. One city council member asked if chromium was still present. David answered with a pivot: "We're focused on opportunity. On what's ahead." Another activist posted drone footage of the site and labeled it Poison Pavillion. David scheduled a closed-door lunch with the mayor and a real estate development lead from Durham. He let them talk about innovation, about health equity. He nodded. He waited. Then he offered to name the pavilion after the mayor's father, a well-liked dentist who'd died in the nineties.

She took the deal.

By spring, the mulch had arrived. By early summer, signage was in production. Future Home of the Wellness Innovation Corridor. Beneath the mulch, the soil remained. Still volatile in places. Still untested in others. David had succeeded not in cleaning the site, but in transforming it into a symbol. The rot, buried deep, was rebranded as history—static, pre-regulatory, irrelevant.

At night, he slept beside a wife who had once asked questions and now asked none. In the morning, he took calls about donor tiers, about seating arrangements for the ribbon-cutting. He practiced the phrase healing environment until it tasted other than deceit. What he had buried wasn't just the data. It was the chance for a reckoning. And in its place he had built something shinier. Something no one wanted to dig into.

The SUV's cabin was sealed in quiet—just enough road rush to remind him of movement, just enough leather to make him feel justified in the space. David sat in the rear passenger seat, angled slightly toward the window, thumb flicking idle against his phone screen. No unread emails. No new crises. His daughter had bounded into the school with a wave and a request for sushi tonight—already negotiating dinner like a lobbyist. He had kissed her forehead, adjusted the strap on her canvas backpack, and reminded her to ask questions. Always ask questions, he said, forgetting the irony as he said it.

Now the car drifted south. Through the tinted glass, the city unfolded in its familiar gradations—north to south, clean to cracked, amenity to absence. Irving Park fell behind them, its winding roads manicured into a kind of architectural lullaby: slate roofs, poured concrete driveways, azaleas trimmed into submission. Then came the medical district—fresh signage, brushed steel, a pharmacy built inside what used to be a grocer. David noted the new awning on the imaging center. Green. Friendly. He'd suggested that color in the branding brief last year. Something about health without saying health.

Downtown proper began near the old Cadillac dealership, a half-preserved façade now leasing as office space for digital consultancies and nonprofits with names that ended in Lab or Collective. There was a new juice bar in the corner storefront of what had once been a bail bond office on Greene Street. Men in logo hoodies and women with structured handbags sipped things that looked like pondwater and called it wellness. David recognized one of the city council staffers at the sidewalk table, AirPods in, nodding along to nothing.

The SUV crept past a mural too bright for the brick it covered—three hands holding a sunflower, underlined by the phrase WE RISE TOGETHER in aggressive font. He thought the kerning was off. Another project pitched by a community arts group, painted over the back wall of a former furniture outlet that had been empty since the first Bush administration. There was a plan to turn the space into a cultural incubator, but no one could define what that meant in measurable terms. He had offered matching funds from the health system's discretionary civic pot, knowing full well it would stretch over five years, then disappear in Phase Three of the corridor rollout.

To the east, he glimpsed the housing tower recently acquired by the redevelopment agency—a Soviet-looking slab softened with fresh siding and a decal campaign. Healthy Homes Start With Us. He'd approved that language himself, the week the eviction notices had gone out. Language first. Then infrastructure.

As they moved closer to the South Elm site, the skyline thinned. The corridor's shell was visible now—steel ribs marking where the wellness pavilion would rise. A wide fence ringed the site, wrapped in vinyl banners printed with smiling children and renderings of greenspace curved like hugging arms. Behind the fence, piles of topsoil waited, imported from a certified source beyond the city limits. David watched a worker maneuver a small excavator toward a drainage trench, slow and careful. The car stopped at the curb. He sat for a breath and let the image arrange itself—cranes, banners, the illusion of momentum.

He tapped his phone, checked the time, and said, "Fifteen minutes." The driver nodded. David looked out the window again, past the banners and mulch, toward the red sluice just visible at the edge of the trench. Brief, a sliver, then gone as the worker moved in front of it. He blinked once, then twice, as if clearing dust.

The phone rang just as his hand met the door handle, the screen flashing DENT. David hesitated for half a breath—enough to consider letting it ring out—but took the call. The driver adjusted the rearview mirror but said nothing. The tinted glass trapped the sound, turned the car into a booth.

"Councilman."

"David." The voice on the line was tight, affected calm. Dent always sounded like a man playing the role of a person in control. "Got a minute?"

"I'm stepping into a site meeting, but for you, sure."

Dent exhaled as if he'd rehearsed the conversation in the shower. "I wanted to flag something before it gets noisy. Hightower's getting aggressive about Bingham. She's starting to frame it as a moral lapse."

David leaned back into the seat, gaze sliding past the crane arm now frozen against the sky. "Bingham's been in holding for years. We're stabilizing the South End. That's where the dollars are working."

"She's not buying the sequencing anymore," Dent said. "And Goldie Hayes is organizing. Not a march, not yet, but something harder to brush off. Letters, legal templates. Residents have started showing up with soil samples in sandwich bags. It's... pointed."

David smiled faintly. "Grassroots documentation. Lovely."

"It's not just optics this time," Dent said. "Goldie's got support from the pulpit forum and at least two deans over at A&T. And she's calling it generational injury. She's connecting dots. Housing, health, land use, zoning. I've seen her pitch. It plays."

David didn't answer immediately. He watched a construction worker lean over a wheelbarrow, adjust his gloves, then begin again with the kind of slow motion that spoke of patience and hourly labor.

Dent filled the silence. "Look, I've kept the thing soft. Redirected the press inquiries. Let staff play musical chairs on the environmental review. But I can't keep putting out the fire."

David closed his eyes for a moment. Then: "Once the last arts grant comes through, we're covered. We'll show active community engagement. Active always wins. They don't have the bandwidth to litigate nuance. We're building a playground and greenspace for them."

"And the bond?"

David opened his eyes again. "We'll need the streetscape bond money once the pavilion's finished. Soft-paved corridors, human-scale lighting. The visual logic has to hold."

"That's a lot of redirect."

David shrugged, though Dent couldn't see it. "We're not taking. We're reallocating."

Dent laughed once. "You say that with a straight face?"

"We're not asking them to disappear," David replied. "We're asking them to trust the future more than the past."

"That's easy to say when the past doesn't smell like an incinerator."

David's voice lowered, cold and exact. "We've always ignored them, Councilman. That's the unspoken contract. The city maintains distance, we give them language. If they ever get organized enough to see the whole structure—how funding flows, how silence pays—we'll have hell to pay."

Dent didn't respond. The silence hummed for a moment, thick.

David glanced again at the trench line. A flag marker fluttered in the soil, the color faded.

"Keep her talking," David said. "Keep Goldie in meetings. Process is the best delay mechanism we have. And the wellness corridor gives us a narrative with texture. Art installations, youth engagement. That buys us time."

"You better hope so," Dent said. "Because the water's rising, David. And people remember who built the levees."

The call ended.

David slid the phone back into his coat pocket and finally opened the door. The sunlight hit his eyes with surgical precision. He buttoned his jacket. The banners flapped in the wind, each one smiling back at him with optimism.

The gravel gave slightly beneath him, the kind of give that signaled recent grading. He was careful of his shoes. Dust lifted at the edges, then settled again. David crossed the site perimeter flanked by the architect, the site foreman, and Cal Danner—a developer he'd known since UNC, now flush off a tobacco mill redevelopment in Durham and sniffing around for whatever came next. Cal wore a performance vest and sunglasses too large for his face, as if he wanted to signal casual authority while still being photographed if it came down to that.

A portable fence panel groaned open and David stepped through, already scanning. The cranes moved overhead with purposeful slowness. A concrete pumping rig stood quiet for now, its arm curled like a muscle at rest. The building's steel frame had reached the third level. Fireproofing wrap glinted against the morning sun, silver in strips where insulation had begun.

"North end core's topped out," said the foreman, a compact man with sun-leathered skin and a voice like crushed aggregate. "Starting curtain wall prep next week. Glazing arrives Tuesday if the weather holds."

David nodded, barely. His eyes were elsewhere—along the line where the pavilion's footprint angled south. The slope had been graded last month. He could see the erosion blankets still pinned like surgical mesh across the hillside.

Cal whistled, scanning the rising beams. "Jesus. This thing's got legs."

"It has to," said David. "Anchor projects don't get second chances."

The architect, a precise woman with minimal affect and a clipboard that looked absurdly analog, pointed to a rendering posted to the back of a concrete form. "We've shifted the flow from linear to more radial," she said. "Encourages circular movement, not just corridor navigation."

David didn't entirely care about movement theory. What mattered was how it photographed from above—curves suggested inclusion. Lines suggested corridors. Inclusion polled better.

"The framing timeline's tight," the foreman added. "We lost three days on the storm delay last week. Still think we can make the November milestone, assuming trades stay ahead of inspection."

David stepped onto a plywood ramp and peered into the open framework. The slab still showed its grid scoring. Workers moved deliberately. One held a clipboard, another pulled cable through a PVC sleeve embedded in the concrete. The choreography was wordless.

"They're pouring the diagnostic wing foundation next week," said the architect. "After that we start trenching for utilities."

"Still waiting on water line permits?" David asked.

"Cleared this morning," the foreman said. "But we've got to cut before the city changes its mind."

David smiled, then looked out past the site fence. From this angle, the lot across the street looked almost benign—grass growing in uneven patches, a hint of red clay near the storm drain. No signage. No protestors. For now.

Cal adjusted his sunglasses, leaned in. "This is going to turn the whole grid, you know that? Once you get the pedestrian traffic right, the rest of downtown flows toward it."

David nodded. He already knew. He turned back to the site. A welder sparked above, a flash of orange-white that seared against the steel. The wellness corridor wasn't hypothetical. It was being bolted into place. He stepped down from the ramp, dust clinging to the edge of his slacks, and kept walking.

They moved without speaking at first, pressing into ground that had been cleared just enough to suggest progress, not so much that it looked finished. The wind picked up at the parcel's edge, where the southern lot dipped toward the chain-link buffer. Beyond it, the street curved into the part of town that had been renamed so many times the real name no longer stuck—now whatever developers chose to write on funding packets. A code-switching landscape.

Cal gestured to the space in front of them, the dirt stamped in neat squares, flagged with pink markers like sprouting ideas. "What's this zone supposed to be?" he asked, squinting.

David slowed. "Playground," he said.

Cal raised an eyebrow. "In a clinical complex?"

"It's a wellness anchor," David replied, automatic. "Whole-family care. Early childhood physical literacy, sensory regulation, intergenerational wellness. It tests well. And we've got grant language around trauma-informed outdoor design. There's a pilot in Charlotte we're modeling against."

Cal gave a soft laugh. "You just stacked ten buzzwords in two sentences. You alright?"

David didn't answer right away. The wind shifted again, bringing with it a scent he couldn't name—maybe old concrete, maybe something earthbound. The red soil here had a memory. Or perhaps he was imagining that. The moment stretched, and something passed across his face. Nothing visible exactly, but Cal saw it, caught it.

"You seem far off," Cal said. "This part of the parcel haunted?"

David exhaled, a single, measured breath. He looked down at the soil, graded, tamped, ready for rubber surfacing. The planned design showed a swing set, a climbing apparatus shaped into a double helix, benches in muted colors, shade structures arched like wings. The plan had passed design review in under twenty minutes. No one ever questioned the moral value of a playground. It was the most reliable form of misdirection available to civic designers.

"This is the part people photograph," David said, voice tight with something approaching honesty. "It's where the mayor cuts the ribbon and a child does something adorable in the background. No one asks about brownfield history when there are kids in face paint drinking juice boxes."

Cal said nothing. They stood on what had once been brownfield and reclamation waste, decades of runoff and municipal shortcuts leaching into the ground. No signage marked the site's past. Only plans for amenities.

David pressed on. "It shows impact. Tangibility. You drop a playground into a project and it becomes a destination. Every funder wants narrative infrastructure now. That's what this is. It completes the optics."

Cal turned, studying him. "You ever think it's too much?"

David blinked. "Too much what?"

"All of it. The polish. The performance. The reframing. We used to build buildings. Now we're building the story of a building."

David didn't answer. Instead he looked out toward the street, where a bus pulled to a stop and a woman stepped off with a toddler in one arm and the transit limit of three grocery bags hanging from the other. She adjusted the child on her hip and walked past the site without looking in. She didn't see the future rising here. She only saw what wasn't.

He returned his gaze to the lot. "We're not building performance," he said, finally. "We're building the conditions that make performance unnecessary."

Cal let that sit a moment, then shook his head. "Jesus, you've still got it."

David smiled, though it didn't travel far. "We all pick our fictions. I just choose the ones that get built."

They stood for a moment at the edge of the lie, staring into the clean geometry of a story that no one would dare question—because children would play here. Because wellness was apolitical. Because once the mulch went down, the past would be buried under three inches of recycled rubber and a commemorative plaque.

He turned away from the footprint, dust besmirching his leather shoes, and didn't look back. At the north end of the lot, the foreman waited with one boot on a cinderblock, half-shielded from the wind. The architect stood beside him, arms folded over her clipboard, a pencil tucked behind one ear, the picture of controlled exasperation. David approached with the crisp gait he reserved for posturing around progress—deliberate, shoulders set, jaw loose enough to read as confident but tight enough to signal he's got places to be.

"We've got a sequencing issue on the utility trench," the foreman said, straight into it. "The line's coming in two feet shallow. Either we regrade the slope, or we cut across the pediatric wing pad and reroute."

The architect spoke before David could weigh in. "We can't regrade. It screws up the drainage calcs. Stormwater compliance was a house of cards already."

David glanced at the laminated site plan. The offending line was marked in green Sharpie, a fragile arc across the page. He didn't care about the trench. He cared about what it meant.

"Do it," he said. "Route through the pad, just keep the visual clean when it's poured. I don't want reporters asking about trenches on walk-through day."

The foreman shrugged. "You got it."

The architect jotted something and David offered a nod, the kind he'd perfected over a decade of pretending to defer.

Cal emerged from behind a port-a-john, brushing dust off his vest. "I'll leave you to your fiefdom," he said, grinning. "See you at the club Saturday? They're doing a bourbon thing."

David smirked, already turning away. "Wouldn't miss it."

Cal vanished through the fence like he knew he'd always land right-side-up. David watched the man's silhouette shrink against the brightness of the morning, then climbed back into the SUV. The interior air was still cool, still clean. His driver offered a silent nod. David waved him on. They pulled away from the site, tires crunching over the gravel he'd personally approved. Each foot of that ground now sealed into memory. He kept his eyes forward, past the cranes and banners, toward the rising skyline ahead.

The guilt didn't arrive as a feeling. It arrived as a fact. Quiet, mechanical, like a building code violation discovered after ribbon-cutting. An awareness too late to prevent, too early to disown. The playground was the fulcrum. The falsity in plain sight. It was where the press would stand, where the children would laugh, where the donors would smile and feel proud of having contributed to something "transformative." It was also where the soil tested worst. He had seen the sampling logs. The core extractions marked elevated metals in precisely the places where they planned to install a slide.

He had moved city money as if sweeping water from a ship deck. Waterline grants. Streetscape bond reallocations. Leftover green infrastructure funds cannibalized from projects in neighborhoods with fewer newsletters, fewer lawyers. Every dollar repurposed with just enough procedural legitimacy to avoid scrutiny—at least from those too tired or too polite to demand the whole spreadsheet.

But Goldie Hayes was not tired. She had the dangerous combination of time and clarity. That was what made her effective. That was what made her a threat. He had seen her three weeks ago at a zoning subcommittee meeting, standing in the back with her arms crossed, saying nothing. Her presence recalibrated the room. The staffers got twitchy. The council members overcorrected.

If she kept pushing—if she rallied the right group of residents, if she published Bingham Park's soil records, if she got Hightower to call for a formal hearing—then everything might stop. The language he'd spent two years drafting could collapse under the weight of a single phrase: They ignored us.

The SUV turned onto Eugene Street, the skyline falling away behind him. He tapped his finger once against the glass and looked out at a woman waiting at a bus stop with a stroller and no shade. He reached for his phone but didn't unlock it. Just held it there, a warm weight in his palm.

The Village Tavern sat behind a row of tasteful hedges and regulation-approved shade trees, its brick facade a simulacrum of Southern gentility stripped of racial memory or culinary risk. It was the kind of place where white wine was still poured with a flourish and the salad forks had never once pierced anything grown in toxic soil. David had been coming here for over a decade—client lunches, reconciliation dinners, discreet collisions with donors who didn't like to park downtown. The waitstaff wore black aprons and communicated in half-nods. The booths had high backs for a reason. Privacy was not an amenity. It was the product.

The driver parked out front without circling. David stepped out and straightened his jacket—not a full suit today, but structured enough to suggest civic responsibility. He preferred neutrality. The look of someone managing infrastructure, not seeking office. His mind ran through the script as he walked—timelines, soft promises, projected public benefit. He needed Councilwoman Hoffman's nod for the bond redirects to hold. The streetscape funding wasn't just cosmetic. It would pave the narrative. No one believed in health equity if the sidewalks cracked.

Inside, the hostess recognized him. Everyone here did. She nodded, murmured "Private room," and led him past the main dining area, where men in retirement khakis argued about university race admissions and second homes with the fervor of people who had never once been denied. The room carried the scent of truffle fries and lightly seared fish, the markers of wealth that had perfected restraint.

He scanned as he walked. Linen napkins perfectly creased. The same oil paintings of imaginary vineyards. Each table a still life of affluence in repose. The walls had seen more public-private deals than the city manager's office.

David moved into pitch posture. He reset his breathing, adjusted the pace of his steps. He reminded himself of Hoffman's political lineage—her grandfather had helped draft the city's 1958 charter revisions. Her husband had once chaired the state university system. She knew how power moved, and more importantly, she knew how to keep it moving without ever making it look like it had changed hands. Her district was engineered with surgical precision: wide-lawn neighborhoods wrapped around one slim corridor of old textile warehouses, just enough downtown brick to justify her involvement in urban renewal, just enough urban population to claim progressive alignment. Her relevance was spatial math, and the voters liked it that way.

The man she'd brought with her—James Picknell, if David remembered the name correctly—was a logistics magnate turned arts philanthropist, the kind of billionaire who liked to be referred to as a "serial entrepreneur." Picknell wasn't on any committee, but he had an account at the community foundation with a seven-figure war chest and a seat on the state transportation board. If he wanted the wellness corridor to succeed, it would. If he didn't, the whole thing could dissolve into a tangle of stalled traffic reviews.

David approached the private room, each step deliberate. He'd rehearsed this: emphasize the walkability index, downplay the driveway variance, quote a metric about reduced cardiac events when shade coverage reaches 30 percent. Mention the sculpture installation. Mention the university partnership. If necessary, invoke children.

He paused outside the room, hand resting on the brass handle. He let himself feel the weight of the next twenty minutes. The ask was delicate—not a direct transfer, but a redirection. Funds marked for general infrastructure, nudged gently toward the corridor's southern edge. A move that would never be called theft, because everyone involved had agreed not to name it.

He opened the door.

Councilwoman Hoffman sat at the head of the table, a napkin already draped across her lap, eyes gleaming above the rim of her water glass. Picknell was mid-sentence, gesturing with one hand and cutting his grilled chicken with the other. Both turned toward him at once, faces composed and expectant. David smiled, the version that showed just enough teeth to read as earnest, and stepped inside.

From above, the private room at the Village Tavern appeared staged—one of four back alcoves cordoned off from the main dining floor by a pane of obscured glass etched with fake colonial laurels. A side entrance through a narrow hallway allowed VIPs to arrive unseen, which meant the real theatre happened out front. At table twelve, two vice provosts from the university picked at identical salads while trading favors that neither would remember next semester. In the far corner, a retired textile executive argued quietly with his son-in-law over charter school tax credits. Waitstaff moved between tables with deference, trained not to interrupt but always to witness.

It was understood, in rooms like these, who was watching whom. The old money watched the young money to see where it would embarrass itself. The young money watched the city staffers to see what they were allowed to manage. Everyone watched the council members—particularly those like Hoffman—because they had the influence to stop momentum, which in Greensboro was as close to power as anyone could get.

David slid into the booth across from her, placing his phone face down on the linen. His jacket stayed on. Hoffman wore a cream blouse with a brooch in the shape of the old city seal. Picknell wore a blazer that looked custom but wasn't—new rich restraint. A server appeared with a refill of iced tea before David could ask.

"Apologies," David said. "Site meeting ran over."

"I admire a man who still visits his projects in the dirt," Hoffman said. Her voice was brittle with amusement. She never let anyone forget she was born in Hamilton Lakes, back when it was still the edge of town and not a golf map subdivision.

Picknell smiled without teeth. "We were just discussing scale. Lynn's concerned the corridor's gotten too ambitious."

David leaned forward slightly. "Not ambitious. Coherent. You can't have impact without scale. Otherwise it reads as pilot."

"And Bingham?" Hoffman asked, buttering a slice of bread with casual grace. "People are starting to notice it hasn't moved."

He shrugged, an elegant deflection. "That site's under legacy restrictions. The city's still parsing what counts as remediation. Legal's sorting it. The wellness corridor, meanwhile, is vertical. It would be irresponsible to pause momentum for a priorities discussion."

Picknell nodded thoughtfully. "Optics?"

"Manageable," David said. "We're spinning the corridor stabilization as proactive. Got a landscape firm prepping renderings that suggest continuity—same palette, same sidewalk design. Once the corridor is complete, the city can put Bingham Park into a 'phase two' narrative. Urban patchwork, scalable interventions. It'll play."

Hoffman took a sip of water, watching him over the rim of her glass. "And the money?"

"We've routed the final grant ask through streetscape. Less scrutiny there. Easier to frame as infrastructure optimization. Technically true."

"You're saying Bingham Park loses funding priority so the wellness corridor downtown can finish its sidewalks," she said.

"I'm saying we optimize downtown infrastructure investments across zones of civic engagement," he said, letting it hang just long enough for her to roll her eyes. "And we do it before the bond language gets messy. Once the streetscape funding's aligned, we can finish the southern span without asking the city to float another appropriation."

Picknell cut his chicken with surprising delicacy. "People forget the bond language doesn't guarantee allocation. It guarantees the pot."

David smiled faintly. "Exactly. We're just managing distribution."

Hoffman set down her fork, placed her napkin over her lap again like a signal. "I can support it. Quietly. The language has to go through committee first. You'll need to massage the memo. Frame it in terms of outcomes and pedestrian safety."

"It's already written."

She paused. "No fuck ups, David. I'm serious. Not one leak. Not one leak that sounds like a leak. I'm not babysitting a salvage operation five months before the next city election. The public comment period is already hot enough."

"It'll be clean," he said. "We'll have the final streetscape draft by the end of next week. After that, we flip the narrative—corridor as prototype, Bingham as Phase II. No one will touch the soil question once we've got street trees and a mural."

Picknell leaned back, impressed or at least amused. "It's a hell of a play."

David allowed himself a sip of tea, cool and unsweetened. "It's Greensboro. You don't sell progress here. You sell consensus."

11

From a bird's eye view, the church looked like any other. A simple brick rectangle softened by a decorated glass front and nascent crepe myrtles, the kind of place built to withstand. It sat in between Bingham Park and Cottage Grove, along South English Street, which had carved the neighborhood in half. The church had a faded white steeple, a white cross bolted on top like punctuation. Inside, the sanctuary swelled. Fans whirred. Children fidgeted in patent leather. A toddler spoke once and was hushed by the full weight of three generations. The sermon had just ended, the final cadence of the pastor's voice still lingering in the rafters. Now the choir was rising.

Ten voices, twelve on good weeks, harmonized into something more than sound. Layered, bone-deep, shaped by lungs that had lived through racism and redevelopment, by women who cooked for each other when husbands vanished and girls who knew the words before they knew what the words meant. The organ held the note and the sopranos rode it, rising above the men, who grounded the harmony with low steadiness, like river stones.

Goldie stood near the third row from the back, beside the old radiator that ticked even in spring. She wore a deep plum dress, faded just enough at the sleeves to suggest long use, not indifference. Her hair was pinned tight. In her hands, she held the bulletin, thumb pressed to the edge. She sang, gentle and sure. A voice meant more for grounding than soloing.

Around her, the congregation drifted into that final melodic moment before release, where the music threatened to lift the room just high enough to forget what waited outside. A woman in the second pew clutched her chest with one hand and raised the other. A boy near the window tapped his shoes to the beat. The choir swayed.

There were no video screens here. No fog machines or guitar feedback. Just the cross at the front, unlit and plain. The pulpit, varnish worn where the pastor's palms had held it week after week. And the stained glass windows casting strips of muted color onto the carpet.

Goldie's eyes were open. She watched. She held it all: the curl of the pastor's voice, the way the choir director signaled with a nod instead of a baton, the cracked spot near the corner pew where someone had once nicked it while moving furniture. She noticed everything. She had trained herself to.

The song came to its close with soft hums and affirmations. The final chord dissolved into silence. The kind of silence that isn't absence, but memory.

"Amen," someone said. Another answered.

Goldie didn't sit. She turned slightly and looked toward the exit, the sun visible through the open door, catching the haze that hung in the air. The congregation moved slow now, stretching toward the end of ritual. Purses closed. Children hushed. The spirit turned to murmurs, hugs, gossip traded gently inside scripture.

She held still a moment. Then she folded the bulletin once more, tucked it into her bag, and stepped into the aisle, already thinking of the names she needed to write down, the stories she needed to collect before they faded or disappeared altogether.

Across the sanctuary, through the dispersal of bodies and laughter and murmured well wishes, Goldie saw her—Yvonne

Hightower, upright and surrounded, as always, by voices leaning in. The pews had emptied into a semi-circle around her. People drew near to her the way they did to warmth in a drafty house. She stood steady in a blue dress and block heels, her purse slung across her shoulder, one hand at her chest, nodding, nodding, listening.

It was always that way with Yvonne. Never checking a watch, never turning away. She'd earned the neighborhood's trust not with platforms or press releases but with a kind of unbreakable presence, forged under pressure no one else saw and few remembered to ask about.

Goldie watched her for a moment. Yvonne hadn't been born into this. She had clawed her way toward it. She had lived in a two-bedroom duplex with a roof that leaked near the stove and a daughter who cried through long nights, and a husband who came home angry five days a week and drunk on the sixth. Goldie had seen the bruises once. Saw how Yvonne covered them with long sleeves and then with a quiet that lasted years. And when he finally left, or when she finally made him leave—it had never been spoken aloud—Yvonne worked doubles at the convalescent center, walking there at five in the morning in shoes that barely held together.

Then came the connector fight—fifteen years back now—when the city had tried to run a road straight through the community's heart, linking East Market Street to the industrial park, calling it mobility, calling it modernization. And Yvonne, still working nights, still raising her girl, still dealing with a car that overheated when you idled too long, stood up at a community meeting and said no.

She hadn't stopped since.

Now she was on council, representing the district they'd tried to redraw her out of twice. They had shortened her precinct list, changed the map, cut it like a salad wedge—but the votes still came in for her, block by block. Not out of loyalty. Out of respect.

Goldie stepped into the aisle and began moving slowly toward the back. She wouldn't interrupt. Yvonne would be there a while. People needed her. Not in the way voters needed officials, but in the way kin needed the strongest back at the table.

As she walked, Goldie caught fragments—"—still no word on the crosstown bus line—" "—told me the permit office lost it—" "—you seen what they're building near the South End?"—and she knew they were not complaints. This was how the neighborhood passed information.

And Yvonne, surrounded now by three more hands reaching out, didn't flinch. She made space for each one. She always had. Goldie moved past, toward the vestibule, her hand tightening briefly on the strap of her bag. She had names to write down. She had a memory to build. And maybe—if it came to that—a reckoning to name.

Outside, the sun heated the pavement, catching on chrome bumpers and windshields and the worn white edges of church paddle fans tucked onto dashboards. The late morning was clean and bright. In the yard beside the sanctuary, children chased each other through dust kicked up by their own feet, their voices high and directionless, like birds startled into flight. A toddler climbed a low concrete step with the skill of a mountain goat, watched by a grandmother pretending not to see.

Goldie lingered near the fence where the crape myrtle leaned in bloom, its pink blossoms drooping with their own abundance. She could smell iron in the dirt, the rich undernote of clay after the early-week rain, the sweet rot of fallen leaves just beginning to darken under the hedge.

Tamara was standing by the curb in a yellow dress that caught the sun like a bell, fanning herself lazily, the way you do when it's not hot enough to complain but too warm not to gesture. Goldie called her name and crossed the lot, flats crunching against loose stone.

"Hey now," Goldie said. "You looking like sunshine itself."

Tamara turned, her smile quick and real. "It's this dress. Foolish to wear something this bright when I'm tired to the bone."

"How's Devin?" Goldie asked, touching her arm, eyes narrowing the way they always did when she asked after someone's child.

Tamara's face flickered, the smile lighting just enough to show the bruise of worry underneath. "Still wheezing. Some days worse than others. The inhaler's working, but the clinic keeps switching brands on us. Say the formulary's changed."

"Again?" Goldie said, not surprised.

Tamara nodded, fanning slower now. "And the bus was late Thursday, so he had to wait in the heat. By the time I got him home he was blue around the lips. I sat him in front of the fan and just prayed over him like I used to do when Mama got those spells."

They stood together in silence for a moment, long enough for the wind to stir the branches, long enough to hear a robin trilling from the telephone wire. The sidewalk was broken where it met the gutter, a crack so familiar it might as well have had a name.

"I keep thinking they'll fix Bingham," Tamara said finally. "Not just for us, but for the kids. That creek's still stinking. Every time Devin plays out back I'm half-watching to make sure he doesn't wander down near it."

"They said they'd start remediation two years ago," Goldie said. "Called it a priority site in the capital budget."

"And yet somehow there's a new parking deck going up across from that boutique hotel on Eugene Street," Tamara said. "Four stories. Got planters on the roof and everything."

"They paid for the concrete before the public hearing was even scheduled."

"And they found the money for that wellness corridor too," Tamara added. "Fast. Like it was already spent before anyone had a chance to weigh in."

Goldie didn't answer. They both knew what it meant when certain neighborhoods got action and others got process. What it meant when bond dollars got repackaged, when grant cycles became excuses. What it meant when your street was marked as transitional but never transformed.

Tamara looked down at her hands. "It's right in our face. Like they're not even pretending no more."

Goldie let her eyes drift to the trees—tall, irregular, their trunks leaning into the years, bark split with the weight of past storms. She reached for Tamara's hand. Held it a moment.

"They keep forgetting who remembers," she said.

And then the children screamed again, laughing this time, chasing each other toward the back of the church, their feet carrying dust into the grass like a kind of joy.

Yvonne emerged from the church doors with her stride intact and her shoulders squared the way they always were after service—renewed by ritual, but not softened by it. She moved through the last of the congregants like a minister of logistics, nodding once, offering brief shoulder touches, promising to follow up. She carried a canvas tote with her council seal stitched onto the side and a fatigue that had learned how to walk upright.

Goldie caught her at the walkway, matching her pace.

"You got a second?"

Yvonne didn't stop walking, but her face turned toward Goldie. "I always got a second for you. That's the problem."

They walked together in the sun, shoes scuffing the sidewalk. Lawns were ragged but proud. The magnolia by the corner hydrant was blooming like it didn't know the apartments behind it had been condemned twice in the last decade.

Goldie waited a beat, then spoke. "You know I don't like to corner folks on Sunday."

"You're not cornering me."

"I just need to ask—what's happening with Bingham Park? Fence is still up. Nothing moved. But they poured concrete over at the health corridor like the city found a secret river of money."

Yvonne stopped beside her car, pulled her keys out, clicked the unlock button. The vehicle chirped once. She opened the door, set her purse on the dash. Didn't get in.

"They're not just building with money," she said. "They're building with momentum. Whole project's like a downhill cart now—nobody dares jump in front of it."

Goldie waited.

Yvonne took a breath, then looked across the street, into the neighborhood. She didn't speak in soundbites. She didn't speak like politicians did on the dais, clipped and media-trained.

"I've been up there ten years now, Goldie. Pushing every week. Cross-town bus routes. Money for mold abatement in rentals. A dedicated housing inspector for the east side. I've written the grant memos, I've chased the consultants, I've sat through development briefings where they don't even show our zip codes on the maps. You think they forgot us, but they didn't. They drew it this way."

Her voice tightened. "Dent and Hoffman run the votes. Not because they're smarter, not because they know the neighborhoods better. Because they control the purse. Dent handles the optics.

Hoffman wrangles the old donors, the arts councils, the foundation boards. And every time we get close—every time I line up something for Bingham Park, or the blight clearance funds, or the rec center—someone calls a work session and pulls it apart."

She crossed her arms, leaning slightly against the door. "Last month I tried to reallocate the leftover climate resiliency bond. It was ours, should've gone toward soil remediation or new sidewalks. Dent motioned for a delay so they could 'consult planning staff.' Two days later, the money's in a line item for pedestrian beautification at the wellness corridor."

Goldie's jaw stayed clenched. She looked toward the park. You couldn't see it clearly from here, not the bad soil or the ash under the mulch. But the fence was visible. Always the fence.

Yvonne followed her gaze. "They want us tired. They want us saying maybe next year. They want us grateful for whatever doesn't collapse."

Goldie's voice was firm now. "So what do we do?"

Yvonne didn't answer immediately. Her eyes moved over the block—over the weathered porches and the kids biking on pavement that hadn't been resurfaced since Clinton was in office. Over the corner lot where the old laundromat once stood, now grown up with stubborn weeds.

"We don't stop," she said. "We don't give them what they want. We get loud, yes, but also smart. They're not scared of speeches anymore. But they're still scared of being seen. Truth makes them flinch. Especially when it's dressed in something they can't dismiss."

Goldie tilted her head. "Meaning?"

"Meaning facts. Meaning memory. Meaning art. Meaning the stories they can't white-paper their way around. If they control the dollars, then we control the narrative. They can bury a park, but they can't bury a story if we tell it right. And we have to tell it so right they can't edit it."

She stepped back from the car, hand on the roof. "That's what we have left. And it's still powerful. We still own that."

Goldie didn't answer. But her eyes had sharpened in the light, fixed now on the idea.

Yvonne opened the door. "I'll back you. Whatever form it takes. I'll put my name on it. Just tell me when you're ready."

Then she got in, started the engine, and pulled away down the block like she'd done a thousand Sundays before. Goldie stood alone for a long moment, the morning still stretching around her. Then she turned and walked back toward the corner.

The lamp in the front room cast a honey-colored circle on the table, soft enough that the rest of the house disappeared into it. The walls breathed with the night heat. Outside, a dog barked once and was answered by another farther off. Goldie sat at the small table she'd kept for forty years and wrote in long, deliberate loops.

He was a child of motion, she wrote. Even when he slept, the toes curled like he was about to run.

She paused. The pen rested against her lip. She could still feel him, in the space beside her knee where he'd used to crouch to draw, elbows planted wide, mouth pursed in concentration. His name was Marquez, though half the teachers called him Marcus and never corrected themselves. He didn't mind. He was polite in that way some Black children learn early—like they're born already translating the world.

She turned the page.

He was six when he got sick. It started with a cough we thought was nothing. No fever or sore throat. Just this dry little bark that made his eyes water.

The memory unspooled in her mind like film. She could still see him under the yellow blanket, curled on the couch watching the nature channel, a bowl of apple slices untouched beside him.

"You okay, baby?" she'd asked.

He nodded, slow. "It just burns when I breathe sometimes."

Sometimes. Not always. The false mercy of early symptoms.

She took him to the clinic, then the urgent care when the clinic said they didn't have the right kind of equipment. Then the hospital, after the breathing got ragged. They ran tests, said the word pneumonitis, said it could've come from allergens, irritants in the air. Said it was rare, but they were seeing more cases on the east side lately. She asked about the soil, the creek near the park, the ash that still blew up from the empty lot after a dry spell.

The doctor had glanced at his chart. "There's no confirmed link," he'd said. "But he's young. He's strong. You're doing all the right things."

They admitted him overnight. Then for three. Then seven.

He was strong, she wrote. And he fought. But his lungs gave out before our insurance did.

She didn't write what happened after. The ventilator. The silence of the room. The nurse who couldn't look her in the eye when they unplugged the beeping.

Instead she wrote, He loved owls. Drew them on every notebook. Said they could see in the dark.

She paused and traced the loop of the "d" in dark, as if lingering might soften it.

He couldn't sleep that month. Said the silence was too loud. He meant the sound in his own chest. I lay beside him with a damp cloth on his head and counted the seconds between each breath. Five seconds. Six. Seven. Then a wheeze.

In the journal, the ink bled a little on the corner where her pen had pressed. She wrote anyway.

His gums turned pale by August. I made him scrambled eggs with cheese and he smiled like it was Sunday. He said, "You're the best chef in town." I said, "Don't make me cry." He said, "But if you cry, I'll cry too."

The words hitched. She pressed the pen harder.

I knew it wasn't asthma by then. He had nosebleeds every other day. His skin turned yellowish. I took him to the ER and they made us wait five hours. When I asked for a second opinion, they sent security.

Then, on the next line, she wrote, They never put his name on any plaque. The playground was promised, then delayed. Then moved.

A moth bumped against the window once, then again. There was a noise, a crack of something outside—maybe a branch or a car door—but she didn't flinch. The house had settled into its age. It made sounds like a body: stretch, release, memory in motion. She set the pen down. The page had dark streaks from where the ink pooled. Her hands looked older in the lamplight. Hands that had cooked and braided hair and packed school lunches and held bodies too cold too early.

The light made her eyes ache, so she leaned back.

He had asked her once—"Nana, how come we live on the poison street?"

She had told him it wasn't poison. That the people who came before had made gardens here. That the park used to have swings that creaked in summer like laughter. That what they called poison was something that hadn't been named right. But later, when he'd gone quiet again, she had looked it up. Chromium. Trivalent, hexavalent, oxidized. She didn't need the science. She'd seen the red sand by the ditch. It didn't blow away. It just sat there, like memory. She turned the page and started a new list.

Names of the taken: Jared. My sister's boy. Tamara's niece. Old Mr. Harris. The baby in the duplex on Spencer Street.

The list would grow. She knew it would. But she would keep writing. Because no one else would. And because she remembered what her mother said after her first baby died of fever: "If they can't count the bodies, they don't have to fix the ground."

So she would count them. Even if it was only her pen scratching in the dark. Even if the paper curled and the ink ran. This was how memory lived. On the page. In the dark. With names spelled clean and deliberate, against the forgetting. She sat back. The journal stayed open, the words cooling on the page. Across the room, on the mantle, was the only photograph she'd ever liked of him—wearing his school shirt crooked, front tooth missing, eyes bright with some private joke. In the morning, the city would still pretend it didn't remember.

The coffee hissed in its maker, a secondhand drip machine with a cracked lid she'd taped shut years ago. The sun had not risen yet—only a slate smear along the bottom edge of the sky—but she was already at the counter, her hands wrapped around the mug, steam lifting into her face. Her bones ached in the places they always did. But this morning the ache felt ceremonial, like her body knew something was about to begin.

She'd had the idea at the edge of sleep, in that drifting place where the mind loosens its grip and memory slips in like a current. She set the mug down and went to the hall closet, where the shelves bowed under years of saved things. She reached for the highest one, brushing past brittle rolls of Christmas paper, a rusted tin of buttons, a basket of broken chargers. The box was there behind it all, its lid soft with dust, corners frayed. She pulled it down slowly, cradling it against her chest as if it might wake something. She carried it to the kitchen table and opened it.

Inside: aged newsletters from New Bethel Baptist, still creased from when they'd been handed out on Sundays, half read and half prayed over. Funeral programs thick with faces. Smiling boys in borrowed suits. Women in church hats the color of robins' eggs and storm clouds. A flyer for a fish fry dated 2007. A photo of the youth choir with her daughter in the back row. Bulletins from candlelight vigils. A birthday card from a girl named Simone who'd died before tenth grade. A laminated bookmark that read: You are the light. Shine anyway.

She sifted slowly, the paper softening as she touched it. The house around her stayed quiet, still curled in its early-morning hush. What was it she was looking for? She didn't know. That didn't matter. This wasn't about evidence.

She laid out the papers in a fan across the table, palms moving like she was anointing something. The photos made her throat catch—children who had smiled once in front of murals now painted over, whose names lived only on church rosters and in the memory of women like her. They hadn't been written down anywhere official. Not the hospital's charts. Not the zoning board's minutes. Not the city's data tables. Just here. In ink on funeral programs. In her box.

A boy named Tyrone who wheezed in every season but spring. Died at seventeen. Complications, they said. She remembered how he'd helped lift folding chairs after church picnics, how his hands shook when he played tambourine. And Little LaShawn, who died in her crib in '96. Her mother said the water smelled like eggs that year. The city said it was nothing. Goldie placed their programs side by side. Noted the years. The addresses. The cause-of-deaths printed like apologies. She felt a tightness in her jaw she hadn't noticed before.

She drank the rest of the coffee cold. This, she thought, was not mourning. This was memory done on purpose. This was the beginning of a map. Not a map like the one Alan had. Not city parcels and red ink. But a different kind—made of names and dates and faces. Made of breath that once lived here. Made of stories that didn't fit in official boxes.

She would write them down. She would ask the mothers and the aunties and the tired men at the VFW who remembered the smell of burning on summer mornings. She would gather what they had: photos in drawers, inhalers kept in memory, clinic bills frayed in wallets. She wouldn't call it a crusade. She wouldn't call it justice. She would call it what it was. The truth. Quiet and wrinkled and ignored too long. But still breathing.

She sat with the papers spread around her like a kind of spell. Outside, the first light finally broke across the roofs. Just light. Clean and fresh and enough.

She whispered to herself, "Let's see what they remember."

The church's folding table was wobbly, the kind that had been hauled out a hundred times before—fish fries, sign-ups, bake sales, coat drives—and always returned to the dark undercroft behind the supply closet. It caught slightly on one leg, so Goldie folded a catalogue beneath it, spine down, pictures to the floor. It steadied. That was enough.

She laid a cloth over it—cream-colored, hemmed with a lace edge frayed from the wash. From her tote she pulled the notebooks: plain-covered, spiral-bound, each one cracked open to the first blank page. A cup of blue pens. Another of black. Beside them, a mason jar with a label she'd lettered in slow cursive: "We Remember Everything." The ink bled slightly on the paper.

The sign, propped by a candlestick, read: "What Do You Remember? Write It Down."

She didn't call it a project. She didn't need the word archive. This was older than that. This was testimony in the ink.

The fellowship hall smelled of starch and perfume, of floor wax and lemon oil from the piano bench. Folding chairs scraped across the tile. Wednesday prayer service had let out gently, people lingering to hug or murmur or pass hands over one another's shoulders. And then they saw her. The table. The question.

The first to stop was Sister Marnelle, who touched the notebooks with both hands before sitting slowly, knees crackling. She wrote for a long time, hand steady despite the tremor she sometimes carried in prayer. When she stood, she nodded once to Goldie, not a smile but something deeper—permission, maybe. Or thanks.

Then came Mr. Tate, the retired bus driver with a limp that ran back to the '60s. He wrote a single line: "I remember when the creek froze solid and the ice looked like colored marbles."

A boy—Jabari, Goldie thought, though she didn't know his people—scrawled in crooked block letters: "I remember Miss Lela's sweet tea and how it made your teeth feel good after."

Someone else wrote: "The first time we saw red dirt, Mama said don't touch it, it don't belong to us."

Another: "The ice cream truck used to skip our street."

Another: "I remember the mural with the birds. They painted over it with a logo. I remember the birds anyway."

Goldie didn't interrupt. She only refilled the pens. Replaced the notebooks when they got full. She kept each page, folding them once and sliding them into a manila envelope marked with that day's date. Just enough to know something was happening. The room filled and emptied. The hum of the soda machine. The clink of chairs being stacked. Someone laughing in the hallway, sharp and sudden.

And still, the table stood. Memory was the thing they made. Line by line. Half-formed and crooked and still sacred. Outside, dusk leaned hard against the stained glass. Somewhere, dinner plates clinked. Goldie closed the last notebook for the night. Ran her hand over the cover like it was a forehead.

This was how it would begin. With the soft scratch of pen on paper, the remembered taste of sweet tea, the ache of a name spoken out loud for the first time in years. A ledger of the lived. She held the jar up to the light. Someone had dropped in a crumpled dollar. Another, a photograph. The picture: a girl in white socks beside a chain-link fence. Smiling. Behind her, the park, blurred and brown.

Goldie whispered, "I see you."

Yvonne arrived as the room was thinning, her heels clicking soft against the tile, coat over her arm, eyes warm but sharp the way women learn to make them after decades of not being believed. She didn't approach the table right away. She stood back, arms crossed beneath her purse strap, taking in the half-used notebooks, the crooked sign.

"Well," she said, voice smooth as ironed linen. "Looks like you decided to take the first step."

Goldie looked up from where she was gathering pens into their mug. Her hands were steadier now than they had been that morning, though her heart still moved strange in her chest, as if she'd held her breath for hours without meaning to. She let out a sound that could've been a laugh.

"They can ignore us," she said. "But they can't stop us."

Yvonne nodded like she'd known that already but still liked to hear it out loud. She walked to the table, brushed a stray crumb from the edge, picked up a pen the way a person might lift a chalice.

"Let me tell it then," she said. "Might as well start before I forget the good parts."

She sat and began to write, her body angled, one foot tucked behind the other. Goldie didn't hover. She just stood beside the jar and watched the light catch in the glass. Someone had left a single red bead at the bottom. Another had torn a grocery list in half and scribbled a name across the back: "Myron Ellison, 1985, nosebleeds every spring."

Around her, the fellowship hall softened into its emptiness. A floorboard creaked once in the back near the pantry, but otherwise it was only the sound of pen to paper, of breath moving through the remembered. Yvonne finished and closed the notebook without flourish. She rose, placed her page gently in Goldie's hands. "You're doing something," she said. "Don't let them tell you it ain't enough."

Then she was gone, coat over her shoulder, perfume faint as magnolia petals after rain. Goldie stood alone at the table. The notebooks were a small mountain now. Ink bleeding through cheap paper, names crowding margins, memories shaped like kitchens, classrooms, street corners, ghosted playgrounds. She gathered them, pressing each one closed as if tucking it into bed. The jar she emptied carefully into her tote, pausing to read nothing, only feel the weight.

She collapsed the table last. It snapped into itself with a reluctant sigh. She held it steady, fingers tight on the metal edge. What was she going to do with all of this? She didn't know. She didn't know who would listen, or how long it would take, or if any office or archive or court would care what Miss Lela's sweet tea meant to a boy with red dust on his shoes.

But she knew this: This was the record before the ruin. This was the ledger before the light. And the pages were hers now. Every single one.

The house was quiet except for the rustle of notebook pages and the occasional snap of the floorboards cooling into night. The lamp on the table cast a circle of light across the stack of papers Goldie had brought home.

She sat at the kitchen table, shoulders rounded, one finger running beneath each line as she read. Some of the memories made her smile—"Brother Leon's cornbread that could fix any argument", "The way the whole neighborhood smelled like hot combs and collards on Easter morning", "The girl who beat three boys in a footrace and still went to prom in heels." Others stung: "The day the creek bubbled red and the dog wouldn't drink from it," "The boy who stopped talking after his cousin passed and never started again," "The little one who called his asthma 'the nighttime ghost.'"

She let those settle. Stacked them. Kept going. One card was heavier than the rest—not physically, but in the way it pressed into her hand. A man's neat handwriting in dark ink, a careful cursive that trailed a little on the y's. The name at the bottom stopped her breath for a beat.

Walter Horn.

She knew of him—everyone did. A widower who came to early service and left just after. Always in a clean button-up, always quiet, the kind of man who had done the work and didn't talk about it. His lawn was edged. His car always washed. The sort of silence you didn't question.

She read.

"1969. I was working sanitation with the city. We were the Black crew—assigned where they didn't want to send anyone else. That year was bad. The kids at Dudley High were marching. The community was thick with police and everyone on edge. They told us to clean up debris from Bingham Park. Not the park itself, but from the creek area. A bunch of broken-up fill and concrete and some things that didn't look right—ash, insulation, what looked like chemical drums with no labels.

"We weren't told much. Just load it up, dump it, don't ask.

"They sent us down to South Elm. To the parcel where the old auto shop burned down. It had tanks in the ground once. They said they'd pulled them, but the dirt still smelled like diesel and fire. We dumped it there. Truckloads. I remember the dust. It wasn't brown—it was like the color of rust on a tool left out in the rain."

Goldie's hand went still. The page fluttered against her thumb like it was alive. She read it again. Then again. The red dust. The same dust that coated the banks behind the hospital corridor. The same dust Ava had tested. The same color that shimmered in Alan's photo. Here it was. In ink. In memory. Before there were records, before there were scans and reports and zoning maps—there was this. A man remembering the dust on his boots.

She reached for her glass of water and found her throat too dry to swallow. Walter Horn. Not a whistleblower. Not a man given to scandal. A man with the kind of quiet that only breaks when the truth has been besmirched. She closed the notebook and pressed her hand flat on the cover, as if to still it. In her chest, a tension gathered, something like reverence.

This, she thought, is what they don't expect. That memory can root deeper than law. That the body remembers where the harm was done. That the truth, once spoken aloud, can't be resealed. She sat there a long time. The night had thickened, stars high and indifferent. But inside, she was awake. Held open. Changed.

She whispered his name once, softly, into the room. "Walter Horn." There were conversations still to have. Voices still to find. And now, she knew, a direction. Red dust. South Elm. A burned-out shop. A name. A start.

The afternoon had leaned toward evening, a slow amber hour where everything—the porch rails, the telephone wires, the lids of trash bins—caught the light like old brass. Goldie moved through the neighborhood like she remembered more than just directions. Her sandals slapped against the pavement. Her left hand curled around a piece of paper, though she hadn't looked at it since lunch. Walter's words were already inscribed.

She passed the vacant lot where Miss Delores used to hold Saturday yard sales, table legs poking up like crooked teeth. The chain-link fence was bent now, zip-tied in places, sprouting tufts of vine. A child's flip-flop lay belly-up near the curb. On the other side of the street, someone had strung a hammock between two trees that didn't look strong enough to hold it, but there it was, sagging with faith. Goldie nodded at it, barely.

Each block summoned its own ghosts. The brick duplex where Little Darian coughed blood into a pillow for three nights before anyone believed it. The stoop where Tamara had scraped her knee the week the creek turned gray. The manhole cover with initials scrawled in it, G.H. & B.H.—her and her brother Bernard, back when they were nine and pretending they owned the world. It wasn't the neglect that hurt most. It was how much of it she still loved.

She reached the edge of Bingham Park and paused. The gate was chained, the lock sun-bleached to a dull green. A sign still read

Closed for Improvements – 2004, though nothing had changed in a dozen years but the rust pattern. The grass beyond had gone wild, swallowing the last of the swing sets, which jutted like broken ribs from the earth. The air around the fence had a smell she couldn't name anymore. Not smoke, not iron, not mildew. Something thinner, older. Absence, maybe. She kept walking.

Bingham Street sloped gently upward, the kind of street that always made strollers groan and mailmen curse. Azaleas flickered pink in two yards; a blue tarp sagged over one roof, its corners held by bricks. A boy rode a bike past her fast, one shoe untied, and she said, "Watch yourself," like it was a spell. He pedaled onward.

Walter's house came into view just as the sun dipped below the tree tops. It was modest, narrow-porched, with white siding the color of old teeth. The trim was freshly painted, though, and the flower beds were neat and tender. She saw him before he saw her—a tall man stooped slightly at the shoulders, trimming back zinnias with a pair of shears. His hands moved with a slowness that spoke of attention.

Goldie paused at the edge of the sidewalk, watching him for a moment. There was something in the line of his back that made her throat pull tight. A man doing something gentle in a place that had known too little gentleness.

She called out, "Walter Horn."

He looked up, shears paused mid-air. His face was unreadable for a moment, then it grew into something close to a smile. He straightened, wiped his hand on his pants, nodded once.

"Miss Goldie."

She stepped forward, the paper in her hand. Her voice felt round in her mouth, careful.

"You got a moment?" she asked. "I wanted to ask you about the dust."

12

Alan parallel parked on East Lewis just past the boarded wine bar that used to be a co-op art gallery, before the grant dried up and the city sold the building to a developer with a recreation brand. The drizzle made everything gleam falsely. Pavement like wet slate, electric scooter wheels ticking past. Shopfront windows fogged with breathless slogans: Local First. Nourish the Now. Curated Healing. A man in joggers passed him holding a mason jar of cold brew as if it were sacred. Alan pulled up his collar and locked the car.

It was just after morning rush hour. The streets were quiet in that liminal way—delivery vans double-parked, retail workers on smoke break under awnings, the sense that something was possible. Ahead, Dame's glowed soft through the mist, its chicken and waffles logo steady in the door glass. He walked toward it out of craving—hope being one of the few things left that hadn't been rebranded.

The call from Goldie had come two nights ago. He'd been grading student essays that barely touched their topics—pages filled with expository urgency and no real heat—when his phone lit up. He'd answered immediately. You didn't let a call from Goldie go to voicemail.

She hadn't started with pleasantries. Just: "I talked to Walter Horn."

Alan paused. "The city worker?"

She let out something between a breath and a scoff. "Sanitation. Back in the sixties. He spoke to me. About Bingham Park. About the dust. He said they dumped fill dirt once at the South Elm site. Called it red like a blood field when it rained."

Alan sat forward on his couch, the laptop sliding slightly off his knees. "Did he say when?"

"Sixty nine. After the riots. Said the city wanted fill dirt moved quick and quiet. No paperwork. Just load and dump."

"Jesus," Alan said. Then added, "He'd know."

"He said it stuck in his throat. The dust. Like it wanted to stay."

Alan didn't say anything to that. The sentence hung there.

Goldie continued, voice even. "He remembers the smell. Not chemical or fire. Just... wrong. Said the dump site had been an old auto shop before it burned down. Tanks were gone, but he didn't trust the ground. Nobody did. He'll show you where it is."

Alan stood then, pacing without realizing it, the carpet soft beneath his heels. "That parcel—524-B—Midland Legacy Trust picked it up in the nineties. It's one of the ones they funneled back into the wellness corridor fund."

"I thought you'd say that," she said. "So I figured it's your turn to look again."

"Goldie—"

"No," she said gently. "You go. See the dirt yourself. Before they roll sod over it again and call it development."

And that was the end of the call. She hung up before he could thank her.

Now, outside Dame's Chicken and Waffles, Alan paused. The sidewalk was slick, and somewhere a pressure washer roared against a brick wall. He looked down the block toward the edge of the construction zone, where a plywood barrier bore a mural of smiling cartoon doctors and a tagline: South End Wellness Corridor: Where Greensboro Heals Together.

The old anger rose, less like fire, more like smelt. What did healing mean, in a city that never cleaned what it poisoned?

He stepped into the restaurant, nodding at the host who didn't look up. Inside, the tables were half full. Contractors in neon vests. A pair of tech guys in softshell jackets whispering over tablets. A mother feeding a toddler a piece of fried dough while scrolling through Zillow listings on her cracked iPhone.

He took a seat by the window. Ordered black coffee. Pulled out his notebook.

Red dust. Blood field. No record. He flipped to the map Goldie had sent him a photo of. Hand-drawn. A triangle sketched with the word DUMP? scrawled beside it.

The waitress brought his coffee. He thanked her, sipped. He stared out the window at the mural again, its pastel promise vibrant through mist. Alan sat with the coffee cooling beside his hand, the notebook open but untouched. The page stared back, stubbornly blank, as if demanding more than facts. Across the windowpane, drops gathered and slid in vertical lines, blurring the mural into soft propaganda. He tapped his pen once, then again. The detail wouldn't let go.

The riots.

Walter hadn't named them that way—he'd just said "after Dudley," the way older men did when history didn't need explanation because it still lived behind their eyes. But Alan knew what it meant. The 1969 uprising at Dudley High School, sparked when a Black student was denied his rightful place as student council president and the administration tried to shut him down. What followed was weeks of protest, street occupation, retaliation. The arrival of the National Guard. Tear gas on school steps. Helicopters over houses. He remembered reading about it in The Fire in the Classroom, Claude Barnes's meticulous book—half oral history, half indictment. Alan had annotated every margin in graduate school, back when he still believed that knowing something thoroughly might help stop it from happening again.

Nelson Johnson had come up through those riots—organizing sit-ins, mobilizing students, defying the city's incremental poison. A decade later he would survive the Greensboro Massacre, when Klan and Nazi Party members shot five anti-racist organizers dead in broad daylight while police looked the other way. Alan had once taught a seminar that paired Johnson's memoir with a GIS mapping of urban renewal zones—his small act of resistance. The students were shocked, which told Alan more about their public education than about the history itself.

But what caught him now, what tightened in his chest as he stared out at the mist-washed sidewalk, was the timeline. 1969: a city on edge, cameras on every corner, energy turned toward protest and panic and spin. If there was ever a perfect time to sneak a quiet crime through the backdoor of chaos—to haul red dust from one poisoned parcel to another, to lose the evidence in the fog of unrest—it would have been then. When everyone was watching Dudley, who was watching the ground?

He pictured the trucks—Walter and his crew, Black men in coveralls, driving through neighborhoods faint with tear gas residue. No one stopping them. Just dump it there, behind the burned-out auto shop. No one's looking. Everyone's afraid.

Alan wrote in the margin: Disaster as diversion. Riot as cover. Red dust beneath protest smoke.

That was Greensboro. Not just a city with a dark past—but a city that had always known how to use its darkness. One hand dangling progress, the other slipping malfeasance beneath the surface.

Historical amnesia wasn't a glitch here—it was municipal practice. Turn the tragedy into a footnote, sell the footnote to a private trust, then pave it with federal grant money and call it healing. He sat back, letting the pen fall against the table.

This wasn't just about Bingham Park. It was about how cities metabolize shame—how they repackage harm as opportunity, how they spin poison into branding. This was the narrative David Moss had mastered. Reframing. Don't say "toxic." Say "pre-regulatory site." Don't say "dumped." Say "transferred." Don't say "massacre." Say "shootout."

Alan looked around the restaurant. At the exposed brick, the Edison bulbs, the reclaimed wood bar. He wondered how many people here had ever read about Claude Barnes. Or knew where the word massacre applied within city limits. He wondered if knowing it mattered, or if the city had finally succeeded in rendering its own history weightless—so thoroughly repaved that the memory faded.

He closed the notebook and reached for his coffee. Lukewarm. Bitter. There was something here. Something more than contamination. A pattern. A timing. A choice. He would go to the parcel on South Elm. He would walk it. He would find the blood field. Because in this city, truth never rose on its own. It had to be dug for, hauled out, named. Before they renamed it again.

Alan saw him from half a block away, emerging through the mist. Walter Horn moved easy but without apology. His steps were deliberate, the way certain men carried age as if it were a medal they never needed to shine. He wore navy slacks pressed at the seams, black shoes polished to a humble glow, and a clean zippered windbreaker—NC A&T in stitched gold letters over his heart.

His hair, once coal-black by all accounts, had gone silvery at the edges and pewter down the middle, cropped close but not shaved, still full. He didn't use a cane, though the sidewalk made him sway slightly, like someone who'd spent too many years on uneven ground. Which, Alan supposed, he had.

Alan rose instinctively, tucking the notebook under his arm. Walter met his eye from twenty paces and nodded once—a gesture that carried nothing of politeness and everything of mutual understanding. Alan waited until the man was close enough that the drizzle no longer muffled his voice.

"Mr. Horn," he said. "Thank you for coming."

Walter's eyes were sharp beneath the brim of his cap, a lined face that gave away very little. He glanced at the window of the restaurant, then back at Alan.

"You the one Goldie said wanted to ask questions," he said. His voice was smooth, but carried the slight gravel of long days spoken through dust masks and over diesel engines.

Alan nodded. "Yes, sir."

Walter looked him over—not hostile but cautious, the way men do when they're trying to decide whether they're being used or heard.

"You university?"

"I teach there. Urban policy. But I'm here because I believe you."

Walter gave a sound that wasn't quite a laugh. "Belief's cheap, son. The city believed in me when I was hauling their trash. Believed I'd shut up too."

Alan opened the door and gestured. "Can I buy you coffee?"

Walter looked past him into the restaurant—contractors, screens, waffles.

"Too noisy," he said. "I like to think when I talk."

Alan motioned down the block. Walter nodded and fell into step beside him, his shoulders square under the A&T jacket. Alan watched him out of the corner of his eye. The way his presence rewrote the street, as if the sidewalk had once known boots like his and stood a little straighter to meet them. There was a royalty to it, yes, but not the kind born of pedigree. The kind earned in rain and filth, on shifts no one else volunteered for.

As they walked, Alan felt the weight of what was coming settle in his chest. The clarity that certain truths weren't found in files or labs. They walked inside people, waiting to be asked.

They crossed toward Martin Luther King Jr. Boulevard at a careful pace, Walter favoring one knee without complaint, Alan shortening his stride to match. The mist had started to thin, the droplets easing from steady to reluctant, the kind of morning light that came with promise. As if the sky had finally agreed to show itself.

On their right, the railroad tracks carved a rusted boundary through the city. Beyond them, the Depot's curved roof caught the wet sun like polished bone. Alan looked north across the rails, toward the clean silhouette of downtown—five towers at most, none of them tall enough to impress but each trying their hardest. The courthouse. The investment firm. The bank building rebranded as Proximity Tower with a mural of clasped hands on its parking deck. A city always rehearsing a bigger future, while its past crumbled just out of frame.

Walter walked with his eyes forward, his face still, but Alan could feel the tightness in the man's body, a pulling inward. Skittish was the wrong word. Wary. Like someone who'd spoken once and been made to regret it.

"I know it's a lot," Alan said finally, softly. "Goldie told me not to push."

Walter didn't look over. "That woman's been pushing since they put the fence up around that park."

Alan smiled. "She has. I've been helping her—writing grants, filing public records requests, some soil testing through my university lab."

Walter nodded, just once. His eyes flicked across the track as a freight train sat still in the distance.

"She told me what you said about South Elm," Alan continued. "About the fill dirt after the riots. I think it matters."

Walter stopped. Not abrupt, just enough for Alan to know the moment had deepened. He turned, the lines in his face cutting sharper in the angled light.

"You the one wrote that piece in the paper?" he asked.

Alan blinked. "Which one?"

"The one about neighborhood redevelopment and buried truth. The part about chromium and asthma kids. I read it twice. Took my time."

Alan's throat caught a little—more than he'd expected.

"That was me," he said. "I didn't name names, but I was thinking of this place. This neighborhood. Goldie, too."

Walter stared at him for a long second, then looked back north, toward the skyline. The buildings shimmered behind the mist. He tilted his chin toward them.

"They never look back, you know," he said. "Those folks up there. They build it forward. That's the trick. Forget what's underfoot."

He began walking again, slower now. His voice, when it came again, had lost its hardness.

"I remember the way that dirt looked when we dropped it. South Elm by the burned auto shop. Looked like rust but felt wrong. Heavy. Like it didn't want to be touched."

Alan said nothing. Let the man move through his own rhythm.

"They didn't tell us what it was. Just to haul and dump. We thought maybe ash from the old incinerator, near the park, before they called it that. Back when it was just fenced ground no one mowed."

Walter's hand went to his jacket zipper, then fell.

"Had a cousin lived near there. Died of kidney failure in '84. Nobody thought to ask why. Just said it ran in the family."

The sun broke through fully now, casting long bars of light across the tracks, as if drawing new lines between where they stood and where the downtown core began.

Alan spoke carefully.

"I think what you remember can help us find the chain. The paper trail. Goldie's been building something. A map of memory. If we can match it to the city's records—"

Walter held up one hand.

"I'm not trying to testify," he said. "I'm not looking to end up in no hearing room while they smile and nod and do what they already planned."

"I get it," Alan said quickly. "I do. But sometimes memory is the only record we have."

Walter looked at him again. This time, something passed between them—recognition, perhaps, or at least the beginning of it.

"Then you better write it down right," he said. "Because this city's got a long history of forgetting loud and remembering quiet."

They reached the edge of South Elm where the road dipped slightly and the sidewalk cracked. The block smelled of distant frying oil. Walter stopped.

At the corner of South Elm and MLK stood the bust—golden, head high, crown of hair tight to the skull, the nose slightly chipped at the bridge. Dr. Martin Luther King Jr. looking north, across the tracks, toward the refurbished towers and municipal buildings that now anchored the city's official self-image. The bust had been donated in the late eighties, after enough time had passed for the city to rename a boulevard without being forced to change its policies. Alan paused. Walter had already stopped. The older man stood before the bust with both hands in his jacket pockets, but after a moment, he pulled one out and touched the edge of the bust's base—two fingers, light as breath.

"My father took me to see him here," Walter said, without looking away. "Nineteen fifty-eight. Day stop on the way back to Atlanta. Spoke to a group of clergy in the basement of Mount Zion."

Alan stayed quiet, letting the moment stretch.

"They said he wasn't going to draw a crowd," Walter added. "Said Greensboro didn't need that kind of heat. So they kept it quiet. But word got out. My father took off work. Put me in a clean shirt. Said, 'You're gonna remember the sound of that voice.'"

He glanced at Alan then, eyes sharp under the bill of his cap.

"I did. I still do. Moved through you like something unforgettable."

Alan nodded, hands in his coat. He looked north, where the street rose toward the train depot and the commercial gloss of downtown—boutique hotels with abstract names, law firms that advertised restorative justice on their Instagram bios, a microbrewery where the mercantile used to be. The skyline looked best in drizzle, when you couldn't see the seams.

"I heard he was supposed to come back in sixty-eight," Alan said.

Walter gave a half-laugh, flat and knowing. "He was. April fourth. We thought we'd see him at Bennett. Girl I was sweet on was a student there. I told her, 'You better wear your best.' Then we turned on the radio and found out he'd stayed in Memphis. Sanitation strike. Said he'd be here next week."

Alan swallowed. The silence between them settled deep. Walter looked south.

Down the slope, South Elm Street fell away in a slow descent, lined with brick storefronts that had once pulsed with trade—furniture shops, record stores, a pharmacy with a soda counter, shoe repair. Now most of them held tax prep storefronts or vape lounges or vacant windows wallpapered with vinyl posters of what they could be if only enough hope could be crowdsourced. The road dipped toward Gate City Boulevard and then, beyond it, the wellness corridor —parcel 524-B—where the dirt waited under a matrix of promises.

Walter's eyes lingered on the curve.

"They put that bust here so it could face north," he said. "Toward the future. Toward what they call opportunity."

He shook his head. "But the truth's down that hill. Always has been."

Alan followed his gaze. Past the bust, past the cracks in the sidewalk and the red brick veneers, down into the lower part of the city that had been zone-coded into neglect. He could feel the day shift. Less mist now. A little warmth coming up. Walter touched the bronze once more, then dropped his hand.

"This way," he said.

The sidewalk dipped into a narrowing thread of South Elm, the buildings crowding close on either side—facades pocked with forgotten signage, iron-grated windows that hadn't held merchandise in decades, boarded-up bars that had once claimed to serve "locals and legends alike." Walter walked with a patient cadence, as if his feet knew the rhythm of this street, and Alan kept pace, half a step behind, notebook tucked beneath one arm.

"You see this curve?" Walter said, gesturing with his chin as they approached the intersection at Arlington. "Used to be a spur line.

Rail ran right through here. Not just freight—trash, too. Sanitation used it up through the sixties. Maybe longer."

Alan scanned the blocks around them. A painted sign still faint on a brick wall read Reliable Tire & Auto—Since 1949. The lot it pointed to was overgrown, half-fenced, a place that had been rezoned so many times it was now classified as "mixed-use aspirational." He made a note of that in his head—aspirational zoning, a term David had used once with a smile at a council work session, as if reality were just a grant away from bending.

Walter kept going.

"That line connected to the east side of town. Curved across Elm below the depot, then straight along Market and ran just past where Bingham Park is now."

Alan felt his breath slow. "Wait. The rail ran directly from here to the park?"

Walter nodded, not breaking stride. "Back then, it wasn't a park. Wasn't much of anything. Just a dump site with a bad fence and a burn barrel every few yards."

Alan imagined it: the slow crawl of freight cars over gravel, the hiss of brakes, the stink of wet ash and fuel-soaked earth. The city's waste, redirected from one Black neighborhood to another.

"I thought the incinerator was decommissioned by the sixties," Alan said.

"Not when I was a kid in the fifties," Walter said. "We'd smell it by mid-morning. Burned everything—household trash, military junk, industrial waste. You ever smell plastic insulation on fire?"

Alan nodded. He could imagine it. Acrid, sick-sweet, the kind of stink that makes a body carry it even after it's gone.

"They'd dump the residue in covered bins," Walter continued. "Load it up on flatbed cars. Some of it stayed put—got piled and buried. Some of it got moved."

Alan stopped.

"You're saying they used this line to move contaminated fill?"

Walter turned, his face unreadable. "I'm saying it was convenient. And when something's convenient, it usually gets used. Nobody asked questions back then. Not if it helped keep downtown pretty for the tournament crowds."

Alan exhaled through his nose. The basketball tournaments—two or three times a year, the city dressed up, swept its corners, borrowed civility from somewhere else and tried it on for a week. His father used to call it "the good behavior season." He never said for whom.

They resumed walking. The street began to slope again, down toward the corridor's anchor point, where chain-link and renderings now promised "a wellness-focused innovation hub" with fiber-optic infrastructure and repurposed warehouse space for minority-owned startups. Alan had read the pitch deck. He'd even taught a student who interned on the community engagement team. The slides were beautiful.

Walter's voice broke through his thoughts again, lower now.

"By the time I started workin' city sanitation, the line was mostly silent. But the rails were still there. I'd walk past 'em every morning. Always wondered what was underneath."

Alan thought of Goldie, her notebooks, the jar on the table labeled We Remember Everything. The past was never gone. It just got boarded up. Labeled under evaluation. Sold to a trust with no listed address.

"Walter," he said, "you've just drawn the map."

Walter didn't answer. Just looked ahead to where the parcel began to come into view, wrapped in a vinyl banner that read Tomorrow's Health Starts Here in block letters above a child on a scooter.

Alan stared at the sign. Then at the ground. He knew what he was standing on. He just didn't yet know how deep it went.

They waited at the light on Gate City Boulevard as cars passed in jolts of morning traffic, each one a metal bubble of distraction—someone tapping a screen, someone eating from a bag, someone nodding along to a podcast about "greening cities through equity-driven capital." The mist was fully gone now, the sky cracking open with a flat, hard light that made nothing look better, only clearer. Across the intersection, the fencing wrapped the corridor site like a promise under arrest.

They crossed on the walk signal, Walter slow but purposeful, his jacket catching the breeze. Alan stayed quiet, the kind of quiet that came from having finally arrived somewhere you suspected might not exist.

The development site was larger than Alan had imagined—four lots total. Two to the north of Arlington Street, where the construction had already begun: poured concrete walls, rebar spines rising from the soil, banners flapping on zip ties with buzzwords too clean to mean much—Anchoring Wellness, Empowering Community, Building Forward. And two lots to the south, where the fence still held and the ground looked like it was waiting to be disguised.

Walter didn't stop at the active site. He veered slightly, across the quiet of Arlington, and walked them to the southern lot—grassless, raked flat, an engineered stillness. A metal sign on the fence displayed a colorful rendering of a future playscape: slides, turf, a splash pad. Children drawn in bright, imprecise skin tones. Behind it, the land was covered in what Alan recognized as standard "cap and cover" materials: geotextile lining, soil packed too neat to be natural, a layer of crushed aggregate raked over with fake irregularity. Walter stopped at the fence and placed one hand on it, the chain link catching the sunlight and his fingers in the same cold geometry.

"Right there," he said.

Alan moved beside him.

"They brought the trucks down in '69. Summer. Maybe late spring. Hard to remember exactly. Everything was upside down that year."

Alan didn't ask. Just listened.

"There were marches. Dudley High, all the trouble. People were watching the schools, the protests, the police. City said this site needed fill. Said it used to be a shop and the tanks were gone and they wanted to level it before it grew over. Said the incinerator site had what they needed."

Walter's voice had no bitterness. Just memory, stated plain.

"They sent us out to the incinerator. Place already smelled like it was ancient. They loaded the trucks full—concrete chunks, insulation, ash, even stuff I didn't recognize. Red dust everywhere. Got into the seat cushions, into your shoes. Stuck in your nose like it didn't want to leave."

Alan's stomach turned gently. "You knew it was bad."

Walter shrugged. "Didn't know what it was. Just knew it wasn't right. But we were told: fill dirt. City-approved. Make it level. Make it safe. And we were twenty years old and trying to keep jobs."

He took his hand off the fence.

"I only worked that job a few days. Three, maybe four. Then I went back to route detail. But I remember it. Clear as anything."

Alan looked over the site, trying to unsee the neatness, to layer it back: the raw soil, the dump trucks, the broken barrels. To see what Walter had seen.

"I was lucky," Walter said. "I never got sick. Least not yet."

Alan turned to him.

"One of the guys—Horace Crump—he ran the loader. Strong as two men, always cracking jokes. He started coughing about six years later. Never stopped. Doctors said lungs, kidneys, couldn't say why. Gone before forty. Wife said he shrank."

The fence rattled slightly in the wind.

"I think about him when I pass this place," Walter said. "All that dirt. All that silence."

Alan looked at the ground and then at the sign promising the play structure. His breath came short.

"They're going to build a playground," he said. It wasn't a question.

Walter nodded. "They call it wellness."

Alan closed the door to his office with deliberate softness, the kind that came from the need to maintain stillness in the wake of something enormous. The campus was quiet, mid-afternoon calm settling over the aging brick halls and ambition-choked green spaces. His own department—a hybrid of urban studies, public policy, and whatever passed these days for civic engagement—was tucked into the third floor of a building that reeked of institutional clean.

He hung his jacket on the hook behind the door. His hands moved automatically: laptop bag on the chair, keys in the drawer, the usual ritual. His body was trying to re-enter normalcy, the muscle memory of professionalism. But his mind was still outside, standing at that chain-link fence with Walter, staring at a capped-over lie branded as health infrastructure.

He sat at the desk and reached for the notebook, intending to transcribe the details while they were still sharp—Walter's voice, the timeline, the red dust, the rail line—but before he could open it, he saw the folder. Manila, crisp, new. Not one of his own. Labeled in Ava's small, tidy script: Parcel 524-B – Crossref / Bingham.

He paused.

Opened it.

Inside, a single page printed from a dot matrix-era state report, the header barely legible. Below that, a note in Ava's handwriting:

"Alan—

Buried in the city's cross-reference index for the baseball stadium site evaluations (1997–99). Parcel 524-B flagged for soils exhibiting residual toxicity consistent with chromium and VOC waste profiles. No follow-up records logged.

—A"

He read the line again. Then a third time. There was a sudden stillness in his mind. Like watching a stain bloom in water. The city knew.

In the late nineties—back when the South End was being floated for a minor league stadium, part of a flurry of speculative boosterism that always came wrapped in the language of civic pride—they had tested the soil. Found contamination consistent with what they now claimed was exclusive to Bingham Park. And instead of remediation, instead of warning, they shelved it. Filed it under a code. Changed their minds about the stadium. Let the parcel sit quiet for two decades. Until someone thought to sell it as "wellness."

Alan stood, then sat again.

Had they... moved the dirt from Bingham Park to 524-B? It sounded paranoid. Conspiratorial. But Walter's story didn't contradict it. It confirmed it. Truckloads. A need for fill. An order from the city. And now—cap and cover. Playground renderings.

He rubbed his eyes. But worse—what if the city hadn't just moved the dirt? What if they'd redirected the money, too? He thought of Goldie's rejected grants. Of the delayed testing at Bingham Park. All while Parcel 524-B—deemed dormant, given funding—was being quietly dressed up under another name.

He looked down at Ava's note again.

Soils exhibiting residual toxicity consistent with chromium and VOC waste profiles.

Alan felt a throb begin at his temple. Volatile organic compounds. He turned to his laptop. Opened the shared project folder. Pulled up the most recent budget line item from the city's environmental services ledger.

Parcel 524-B was listed nowhere.

But "Wellness Corridor Stabilization" had received $1.2 million in supplemental funding the same year Bingham's remediation request was again denied. His fingers hovered over the keys. Then stopped. Because suddenly, it wasn't just about dirt. It wasn't even about the city's failure anymore. It was about something else.

The sun had begun its descent over the campus green, glazing the buildings in that late-afternoon gold that made everything look softer than it was. Alan walked from his office toward the Weatherspoon Gallery, hands in his coat pockets, trying to let the light work on his thoughts. He passed a tour group of prospective students and their parents—father in wraparound shades, mother with a reusable water bottle and a rehearsed enthusiasm. The guide, a theater major with a clipped voice, pointed to the student union and said the word "innovation" three times in one breath. No one flinched.

Alan let himself drift, the way people do when they want to feel less responsible for their surroundings. He cut across a lawn that used to be a parking lot and now featured a sculpture of three welded circles titled Gravitational Nest #7, funded by a grant from a corporation that also made fracking equipment. The absurdity didn't bother him anymore. That was the trick of working in a university. Eventually the contradictions stopped being friction and became landscape.

The folder from Ava was in his bag. He hadn't reread it since lunch. The words were already installed—residual toxicity, VOC waste profiles, no follow-up records. Walter's voice echoed beneath it, irrevocable. But as he neared the museum steps, the pressure dulled. Not gone. Just... suspended. Some part of his mind placing the horror in a holding pattern to make room for art, for small talk, for wine in plastic cups and the sound of an academic saying the phrase "post-spatial gesture" with a straight face.

Inside, the air was climate-controlled and hushed, the kind of silence that made your steps louder. The exhibit's first room held a series of blown-up cyanotypes of aged mill machinery, filtered through sheets of frosted mylar. A man in a tight blazer stood before one and said "palimpsest" as if summoning a spell.

Alan turned toward the next gallery, but his thoughts stayed lodged somewhere between the red dust and the rendering of the future playground. He let the art wash over him—composed chaos, curated ruin. The state had found a way to aestheticize decay and sell it as insight. Goldie had found a way to name it and keep it from being forgotten. He wasn't sure why both saddled him with shame.

He reached for the wine. He smiled at someone's joke. He walked into the next room and stood before an installation titled Memory as Infrastructure.

The exhibit had its moments. An installation of archived protest fliers suspended from fishing line, rotating slowly under a ceiling fan as if revolution needed ventilation; a looping video of public housing demolition slowed to such a degree that each puff of concrete bloom resembled a time-lapse of grief. He stopped to read a wall label that quoted a theory of civic disappearance and considered, for a second, the possibility that someone had done their homework.

But then he turned and saw the mayor.

She stood by the room's north wall near a grid of color-coded zoning maps printed on silk. Mayor Bramlett, in her off-the-rack polish—beige pantsuit, matching pearls, every gesture a campaign ad rehearsal. She was talking to Councilwoman Hoffman, who smiled the way only career public servants smile when they think the event photographer might be near. Alan felt his stomach lurch with anger that had metabolized into something more durable than fury.

They were probably talking about "impact." About "cultural partnerships." Maybe about how wonderful it was that the university continued to engage with "challenging histories" while keeping the noise buffered within the polite acoustics of gallery space. Alan didn't need to hear it to know. The language had become too familiar. Cities learned how to sound accountable while investing in their own immunity. He turned away, back toward the exhibit, then froze.

Paula Moss.

It was almost cinematic, the way she entered the frame with that particular gravity certain people develop when enough doors have been opened for them on arrival. She was speaking to a junior dean from advancement, nodding warmly, teeth bared in a way that suggested agreement, not joy. Her voice didn't carry, but her presence did.

Alan hadn't seen her in five years. Maybe longer. But here she was, in all her calibrated glory, stepping through an art exhibit about memory and displacement while the truth beneath her public statements was toxic.

He felt the surge—anger, yes, but also disbelief, the absurdity of it. Paula Moss, the self-appointed conscience of municipal renewal, surrounded by abstractions of the violence her kind had paved over. She had perfected the art of civic performance. Could say "racial equity" with a straight face while boosting a wellness corridor that reallocated brownfield funds to a sanitized playground on toxic dirt. She was a master of misdirection, always one sentence ahead of accountability, her language engineered for the grant cycle and the editorial board.

Alan watched her move. She shook a hand, accepted a card, posed for a photo with someone from the local arts council. Her body language was flawless—open palms, slight lean forward, eyes lit just enough to imply listening. She looked like she belonged here because she did. This was her terrain: clean walls, funded expressions, polite applause.

And all Alan could think about was Goldie's table in the church basement. Spiral notebooks with bent spines. Handwritten stories slipped into a mason jar. Names of the dead scribbled in the margins of funeral programs. No grants. No press. No launch gala.

He looked again at the installation near the center of the room—steel barrels arranged in a circle, filled with soil and sound. From inside, a speaker played looped audio fragments: voices recalling mill creeks that ran the wrong color, a child's inhaler clicks, a grandmother naming the cancer cluster street by street. It was beautiful. It was moving. And none of it, he thought, would change a damn thing if the mayor could smile at it and call it progress.

Paula laughed lightly at something. Tilted her head in that way she had when she wanted to seem charmed. Alan looked at her, his hand unconsciously closing around Ava's folder in his bag.

Their eyes met across the gallery, sudden and unmistakable, like the shock of your name whispered in a room where you thought yourself invisible. Paula's soft eyes landed on him, and then, just as quickly, she smiled.

It wasn't theatrical, wasn't strategic. It was that devastating smile she used to give him when they'd been in the same room at late meetings or receptions or public hearings, when she wanted him to know she'd seen him and, more than that, remembered. It was the smile she wore when she wasn't selling anything.

Alan felt it hit—first in the chest, then the throat. That brief, unwelcome warmth. Not longing. Something gentler, more dangerous. It disarmed him, instantly, the pressure in his spine slackening, the intellectual fury dissolving at the edges like salt in warm water. For one second, the whole museum, with its pristine walls and artistic grief, disappeared behind the brightness of her expression.

She hadn't changed. The eyes still searching, alert, never quite at rest. The smile that told the truth by pretending not to. That smile had once leveled him across a panel on environmental justice funding four minutes before she'd stood to oppose the very thing he was fighting for. He'd fallen anyway, into something like admiration. Or worse, the suspicion that she, too, had once believed in the same things and had only learned better. He looked down for a moment, then back up, and she was still watching him, the corner of her mouth lifted, eyes narrowed just slightly in the old familiar way that asked: Will you come over, or will you let me go?

Alan felt pulled across the distance. The outrage, the folder in his bag, the contaminated soil and Goldie's righteous fury, the memory of Walter's hand on the fence—it all quieted, momentarily displaced by the gravity of her. Because for all the harm she might've signed off on, for all the cold calculations dressed in equity language, Paula Moss still moved like she remembered when they used to dream of saving things. And some part of him, traitorous and aching, still wanted to believe that wasn't entirely gone.

She crossed the room without haste, as if walking toward him were the most natural thing in the world, though he could tell by the slight stiffness in her posture that his presence had caught her off guard. They met in the narrow space between two installations, beside a column wrapped in archival photographs of vanished homes. Her perfume was faint—something floral, too elegant for the season—and he inhaled it like memory.

"Alan," she said, her voice smooth, a little breathless with effort. "Didn't expect to see you here."

"I didn't expect to be here," he said, and his voice came out too fast. He tried to smile.

Her eyes scanned his face, the way she used to when she was deciding whether to push him or let him be. "Still out chasing ghosts?"

His face flushed, an adolescent betrayal of composure. His ears warmed, his jaw tightened in that helpless way embarrassment moves through the body when you still care how someone sees you.

He cleared his throat. "Actually," he said, trying for evenness, "I've been working with Goldie Hayes. On Bingham Park."

Something lifted in her then. The flint in her expression softened. Her posture loosened, the corners of her mouth relaxing from their poised elevation. She looked past him for a beat, as if seeing something else—an older woman at a folding table, perhaps, or a memory she wasn't expecting.

"I heard she was collecting stories," Paula said. Her voice had grown gentler. "I didn't know you were involved."

He shrugged, though there was nothing casual about it. "I'm helping where I can. Some of the things people remember, what's been buried."

She nodded, not dismissive but careful. Measured. The politician in her still alive and well, but less guarded now. Her gaze flicked briefly to the floor, then back to his. For a second, the old familiarity settled between them.

"She always did have more courage than most of us," Paula said quietly. "And a better memory."

Alan searched her face. There was something behind her words—regret maybe, or weariness—but he didn't press. The moment held them, delicate and brief. Then someone called her name from across the gallery. Paula looked toward the voice, then back at him, offering the rest of her smile.

For a moment, Alan thought she might actually stay. Something behind her eyes flickering open, just for a second, like a window unlatched in a locked room. When he mentioned Bingham Park, the usual sleekness in her posture had wavered. Her hands, always elegant, always at rest, had come together lightly at her waist, a gesture that told him she was thinking.

"How far along is the work?" she asked, eyes narrowing in something close to interest. Real, measured interest. It startled him.

He treaded carefully. "We've been gathering testimony. Goldie's put together something... remarkable. It's not formal. Not funded. But it's honest."

Paula nodded. Her gaze set to a point just past his shoulder, as if calculating what it might mean if the wrong person heard them. Her expression was no longer just polite, no longer administrative. She seemed—curious. Maybe even stirred. He didn't dare bring up the corridor. Didn't mention Parcel 524-B. Didn't say

David's name. The risk was too great, the terrain too sensitive, and he couldn't tell yet if her curiosity was personal, professional, or something stranger.

She took a breath, stepped a shade closer. The chatter in the gallery blurred behind them. Other people's voices, other people's wine and outrage. Then she reached out—brief, unassuming—and touched his arm. Her fingers, light as a comma, pressed just above his wrist, not possessive but anchoring.

"Cities hide what they can't clean," she said.

The words came so easily, so gently, that Alan almost didn't register them at first. They didn't feel like deflection. They felt like something she'd been waiting to say, and maybe couldn't say anywhere else. And then she was gone, walking back toward the group at the far side of the gallery, where the mayor had reappeared near the wine. Her gait was elegant again, unhurried. She joined the cluster of people nodding over public-private partnerships and tax credit strategies dressed in nonprofit verbiage. It was as if she had never stepped away. Never leaned in. Never said anything.

Alan stood there, her words lingering just above his skin. Cities hide what they can't clean. It landed subtle. The sentence unraveling itself in his mind. They couldn't clean Bingham Park. Couldn't scrub the chromium out of the soil or the toxins out of the air. So they covered it in time, and signage, and silence. They couldn't clean 524-B. So they renamed it. Repackaged it. Redirected the cleanup budget and crafted the press release. They couldn't clean what was done. So they hid it.

He thought of Walter's hand on the fence. Of Ava's folder. Of Goldie in the church basement with her ink-streaked fingers and her jaw set in stone. He looked around the gallery again, at the clean walls and the safe metaphors, and felt the gravity return. The mask of the city wasn't cracking. It was evolving. The performance had just entered its next act. He didn't move. Didn't leave. Because something in her voice—something in that brief, precise phrase—had sounded not just like complicity. It sounded like a warning.

Part Three

13

Paula stood in the bedroom, the light from the sconces catching the gleam along the molding. The room's air held the trace of cardamom from a candle she hadn't relit in weeks. Outside, the sounds of the city thinned to their evening register—distant tires over wet asphalt, a neighbor's door latch catching, the drone of an air conditioning unit nearing the end of its cycle.

She unfastened the clasp of one earring. The dinner had been dull in the exact way such dinners were meant to be—polished language, agreeable outcomes, foundation rhetoric about leveraging civic assets through public-private alignment. A glass of pinot, a plate of wild rice, someone quoting Baldwin in a way that made her want to leave her body. And she had smiled, and nodded, and spoken as if she still believed in the structure of change.

The earring slipped between her fingers as she reached for the velvet-lined tray inside the jewelry box. It was small, shaped like a tear, the metal warm from her skin. She moved to place it, then paused. Her hand had brushed the edge of the photograph. It was wedged along the back wall of the box, behind a bracelet she hadn't worn since the last board appointment. The photograph slightly warped, the paper soft with age. She knew it too well. Alan beside her, both of them younger, less jaded. It had been early spring, years ago, at a protest neither of them organized but both of them had shown up for, with the kind of open-throated urgency they used to call conviction. He was caught mid-sentence, face turned toward her with certainty. Her mouth half-open. A sign overhead blurred in the motion of the shot.

She let her fingers rest on the edge of the photo. There was no regret. That had never been the shape of it. What passed between them had simply refused to become anything sustainable. Their work had outrun their timing. They had chosen the clarity of distance. But something inside her shifted, small and deliberate. A feeling unnamed. She pulled her hand back and closed the lid of the box with care, aligning it until it sat flush.

Across the room, her phone buzzed once against the dresser. She didn't reach for it. Instead, she moved to the mirror and looked at herself the way one might look at a painting re-hung in a familiar space. She exhaled. The quiet held. Then she reached for the other earring.

She looked at herself in the mirror again. The light caught at her cheekbones, just enough to remind her of how often she'd been told she looked composed when she was simply tired. The face looking back at her was the same one she offered to donors and camera crews, to staff briefings and ribbon cuttings—serene, precise, untroubled. But the stillness behind her eyes tonight felt a degree off, not enough to call a fracture, but enough to mark.

Her gaze held. She thought of earlier that evening—just before they'd stepped out of the restaurant. She'd been standing beside David in the vestibule of 1618 West, the glass doors beaded with rain, and he'd been tugging at the cuff of his sleeve like he always did when waiting on the car. They'd been half-listening to a pair of local investors recount their plans to open a mid-century jazz lounge in the wellness corridor's southern block, complete with "Black heritage-themed cocktails." Paula had smiled, eyes steady, mouth composed, while David murmured affirmations.

Councilwoman Hoffman had arrived just as they were preparing to leave—coat unbuttoned, earrings still swinging from whatever reception she'd attended before. She smelled of some sharp, expensive scent and looked over David's shoulder like a woman who always assumed she was interrupting something lesser.

"Well," Hoffman said, eyes gleaming, voice pitched just high enough to carry. "I hope you're keeping tabs on your historian friend. Word is she's taking up space again. Memory jars and kitchen table meetings and all that charming nostalgia."

David's smile didn't move past the corners of his mouth. "Goldie's committed," he said, his voice mild, almost affectionate. "But the circle's nearly complete. Once the anchor site clears phase two, the rest will follow."

Hoffman tilted her head, mouth pursed. "Let's hope you're right. Because sentiment's gathering like a storm. And if we're caught under it without an umbrella, your little corridor is going to look like a monument to miscalculation."

Paula hadn't spoken. She stood beside David with her arms crossed lightly at the wrist, a posture that suggested discretion. But she'd watched the exchange, every flicker of tone and half-swallowed pause, and felt the way the air charged around it.

Hoffman turned to her before leaving. "You look lovely, Paula. As always."

Hoffman smiled and slipped past the doors into the restaurant.

Now, alone, Paula blinked at her reflection. She reached for her moisturizer but didn't apply it. Instead, she let her fingers rest lightly against the rim of the jar, her mind still hearing the phrase: "the circle's nearly complete."

The city was soft with morning when Paula pulled onto Summit Avenue. Light crept across the hoods of parked cars, collected on the windows of closed storefronts, turned brick bright where the sun caught. She wore her casual jacket, unbuttoned. No need for polish in the early hours. The radio was off. Her daughter had left with David just after seven, backpack swinging, cereal unfinished on the counter. He'd said something about needing to stop by the site, voice tight from too little sleep or too much pressure. She hadn't asked which.

The car interior was quiet, the dashboard ticking as the system warmed. She drove with one hand, the other resting on her leg, fingers curled from habit. Traffic was thin. At a stoplight, a man on a bike passed her on the right, standing in the pedals, hoodie drawn tight. A woman walked a dog without a leash near the corner where the new murals had gone up last week, funded through a grant program repackaged three times before it passed council.

Her phone lit up on the console just before the turn onto Yanceyville. David. She picked up.

"Hey," he said. His voice pitched carefully. "I know you're en route."

"Already halfway there," Paula said. "What is it?"

He cleared his throat. "You know what's on the docket. The Alliance report will be on the table. It's not just metrics anymore. We're moving into implementation. Site assessments. Outreach. Once this clears, we'll be past the threshold."

"I chaired the subcommittee that wrote the agenda."

"I know," he said. "I just—listen, this is the moment. Once the Alliance signs off on the playground package, everything moves."

She didn't answer.

"We hit capacity on wellness indicators," he continued. "Community engagement's up. The anchor site clears final inspection this week. And parcel builds are already queued for Q4. We've got a clean path."

He paused, waiting.

"We're almost past the point of resistance," he said. "Once this meeting's done, the project runs itself."

She drove past the park-and-ride, where the pavement was still striped with yesterday's puddles. Two people sat on a bench under the shelter, heads tilted toward their phones, knees close. She thought of how long David had been using that phrase "past the point of resistance" as though the thing they were building was gravity itself.

"I've been running cover for you since phase one," Paula said. "Since the title transfer went to Dent's shell company and you told me not to ask who drafted the memo."

"I know you've done the work," he shot back. "But we need to tighten right now. Hoffman's nervous. She's hearing noise. People whispering about Goldie's project. Alan showing up at meetings. There's a narrative brewing, and we need to get ahead of it."

"I've smoothed language. Shifted timelines. Sat through stakeholder meetings where I let them think I was the architect," she said. "Don't tell me about narrative."

She changed lanes. The roads were clean this morning, the city's schedule running on time.

"I've carried this in committee, in press, in closed session. I've endorsed deliverables I never saw. You're not reminding me," she said, flat. "You're asking if I'm still on script."

There was silence.

Then, softer: "I'm saying the story needs to hold. Just a few more steps," he said. "A few more months. After that, we're running on momentum. The anchor's complete, the funders stay quiet, the Corridor brand becomes the story."

The road curved past the county building. Her turn was next. She signaled. Looked once in the mirror.

"You with me?" he asked.

"I'll chair the meeting," she said. "I'll hold the language. But don't forget who's taken the risk."

"I haven't," he said. "I won't."

The line went dead. The screen dimmed. Her reflection hovered in the black glass. She drove the last stretch in silence.

She turned into the community foundation lot. A few other cars already parked. The lot had been repaved last spring with state dollars earmarked for climate change. No one had explained how. She gathered her bag, checked her watch, and stepped out.

The delegation from the school system was on slide twenty-two of a thirty-slide deck. The font was too small, the bullet points redundant. One of the presenters, a man in a blue fleece vest with the district's logo stitched above his heart, read directly from the screen. His colleague stood beside him, nodding, as if seconding each line of text would add meaning.

The free lunch extension was a three-year request, a continuation of a federal pilot that had expired. They were asking for bridge funding. The ask was modest, framed as strategic. "Food as foundation," one slide said. Another read, "Nutritional Equity Through Scalable Solutions." The only compelling image—a photo of a child holding a half-eaten peach—had been reused four times.

Paula sat at the head of the table, spine straight, eyes forward. She had perfected the art of active listening with minimal expenditure—chin tilted slightly, fingers laced, a calm blink every ten seconds. The clock on the far wall read 10:57. They were behind schedule.

Keith Collins, the board's treasurer, adjusted his glasses for the third time in ten minutes. His pad sat in front of him, half a page of notes in neat, pointed script. He had a gift for translating bureaucratic passion into numbers, and he looked like a man deciding whether to be generous or precise.

Keith always arrived five minutes early. He took the same seat each meeting—second from Paula's left, close enough to speak but far enough not to seem eager. His notebooks were identical each quarter, black hardcovers labeled in small block letters by date. He opened them calmly, wrote with a fine-point pen, and never doodled. This morning, he wore a navy suit with a green tie and looked like a man who had never once raised his voice in a public setting. He greeted the program officers with a nod. When the pediatrician, Dr. Rowley, asked about his oldest, he answered briefly "Freshman year, public health track. Doing well." Then turned back to his notes.

Paula watched him as the meeting droned on. She had come to rely on Keith in the way people rely on properly calibrated machines. A quiet, sustaining certainty. He understood the financial structure of the wellness corridor project better than anyone at the table. Maybe better than David. He had read every site report, scanned every line item, cross-checked every regulatory appendix tacked on to the 524-B parcel documentation since the beginning of phase two. He hadn't needed to be asked.

When the first concerns had surfaced—questions about overlapping remediations, the sequence of state filings, the language in the cap-and-cover certifications—it was Keith who held the line. Not defensively. Just with data. He'd presented a one-page summary to the Guilford Health Alliance board three months earlier, mapping the movement of funds, the audit trail from the federal stabilization grant to the wellness infrastructure line item. "It's contained. It's sound. The risk is reputational, not structural," he'd said, with cool finality.

The board had relaxed after that. Even Dr. Rowley. Even Tanisha, for a while.

Today, Keith sat with his hands folded over his notebook, fingers still. His glasses caught the overhead light. He hadn't spoken yet, but his presence was already a kind of reassurance. He had been the steady voice in backroom calls and pre-meeting summaries, the one who reminded them that wellness optics were easiest to defend when the money stayed on schedule.

Paula glanced at the agenda. Parcel 524-B was near the bottom. Keith knew that, of course. He'd prepared her for the vote in three bullet points, texted the night before.

—Permits cleared.

—Contractor verified.

—Timeline holds.

He hadn't said anything about Hoffman. Or about Goldie. Keith didn't deal in personalities. He dealt in systems. Paula leaned back slightly, spine tall, expression unreadable. She trusted him. But trust, she was beginning to remember, wasn't the same as immunity.

To Paula's left, the two mid-level program officers, both women in smart blouses with lanyards still on, offered encouraging smiles at appropriate intervals. They worked from laptops. Neither had spoken since the meeting started. Their job was to carry weight without exerting influence.

Dr. Rowley, leaned forward now. He tapped a pen against his binder once, then spoke.

"I just want to say I've seen firsthand what this nutrition program does. We can argue scale and metrics, but hungry children don't care about metrics."

A soft murmur of assent followed. Rowley was old enough that his opinions carried the aura of having been earned. Then the younger board member, Tanisha, cleared her throat. She was the only one under forty in the room, and it showed in her posture—eager, upright, alert to nuance. She'd been Goldie's mentee once, something Paula never forgot but never named.

"I just want to add," Tanisha said, her voice firm, "this isn't just a continuation. It's a line in the sand. If we fund this, we say feeding children matters more than waiting for the next grant cycle."

Paula watched her without reaction. The statement hung there. No one countered. After a pause, Paula nodded.

"Thank you," she said. "Any further discussion?"

No one spoke.

"All in favor?"

Hands rose. Unanimous.

"Approved," Paula said, and made a note in the ledger. The school officials packed up their slides with quiet relief, thanked the board, exited with binders clutched like proof of relevance.

There was a brief shuffle, water poured into paper cups, pages turned. Paula moved her fingers lightly across the agenda. One item left. Paula's pen already hovering over the ledger. The energy in the room had begun to fade, the subtle exhale that follows decision-making, where people mentally pack their bags. She cleared her throat, ready to continue.

But then Tanisha lifted one hand.

"Madam Chair," she said. "Point of personal privilege."

Paula paused, nodded, prepared for a passing comment, something easily merged back into the rhythm of the agenda.

"I've been following the work Goldie Hayes is doing with that Cottage Grove coalition," Tanisha said, her voice steady. "Why aren't we supporting Bingham Park remediation? Her presentation to City Council last month was serious. People were listening. She laid out the health risks tied to Bingham Park, connected the community reports with pediatric asthma data, brought in historical testimony. It wasn't anecdotal—it was documented. She's building an archive, and now there's a plan in motion for public displays, art installations, field reports from families. It's grown beyond storytelling. It's becoming civic record."

The words landed in the room with precision. Not aggressive. The sound of a fork dropped onto tile—enough to freeze motion. Paula's mouth opened slightly. The tip of her tongue pressed behind her front teeth, looking for the phrase she had prepared for this—something to nod toward inclusivity, to gesture at the shape of the thing without naming it. Nothing arrived.

She said, "We've... been aligning our funding priorities more broadly with... infrastructural impact zones."

It was soft. Measured. But it came too slowly. The stammer showed hesitation. The kind that makes people glance at each other. Dr. Rowley frowned. A mild tightening at the corners of his eyes. He straightened in his seat.

"But that's exactly where the asthma cases are climbing," he said. "Bingham Park is the impact zone."

No one responded.

Paula glanced at Keith. He didn't lift his eyes. His pen rested on the agenda, unmoving. A second later, he tapped it once against the table. Someone else adjusted their chair. A paper rustled. The room, so recently orderly, now carried the unease of something being withheld. Paula inhaled, lifted her shoulders slightly, reasserted the position of her spine. She could feel every face on her. Not hostile. But alert. She'd been presiding over this room for four years. The confidence they placed in her had never felt unearned. Until now.

Because this wasn't a challenge. It was a correction. They were reminding her, with their silence, of what she was expected to manage. And for the first time since she had stepped into leadership, she understood that what she possessed wasn't authority. The board's trust was a transaction. She was there to hold the line. Until she couldn't.

Paula exhaled quietly through her nose, recalibrated.

"We can add a discussion item for Bingham Park to next month's agenda," she said. Her voice was measured again, recovered, the edges smoothed. "There's room in the policy window for us to examine overlapping community health zones and see where alignment is possible."

It was the tone of a concession without any of the substance. Something borrowed from prior meetings, from a shelf of placeholder phrases that had served her well before. She moved to turn the page in her notes, a gesture meant to close the moment.

But Dr. Rowley didn't let it go. He looked directly at her now, arms crossed with fatigue.

"That neighborhood's been waiting for years," he said. "Waiting for testing, for remediation, for visibility. Goldie's not creating problems—she's documenting them. And we're still acting like it's a novelty."

Paula kept her face still. There was a slight heat rising under her blouse collar. She folded her hands again. Leaned forward.

"We'll prioritize it for the next grant cycle," she said. "That's the cleanest mechanism we have."

No one replied. Tanisha nodded once but did not smile. The program officers kept their heads down. Keith had returned to his notes. He was flipping a page without urgency, his pen now idle on the table. The ledger in front of her held its clean lines, each item squared and marked. A record of action taken. But the room had changed. There was no vote here. Just the hollow shape of one avoided. Paula turned the page in her binder with more force than necessary, the paper catching against her thumbnail. The motion, like the voice that followed it, was smooth but fast. Too fast.

"Keith," she said, with a pivot, "can we move to the development update on the wellness corridor playground? Let's walk through the current timeline."

A redirect disguised as momentum. Eyes turned to Keith, whose laptop was already open, cursor blinking in a spreadsheet docked on the lower third of the shared screen. He adjusted his glasses and cleared his throat with habitual rasp.

"Right," he said. "This is from this morning's upload. Development sequence updated for Phases I and II."

He began scrolling, the spreadsheet now projected above the board's heads. Rows of white and gray cells, a quiet field of numbers and project codes. He moved to the section marked "Wellness & Innovation Zone – Parcel 524-B." His voice had that reliable cadence again, dense but steady.

"As you can see, Parcel 524-B—now formally listed as part of the Wellness & Innovation Zone—is slated for Phase II utility alignment. The original language on—wait..."

He stopped. The mouse hovered. He scrolled once. Then again. His shoulders hunched.

"That's... strange," he said, quieter now. "The remediation clause is gone."

Silence. He leaned forward. Eyes narrowing.

"It was in the draft from two weeks ago. I had a line item for subsoil stabilization—under community wellness infrastructure. I remember because I flagged the phrasing. It was awkward."

He tapped twice on the cell and brought up the metadata. No comment tags. No revision history.

"It's not here."

The room didn't move. No pens tapped. Paula sat motionless, her fingers locked loosely at the edge of her binder. Her pulse gathered behind her ears. She thought about asking him to refresh the file. To check the previous version. To remind them all that language moves in and out of drafts in early planning stages.

Keith looked up. Met her eyes for the first time since the meeting began.

"I'm telling you," he said. "It was there."

Across the table, Tanisha pushed her binder an inch forward, hands flat against the cover. And the room, once responsive to her voice alone, now watched Paula and waited.

Paula leaned forward, elbows close, fingers steepled just above the closed edge of her notes. The dynamic in the room had changed. Some intangible register of attention that no longer belonged to her. The pulse behind her breast beat too loud, too steady, impossible to ignore. She didn't touch her face. She didn't blink effusive.

"Perhaps it was consolidated under environmental compliance—" she said, low, even.

Keith didn't let her finish.

"No," he said, flatly. "It's not. It's deleted."

He tapped a key again. Scrolled down, then back. "That language was there. Specific reference to subsoil remediation. A clause. With the DEQ tracking number in parentheses. It's gone."

He didn't look at anyone now. His tone didn't rise. He spoke like someone confirming the location of a missing stair. The silence persisted. Everyone in the room understood that something real had just changed. Even those who didn't understand the stakes yet felt it.

Then, from the far end of the table, one of the junior board members—Paula thought her name was Ellie, recent hire, sharp, idealistic—spoke without looking up.

"Is this connected to the Goldie Hayes project?"

Her voice was quiet, but the sentence carried. The room absorbed it completely. No one answered. Not Paula. Not Keith. A rustle of paper. Then a man's voice—mid-table, Dr. Rowley, measured.

"Wasn't 524-B considered brownfield status at one point?"

Still no one looked directly at Paula. But the center of gravity had shifted toward her chair, whether they faced her or not. She could feel her throat constrict. The pressure of calculation with no clear direction. Her authority, a given until seconds ago, now felt contingent, as though someone had unplugged the circuitry behind it.

She heard herself say, too lightly, "That classification was temporary. Based on a pre-regulatory status." But no one asked her to elaborate. The spreadsheet remained on the screen—cells blinking, lines unspooling. She reached for her pen just to hold something.

Paula's breath shortened, clipped at the top of the inhale. Words continued around her—deleted, remediation, Goldie—but they no longer held context. They floated, submerged, a muffled litany dissolving beneath the surface of time beyond her control. The room, once responsive to her modulation, had turned opaque. The edges of the table blurred. Faces smeared at the edges.

Her eyes fell to the corner of the presentation slide still glowing on the wall. Lower left, pale gray on white. An image of an old consultancy logo—David's. Not current. Outdated branding, something that should have been scrubbed when the design firm pushed out the final graphics. But it remained, a ghostprint. A fingerprint.

She remembered him in the kitchen. Late, distracted, reading through project notes and rifling for tea bags. "That parcel's undervalued in all the right ways," he'd said. He'd been speaking to the idea of the thing, not the woman beside him. She remembered the weight of that moment. How she had let it pass without stopping him. Without asking.

He knew.

The thought didn't rise like revelation. It was dropped into her. The language, the omissions, the way everything had moved too cleanly, too quickly, across too many desks. He had built the narrative from the inside and let her carry the story. Her stomach turned. Her hands went cold. The pen slipped from her fingers and struck the table with a clatter that filled the room. It rolled, then stopped, pointing nowhere.

No one moved. She heard herself speak, and the voice was her own, but foreign in its brittleness.

"Excuse me."

She pushed back from the table. The legs of the chair scraped against the carpet. She stood without grace. Behind her, the screen still held the spreadsheet. Parcel 524-B glowed at the center, emptied of what had once been real.

The boardroom door swung shut behind her with institutional calm. Paula stood in the corridor, alone, the strip lighting overhead now blinding her, the carpet dull beneath her heels. Everything rendered in the artificial clarity of a building not meant to hold emotion. Her breath came fast, shallow, soundless. She pressed her fingers into her temples hard enough to hurt, harder still when it didn't clear the pressure behind her eyes. The burn gathered at the base of her neck, climbed toward her scalp in waves.

Her blazer felt too tight at the shoulders, though it hadn't shrunk. Too fitted, too sharp, a decision made in the confidence of the morning that now struck her as cruel. Her mouth was dry. Behind the wall, she could hear Keith's voice doing what she was supposed to be doing. Holding the line. Explaining away the absence of language that never should have disappeared.

She leaned against the wall, her weight uncertain. Her spine curved just slightly. Just enough to break posture. A temporary defiance. Her body trying to create distance from itself. The cool of the paint bled through the sleeve of her jacket. She exhaled through clenched teeth.

A janitor passed, pulling a cart stacked with paper towels and plastic bottles of diluted solution. He didn't speak. She was grateful. She couldn't have spoken if she tried. She nodded, eyes wide but controlled, rehearsing the face of composure. He kept walking. She stayed there, still halfway upright. Her phone buzzed in her pocket. She pulled it out with one hand, already knowing. David.

"Dinner with Dent confirmed. Proud of you today. Big moves."

The message sat on the screen without ceremony. As if her complicity had earned its own syntax. She stared at it. The screen blurred. Her vision narrowed at the edges. Her lungs forgot the pattern. A rushing sound filled her ears, pulsing and relentless, like machinery inside a locked utility room.

He had sent that message knowing what had been removed. Not speculatively. With confidence. With ease. She stared as her breath shortened further, the pressure in her chest tightening into something unmanageable. Her legs began to shake. Proud of you.

She bent slightly at the waist. Just enough to feel the blood change direction. Her knees stayed locked, but she wasn't sure how long they would hold. The skin at her neck flushed, then cooled, then flushed again. Her fingers felt distant. Detached. Everything in her wanted to turn back through that door, to reclaim something—position, language, the last sentence said in her name. But her feet didn't move. She read the message again. Watched it remain. Her thumb hovered over the screen with the realization that the words, like the clause in the spreadsheet, would not disappear just because no one acknowledged them.

The hallway stretched long in both directions, sterile and calm, a place between destinations. The edges of her vision dimmed. Her jaw clenched. A wave of nausea rolled through her, fast and mean. Paula thought, for one second, she might black out. Then the screen went dark. Silence returned. She kept walking.

The foundation's bathroom was cold, too white. The kind of white that felt imposed, fluorescent and brittle, with grout lines too clean to trust. Paula pushed the door open. No one inside. The quiet of the air vent and the drip of one faucet—water against porcelain, irregular but persistent. She stepped to the sink, both hands on the counter now, weight forward. The mirror above the basin was wide and without frame. It gave nothing. It offered everything. Her reflection was still.

The lipstick had bled slightly—just at the crease of her mouth, where the skin folded naturally into itself. A thin red line. Not quite a smear, not dramatic. Just enough to suggest movement. The trace of something unstopped. Like a line drawn backward from the corner of silence. She stared at it. Her breath was shallow. Her pulse had settled into the back of her jaw, a dull percussion. She took a tissue from the dispenser, wiped carefully at the corner. Once. Again. The stain came away. But the mark remained. A refusal. Her face had not changed. And yet? The eyes held less light. The jaw looked braced for something. The forehead, always smooth, now creased at the edges with questions she hadn't considered. A woman stared back. Dressed well. Composed. Empty.

She studied her own image the way one studies a room after someone has left it. Taking in the shadow, the dent in the cushion, the door open. For the first time since the beginning of all of it—before the meetings, before the wellness corridor plans, before the fundraisers and the clean phrases and the full-color renderings—Paula didn't recognize the woman looking back.

She pressed the tissue into the trash, turned off the tap, and left the light on behind her.

14

Keith closed his laptop without looking up. The spreadsheet still projected on the wall, casting light across the conference table in bars of white and pale green, but the numbers no longer meant anything. Not to the room. Not to him. The cell that once held Remediation – Parcel 524-B – Subsoil was blank, and now the space around it was collapsing.

No one spoke when Paula left. They had watched her rise quickly, leave her purse behind, the chair pushed just out of alignment. The silence had calcified around the door's slow swing. It hadn't latched fully. Keith could still hear the noise of the hallway beyond it. Across the table, Rowley sat with his arms crossed, expression unreadable. Tanisha kept her gaze steady, focused, her binder open to the page with the audit notes, Goldie's name scribbled in the margin.

Keith adjusted his glasses. He'd meant to speak sooner. He hadn't.

"She'll be back in a minute," one of the program officers said, too hopeful.

He looked at his watch, then at the screen again. He knew the pattern. This was where damage could be minimized. This was where the formal voice reasserted order. But his mouth felt dry. There was an edge of nausea.

"We'll take five," he said.

The words hung there.

"I'm calling a recess."

Chairs creaked, bodies moved. No one objected. He reached for Paula's pen, rolled it between his fingers once, then placed it in the spine of her ledger. The page was open to the 524-B playground allocation. The signature line was still blank. The room emptied, cautious steps over carpet, muted greetings exchanged. The spreadsheet, still on the screen, waited to be explained.

Keith stepped into the hallway just as Paula was coming back down the corridor, her pace composed but not brisk, shoulders squared. She was paler than usual. Her mouth was set, contained, and the hand not holding her phone was balled into something approximate to grace.

She offered a nod, just enough to acknowledge the gap she'd left.

"You alright?" he asked.

She gave the sort of laugh that ended before it began. "Fine," she said, quickly. "Let's just get this done."

Keith didn't believe her, but he didn't expect truth. He knew the calculus behind that particular tone. What it cost a person like Paula to say anything resembling vulnerability. She looked like she'd aged a year in the five minutes since she left, but the jacket still sat perfectly on her shoulders. They walked back toward the boardroom together. The silence between them a kind of pact.

He thought, as they approached the door, about the notes that had disappeared from the spreadsheet. The language that had been present two weeks ago and now wasn't. He thought about the DEQ tracking number he'd highlighted in a note to himself, the one he'd intended to bring up if anyone had questioned the vote earlier. No one had. Until Tanisha. Until the board stopped operating like a body and began behaving like a room full of people.

He thought about the subsoil. The 524-B site, resurfaced and renamed a playground, sealed in the language of improvement. He'd read the site reports twice. He'd seen the consultant's seal, the geotechnical summary, the deferral language tucked at the end of the public copy. He had known what the omissions meant.

He could feel the weight of it now, dull and square in the center of his chest. There was a moment, he knew, when someone like him could say something. Could pull the brake. Could name the thing out loud, even if it came at the cost of the vote, the playground funding, the board's manufactured consensus. It would not have undone the structure. But it would have signaled a refusal to carry its deception further.

Instead, he'd called a recess.

He opened the door for her. They walked in together. The board members were returning to their seats, leafing through papers, resettling into the posture of governance. The screen still showed the spreadsheet. The cell still blank. Keith sat. Paula took her chair. He looked at her, once. Then turned to the room.

"Let's resume," he said.

The rustle of papers was sharper, the water cups less full. Even the air, managed by the building's central system and timed to cycle every twenty-seven minutes, felt heavier. Keith watched the numbers reappear on the screen as the projector blinked awake. It was the same spreadsheet—columns for cost, contractor timelines, percent complete—flattened language engineered to make nothing seem urgent. Parcel 524-B was still there, mid-column, stripped of its one ethically complicated phrase.

Paula sat at the head of the table with her hands folded on her closed binder. She hadn't reopened it. Her face was composed in the way only exhaustion can produce—features aligned but hollowed, the facade of stability held by muscle memory alone. Every person in the room saw what it cost her to remain still.

Paula spoke at last. Her voice was softer than before, the polish dulled. "We'll return to the agenda item—approval of the wellness infrastructure sub-grant tied to Parcel 524-B of the anchor site. The proposed spend is earmarked for playground equipment and mural installations."

She stopped there. No elaboration or guiding statement. The old rhythm wasn't there.

Keith cleared his throat. He didn't look at her. He looked instead at the group, at the collapse of consensus. The pediatrician was already leaning forward, his pen angled across the page.

"I'd like to revisit the 524-B motion before we proceed," Rowley said. "I understand its importance, but new information's been introduced. We ought to reconsider."

Tanisha followed before Keith could respond.

"I still have questions about funding overlap. If the remediation plan is gone, what are we building on? Is the playground meant to signal closure? Because it looks like staging—like the beginning of something that's already been decided without us."

One of the program officers shifted in her seat, murmured something about grant alignment. No one acknowledged it. Keith adjusted his glasses, slid his notebook to the side. His hand rested on the table, palm down, fingers spread. He could feel the tremor that hadn't left since the language vanished from the cell.

"The item remains within budget and scope," he said. "As of last update, all permitting is in place. Site inspection cleared for non-invasive installations. Modular equipment avoids soil penetration. Funding moves the project to readiness for public use."

He said it calmly, like he'd said a hundred other things over the years—capital disbursement for outreach vans, mobile dental services, back-end financing for a pilot shuttle route that lasted six weeks and was quietly folded. Say it clearly. Keep your voice low. Make it seem inevitable. But as he said it, he thought of the line that had disappeared. He thought of the phrase subsoil remediation and how it had been reduced to absence. He had flagged it. He had made a note. He had chosen not to ask who deleted it.

"The project is nearing completion," he said, calmly. "Parcel 524-B has been integrated into the Corridor's wellness infrastructure since Phase II. The vote is procedural, yes, but also essential. Equipment's ordered. Contractors scheduled. Backing out now introduces a different kind of liability."

He watched their faces, measured the weight of each blink, each still pen.

"We've passed the stage of questions," he said. "The public sees momentum. If we pull back now, we're not just pausing—we're rewriting a process that's already met its approvals."

He didn't say what he was thinking: that his own voice sounded foreign to him. That he heard the word liability and wanted to stand up and leave the room. That his daughter—now in undergrad, now asking him questions about urban policy over Sunday brunch—would hear about this vote eventually, and he wouldn't know how to explain it without reducing himself to systems and constraints.

"I know it's uncomfortable," he said, quieter now. "But governance isn't clarity. It's sequence."

Across the table, Rowley leaned back, lips pressed thin. Tanisha didn't look convinced. But she closed her binder.

"But the soil data for that site hasn't been updated," Tanisha said. "We're greenlighting community use before confirming the remediation is complete."

Her tone was even, but there was a clarity to it. She had stopped trying to couch it in optimism. Paula looked at her, said nothing. Dr. Rowley followed. "And this is the same parcel flagged in '99? Near the old brownfield site that stopped the baseball stadium? I'm not opposed to the investment, but you're asking us to validate something we haven't verified."

Keith nodded once.

"The investment isn't the issue," he said. "It's the timing. We're at the edge of the funding window. If we delay, we risk losing contractor availability. That restarts procurement. Which collapses the construction timeline. Which pushes us out of compliance with the Phase III objectives."

He knew how it sounded. It was true. It was also evasive. He pushed forward.

"We don't have evidence the site is unsafe," he said. "We do have documentation that the surface is capped and sealed. What we're funding—equipment, murals—doesn't engage the subsoil. It meets code. We've met every procedural obligation."

There was a silence. Just enough to hold everything that wasn't being said. Keith looked at Paula. Her hands were still. Her face unreadable. He turned to the board.

"We can't answer the city's history in this vote," he said. "We can only move the work forward. We have families waiting for amenities we already promised."

He said it cleanly. Authoritatively. The room responded. The vote was called without drama.

One of the program officers raised her hand first. Then Rowley. Then Ellie. Tanisha hesitated. Then lifted her hand, slowly. Keith didn't raise his own. He just recorded the vote. They moved on. The spreadsheet remained open. The cell didn't refill. No one mentioned it again.

Afterward, as they gathered their papers and thanked each other with the usual murmured professionalism, Keith thought about the word anchor. How it always sounded like stability when really, it just meant something was being held in place. No matter what was buried underneath.

How does a man get to become a coward? Keith walked with his head bowed, not from shame—he couldn't even feel that yet—but from the weight of internal collapse that hadn't settled into belief. The vote had ended fifteen minutes ago. His voice had been clear. His hand steady. No one had seen him hesitate. And yet he was peeled open with violent precision. The kind of undoing that happens when a man keeps choosing safety over clarity until there's nothing left.

The sidewalk was hot even in shade, the light hard-edged across the pavement, the breeze useless. His dress shirt stuck to his lower back. His tie loosened just enough to signal that the day was ending, but not enough to unfasten the pressure at his throat. There was sweat along his hairline. He hadn't noticed until now.

His father would've found all of this ridiculous. All this conscience, this interior turmoil. The man had run a logistics firm for forty-three years, controlled five regional warehouses, sent drivers into hurricane zones without blinking. "What good's a decision if you second-guess it," he used to say, eyes flat, fork suspended over dry pork chop. His father wasn't unkind. He simply believed the world sorted itself around men who moved forward.

Keith had inherited the belief, if not the spine. The degrees, the roles, the position on this board and others—he could fill the outlines of the man he was supposed to be, but the moral conviction never quite arrived. He had learned to approximate resolve. To nod in the right places. To explain risk in ways that felt like protection.

The sidewalk veered north, past the new urban green. Three acres of reclaimed real estate turned public promenade. Native grasses, a kinetic net sculpture, a water feature that gurgled like it was swallowing the past. The signage called it The Commons. A four-million-dollar private donation made it happen. The city threw in another two for infrastructure—lighting, concrete work, custom benches sealed with a protective polymer. He stopped at the corner. Across the street, a mother pushed a child on a swing that cost more than a month's wages in Cottage Grove. There had been no swing sets there. No splash pad. No turf engineered for impact absorption. Just red clay, some broken fencing, a trash can fused to the ground with rust.

He thought, not for the first time, that the city wasn't so much misgoverned as misaligned. The money always flowed downhill—down the slopes of power, familiarity, whiteness. And he had learned to speak that fluently. Had built a career on the steady, quiet redirection of funds from the urgent to the inevitable. He crossed toward the office tower. Glass and steel, twenty-two stories of promise and leverage. The cock from which the city's power pulsed. Contracts written here, zoning interpretations massaged, equity branded and sold in half-day summits with pastry trays and name tags.

The revolving doors hissed open. The lobby was cool and indifferent. He thought about what it meant to live in a city that buried its poisons and dressed the edge with murals. The elevator arrived. He stepped in. He told himself he still had time to do something right. But the thought sounded rehearsed, a prayer recited in a language no longer believed.

The elevator ticked off the floors one by one—13, 14, 15—each number glowing red for a second before being replaced by the next, an official rhythm that gave the illusion of progress. Keith stood alone inside the metal box, arms crossed across his chest, one shoe angled outward as if his body were ready to leave before his mind had caught up.

Somewhere around 17, it hit him. The night in Burlington. The secretary, half his age and just as complicit. She had laughed at something trivial in the car, and he had gripped the wheel a little harder. Not out of anxiety, but control. He could still remember the moment he realized that the pleasure wasn't in the body beside him but in the act of holding the lie. He had orchestrated it, managed it. Power wrapped in discretion. The feeling was cleaner than desire. Almost elegant.

But after, the silence had been different. A sense that something private had been displaced. Something unseen, but known. When he got home, he had told his wife that the meeting was productive. She had believed him. Or said she did. They'd had dinner on the porch, salmon and couscous, and she'd complimented his patience with the kids. It was the first time in years he'd wanted her to yell.

The elevator slowed. He recognized the feeling now. That same grim awareness of his own capacity for deceit. That old instinct to manipulate the narrative just enough to survive it. But what had once been a private skill now pressed against him like a guilt he couldn't blame on anyone else. He had spent years in rooms where his voice was treated as ballast—calm, measured, useful. And now that same voice had helped erase a clause about toxic soil.

What was the cost of comfort if it came at the price of integrity? The elevator dinged. 22. He would emerge different. That much he could still control. He would find out what David Moss had done. Not just the missing language. Not just the funding trails. All of it. The way the wellness corridor had been built—who had written the story, who had been erased from it, and who was still standing on poisoned ground while the renderings went live.

He stepped off the elevator. The office was hollowed out by late afternoon. Desks sat in their after-hours posture—monitors dimmed, chairs tucked in, half-finished projects paused in states of polite abandonment. A water bottle sat sweating on the reception counter. A sweater hung over the back of a chair like a flag of resignation. Down the hallway, Keith passed no one. He closed his door. He lowered the blinds one slat at a time, pulling the cord with even focus. The light in the room took on a blue edge from the monitor's glow. He sat down without removing his coat. No breath deeper than necessary. No sound but the clicking of the mouse. His hands moved with surgical calm.

The first search: UWC-17.

The Urban Wellness Corridor. Phase I. 2017. He typed it with deliberate keystrokes, resisting the impulse to rush. The internal document archive accepted the query and returned a stack of digital folders. Environmental compliance. Site assessments. Remediation status logs. All marked complete.

"Start with what they wanted us to see."

He opened the final Phase I remediation report. A PDF, sixty pages. The summary page scrolled down the screen. Site contamination pre-regulatory. No actionable contaminants detected. The phrase was bureaucratic glass—clear, smooth, hard enough to shield liability from view. But at the bottom, in the footer, barely noticed—Compiled by: SiteOps LLC (Third-party review).

He went backwards. Opened a draft two months older. Then one more. Found what he was looking for: the initial language, plainer, untouched. Chromium VI detected in 3 of 9 deep core samples. Further action pending. He stared at the sentence. His jaw tightened. The final report had buried this entirely. Rewritten. Paved over. There, in the margin of draft two, a comment in red:

Language restructured for stakeholder comfort. See legal approval thread.

He whispered it once. "Stakeholder comfort."

He clicked open a second tab and dove into the legal archive. He still had admin access from his previous post in capital projects. A convenience no one had remembered to revoke. The search took time. He refined the parameters: UWC-17 + Cr(VI) + stabilization. Filtered by date. An accumulation of matching threads.

He found it. A redacted email from David Moss's chief of staff to the legal liaison.

"We're framing the soil material as pre-regulatory mineral density. Language has been cleared. Please avoid reference to toxins unless in technical annex."

Another message, less formal, forwarded from David to his CFO.

"Let's keep messaging on brand. Focus on access and wellness, not what we had to clean to get there."

Keith's hand hovered above the mouse. The screen felt warmer now, the light sticking to his skin. This wasn't sloppiness. It was a plan. He scrolled back. Read the same lines twice. David hadn't lied outright. He had subcontracted the deceit. Passed it like a brief, dressed it in the language of progress. The architecture of misdirection done in clean lines.

Keith opened the GIS viewer next. Pulled up the corridor map, the site overlay. Entered the coordinates from the test samples. Layered them over the updated parcel design. The deepest core samples—the ones that had returned positive for Cr(VI)—lined up directly beneath the project's south lot. Parcel 524-B. Right under the playground. Where the splash pad would go with the mural of the dancing children. All just funded by unanimous vote. He leaned back in his chair. Breath shallow now. Hands loose and twitching in his lap.

Last fall, his younger daughter's class had visited the site, then a gravel lot for downtown parking. There had been a health fair, glossy brochures, a smoothie truck parked near the greenway trail. His wife had sent photos—children with painted faces, standing in front of the Healing Begins Here mural. She had texted "This actually looks great." And he had believed it.

He whispered, "I signed off on this."

He minimized the maps. Opened a new folder on the desktop. Dragged the original remediation draft into it. The redacted email from legal. The internal memo with stakeholder comfort language. The map overlay. The original test result flagged pre-regulatory. He timestamped each file. Labeled them precisely. Put a note on the folder: For Alan.

He sat back again. The blinds filtered the last light from the room into narrow vertical shadows across the floor. This wasn't redemption. This wasn't even resistance. But it was the beginning of something that might, eventually, contain the truth.

Keith pulled into the driveway just past seven. The garage lights clicked on before he opened the door, sensors accommodating his arrival. The house, all brick façade and decorative stonework, loomed with manufactured elegance—a build too young to be tasteful, too expensive to be denied. They'd chosen it six years ago, during the peak of his consultancy earnings, in the phase when Allison was still sold on square footage as evidence of upward mobility. The lawn had been reseeded in March and already looked synthetic. The manicured edges of the yard were sharp enough to shame the neighbors.

He stepped out of the car and let the door shut behind him. The sky was fading to violet. The grass smelled chemically crisp. He looked across the lawn to the porch and thought of his oldest daughter, now a freshman at a private college in the Triangle. Public health major, gender studies minor. She had stopped calling after the holidays. A few texts, always polite. He hadn't asked for more. He wasn't sure what he'd say. Was he a good father to her? The question came suddenly. He'd paid what needed paying. Co-signed what needed co-signing. Had picked her up from rehearsals and taught her how to hold a steering wheel. He had never once screamed. But he'd also rarely been home before dark.

Inside, the silence was full. The kind of quiet that arrives when everything is functioning but nothing is connected. He dropped his keys in the ceramic bowl on the entry table and walked through the kitchen. Lights on, a few dishes in the sink. No sign of Allison.

"Anna?" he called, gently.

Her voice came from the den, flat and unbothered. "In here."

He found her at the dining table, school-issued laptop open, hair pulled back in a loose knot. She looked up, saw it was him, and then returned to the screen. Her shoulders had a language he was just learning: adolescent withdrawal, cloaked in efficiency.

"Hey," he said. "Where's your mom?"

"She's at the auditorium," Anna said, not looking up. "Sound check or lighting or something. She said it'd be late."

Keith nodded, though the answer sat strangely. Allison had been in production and tech support for the community theater program for years now. He couldn't remember the last time she'd attended a show without a headset or being in the spotlight.

He stepped closer. "You've got a lot of homework?"

"Some."

"What are you working on?"

She shrugged, still typing. "Math."

"Want help?"

She hesitated just long enough for the rejection to sting. "I'm good."

Keith moved toward the kitchen island, pulled out a stool, and sat. She didn't look at him. Her fingers moved across the keyboard.

He studied her—the narrow face, the eyes that moved without urgency, the jaw set like her mother's when she didn't want to argue. He tried to remember the last time he had taken her somewhere, just the two of them. The zoo, maybe, before third grade. The memory blurred into traffic, ice cream, a work call he'd taken while she stared at zebras.

"I was thinking we could maybe go out this weekend," he said. "Just the two of us."

She paused, looked at him over the screen. "Maybe."

It wasn't sarcasm. Mere indifference.

He nodded. "I want to do better," he said, not even realizing the words had formed.

She looked at him again, this time longer, and then returned to her math.

"Okay," she said.

It was the smallest word. But it hung heavier than the evening light pushing across the window sills. He sat there, watching her shoulders rise and fall in the glow of the screen, and thought—I have time. I still have time.

He changed upstairs without turning on the main lights. The ambient LED from the closet was enough. Gym shorts, old Carolina t-shirt, socks thin at the heel. In the mirror above the dresser he caught a glimpse of himself—shoulders rounded, chest softer, neck starting to fold where muscle used to stretch. A man of influence with a calendar full of meetings and nothing sacred on it.

Down in the garage, the elliptical waited. Behind it, the industrial shelves Allison had insisted they install held storage bins labeled by quarter: Summer Gear, Fall Decor, Storm Prep. He stepped onto the machine, pulled the earbuds from the drawer under the workbench, synced them with his phone, and thumbed through a menu of economic podcasts. Settled on Bloomberg's overnight brief. Global recap, forty-five minutes. He started pedaling. The machine chirped once, then fell into motion.

The host's voice cut through—market tightness, macro pressures, Yen movement, the Nikkei expected to open cautious. London would roll in a few hours. There was mention of Turkish inflation and carbon futures in Germany. He adjusted the incline and picked up speed. The machine groaned under him. His shirt clung to his back. Sweat gathered quickly, pushed through pores like something hunted out of him. He pressed harder. He thought about the folder. He thought about the emails—David's careful tone, the redacted legal language, the quiet choreography of erasure performed without smudges.

He thought about Parcel 524-B and the children who would run across that soft-covered ground in shoes their parents had bought on credit. He thought about the vote. About Paula, depleted. About Tanisha, angry but too late. About his own voice, steady, finishing what no one wanted to name. He had built his adult life in small, rational increments. A resume of cautions. A marriage of managed expectations. A fatherhood constructed more from financial compliance than spiritual engagement. He had served the systems that rewarded that shape of man.

The elliptical creaked as he pushed harder. His calves burned. His breath came faster. The voice in his ears touched on commodities, then global tech indices. He caught a phrase: data tells its own story. He almost laughed. He increased the incline again. This would not atone for the affair. It would not return the things left unsaid to his wife. It would not undo the calls he hadn't answered from his daughter at school or the times he'd looked away when Goldie's name came up at the table. But tomorrow, he would give the folder to Alan. He wouldn't prepare a speech. He wouldn't ask for anything in return. He would put the truth, as much of it as he could bear to name, in the hands of someone who knew what to do with it.

The podcast ended. The room fell into a mechanical quiet, no voice in his ears now to soften the churn of his pulse, no data to frame the evening's sweat in something larger. Keith reached for his towel, wiped the sweat from his brow and neck, the skin red and salted and tender with exertion. He was about to dismount when he heard it—the garage door rising in its uneven track, the sound of Allison's car lurching into place. She parked too close to the workbench, crooked, the bumper nearly kissing the storage shelves. A clumsy arrival, or deliberate. Something in the way the engine cut too fast, the silence that followed.

She opened the door without looking his way. The cabin light spilled around her, pale and accusatory. Her hair was pulled back in a clip that had lost its grip; strands clung to her neck, clumped near her ear. One side of her blouse hung loose from her pants, untucked and wrinkled. The shoes she wore now scuffed along the side. He noticed these things without deciding to.

"You okay?" he asked.

She paused. Just long enough to register the question as one that required deflection.

"I'm fine," she said, voice thin. "Just...chaotic. Tech stuff. Everyone wants a miracle at the last minute."

Her keys jingled. She still hadn't looked at him.

"You're late."

"So are half the lights. And the sound board wasn't grounding right. It took forever to fix."

He stepped off the elliptical, legs wobbled briefly. The space between them thick with unspoken things. She moved past the car, then stopped—realized there wasn't enough room between his machine and the front bumper. Her body stilled for half a beat.

"You sure you're okay?"

"I said I'm fine."

Her blouse had twisted around her waist. There was a reddish mark just above her collarbone, the kind of thing that didn't show in fluorescent light unless someone was looking. He hadn't been looking for it. But there it was. She caught him staring. Her eyes hardened.

"I was moving scaffolding," she said. "I bumped into it. It's not a big deal."

"That where you got that?"

She shrugged. "What?"

"That."

She touched her collarbone. Didn't flinch. "I told you. It's nothing."

They stood like that—two people surrounded by expensive cars and controlled climate, with nowhere to go but sideways. The air compressor kicked on near the freezer. She moved first.

"I can't get through there," she said, gesturing at the gap between the elliptical and the hood of her car. "I'll just go around."

She turned, walked briskly to the side door, didn't look back. He watched her go. Her shoes sounded different on the gravel path outside. A flat rhythm, fast and off. He stayed there, chest still rising. He hadn't asked the question he wanted to ask. Not out of fear. Something worse: the suspicion that he already knew the answer. And that if he pressed her, if he pushed even a little, they'd both have to say things that would break the last structure still standing between them.

She disappeared around the corner of the house. The side door clicked shut. He stared at the closed door as if it might open again. The silence wrapped around him. It pulsed with absences, held a kind of decay that stiffened. The elliptical blinked its cool blue readout—45 minutes, 514 calories burned, average incline 5.2—and shut itself off. Even the machine wanted no part of this.

Keith remained standing, hands on his hips, shirt damp and clinging. His legs ached. His chest itched with sweat. The residue of the workout clung to him. He had convinced himself, just an hour before, that he was reassembling something—dignity, maybe, or something adjacent. That if he gave Alan the folder tomorrow, if he stood beside the truth long enough, it would rinse him clean. But here it was again: that crack in the domestic wall, not visible to the neighbors, just the widening space between footsteps and replies. He couldn't explain to himself why this moment—his wife's shoulder turning, her voice clipped and effortful—hurt more than the vote, more than the buried toxins, more than what he had helped facilitate.

He thought of the mark on her collarbone. Her reaction flat, defensive, prewritten. It was the same tone he used in meetings when his decisions came under scrutiny. The tone that said we're not doing this here. And then the question, sharp as glass: Is this what I taught her? Had she learned it from him, this way of cloaking betrayal in logistics, of managing consequence through tone?

Keith sat on the edge of the weight bench, let his elbows drop to his knees, hands limp between them. His fingers trembled, just enough that he noticed. He'd walked closer to clarity in the afternoon. Had believed, truly, that he was nearing some moral threshold. That if he could name the lie in the soil, if he could lift that truth into someone else's hands, he might begin to reclaim the version of himself that once deserved the life he'd built.

But now, in the wake of her retreat, the bottom fell out of belief. Because it had never been about one choice. It was about the long erosion. The small permissions he'd granted himself. The children he barely knew. The woman who no longer trusted him enough to lie well. He thought about asking her. About following her into the house, into the kitchen where she'd pretend to make tea, where she'd keep her back to him while the water warmed, and asking her straight. Are you with someone else?

And he thought about what she might say. And how he would survive it. And whether he even deserved to. He reached for the towel, wiped his face again, deliberate this time, then folded it in half with shaking hands and set it on the bench beside him.

15

The Commons was immaculate, unnaturally so. Thirty-five thousand square feet of tiered turf engineered for drainage, bordered by planter beds that cost more than most single-family homes east of Summit Avenue. The city called it an urban greenspace, a "shared cultural infrastructure," though everyone knew the programming ended by seven and the gates locked automatically.

The yoga mats were unrolled in uniform rows, sponsored by a local athleisure brand whose logo adorned the lavender grip surfaces like a watermark. Above them, a suspended mesh of woven steel and netting undulated in the morning wind—shades of orange, magenta, and the bruised violet of curated optimism. It had a name, the sculpture, something meant to evoke "lift" or "weave," though no one used it. To most, it was just the net. Its presence loomed but didn't overwhelm. It was expensive, beautiful, and utterly forgettable, which was exactly the point.

Allison moved into downward dog, heels flexed toward the false grass, sweat tracking down her spine in pointed rivulets. The instructor's voice floated above the movement, amplified through a wireless mic clipped to her bra strap. Inhale, reach, elongate the body, hold. Allison watched as the sun flickered between high-rise reflections, cutting through the colored mesh in shafts of fractured light.

She focused on her breath, tried to quiet the stutter of thoughts still pinballing through her skull. It had taken everything to leave the house that morning. The way Keith had looked at her. Like he finally saw her. She had washed the mark away in the shower, bruised skin fading into concealer and a high-collared zip. Drew hadn't texted. She hadn't expected him to. Last night had been a mistake, or the continuation of a mistake. Either way, it now had a specific shape and a location on her body.

The woman next to her adjusted her stance, her mat creaking with the redistribution of weight. Rows of bodies moved together. An orchestrated sweat, arms outstretched, lungs synchronized under the hum of city mechanics: HVAC systems for the towers nearby, a distant service truck reversing into the underground parking deck, the quiet glide of a drone camera tracking morning in 4K.

Allison shifted into warrior two, thighs burning, her breath audible now in the chamber of her own chest. She knew she was strong. She had always been strong. But strength had become moral cosplay in middle age. A thing proven in public. At yoga, at volunteer sign-ins, at school board meetings. Not something lived quietly at home, where the truth had started to ooze between the silence and civility. She hadn't loved Keith in years. Not with her full self. But she hadn't planned on Drew. He was supposed to be a flirt, a joke, an indulgence with a clear endpoint. Now, she couldn't tell what it was.

The instructor's voice cut in again, guiding them toward pigeon pose. Allison dropped her right leg forward, pressed her palms into the mat. Her body bent forward into the shape of surrender. Around her, the city gleamed with its clean geometry. Glass towers reflecting blue sky, every surface scrubbed of history, every inch accounted for. She stared into the grass. It smelled like heated rubber. Nothing about it was alive. She inhaled again. Deeper this time. Let herself disappear into the motion.

The phone vibrated, a short rattle against the edge of the mat. Allison tried to ignore it. She pressed deeper into her pose, breath clenched, the weight of her own body demanding focus. But the sound kept cutting through the rhythm. Once, twice, then silence, then again. The screen lit up with each wave, throwing her own face back at her from the lock screen, its blue glow pulsing through the weave of her tote bag.

The instructor's voice climbed above the crowd—inhale, sweep the arms forward, feel the light travel from your fingertips to the spine—but the illusion was broken. The woman on the mat beside her, tight-bodied and middle-aged in coordinated separates, turned her head slightly without breaking form.

"Is that you?" she asked, sharp at the edges. "It's kind of... distracting."

Allison exhaled, more of a puff than breath. "Sorry," she said. "Sorry." She untangled from the twist of limbs, planted her palms, pushed up from the mat. Her hip cracked. Her phone was buzzing again by the time she reached for it.

She gathered her towel, slung it over one shoulder, grabbed the water bottle and the tote, the mat still unrolled behind her like an abandoned project. The grass was damp. The bottom of her foot picked up something slick. She stepped away from the formation, toward the shaded edge where the pavers gave way to a small patch of native plantings and a sign explaining the ecological history of the creek that once ran beneath the city.

She glanced down at the phone. Three missed calls.

Allison stood just beyond the edge of the green, half in sun, half in the thin shadow cast by a metal placard explaining the park's LEED certification. She stared at her phone, thumb hovering just above the glass like. Two of the calls were from Melanie Rowe, one of the more excitable theatre board members. Melanie had a permanent forward lean in her voice, the cadence narrating her own ascent to regional influence. She hadn't left a message.

The third number she didn't recognize. But it had left a voicemail. She tapped play. The voice was young, crisp, carefully modulated. Trained in the art of polite confrontation.

"Hi, Ms. Collins, this is Leah from the Gate City Observer. I'm a reporter on the civic affairs team. We're working on a developing story related to Prescott Brooks and hoping you might be willing to provide comment. Please feel free to call or text me at—"

She stopped the message before it finished. She didn't need the number again. She wouldn't call it.

Prescott. Her spine stiffened. She hadn't spoken to him in a few days, but they'd texted often. She had stood beside him in every grant meeting, every board pitch, had helped him rewrite the language on two donor packets last month. They had weathered hard seasons—this one harder than most. The theatre's operating budget had slipped dangerously close to the edge. Attendance was down. Foundations were circling, murmuring about rebranding. The mural campaign had been half publicity stunt, half lifeline.

She'd known he was under pressure. He carried it differently now. Shorter sentences. Less appetite for rehearsal feedback. She had assumed it was the usual nonprofit fatigue—that civic burnout particular to men who say things plainly in rooms that don't reward it. What would the Observer want from him? Or from her? It wasn't like Prescott chased scandal. He was allergic to ego. His only vice, if you could call it that, was stubbornness—the kind that refused to soften truth just to keep donor checks flowing. A twinge of sickness twisted in her gut. Something had happened.

The sound of a child yelling from across the lawn snapped her back. A toddler chased a soccer ball under the shade net, oblivious to structure, to funding cycles, to the editorial schedule of the

Observer. Allison turned the phone over in her hand. The plastic case was warm now. She took a breath. Held it. Released. Then she walked back to her mat, barefoot on grass that wasn't really grass, rehearsing the silence she'd offer when the paper called back.

The class had dissolved while she was at the edge of the lawn, the rows broken, the bodies dispersing like a closing ceremony. People were chatting, stretching casually, spritzing wrists with essential oils from tiny labeled bottles. The instructor was already packing up her speaker and rolled demo mat, her ponytail dark with sweat at the nape. Allison reached her own mat as the woman who'd called her out earlier was bending to fold hers. Matching towel, aluminum water bottle in a monogrammed sleeve. The woman straightened and smiled, benign now, her earlier edge released via completed exercise.

"That was a good one, right?" she said, fanning herself with one hand. "And the park—God, it's just incredible. Every time I'm here I think, this is the kind of city we're becoming, you know?"

Allison nodded, crouched to roll her mat tight, focused on the straightness of the edges.

"The sculpture," the woman continued, nodding upward at the overhead netting, "it's just—like, how lucky are we to have this as our backdrop? I mean, Charlotte's got nothing like this. And it feels safe here. You can just tell."

Allison forced a half-smile, her hands busy with the straps of her tote. "It's definitely... polished."

The woman laughed. "Right? My husband says it looks like something you'd build if money didn't matter and feedback wasn't allowed."

"That's... not far off," Allison said.

They stood for a beat in the shade of a planted magnolia. The woman slipped on her sunglasses, flipped her ponytail over one shoulder, and offered a breezy "See you next week!" before walking off, already unlocking her phone, already somewhere else. Allison stayed behind. She looked up at the sweep of color caught in the rigging above. The orange, the violet, the engineered flutter of suspended design. It moved as if weightless.

She took one last look and slung her bag over her shoulder. There was still voicemail residue in her ears, still the name Prescott Brooks clanging against her mind. The grass bent easily under her feet as she stepped toward the sidewalk, past the donation plaque, past the benches named for families she knew only by reputation.

A city becoming something, the woman had said. Becoming what? And for whom?

She was halfway down Summit, walking in the narrow shade sliver cast by parking kiosks and the old brick facades still untouched by redevelopment. A food truck labeled "Grain & Ghee" idled at the curb, spewing the smell of clarified butter and turmeric into the high-end air. Somewhere nearby, a busker was playing saxophone badly—"My Favorite Things," melting at the high notes. The luxury pet groomer on the corner had put out a collapsible water bowl for passing animal lovers.

Her phone rang. Melanie Rowe. Allison stopped. Pressed answer. Brought the phone to her ear.

"Allison—oh my God, have you seen it yet?" Melanie's voice was half-hysterical, pitched for breathless effect. "The article. The Observer just dropped it. Prescott. It's Prescott."

"What?" Allison said, flat. "What about Prescott?"

"He's resigned. Effective immediately. They just made it public. They're saying—Christ—they're saying he sexually assaulted multiple male interns. From the university program. From our program. I mean—what the hell is happening?"

The words split the air. Allison had to sit down. She spotted a bench outside the dog boutique, between two planters shaped like terriers, and lowered herself, gripping the edge with her hand.

"Melanie, slow down."

"No, no, I can't slow down, I just got off the phone with Virginia and she's in shock, we're all in shock. Apparently the interns—plural—have been giving statements for weeks and the Observer was holding it until they could get quotes from legal. It's—God, Allison. It's bad. And we just had him featured in that video with the mural kids."

Allison blinked. "Do you believe it?"

"I mean—no. Of course not. But—God, they always said he was kind of... you know."

"No," Allison said, still staring straight ahead. "I don't know."

Melanie dropped her voice. "I mean, he's always been so... particular. Private. And he did hand-pick the interns. And those weird evening rehearsals, and the way he got so controlling about the costumes this year—"

"He's gay, Melanie. Not criminal."

"I know, I know. That's not what I mean. But still—it's not a great look, Allison. And the board has to make decisions. They're already getting calls from parents. Donors."

A cyclist passed, ringing a bell with forced cheer, and nearly clipped a small child holding a matcha soft-serve. A BMW SUV with state legislative tags double-parked in front of the juice co-op. A squirrel darted under the bench and out again, pursued by nothing. Allison closed her eyes. Her heart was going too fast again, skipping unevenly. "Did Prescott say anything? Did they even let him respond?"

Melanie exhaled dramatically. "I guess he's denying everything. Of course. But the article—Allison, it has details. Names withheld, but enough to know it's real. One said Prescott asked him to come to his apartment after a lighting meeting. That he tried to—ugh—massage him. It's all gross. And this is going to kill our funding, I mean kill it. Who's going to donate to a theater that lets predators direct teenagers?"

Allison stood up. Her legs wobbled. She walked forward without a destination, phone still pressed to her ear.

"I don't believe it," she said, voice sharper now. "There has to be more to this."

"Well," Melanie said, with a tone designed for plausible deniability, "there's always more."

The call ended a few minutes later with promises of an emergency board meeting and talk of damage control. Allison didn't remember where she'd walked to—only that her shoes were pinching, her hands were cold, and that something large and invisible had just shattered the center of her known world.

The text came at a red light on Lawndale, where the landscaped medians held a new set of banners, "City of Innovation," that flapped from the poles. She read it twice.

Melanie Rowe: "Emergency board meeting. 2 p.m. At the theater."

By the time she pulled into the lot behind the community theatre—three cracked spaces, one reserved with a peeling placard for "Artistic Director"—the clock read 2:06. Melanie's car wasn't there yet. Neither was the treasurer's.

Inside, the theater's back office felt more oppressive than she remembered. A square room wedged between the greenroom and the storage closet, its walls covered in aged production posters from better years. The Piano Lesson, A Midsummer Night's Dream, Raisin, all mounted askew in matching black frames, the matting yellowing from the poor lighting and humidity. The long side table had been repurposed as a snack station for meetings since last spring—now buried under a rotating collection of tea boxes, paper napkins, unopened crackers, and a half-dozen unclaimed mugs. The folding chairs were arranged in a circle, uneven legs clattering against the warped floor. A stack of unopened programs from Much Ado leaned against the back wall, and in the corner, a foam bust of Shakespeare looked down at them.

Five board members were already there, seated stiffly, the kind of people who came to emergency meetings with pre-drafted statements. One woman wore sunglasses indoors. Another was already holding a printed copy of the Observer article, highlighted. Allison sat down, adjusted her sleeves, folded her hands. The room smelled of must. A box fan ran in the corner. Someone had brought lemon seltzer.

The door swung open and Melanie arrived, sunglasses perched on her head like an antenna, phone in one hand, legal pad in the other. Her lips were pressed into an expression of solemn authority, the kind cultivated over years of local philanthropy and mid-tier scandal.

"Okay," Melanie said, barely seated before starting. "We're all here. Let's begin."

Melanie cleared her throat like a podium had just materialized. She stood, though no one else had, and gestured toward the man who followed her in, a tall, overly tanned figure with silver hair shellacked into compliance and a leather portfolio tucked beneath one arm.

"This is Victor Ramsey," she said, lips forming the name like a film credit. "He's here to advise us on the legal implications of the current situation. Just to be clear—he is not pro bono."

A few brows lifted. Someone coughed. Allison glanced at the treasurer, who had suddenly taken interest in the condition of her pen. Victor didn't smile. He nodded once to the group, set the portfolio down on a stack of unopened programs, and leaned in.

"You've all read the article," he began. "I'm here to walk you through board exposure, organizational liability, and reputational risk. First, and most importantly: until an internal investigation has concluded and any potential civil action is resolved, you are all advised not to make public statements."

He looked directly at Allison, who held his gaze, then looked away.

"That includes press," he continued. "Social media, community partners, even donor communications. One misstatement could compromise the organization's standing, not to mention your personal indemnity."

A woman across the circle raised her hand. "Wait—so if someone from Spectrum News calls me and asks if Prescott really did it, I can't say he didn't?"

Victor didn't sigh, but he gave the verbal equivalent. "You can say: 'The matter is under review, and the board is committed to transparency and due process.' Nothing more."

Another board member, the one with the sunglasses now on her head, leaned forward. "But what if someone asks whether we knew? About the interns, I mean. Because we didn't. We didn't, right?"

That last note carried a tremor. Victor opened his portfolio and removed a thick sheaf of paper. "There are board liability standards," he said, "that hinge not on what you knew, but what a reasonable person in your position should have known."

"Jesus," someone muttered.

Allison sat motionless. The heat in the room had risen, or maybe it was just the fan pushing the same air around in circles. A single program fell from the stack behind Victor's elbow and landed flat on the floor. He paused, glanced down, ignored it.

"Any indication that complaints were filed and ignored—even informally—exposes the organization. And if any board member knew of behavior that could be construed as grooming, coercion, or hostile work environment and failed to act, the liability extends personally."

Melanie's voice broke in, soft but urgent. "That's not what happened here. Prescott was private, yes. But there were never complaints. Never paperwork. And the interns—he mentored them. We saw it."

Victor held up a hand. "I'm not here to adjudicate facts. That's not my role. I'm here to outline what happens next."

And then, as if by script, the questions came—not quite in panic, but in a kind of polite unraveling: Who's in charge of communication now? Do we need to alert insurance? Will our funding freeze? Can we access the interns' contracts? Should we suspend programming? Who makes that call? The room swelled with it. Allison said nothing. No one was asking the question that mattered most. What if it wasn't true?

Melanie stood again, this time with less grandeur, the lean of the room now tilting into the real problem: not the scandal, but the vacuum.

"We need to talk about leadership," she said, hands clasped in front of her, as if delivering bad news at a wake. "Prescott's removal—effective today—means we don't just have a PR issue. We have an operational cliff. Payroll. Programming. The Virginia Woolf production is mid-rehearsal. We still owe the mural grant a final report. And we're—" she paused, flicking her eyes toward the treasurer, "—under considerable financial strain."

No one needed the balance sheet read aloud. Everyone in the room knew the margins. The spring fundraiser had underperformed. Ticket sales were flat. The gala had been salvaged by an anonymous check—Allison knew whose hand had written it, and she could still feel the warmth of Drew pressed between her that afternoon, the moment she stepped away from the third glass of wine.

"We need someone to keep us on track, quickly," Melanie said. "Even if it's temporary. Just through this stretch."

A pause. Silence wrapped in discomfort. Eyes down. A cell phone buzzed—ignored. No one volunteered. No one even stirred. Then Melanie turned toward her.

"Allison," she said. "You've been here longer than anyone. You know the space. You've built donor relationships, managed productions, you've literally painted the stage. And—" she added with urgency, "—you have the sweat equity. No one else can step in like you can."

All heads turned. And in the middle of that long, wide silence, Allison said yes before she even realized. It wasn't ambition. It was muscle memory. She had spent years filling gaps, smoothing over tension with decisiveness. In board meetings, in committee crises, in her own home. The yes came out of her like a reflex.

"I'll do it," she said, and it felt like someone else's voice. Clear, calm, positioned.

Melanie smiled, but the relief in it was transactional.

"We'll draft an announcement this afternoon," she said. "It'll reassure the funders. We'll need you to speak at the donor's circle next week."

Allison nodded. She sat back. Her thoughts finally came. The lead role again. The deference of a costume no one else wanted to wear. The chairs were still warm when people began to scatter, murmuring fatigued goodbyes. Half the board avoided Allison's eyes. One man patted her shoulder with the same limp reassurance one offers to someone heading into surgery.

Melanie was already in motion, gathering her binder, smoothing the front of her dress as if preparing for a different meeting. "Come on," she said, tapping Allison's elbow. "Let's get you in your new office."

They moved out of the board room and into the corridor that led toward the lobby. The smell changed—less must and old carpet, more mildew and afternoon heat. Posters lined the walls here too, brittle and curling at the edges. One for a 2009 production of Les Misérables was marked with peeling gold stars. A crack ran along the baseboard, patched once and then forgotten.

Victor Ramsey, the attorney, was already halfway down the hall, portfolio tucked under one arm. He paused when he passed them.

"Good luck," he said to Allison, with a smile that wasn't really a smile. "You'll need it."

Then he was out through the main entrance, past the long glass doors streaked from years of irregular maintenance. The outer foyer—the once-grand welcome hall—was all shadow and stale air, its chandelier unlit, its coat check desk now a disused box of old programs and raffle tickets from a holiday fundraiser. Melanie gestured toward the windowless office behind the concessions stand. "Here we are."

Allison stepped inside. The air was ten degrees warmer than the hallway. One desk, two chairs, three dead houseplants. A corkboard with faded pushpins. A whiteboard bearing Prescott's faded handwriting: Next season projections – do not erase.

Melanie leaned against the doorframe. "We'll get someone in to clean. It's been, well, a while. He didn't love administrative space. Always said it killed his momentum."

Allison touched the back of the desk chair, didn't sit. "Did you know?"

Melanie blinked. "Know what?"

"About any of it."

There was a long pause. Then Melanie pulled at her necklace, gave a soft sigh.

"I knew he was... intense. Territorial. I mean, he had those kids working insane hours. I told him once—twice?—that the optics were bad. But no one ever said anything formal. Nothing written. You understand, right? There's a difference between suspicion and responsibility."

Allison didn't reply.

"You'll be great at this," Melanie said, brightening her voice like it might carry. "Really. The board's behind you. And I think this will actually be good for the theatre. Reset the narrative. A woman director. A mother, for God's sake. It's stabilizing. People like stability."

Allison gave her a look. The kind that comes just before truth or retreat.

Melanie smiled. "Anyway. You have the keys. Literally and figuratively."

And then she was gone. Off down the hall, heels clicking, the dance complete. Allison stood alone in the office, surrounded by the remnants of half-funded dreams and season brochures that hadn't aged well. The computer monitor blinked once. The phone on the desk had a sticky note on it that said line 2 is dead. She sat. Just to see how it felt.

The office smelled like aged sweat sealed in upholstery and aftershave cheap enough to linger past midnight. The desk had one working drawer, sticky from a spill never cleaned. She pulled it open and found receipts folded into quarters, illegible sticky notes, an inhaler, two corks, and a mostly faded gift card for a fusion ramen bar that closed two years ago.

The computer booted, wheezing through its start-up, desktop wallpaper still a promotional image from A Doll's House, Part 2, Nora mid-exit, defiant and pixellated. The file folders were all unlabeled in the drawer—just strings of initials and date stamps. Prescott's way of organizing.

She opened one at random: invoices. Unpaid. Dozens. Lighting rentals, costume suppliers, a muralist with an impossible name and a deadline from April. Some stamped past due, others marked with question marks and vague notations in Prescott's jagged shorthand. The financial logic was not logic. It was a fever.

The message light blinked on the desk phone. She found the voicemail tab by accident, toggling through a misaligned menu. There was one new message.

"Hey, Prescott, it's Diego. Again. Look, I've been patient, man, but it's been six weeks. I know this wasn't the plan—like, I get how grants work—but I can't float the whole wiring bill. If you can't pay this week, just let me know, okay? Just... be straight. Call me."

The message ended with a long, shaky sigh.

Allison stared at the screen. Her stomach turned. She reached for the printouts stacked behind the monitor, unfiled and damp at the corners. A spreadsheet—black and white, numbers tight against the gridlines. Titled "CF_ED_Sched3." It looked innocuous. Boring, even. She scanned it quickly, then again. Line items read like expenses—paint, fabric, catering—but the vendors didn't match anything she'd seen before. One listed address was a mailbox center in High Point. Another was a shell company for Creative Futures LLC, which she remembered only vaguely as the outfit Drew mentioned during their first post-rehearsal drink, something about brand elevation and community assets. The skin behind her ears burned.

The columns ended with totals that didn't match the ledger. Not even close. Prescott hadn't just mismanaged the books. He had moved money. Quietly. Repeatedly. Across programs, across fiscal years. Personal expenditures buried under production categories, the kind of manipulation you could only pull off if you had everyone's trust and no oversight. Thousands. Maybe more. Her breath waned.

She crouched beside the desk, then sat fully on the floor, her back against the filing cabinet. The cheap metal pressed cold against her spine. She could smell the sourness of the rug now. The spreadsheet lay beside her, the paper weightless and radioactive. She tried to do the math. She failed. She let her head fall forward. For ten full seconds, she said nothing. Then her face crumpled. And she wept. Not because she had trusted him. But because she had belonged to the theatre. Because it had been her excuse, her refuge, her justifiable absence from home. Because she had believed, even in bitterness, that she was tethered to something worthy.

After several minutes, she stood. Wiped her face with the sleeve of her blazer. Pulled the mirror from her purse and fixed her eyeliner. Outside, the cast would be arriving. Tech week. Half the costumes still needed steaming. She knew someone would be asking about the projector. She folded the spreadsheet once, slid it into her bag, and walked out of the office.

16

Goldie parked in the dappled shade of a crepe myrtle that hadn't bloomed properly in years. The canopy overhead was sparse, patchy like the hair on the back of her brother's head. The sun hit the windshield hot and sharp, and she reached for the fabric strap of her purse. Across the lot, the grocery co-op sat square and squat, its mural of fruit and neighborhood slogans faded, the bananas more gray than yellow. Vandals had tagged the bottom corner again with silver paint looping through a word she didn't recognize.

Walter's list was short, handwritten in block letters that leaned left: apples, whole wheat bread, sugar-free jam, two bags of those little nuts he liked that made his mouth feel "less wrong" after insulin. His health had been visibly slipping. He'd fainted at church two Sundays ago, too proud to call it that. Said he just "got up a little too quick." She'd watched him sweat through his collar and smile like it didn't bother him.

Their friendship had grown in the time since that afternoon visit weeks ago. He called her now. Let her sit on his porch. Let her bring him things.

The parking lot was half-full. She recognized one of the older cashiers through the glass doors stacking paper bags near the front. A little girl came out carrying a juice with both hands, dragging a woman's shadow behind her. The door opened with a mechanical whine, and inside, the air was cool. It always smelled like cardamom and cleaner in here. The produce looked just shy of proud. She moved through the aisles, her basket light but deliberate. She liked this place. Not for the prices—those could make you curse—but for the quiet, for the way people didn't pretend not to see each other. A man she didn't know nodded at her near the grains. A woman she hadn't seen since the last neighborhood meeting smiled, a close-lipped expression that seemed to say "you still at it?" Goldie adjusted the basket on her arm and gave a nod.

"Goldie Hayes," the woman said, coming in at a diagonal from the bulk bins. She wore a church choir tee-shirt under an open denim vest, her edges angular, her voice weathered smooth. "I was wondering when I'd run into you. My cousin said you stopped by Dunbar Street last week. Left that notebook with Mama."

"I did," Goldie said. "Your mama wrote a full page. Took her time, too."

"She been talking about it every day since. Talking about Mr. Womack's plum tree and how it used to lean over the fence. Said she hadn't thought about that plum tree in forty years." The woman smiled broader now, but there was something in her eyes, a glint of distance. "She got mad all over again about the dog that jumped the fence and tore up her garden. Said, 'he didn't even bark. Just walked in like he paid the rent.'"

Goldie laughed, soft in her throat. "That's the kind of memory we need. The ones that don't make the books. The ones they think don't matter."

"Well, it mattered to her. And to me, too. Made me realize I forgot what color the old fire hydrants were. Ain't that something? All that time walking past them."

"They used to be green," Goldie said, quick as you please.

The woman snapped her fingers. "That's it. Green. Not lime, not hunter—just green. You see what I'm saying? You jog something loose, and the rest follows."

"I hope it keeps following," Goldie said. "We're putting them on the wall next month. In the fellowship hall. Just until we can get a permanent space."

"I'll bring my niece by. She's learning how to draw now. Sketching old porches and chimney stacks. Might be something for her to see what memory looks like when it stands up."

Goldie nodded, her chest warming in the co-op's frigid air.

"I'd like that," she said. "We need young hands."

She thought back on Walter. About the way he'd looked out the window yesterday while telling her something she already knew—how memory wasn't just what stayed, but what kept showing up, uninvited, in the middle of making toast or washing a dish. He told her about a boy he knew from the sanitation crew, soft-voiced and bow-legged, who used to whistle in the morning while they drove out to the dump. The boy died in '81. Just another line dropped from the city's rough draft.

Goldie picked up the jam. Strawberry, no sugar added. She added another jar to the basket for herself. Something about that felt right.

Tanisha came around the corner from the grains aisle with a small canvas tote slung over her shoulder, a bunch of greens poking up like flags. She walked with the same no-nonsense posture Goldie remembered from the years after Tanisha graduated from Bennett, eyes alert, like she was always ten steps ahead of the room she'd just entered.

"Goldie," she said. "I figured I'd see you eventually if I kept showing up where people still believe in fresh vegetables."

Goldie smiled and shifted her basket. "And the stubborn ones come for the vinegar and protest flyers."

Tanisha gave a quick laugh. "You're not wrong."

They stood there a moment, between lentils and nut butters, the air full with the scent of ground sesame and bulk tea.

"I've been meeting with Yvonne," Tanisha said, leaning against the shelves like her news had weight. "Trying to carve a path through the sludge—literal and political. The Bingham Park remediation? They're stalling. She's pushing, but they keep diverting attention. Money, too. Projects downtown getting fast-tracked like somebody flipped a switch."

Goldie watched her, listened without blinking.

"I don't have proof," Tanisha continued. "But something's wrong. We think there's a reason cleanup keeps slipping. Maybe it's a budget thing. Maybe it's something worse. But we're tired of waiting to be told next quarter." She sighed, straightened. "Some of us are speaking at council next week. Not to plead. To press."

Goldie nodded. "Good. They need to see your faces."

Tanisha lowered her voice. "I thought you might say something, too. Not for us—just... you have a way of making their silence seem dishonest."

Goldie adjusted the weight of her basket again, the jars knocking together in a soft clink. "I've got something planned," she said. "At the church. Saturday after the council meeting. We're putting up the first set of memory panels—photographs, written pieces, some of the children's sketches. We've invited folks to walk through, write their own. Nothing fancy. Just real talk."

"That's more than enough," Tanisha said. "That's momentum."

"It's a warning," Goldie said, her voice like thread pulled taut. "We remember what they'd rather we didn't."

Tanisha touched her arm lightly, a brief weight. "Then I'll see you there."

The yogurt shelf was too cold, blown stiff with air from a duct overhead that blasted no matter the season. Goldie hunched into it, fingers skimming over rows of plastic cups with branding that sounded like apologies: "no added anything, guilt-free, gut-smart." She found the one Walter liked, the plain kind with the blue lid and the grainy texture he claimed "felt honest." She dropped two into the basket. The first one landed crooked against the jam.

"Diabetes gon' kill you if the city don't," she muttered, half-fussing, half-laughing, the words catching in her throat. The man standing by the dairy case glanced over. She didn't care. Talking to herself had become habit lately. She checked the list again—written in Walter's careful script like he was still filling out work orders—and found the last thing: low-sodium soup. She turned the corner and scanned the shelf, eyes quick. Same brand, different flavor. Chicken or lentil. Lentil would make him feel scolded. Chicken it was. She pulled three cans and stacked them tight.

The basket was nearly full now. Nothing indulgent, all of it careful. She looked down at it and saw a list written by a man who used to shovel slag from the edge of town, who knew how to sweep his own stoop before sunup, who remembered what it meant when dirt turned red in the rain. She had the names. She had the lab reports. She had the funeral programs in her drawer. She moved toward checkout, her joints stiff from the cold.

The automatic doors parted with a wheeze. Goldie stepped into the vestibule, sunlight waiting like it always did. Bright, too sharp, exposing what most folks preferred not to think about before noon. She paused just inside, adjusting the paper bag on her hip, her keys in one hand, the strap of her purse slipping. That's when she saw it, half-tacked, stressed at the edges under the weight of air and neglect: a city flyer stapled crooked to the corkboard beside the community bulletin.

Building a Brighter Future Together – Wellness Corridor Update.

Block lettering, teal and orange. A rendering of a smiling child skipping across some landscaped plaza that looked nothing like anywhere she'd ever stood. There was a doctored skyline in the background with buildings taller than they really were, as if the artist had drawn from ambition instead of understanding. Goldie stared at it a moment, jaw set. No one else in the vestibule noticed. One man was loading groceries into his trunk, earbuds in. Another passed behind her, hands full of something compostable. She reached up and took the flyer down, one hard tug from the top corner. The staple tore through the paper with a sound that made her teeth tighten. She folded it once, then again, tucking it into the side pocket of her purse without ceremony.

"We'll see about that," she said.

Walter was on the porch when she pulled up, his long frame bent into the same aluminum chair he always used, the one with the cracked green webbing and the legs that never sat flat. His hands rested on his thighs, wide-knuckled and open, like he was waiting on news or the weather. The porch had been swept, but the corners still held spider threads, brittle as memory. A Styrofoam cup rested on the rail beside him.

"You're late," he joked without looking.

"I'm generous," Goldie replied, approaching the porch, bag tucked in the crook of her arm. "You want exactness, get a delivery service."

He grunted, not in disagreement, but the sound of a man glad to see her. She came up the steps, knees stiff from the cold that always found its way to her joints. She passed him the bag and he took it without ceremony, setting it at his feet.

"You get the jam?"

"Two. I know how you are with toast. You treat it like communion."

He gave a small chuckle. "You know me."

She looked out over the yard, where the sidewalk buckled up around the roots of a maple that had outlived the streetscape. Somewhere, a radio spilled out gospel.

"I found something today," she said finally, pulling the folded flyer from her purse. She handed it to him the way you hand a letter from someone who doesn't write anymore.

He unfolded it, the corners catching on his calloused fingers. Read the headline. Took in the image. Sat with it a moment.

"That's the Corridor mess?"

"Supposed to be."

He shifted in the chair. "I don't see no mention of Bingham Park. Or the White Street landfill. Or anything east of Murrow, for that matter."

"You surprised?"

"No. Just tired of their empty gestures."

She nodded. "They always call it something noble. Wellness, innovation, community uplift. Like it's rude to ask what's in the runoff."

Walter folded the flyer again, tighter this time, until it fit into his palm.

"They think naming it nice is the same as cleaning it."

Goldie sat next to him, her weight creaking into the plastic chair. A breeze moved the porch's hanging fern, brushing the air just enough to remind them it was still spring.

"We're gonna speak," she said. "Next week. At council."

"You ready for all that?"

She turned her face toward him, eyes steady. "I been ready. I was just waiting on their lies to stop sounding so reasonable."

The kitchen was quiet except for the rattle of paper as she spread her lists across the table. Goldie wore her house sweater—pilled at the sleeves, thin at the elbows, still smelling of whatever she'd cooked two nights ago. There were four legal pads open in front of her, a stack of handwritten cards clipped with a black binder, and a shoebox filled with photos in no discernible order. The effect was a kind of private cartography.

They had decided, at last, to call it Cottage Grove Living Memory. Not an archive or a history project, but something still beating. A place to house what refused to be discarded. She had written the name at the top of the newest page in cursive and underlined it twice. The ink had bled a little.

She read back through her categories: Oral Testimonies. Funeral Programs. Photographs. Recipes. Street Names Lost to Redevelopment. She paused at that one. Lost to Redevelopment. She didn't know when she had first started naming the displacements like that, but it sounded right. Talleyrand Avenue, gone under the bypass. Walnut Court, now the gravel behind a dollar store. It was easier to remember when you wrote it down.

A stack of index cards rested near her teacup. She picked one at random. Elijah T. – says he remembers the park before the swings. Says it used to smell like burning tires at night. Another: Tiffany S. – Miss Lela's sweet tea. Two cups sugar to the gallon. Mint leaves if she was feeling generous. She let her hand hover over another but didn't flip it.

Her throat ached with something unnameable. The grief came and went, but what stayed was something closer to fury. The quiet, rooted kind. The kind that grows in the cracks of sidewalks, out of the places nobody bothered to pave right. She thought of her grandson again. His hands clutching his little chest, the way he had looked at her at the end like "did we lose?"

Goldie pressed her hand to the table, fingers splayed. Her nails were clean, short, ridged with the years. She thought of Walter, and the soup in his cupboard. She thought of the children who would read the words tacked to the church walls and ask who Miss Lela was, or why there used to be a park on a toxic landfill they never knew was there. She thought of the paper flyer in her purse and the word wellness printed like it could be true just because it was centered. She picked up her pen and wrote another heading: Buried Things. Then underlined it, once. Sat back. Let the pen fall. Her chest tightened and her vision blurred just enough that the page lost its edges. The anger didn't rise all at once. It leaked in, steady. Like groundwater.

The Melvin Municipal Building looked less like a seat of power than a failed Brutalist experiment softened by decades of bureaucratic compromise. Everything about it reeked of procedural delay. The lobby still bore the ghost of 1990s optimism—an information desk staffed by a lone intern and a framed photo of some former mayor posed with an American Idol celebrity no one remembered. Upstairs, the council chambers spread out in the shape of polite control: wood veneer panels, fixed seating, a row of dais microphones that gave every speaker the voice of someone apologizing for their own civic engagement.

Outside, the banners still read One Greensboro, though depending on which side of Church Street you were born on, you knew there were at least three.

Goldie entered without pretense. She carried a bag with nothing in it for show. In her coat pocket, she had the folded flyer from the wellness corridor campaign. The corners were soft now. She'd carried it like a memento she meant to show someone eventually.

The chamber air was dry in a way that made people cough more than usual, and the acoustics, despite three expensive remodels, still flattened every public comment into a version of "thank you for your time."

The gallery seats were half full—retired teachers, clergy, a man in a Panthers jersey who came bi-weekly to shout about code enforcement. A few staffers scurried like ants behind the glass. The mayor was already seated, blinking into her iPad, scrolling with the detached rhythm of a woman checking her 401k before voting on sewer allocations. Lyle Dent and Kathy Hoffman chatted in staged whispers about a downtown bid for a new parking deck that would anchor the latest hotel project near the baseball stadium.

A new mural had been installed in the hallway—a vaguely triumphant landscape of civil rights icons standing just slightly apart from one another, each rendered in pastel defiance, their gazes directed upward, away from the broken air vent in the corner. There was no plaque acknowledging the 1979 Greensboro Massacre, nor any mention of how the police had, back then, taken lunch breaks while the Klan reloaded.

But progress, they liked to say, was a long arc. They printed that phrase on grant applications. They said it during ribbon cuttings and when canceling bus routes that once reached Cottage Grove. The chamber lights dimmed as the city clerk read the meeting's opening lines with the tone of someone trying not to wake a baby.

Goldie found a seat in the second row, center left, behind the same man who used to run the soundboard at her church before he left for Charlotte and a job that didn't require miracles. He turned and gave her a nod. She returned it. She had no speech written. She didn't need one. This was the kind of room where lies dressed themselves in progress and hoped no one would notice. But she hadn't come to be noticed. She had come to be remembered.

The press row, such as it was, stretched along the left flank of the chamber. Two tables pushed together amidst a tangle of power strips and plastic badges. The reporters arrived with the choreography of people who'd done this enough times to know where the outlets were and which chairs didn't creak. There was the girl from the student paper at A&T, tapping furiously on a borrowed MacBook with a cracked screen. Next to her, a man from the Observer, gray at the temples, already frowning like the meeting owed him something. A freelancer from one of the weekly outlets came late, carrying a messenger bag and the kind of camera that signaled he once covered protests in cities that mattered more. He scanned the room through the lens, adjusting the aperture like anticipating disaster. Further down, a blogger known mostly for exposing convenient municipal contracts set up a tripod with a shotgun mic and the confidence of knowing just how far you could push a public records request.

They didn't speak to each other. They rarely did. They communicated in glances, sighs, and the occasional side-eye during long proclamations. They wore blazers, utility jackets, press badges with peeling stickers. Most of them had written about the wellness corridor project at least once. Soft features spun from press releases, cut with one quote from a concerned neighbor. The hard stuff never made print. The hard stuff didn't sell ads.

At the dais, the mayor raised her chin, tapping the gavel once.

"We'd like to begin tonight by recognizing the volunteers from this year's citywide clean-up initiative. If the team from Action Greensboro would please stand..."

Scattered applause. A dozen young professionals in branded polos rose in unison, smiling like interns. Behind them, a small cluster of fifth graders from Hampton Elementary fidgeted in matching t-shirts, trying to look attentive as the mayor mispronounced their teacher's name. Goldie waited in her seat. The speechifying would take ten minutes, maybe fifteen. A parade of acknowledgments before they opened the floor to people who didn't smile for ribbon cuttings. She glanced at the press row. One reporter already had his hand over his mouth, mouthing the lines he'd heard a dozen times before. The cameras weren't rolling yet. But they would be.

Tanisha's name was called just as the last round of civic acknowledgments fizzled into a polite murmur. Four young scholars from a middle school coding program had received commendation plaques the size of cafeteria trays, and one was still cradling hers like a fragile heirloom. The mayor leaned forward, scanned the sign-up sheet, and read her name without pause or inflection.

"Tanisha Clarke. You have three minutes."

She walked to the podium with her back straight, deliberate. Her blazer was navy, fitted, and her braids were pulled back with precision. Her face betrayed nothing. Only focus. A woman familiar with rooms like this and unimpressed by their rituals. She adjusted the mic. A screech of feedback. The council flinched.

"Good evening," she said, voice steady. "My name is Tanisha Clarke. I serve on the board of the Guilford Wellness Alliance, and I'm also a resident of East Greensboro."

She let that last part sit a second.

"I'm here tonight to ask a question that's been asked before, probably in this very chamber. Why does the east side of town wait years for environmental remediation while the west side receives landscape architects, lighting consultants, and community branding experts within a single fiscal cycle?"

She looked down the row of council members. Most were still, eyes softening into that attentiveness public officials cultivate when confronted with facts they have no current intention of acting on.

"I've compared the public funding breakdown for the South Elm Wellness Corridor and the Bingham Park remediation. The numbers don't lie. More money has been spent on playground renderings, street banners, and bike-share pilot programs downtown than has been allocated to clean up a public neighborhood park with known soil contamination."

There was a flicker of movement—one of the at-large members glanced toward an aide, who showed him something on a tablet.

"I'm not here to assign motives," Tanisha continued, keeping her hands loosely clasped in front of her. "I'm here to point out patterns. I'm here to remind this council that environmental wellness doesn't mean new signage or another art walk. It means equitable investment. It means that the zip code you live in should not determine the air your children breathe or the soil they play on."

She didn't raise her voice.

"We are not asking for more. We are asking for fair. And if the word wellness is going to be printed on every grant application, website banner, and utility bill, then I suggest it be reflected in the budget."

Tanisha stepped back. Nodded once. And returned to her seat. No flourish. Light applause.

The room held a beat of real silence.

Then the mayor blinked, looked down again, and called the next name.

"Goldie Hayes."

Goldie rose slowly, not because she was unsure but because her knees demanded it. The second row chair creaked as she lifted her weight forward, one hand steadying the strap of her purse, the other brushing against the folded flyer tucked in the pocket of her coat. The room hadn't gone quiet—nothing ever truly quieted in this place—but there was a perceptible pause, the way a room leans before the words come.

The aisle between rows was narrow, upholstered chairs on either side stiff and too close, the carpet worn into a matted path. She walked it with the measured cadence of church aisles and cemetery grass, to processions that meant something. A camera clicked twice from press row. Yvonne Hightower caught her eye and nodded from the dais, warm at the edges, a nod of encouragement and witness. Dent pretended to glance at his notes but didn't flip the page. Hoffman looked past her entirely, eyes fixed on a point three inches above Goldie's shoulder as though she were reading an invisible teleprompter.

Goldie's pulse thumped in her ears as the steps brought her closer. As she approached the podium, her body betrayed her with a flicker of memory: her grandson in his Halloween costume, cardboard robot arms painted silver, his laugh sharp and high as he ran crooked down her front walk. Then, without warning, the hospital bed. The beeping. The small, wild silence of his hand in hers. She didn't cry. But the breath that came next snagged in her chest. The microphone loomed like it knew the whole story already. The TV monitor above the council zoomed in, mechanically, her face blooming in pixelated closeness. She stopped. Centered herself and took a breath. A deep one. Anchored, pulled from the bottom of her feet. Then she leaned forward. Not toward the mic, but toward destiny.

"Good evening. My name is Goldie Hayes. I was born three miles from here and I've lived my whole life in Greensboro, except for the years we followed my husband's work up and down I-40. I buried him in 1998, and I buried my grandson in 2001. He was eleven years old, and by the time we knew what was eating him alive, there was nothing the doctors could reverse. They said it was environmental. Said it like a thunderstorm. Like it just happened.

"Now, I didn't come here tonight for comfort. I came for the record. For memory. Because y'all have made it clear what's convenient to forget.

"The park I live next to—Bingham Park—used to be a landfill, and before that it was the incinerator site for the city's refuse. But it wasn't just trash. It was chemical waste, ash, scrapings from vehicles, runoff from factories, incinerated rubber, debris from riots and burnouts. You dumped your mess there for thirty years and then you called it a park. You slapped grass over it and built a playground on top. For the Black kids. The poor kids. The disposable ones.

"You didn't clean it. You renamed it.

"I am not a scientist, but I can read a report. I can see the red runoff that still comes up in the rain. I have watched the kids get sick. I have walked the path where no grass grows no matter how many seedings. I have counted the names on the funeral programs in my church. You don't need degrees to recognize a pattern. You just need to live long enough.

"What makes this city beautiful—what made it beautiful—was not your vision statements or your wellness corridors or your innovation zones. It was the people who held the memory. Who stayed. Who kept the doors of the church open when the pews were almost empty. Who passed down stories because the official version kept revising itself.

"We remember everything.

"We remember when Martin Luther King was supposed to come here in '68 but didn't because Memphis was calling. We remember the armored vehicles rolling through East Market in 1969. We remember the lies they told about the riot at Dudley. We remember the massacre in 1979 that you still can't say out loud. You keep naming buildings after people while poisoning the ground others stood on.

"And now, with Bingham Park, you are doing it again. But slicker. You move the cleanup funds down the street to a parcel you actually want to redevelop. You cap the land, not to heal it, but to profit from it. And you leave us breathing it in. Again. You sit up there and call it revitalization. You write grants in the name of communities you've never walked through without a ribbon to cut.

"You don't get to poison our children and then rebrand our neighborhoods as opportunities.

"You don't get to disappear the dead.

"You don't get to memory-hole your mistakes and pave the grief of a people into something marketable.

"This isn't me asking. This is me witnessing.

"You can nod. You can scribble your notes. You can thank me for my time. But when you sleep tonight—and every night after—I hope you dream of toxic dirt that won't stay buried.

"I hope you dream of the names. Because we'll still be saying them long after the last mural fades. And when the reckoning comes, don't say you weren't told.

"I just told you."

17

Alan crossed the quad with his coat half-buttoned and a cup of coffee gone lukewarm in one hand, the sleeve of his other arm pushed back to check the time every few steps though he already knew he was early. Spring had broken open in the most dramatic way—crabapple trees broadcasting pink like they'd been coached, students in shorts pretending it wasn't still fifty-two degrees, campus tour groups stopping mid-path to marvel at sustainability signage installed by the latest facilities initiative no one had voted on. A new sculpture had gone up outside the student union: three interlocking metal rings titled Emergent Possibility by someone with a Guggenheim grant and no roots in the Piedmont. Alan nodded at it as he passed, unsure whether the rings were meant to represent collaboration or just take up space.

The brick path glistened where the maintenance crew had pressure-washed it over the weekend, erasing whatever protest chalk had been scribbled down before alumni day. He passed two faculty members from the business school deep in discussion about converting unused lecture space into a "flexible innovation lounge." Another clutched a tote full of glossy university magazines featuring a Black alumnus on the cover and seven pages of content about new donor-facing partnerships with biotech firms from Raleigh.

Alan didn't mind the pageantry. He minded the amnesia.

He was still riding the clarity of Goldie's speech. He'd watched it twice on WFMY's website, once casually while making toast, then again with the volume up loud, alone in his kitchen, muttering agreement before she even reached the midpoint. The paper's coverage had been better than expected. A full column above the fold. They had chosen a still frame where her eyes locked on the dais—serious, unreadable. She'd said what he'd never managed to fit into four op-eds and a panel at the historical society. And she'd done it with the city's logo displayed behind her in high definition. Tonight was her exhibit. He looked forward to it with the anticipation he reserved for things that weren't designed by committee. It had been years since he'd attended anything that felt handmade.

He reached the side door of the urban studies building, badge clipped to his belt, a sleeve of papers tucked under his arm. The building's facade had been updated last year with funds from a regional rebranding campaign—new signage, ADA-accessible walkways, planters filled with drought-tolerant sedge. The interior still smelled like old photocopiers and whatever glue they used to hold carpet to concrete.

Inside, the hallway was quiet. Office doors closed. The world was elsewhere. Alan moved at his usual pace, deliberate, but alert. He still believed in presence. The daily act of showing up. He opened his office and found it unchanged. A chair, a desk, the return of air through a vent that had been broken since October. A manila envelope sat on his keyboard.

He removed his coat, draped it over the back of the chair, and placed the coffee down without looking at the envelope again just yet. He was still thinking about Goldie. That was where the day would begin. With her voice, still echoing where it mattered. He turned toward his computer, the screen blinking sleepily to life. He nudged the envelope aside with the back of his hand—too light to be threatening, too dull in shape to stir interest. Likely a galley copy of a new book on urban renewal from some think tank out of Atlanta or Austin, the kind that argued you could gentrify ethically if only you invited enough artists and farmers' markets to the opening ceremony. Or else it was from a student who still believed "final project" had a floating deadline.

The computer password box blinked twice, as if asking whether today really required logging in. He entered it without ceremony. Two browser tabs sprang to life: his email inbox—full of committee agendas and uninvited panel solicitations—and the open thread he'd left running on a social media app.

Goldie had detonated.

Her name was trending locally. The local TV news clip had been re-shared by housing advocates, climate justice groups, a food pantry, and one statewide candidate who had clearly not watched the whole thing but had decided her line about dirt and memory was quote-friendly. Some of the usual ghouls in the comments were seeding cynical doubt—do we have confirmation on the contamination levels?—but they were being outpaced, for once, by people repeating her words with reverence usually reserved for protest chants and scripture.

He scrolled through tags: @cottagegrovecoalition, @greensboroiswakingup, @wearethestudy. The last one had posted a photo from inside the council chamber, Goldie at the podium, eyes sharp and chin set. The caption read: Say her name. Then listen. A hundred and eighty-six shares.

Alan felt a twitch behind his left eye. Joy, maybe. But also a low-grade panic, the kind that came when you knew the moment was rising and you weren't entirely sure if you were meant to speak into it or stay the hell out of its way. He clicked through the coverage. The Observer had run her image above the fold. WFMY ran a short segment calling her "a community elder and environmental memory-keeper." Lyle Dent had made a statement about transparency in development that read like it had been drafted in the back seat of his Uber.

Alan sipped his coffee. Cold. Bitter in that particular office way, as if punishment had been engineered into the brewing system. Then he turned to the envelope. He slid it forward with both hands, the seal already loosened. No return address. No label. Not unusual. Academics sent things like they assumed everyone had limitless time and curiosity.

He opened the flap. Inside was a thumb drive and a stack of printed documents, binder clipped. The top page was a city memo. The header looked familiar. Alan froze, then leaned back in his chair. He set down the coffee without drinking. This was not a book. This was not a student project. This was something else.

He laid everything out with care. The USB drive, matte black and unbranded, cold to the touch. The spreadsheet, printed in grayscale, lines too tight, title cell too vague to read. The GIS parcel overlay—map grid with numbered sectors, a shaded blot in the lower quadrant that meant something if you already knew what you were looking for. The post-it note, off-yellow, the ink slightly smeared but unmistakably Keith's: You were right. You just didn't have the whole map. —K.

Alan stared at the note for a full thirty seconds before touching anything else. Keith. Not a man of risk or a man of drama. The kind of man who always brought his own pen to meetings and read bylaws aloud. For him to send this—anonymously, no less—meant the contents weren't conjecture. They were pressure points.

He started with the spreadsheet. The label—UWC_ParcelB_RECLASS_final.xls—told him immediately that it wasn't meant for public eyes. "Reclass" wasn't a term that made it through press releases. It was internal shorthand. Obfuscation packaged as process.

The rows listed cost centers, soil data, funding reallocations coded in numerical shorthand. It took him a minute to orient himself. Then he saw it—two lines separated by three fiscal quarters. One labeled Bingham Park Soil Remediation, Phase I. The other, six cells down, Parcel 524-B Site Prep – Community Wellness Zone. The numbers were identical. Down to the cent. He blinked. Ran a finger down both columns. Not a pivot. A rebranding. They had moved the funds. Quietly, surgically. Not stolen, exactly. Just... redirected. Bingham Park had been repurposed on paper without anyone telling the neighborhood.

The map clarified it. GIS layers stacked with false neutrality—parcels shaded in blue for "under development," green for "remediated," and an off-white void for what didn't count. Parcel 524-B had a green tag now. A cap-and-cover designation. But the underlying core samples—he could see the old borehole sites on the overlay—mapped directly over the planned playground and mural installation. And it wasn't cleaned. It was covered. He sat back. Mind ticking. He pulled open his laptop and inserted the USB drive.

Three folders: Legal, Correspondence, Photos.

Inside Legal: redlined drafts of the environmental impact report, one version with a clause about chromium levels struck clean through. Inside Correspondence: email chains, many from domain names ending in .gov and .org, about messaging strategy and "risk perception management." David Moss's name appeared six times. One note read: "Frame 524-B as part of the 'wellness arc'—avoid toxic associations in all public materials."

Photos folder: aerial images, timestamped, of soil dumpsites and excavation trucks. One labeled May1969_Bingham-Fill_SouthElm.tif.

He stood. He walked to the window and stared out across the quad. Students lounged in the sun like it was any other Thursday. A girl was practicing clarinet under the trees near the history building. Someone rode past on a scooter that bore the city's new wellness logo, printed in kelly green. Alan ran a hand through his hair, then back over his face. His mouth was dry. He turned, sat again. The folder sat open on his desk. Keith's note was still there, his tidy guilt scrawled in Sharpie.

Alan whispered once, aloud, not in awe, not in anger—just to say it in the room:

"They fucking buried it."

He double-clicked the first file and the screen filled with the kind of memo that didn't get printed unless someone was worried about being caught. The header read CONFIDENTIAL – LEGAL REVIEW – DO NOT DISTRIBUTE, followed by a list of recipients who all had job titles ending in strategic advisor or project counsel. Alan scanned it slowly, line by line. The language was bloodless, lawyered to death and then reanimated into euphemism.

"In external-facing materials, references to soil composition at 524-B should adopt the 'pre-regulatory mineral presence' framework approved in Item 4c."

Pre-regulatory mineral presence. Not toxicity. Not Chromium VI. Not carcinogenic compounds in playground soil. No, the term had been reshaped into something both dignified and meaningless. An inheritance of inconvenience. Language meant to stand in place of accountability, sculpted like corporate signage, full of curves and no edges. He opened the next file. A map rendered in grayscale, 524-B in the center, boreholes marked like old wounds. Six were labeled with red dots. Below, a caption: Cr(VI) levels exceed baseline in 6 of 9 core samples. Depth: 3.2–5.6 meters.

He toggled to the final report the city released—the one Goldie had tried to get through public records and was told was still "under legal review." No red dots. No caption. The same map, sterilized. Parcel 524-B shaded a reassuring mint green with a footnote: All readings within acceptable environmental standards.

He leaned in. Clicked next. The side-by-side comparison file. A split screen of public versus internal filings. On the left, the press release: The 524-B site has undergone necessary environmental review and meets the city's commitment to community health and wellness. On the right, the internal draft: Remediation incomplete. Recommend cap-and-cover approach. Avoid further excavation due to pre-regulatory chemical absorption. That line was cut from the final version. The lie wasn't in omission. It was in the architecture.

Another file. Budget reallocation documents. He read the line deliberately. Twice.

Transfer: $822,000 from Bingham Park Environmental Remediation, Phase I → Wellness Corridor Anchor, Parcel 524-B – Site Prep and Public Engagement (Murals & Playground).

Date: Nine months ago. Before the mayor's photo-op. Before the fake groundbreaking. Before Goldie stood at the podium with her dead grandson on her tongue. The screen glared back at him. Nothing in bold. Nothing in red. Only plain numbers and unremarkable rows. Except this was the moment. This was where it happened. Not in smoke-filled rooms, not behind locked doors, but right here—in a spreadsheet cell on a Thursday at 3:42 p.m., logged and initialed by a senior budget analyst with a Gmail alias.

He sat still. His breath shallow. Everything Walter had said. The red dust. The trucks. The timing. Everything Goldie suspected. Buried soil. Quiet rerouting of the community's money. Everything Alan had intuited in half-read editorials and roundtable panel critiques, now printed in twelve-point Arial on a PDF no one had ever meant to be read.

His pulse quickened. He looked again at the file tree. Each document opened was a hinge. A small, unforgiving turn.

He pulled Walter's notes from the manila folder where he kept old field memos and recorded interviews. The kind of archive he never trusted to the cloud. Walter's voice still lived in the margins: Red clay, south of the textile spur, creek cutting east. That part had sounded too specific when he first heard it, like the kind of detail invented to make a story sound believable.

He opened his file drawer and found the student lab notes from six years back—notes he'd dismissed as overcautious, inconclusive. The photos were low-res, time-stamped, taken with a borrowed camera during a class project on historical industrial waste sites. The dirt in one was vivid, unmistakable. Not rust. Not clay. Runoff, red as brick powder, spread across a ditch as if someone had spilled a story and walked away. The chemical analysis below it—barely legible in pencil—listed Cr(VI) with an asterisk: "possible contaminated fill, source not confirmed." No one followed up. The semester ended. The class moved on.

He reached for Keith's map, unfolded it across his desk. He brought up the GIS parcel data, zoomed in, south of the old textile spur line, the creek cutting east behind the burned-out auto yard. The coordinates lined up exactly. Every pin. Every line. Walter's memory had been precise, down to the bend in the slope where runoff would have naturally pooled before seeping toward the gutter.

The student's blurry photograph. Keith's reclassified map. Walter's story, told like a confession. They were all describing the same act. It was never two sites. It was one. Bingham Park's red dirt, dug up under cover of crisis in 1969, trucked across the city, dumped south of the tracks, and then—forty years later—resurrected, capped, landscaped, and reborn as the center of a wellness corridor.

He whispered it once, the phrase barely audible even to himself.

"They buried the same dirt twice."

Then louder, not in anger, but in awe at the scope of it.

"And this time, they landscaped it."

He printed the map without adjusting the margins. Let it cut off slightly at the edges, just enough to feel unresolved. The ink still wet when he pinned it to the corkboard beside his desk. Thumbtacks pressed in with his palm, firm and without hesitation. On the left side: Bingham Park, the chain-link fence still visible in the aerial, the same one that had rusted down the middle like it had been split on purpose. On the right: Parcel 524-B, labeled in clean sans-serif font as part of the Wellness Corridor Community Zone. On the new marketing materials, it had a micro-theater now. Outdoor seating arranged in semicircles like something holy might happen there. He took the Sharpie from the drawer. The thick one, the one that bled through paper if held too long. Wrote in block letters above the map, pressed harder on the final word.

EQUIVALENT CONTAMINATION. UNEQUAL RESPONSE.

He stepped back. Just enough to see the page as an artifact. There was no diagram left to draw. No argument left to map. It was all there. Parallel outcomes. Divergent care. Then he sat. Hands flat on the desk. Breathing low, long, pressed out. The kind of breath that came after certainty. There was no need to pace. No urge to call. No instinct to explain. He looked straight ahead, past the map, into the dead wall space that carried nothing.

"They knew," he said, the words shaping in the back of his throat before they left his mouth. "Keith knew. Paula probably knew. And they let it happen anyway."

No one was there to hear it. That was fine.

Outside his window, the quad carried on. A group of students passed, their playful voices rising in a way that made the quiet in the office seem tighter. Somewhere beyond that, the city kept moving. The planning board. The zoning committee. The next press release already halfway drafted. He thought of Bingham Park. The sinking basketball court. The fence sagging where someone had kicked a ball too hard. The memorial bench with no name engraved, just IN LOVING MEMORY and a date range.

He had always suspected. But now he was finished suspecting. Now he knew.

He closed each window with precision, the cursor hovering over each red X like it was marking something for burial. The desktop returned to its static blue silence. He didn't need the screen anymore.

The USB drive sat warm in his palm before he put it into the drawer, tucked beside a paperclip coil and a half-empty pack of mints, domestic clutter that had never carried consequence.

The room felt clearer now. As if everything he had suspected had been scooped out and named, made firm and knowable. There was no argument left to construct, only the truth to place—gently, like a stone—where everyone could see it. He reached for the legal pad, a fresh sheet open before him. He wrote without lifting his wrist:

Publish with Goldie before the next city meeting.

The words looked stable there, unadorned. An intention, fully formed. He underlined it once. He looked at the line a moment more, then reached for the desk phone. He lifted the receiver and dialed. The plastic cool against his ear. The tone steady.

It rang once.

Then Ava's voice—alive, direct, unguarded:

"Alan?"

He inhaled once. Held it. And then he spoke.

Alan parked two blocks south, just past a cinderblock hair salon and a vinyl-sided duplex with a tarp covering half of the roof. The church lot was already packed with SUVs, an aging Buick with peeling clear coat, two electric vehicles straddling a gravel patch someone had tried to landscape with river rock and hope. He hadn't expected this. A Thursday night. A church basement. He'd assumed twenty people, maybe thirty. Finger snacks. Maybe a pitcher of tea.

He walked reverently, hands in his jacket pockets, the sidewalk cracked and heaving from root systems older than the wellness corridor project's branding consultants. The early evening air still held warmth. Porch lights flicked on down the block like a pulse. Outside the church, voices spilled out through the open doors—laughter, the scrape of metal chair legs, someone calling out a name over the music. The sign above the entry was hand-painted on muslin: What We've Lived, What We Carry. The font was uneven, deliberate. No grant-funded design firm had laid this out in Adobe. It had been made by hand. The brushstrokes still visible. He paused just before the threshold. He adjusted his collar, exhaled once, and stepped into the light spilling from the church vestibule, warm and wide and unashamed.

The fellowship hall had been remade. Not decorated but transformed. The tables were gone, the linoleum floors buffed to a shine that reflected the warm flood of light. The air smelled like glue sticks and acrylic, and whatever cheap markers the kids had used in long streaks across the butcher paper taped to every vertical surface.

Quotes looped the room in handwriting that varied from reverent cursive to sharp block letters. My mama never trusted the city's water, read one. They only paved our street after the mayor's cousin moved in, said another. Some were signed. Some anonymous. All unapologetic.

To his left, a memory wall—collages assembled on foam board, snapshots layered without symmetry: kids in church shirts, faded birthday parties, plastic lawn chairs, parking lots before they became redevelopment targets. Elders stood around one of the boards, pointing at faces, arguing about who had the better jump shot in '73. A woman in a green sweater said, "That's when we still had the big sycamore in front of 1310," and a man beside her replied, "That tree got taken down like it owed somebody money."

Near the far wall, a teenager sat at a folding table with an iPad, typing quickly, eyes flicking up only to ask, "What year was that again?" Another leaned over a map of Bingham Park printed in black and white, adding colored pins where residents had reported ooze, leachate smells, or soil collapses. Each pin had a Post-it attached with a first name and an age.

A girl, maybe sixteen, scanned a QR code printed on the wall above a collage labeled WATERLINES. Alan heard the voice from a recessed speaker: a recording of an old man, dry-voiced and exacting, describing how the pipes used to whistle in the winter and turn the sink water yellow when the furnace kicked on. The girl listened, nodded, then tapped a checkbox on the screen beside her. It synced. Documented. Lived and now stored.

Alan stood just inside the door, still holding his coat. This wasn't documentation. It wasn't grievance. It wasn't even resistance—not the way power meant the word. It was something older, and far more difficult to refute. This was governance without permission. Policy by memory. Testimony made physical. A room that no longer needed to demand justice because it had begun to build its own.

Alan wove through the clusters, shoulder brushing against canvas and paper and life. The room had no formal aisles, just pathways made by presence, and every table demanded pause. He passed one covered in brown craft paper layered with hand-drawn maps. Neighbors had written in their own street names, their own corner stores, their own erased landmarks in red Sharpie and pencil. A little boy was tracing one with a marker, tongue between his teeth, while his grandmother narrated which houses used to have popular porches and which ones had vanished in silence.

Toward the back of the room, near a table repurposed as an archival display, stood Goldie—coat off, sleeves rolled, notebook tucked under one arm. Three women leaned in close, one with a hand resting lightly on Goldie's shoulder, another laughing so hard she'd started to tear up. A young man nearby was nodding, taking notes on his phone, like the stories might vanish if he didn't catch them fast enough. Beside the table sat Walter, legs stretched out, cane leaning against the folding chair. He wore a clean windbreaker zipped to the top, eyes bright, like he was watching his own party and it was going better than he expected. Alan approached in wonder. Goldie saw him before he spoke, nodded once with a quiet kind of warmth, and turned to finish a sentence. When she did face him, it was with neither surprise nor ceremony.

"You made it," she said.

"I wouldn't have missed it," Alan replied. He looked around. "This is—this is more than a presentation."

Goldie shrugged like she'd already worked through the awe. "It was just the notebooks at first. People wrote more than I thought they would. Then we ran out of space. Then people started bringing their own stories. Photos. Letters. A woman brought her mother's recipe for vinegar pie and said, this is memory too. And she was right."

Walter chuckled beside her. "Some folks needed a place to tell it. Others just needed to be asked."

Alan turned to him. "You're part of this, then."

Walter leaned back slightly, fingers laced over his stomach. "I remember things. That's all. Turns out remembering out loud is more dangerous than people thought."

Goldie gestured around them. "We've had schoolkids come in to draw what they think their street looked like before the warehouses. Elders leave voicemail stories. We're working with a coder to build a walking tour app—just audio and location. You stand on a corner and it tells you what used to be there."

Alan blinked. "How did you scale this so fast?"

Goldie glanced around. "We didn't scale it. It just kept growing. It's what happens when you stop asking for permission and start writing your own record."

Walter added, "They can call it a corridor if they want. We've got one too. Ours starts here."

Alan didn't respond right away. The table in front of them was covered in photos, quotes, fragments written in child and elder hands. There was no masterplan, no five-figure consultant. And still, it was whole. He glanced at Goldie again. She didn't look triumphant. She looked busy. Like this was only the beginning. There was no announcement or spotlight. There was a lull in the sound—the way voices still when something is about to begin—and Goldie stepped toward the podium near the altar steps. The room leaned in with her.

Alan was standing near the memory quilt display, half-hidden by a poster board of obituaries arranged by street. When she began to speak, he moved no closer. He wanted to see her from the edge. Wanted to feel the current without interfering with it. Goldie's voice rose, steady, the kind of cadence shaped by real use, like a tool passed down until it fits in the hand without effort.

"I want to thank the mothers who left work and came straight here, uniforms still on, tags still clipped to their collars. I want to thank the teenagers who took time from whatever else they had going and decided that listening to their elders wasn't beneath them."

A few heads nodded. A woman near the piano murmured, "Go on, now."

"I want to thank the artists who didn't ask what the budget was. Who brought tape, and chalk, and whatever else they had, and made it work. I want to thank the students who asked the right kind of questions. The kind that don't come with funding."

The crowd had gone still, not quiet—there was always the shuffle of feet, the energy of children near the back—but still in that way that means a room is paying attention with more than ears.

"We've been told this story was marginal. That memory is nostalgia. That if we want investment, we have to erase the parts of ourselves that came before the grant cycle. We've been asked to make ourselves legible to systems that never saw us."

Her voice didn't rise, but it deepened, grounded itself.

"This? This is us seeing ourselves. Fully. Not filtered through metrics. Not cleaned up for redevelopment. This is us naming what was stolen and where it was buried. Not just the soil. The futures. The life."

Alan could feel it in his chest. A deep, involuntary understanding that what she was building couldn't be absorbed, couldn't be managed, couldn't be folded into the wellness corridor and renamed success. Goldie took one step forward, hands at her sides, eyes sweeping the room.

"This is just the first," she said. "This is the soft light before the fire."

A pause.

"We are going to map our grief into their infrastructure. You hear me? Our pain is going to be load-bearing."

And then the room broke open.

Not with clapping alone—though there was that, hard and full—but with voices. With foot stomps. With the sound of presence affirming itself. It wasn't polite. It wasn't planned. It had nothing to do with politics and everything to do with memory becoming matter.

Alan bore witness. He stayed near the back wall, just behind a taped grid where kids had drawn hopscotch beside quotes from people born long before asphalt. The room had settled again, the applause morphing into conversation, the chairs shifting, someone pressing play on another recording loop.

Goldie stepped down from the podium without fanfare. She didn't retreat. She re-entered. First to the boy with the marker-stained fingers, crouching to look at his drawing. Then to the woman who had spoken during the early testimony hour, the one who had described the smell of soil like a burnt iron. They embraced quickly, like people who didn't need to explain.

She answered a question from a student with a lanyard and a notepad, nodded once, pointed toward a display about zoning changes from 1984. She rested her hand lightly on an elder's shoulder, tilted her head to hear a question without asking the person to speak up. She picked up a dropped program from the floor and slid it onto a table without breaking stride. Alan watched all of it with that specific kind of clarity that arrives too late to be useful and too exact to ignore. He had brought data. Footnotes. Annotated reports. He had written op-eds with compound sentences and quiet outrage. And she—she had brought presence. She wasn't arguing for legitimacy. She embodied it.

He thought: This is what leadership looks like. Not titles. Not budget line items. This.

She moved through the space as if nothing about her asked to be noticed. Everything about her made the noticing unavoidable. He felt admiration. And also something closer to shame. He had been looking for allies. For someone to amplify. She didn't need him.

Near the exit, beside a folding table draped with a vinyl cloth and a shallow plastic tub of name-tags, Alan stood with his coat slung over one shoulder. The Sharpie lay uncapped on the edge, bleeding into the paper like it had decided it was done being useful. Most of the labels had been filled in with first names only—Miss Lela, Andre, Yvonne, Keisha with an asterisk—as if surnames had always belonged more to bureaucracy than to the community inside this room.

Goldie joined him. Her blouse was lightly creased at the hem, a mark of movement, not disorder. Her shoes were sensible, worn but clean. She'd stood for hours. There was no sign she'd felt it. Alan watched the last few attendees funnel out, offering thank-yous to the volunteers and hugging each other like they were leaving church after an altar call that had somehow spilled into urban reform. He had the brief, idiotic urge to say something academic about narrative space, to find the perfect phrasing for what she'd constructed—community as method, storytelling as infrastructure—but stopped himself just in time.

He nodded toward the room, the walls thick with taped memory and unsanctioned truth.

"It's incredible," he said. "You did it."

Goldie didn't look away. "We're just getting started."

She turned slightly, enough to catch his profile.

"You ready to publish?"

He didn't hesitate. Not because it was simple—nothing about this was simple—but because the toxic park no longer permitted delay. He'd stood inside something tonight that left no room for abstraction. He turned to her, full weight of the thing behind his words now.

"With this behind it?" he said. "Absolutely. But I've got one more field sample to secure."

The rain hadn't let up all evening. It was just enough to soak without offering the excitement of a storm. Water streamed down the gutters on South Elm in thin, continuous lines, carrying leaf pulp and construction dust to the lowest point it could find. The sky was heavy, as if held aloft by indifference. Alan pulled his hood tighter around his neck as he approached the agreed-upon corner—a small utilities shed tagged with initials from someone still defiant enough to spray paint government boxes. Ava was already there, back pressed against the cinderblock wall, hair damp but not dripping, phone off, bag zipped and worn close. They exchanged a nod.

"This city doesn't even bother to hide things anymore," she said.

Alan glanced past her to the corridor anchor site. The banners flapped, sodden, the logos already peeling at the corners. WELL-

NESS & INNOVATION ZONE – PHASE II in dull type over an artist's rendering of a child spinning beneath a trellis of flowering vines. The real vines had yet to arrive.

"What are we walking into?" he asked, not because he didn't know, but because he wanted her to say it aloud.

She adjusted the strap of her bag and started forward. "A clean site. According to every public file."

They moved together along the perimeter, following the line of chain-link fence that bordered the south side of parcel 524-B. No lighting on this side. Just runoff and signage. The soil sloped here—bad grading—and water pooled in the corners where the fill hadn't settled right. The ground was already giving off a sour mineral smell, something between ash and copper. Alan stepped carefully, eyes scanning the cracks in the pavement where grass had tried and failed to root. Every inch of the parcel had been curated to appear stable. Even now, in rain and absence, it maintained the posture of wellness.

He could feel it already, though. They weren't alone. Not in the surveillance sense. In the civic one. The kind of space that pretends not to remember what was done to it. Ava glanced sideways at him as they reached the back fence line.

"You sure you're still with me on this?" she asked.

Alan looked past the fencing, toward the playground footings still half-set in their concrete collars. Toward the site that no longer bothered with the lie.

"I'm here," he said. "Let's see what they paved over."

Ava crouched beside the fence where the wire had buckled, worn into slackness by wind, rain, and bureaucratic delay. One of the posts leaned outward at a strange angle, as if even the fencing had grown tired of its assignment. She pushed the metal aside with her forearm and slid through with ease.

Alan stood still for a moment. The entry point gaped like a question. He looked once over his shoulder. No headlights on patrol, only the empty rhythm of South Elm dripping against itself. Then he stepped forward, ducked under the torn mesh, his hand brushing the rusted end of a bent tie.

Inside, the site held a strange tension—like walking into a house where someone had just stormed out. Materials everywhere. A pallet of playground surfacing, still in plastic. Piles of fresh sod waiting for placement, the undersides already black with rot. Orange mesh fencing sagged between temporary stakes, some fallen, others upright as if by accident. A painted utility box stood ten yards off, its mural mid-image: a child with one hand raised, the rest of the arm still missing. The primer line visible, uncorrected. Brush strokes left open to the rain.

Alan scanned the horizon of the parcel. The half-completed walkway stretched about twenty feet then stopped. Just a poured slab into mud. The edges had started to wash out. This wasn't blight, and it wasn't progress. It was civic theater half-struck. An illusion suspended mid-construction.

He stepped lightly. The soil gave under his weight. His boot came up slick. Ava kept walking, observant and sure, reading the ground with the same eyes she used on soil reports and property deeds. Alan moved closer to the utility box, watching the rain slide down the unfinished paint, cutting thin streaks through the color. The child's eyes were complete—black dots with a single white point of reflection—watching something that wasn't there.

Alan whispered to no one, "This place wants to forget itself."

And then he kept walking. Ava stopped mid-step, the way someone does when a memory catches before a word. She turned slightly, then dropped to a squat without announcing it, her knees pressed close together, one hand bracing against the damp slope.

"Look," she whispered.

Alan crossed to where she crouched, boots slipping in the soft ground. The turf plugs beside them had loosened in the rain, one corner collapsed, sod peeling like carpet rolled too long. Near its base, the slope had given way. Just a finger's width of erosion, but enough. The land had cracked open a seam. The dirt beneath wasn't new. It wasn't even ambiguous. It was red, too red, packed dense and slick with ooze, the kind that didn't occur naturally this shallow unless someone had moved it. The kind that bore a memory of being somewhere else.

Ava pulled a scrap from her notebook, tore it in half, pressed one edge to the soil and dragged. A smear bloomed across the paper—thick, brick-colored, uneven. She looked at it once, then wiped her fingers on her jeans. Alan dropped to one knee, leaned in, letting the rain tap the back of his jacket. The smell was sharp—metallic, old. Familiar. He reached down, broke a small clod loose, rubbed it between his fingers. Grit gave way to fine powder. Beneath it, the iron sheen.

He closed his fist around it.

"It's the same soil," he said quietly. "It's the same damn soil."

Ava didn't answer. The slope held its secret. The site around them pretended not to notice. They stayed crouched there, listening to the tap of rain on engineered turf and half-set concrete. Ava reached into her pack, pulling out a plastic sample container with a screw-top lid and labeling strip already half-filled in—she had planned this, expected this, maybe even needed it to happen like this. She set it on the pallet's edge and unscrewed the lid with dry fingers, movements quick but unpanicked. It wasn't adrenaline. It was protocol. Alan watched her crouch again, open her notebook with one hand and slide a clean plastic spoon from a side pocket stitched for this exact purpose.

"You came ready," he said, suddenly aware of how far behind he still was in the practice of resistance. He had files. She had tools.

"I don't walk into a site blind," she said, sliding the spoon through the top layer of clay and packing it into the container. "Especially not one this manicured."

He handed her a clean Ziplock from his own coat pocket—he'd brought them in case of notes, maybe flyers. She double-sealed the first container, labeled it A1 – Parcel 524-B SE Slope – Visual Contam, and dropped it into the plastic. The second sample went into a generic bag, no label yet. She paused with the bag open.

"Redundancy matters," she said. "Lab gets one. We keep one. In case something gets lost."

Alan nodded. His phone was already out. He stepped back, framed the pallet, the landslip, the mural half-visible in the background. He took three photos wide, two close. Shot the run-off trail leading toward the storm drain at the lot's edge. Captured the angle of the slope, the imprint of their footprints, the red stains visible.

Ava sealed the second sample, stood up, and wiped her hands again, first on her jeans, then on the inside lining of her jacket. The rain still fell—steady now, a rhythm that couldn't be ignored.

"This is it," she said, her voice now edged with the kind of certainty Alan had only ever found in footnotes. "We're not guessing anymore."

He looked down at the mud, the stain, the sample in her hand. He thought of the overlay Keith had given him. Of Walter's voice describing red dust and quiet instructions. Of Goldie, standing at a podium built for worship, declaring that grief was now structural. He took one last photo and followed her toward the fence.

The rain picked up. The kind that blurred signs, softened angles, made buildings seem further away than they were. Drops dimpled the rolls of sod stacked by the temporary fence, spread across the site like apology rugs. Ava didn't flinch as she passed through the split in the chain-link. She pushed it open with her shoulder and ducked through in one motion. Alan followed, catching the edge of the wire with his coat, tugging a thin tear into the hem.

They stepped back onto the public sidewalk like people exiting a ceremony they hadn't been invited to. The concrete was slick beneath them, runoff pooling where the curb dipped toward a storm drain stamped with the city's recycling logo.

Alan pulled his hood up again. His breath fogged in the damp. Behind them, the site sat quiet, stage-lit by the city's amber streetlamps. The mural on the utility box had gone reflective in the wet—the child's half-painted arm now streaked with black drip lines, the unfinished smile distorted by the sheen.

They stopped at the corner, just past a light pole wrapped in a plastic banner for the Wellness Corridor Spring Showcase. The soil they'd disturbed was already darkening back to uniformity under the rain. The red clay, once exposed, now dulled by the moisture, tamped by the weight of sod not yet rooted.

Alan looked back. Shook his head.

"They almost got away with it," he said, quiet but firm, as if speaking to the block itself.

Ava's eyes didn't leave the site. "Almost."

They stood there a moment longer, the kind that lets you listen for what isn't being said.

He broke the silence first. "We get it tested. Then we get it published."

She nodded. "Then we get it into the record."

Alan took a slow step forward, turning his back to the parcel for the first time all evening. "Do we send it to the city?"

"Eventually," Ava said. "But not first. First, we send it to the people who'll make sure it doesn't disappear."

Alan looked over. "Goldie."

Ava didn't smile. "And whoever else will listen."

The rain threaded between them as they walked north, their shoes slapping on the wet pavement. They didn't speak again until the corner turned dark and the mural faded from view.

Alan sat with the desk lamp angled low. His office was quiet except for the whine of the hard drive waking from sleep, the screen blinking back to life as if reluctant to bear what it had been made to hold.

He opened the photo first. The playground site, shot in the rain—mud sliding from the pallet edge, the red clay visible beneath the slope, stained paper and Ava's knuckles still smudged in the frame. The rain had flattened the color but not erased it. Red not as symbol but as fact. Red as signature.

Next, the old scan from Bingham Park. A student lab test, six years old, conducted under lab lights with latex gloves and off-brand reagents. Alan had filed it away when no one returned his calls. The city said the report was "under legal review." It had stayed in the bottom drawer until now.

He dragged one image beside the other. Adjusted scale. Aligned the horizon lines. Same depth. Same saturation. Same trace mineral pattern. Two sites. One source. He didn't need a legend. The story was already encoded in the color. He opened a new document, the blank page starker than he remembered. He typed with fervor.

"You paved over a wound and called it wellness. We are here to reopen the record."

Outside the window, the rain had stopped. Pavement gleamed under the sodium bulbs, the corridor site somewhere beyond the skyline, still waiting with the manufactured quiet of capital ready for ribbon-cuttings and choreographed smiles. But Alan knew what lay beneath it now, compact and unacknowledged. Red clay tamped beneath sod. A city's self-mythology cracking at the seam.

He leaned back. The prism had shattered. What remained were fragments. He turned off the lamp. Left the file open. Let the light from the screen tell the story until morning.

Part Four

18

It was twelve-thirty, and the Commons greenspace was performing wellness on schedule. A line of seniors in coordinated athleisure mimicked arm circles beneath the stylized shade of a netted installation that resembled either a deconstructed vertebra or the world's most tasteful poultry trap. The netting had been installed last year with a placard quoting someone from the design school—"modular elasticity in communal tension." Keith read it once and never again. The net swayed slightly in the breeze, its cables taut in places, sagging in others, like something trying to mean more than it did.

He stood on the brickwork apron of the park's edge, watching the seniors twist at the waist in geriatric unity. The instructor, a woman with a wireless mic and the controlled cheer of a flight attendant who'd seen too much turbulence, called out motions with professional encouragement. Breathe in, reach up, expand through the ribs. No one looked happy, but no one left. That was the magic of sanctioned movement. Participation counted as belief.

The food trucks formed a crescent at the southwest entrance, their decals loud against the municipal brick of the library wall. Korean BBQ, falafel, vegan "melts" spelled in cursive. Keith chose the BBQ truck because the line was shorter and he didn't have the heart to pretend tofu had appeal. The man inside the truck wore a bandana and moved like someone who measured success in transactions-per-minute. Keith read the chalkboard menu—gochujang pork belly tacos, kimchi fries, heritage rice bowls—and picked the tacos, not because he wanted them, but because the word "bowl" triggered a vague weariness.

"Name?" the cashier asked.

"Keith."

She typed it into a tablet without looking. Her fingernails were silver and square. The screen chirped as his card cleared. The speaker near the register played a lo-fi instrumental remix of something that might have once been Alicia Keys. Keith stepped aside and watched a pair of consultants in high-end sneakers debate side dishes. One of them wore a lanyard for the innovation summit that was happening three blocks over. The other kept adjusting his blazer like it irritated him.

A boy with an upcycled lemonade cart passed, hawking turmeric spritzers from a reclaimed wood frame. He called out a price, then added "organic and donation-based" in the same breath. Keith took his order number and drifted toward the seating.

The park's "mixed-modal lounge furniture"—a phrase he remembered from the public hearing—consisted of oversized steel discs with embedded cushions that resisted comfort with bureaucratic discipline. Keith chose one on the far edge, where the astroturf met the first row of street trees planted for carbon offset. His view took in the full scene: seniors still twisting; a man on a city-issued bicycle doing laps without sweat; two children in matching jumpsuits feeding pigeons bread from bags labeled low sodium.

He opened the compostable container. The tacos were aggressively composed—drizzled, stacked, garnished with microgreens. He lifted one, the tortilla already softening. A piece of pickled radish slipped out and landed on the tray. For a moment, he sat still. Just chewing. Then the thoughts came, like they always did.

That he used to come to this park when it was just real grass and dogwalkers. That the plot had once been flagged as unsuitable for development—too narrow, too close to the runoff ditch, the soil marked with trace petroleum from a service station long demolished. That the developer who'd won the contract had married the deputy zoning commissioner's daughter. That the "urban green zone" was pitched as a public-private prototype in a slideshow funded by a mobility grant with no mobility metrics. That none of it mattered now, because the shade was pleasant, the net photographed well, and the tax credits had cleared. He bit into the taco again. Sweet, salt, heat. The flavors collided in three-part harmony.

Across the green, a drone hovered briefly to film the exercise class. One of the seniors looked up, then looked away. The instructor didn't pause. Keith watched the little machine tilt, then rise, then vanish into the blue above the library. The taco dripped onto the cardboard tray.

Keith wiped his hand on the branded napkin—Smoke Seoul'd: Tradition With a Twist—and leaned back against the cold curve of the bench. From here, the net installation framed the skyline in soft ellipses. The glass buildings gleamed like they believed in themselves. He didn't. But he was still here. Eating, watching, remembering the lines that had been drawn long before anyone here arrived. He took another bite and chewed slowly, the kind of slow that wasn't about taste but about delay. A breeze passed. The net undulated. The seniors reached toward the sun like they'd been told something waited up there. Keith stayed seated. He had nowhere to be for another twenty minutes. He watched the park rearrange itself in motions that looked almost meaningful.

The taco cooled in its own oils, and Keith let it. He pulled out his phone—face ID still sluggish in sunlight—and swiped past unread emails and a half-drafted apology to his older daughter, lingering finally on the local news feed. Third headline down: "Curtains and Cracks: Community Theater's Interim Director Speaks on Financial Challenges." A photo of Allison accompanied it, windswept on the front steps of the playhouse. She looked like herself, but framed for public sympathy—chin raised, a little too much eyeliner for day. It was the first article published a week ago.

He tapped it open. The quotes read rehearsed. "We're committed to transparency." "Every dollar will be accounted for." The language of a woman who had never balanced a budget but knew how to look unflustered in front of donor plaques. The memory dropped in like a curtain: Allison, backlit by the kitchen window a week earlier, tossing her keys in the ceramic bowl, humming something tuneless.

"I have never, in my entire life, seen anything so completely, fabulously fucked."

She said it like a toast.

Keith looked up from his laptop. "Welcome home?"

Allison dropped her bag on the island and opened the fridge with the force of a prosecutor unsealing evidence. "I made it four hours before someone used the word 'exposure' as a justification for not paying the lighting tech." She pulled out a bottle of chardonnay and checked the label. "This is the bottle I said we'd save for Thanksgiving, right?"

"I think so."

"Great." She opened it anyway and poured half into a mug emblazoned with GREENSBORO PTA—WE SHOW UP!

Keith closed the laptop. "So... first day as interim?"

"Prescott's office still smells like clove cigarettes and cedar balls. And I found a drawer—Keith, a drawer—full of uncashed checks dating back to June. One from a woman who died in August. That's the level of tragedy we're working with."

She drank. It wasn't performative. It was hydraulic.

"I take it there's no transition memo?"

"There's a sticky note that says 'Don't let the grantors eat you alive.' That's it. That's the whole onboarding process."

He tried not to smile. "That's... theater."

There was a silence. Allison drained her mug and refilled it. She leaned back against the counter, her heels slipping off as she flattened her feet to the tile. "Do you know what the budget line for costuming is this season?"

"I have no idea."

"Two thousand dollars. Total. For five shows. I could spend more at Target in twenty minutes."

Keith hesitated. "So... are you walking away?"

Allison looked at him like he'd suggested she sleep in her car for fun. "No. I'm going to direct Virginia Woolf with a busted board, a seventeen-year-old prop manager, and a cast of women who think blush is a character trait. And I'm going to make it good. Or at least loud."

He nodded, but she was already walking out of the kitchen, mug in hand, calling over her shoulder: "Also, I told Channel 12 I'd do a statement this week. If you see me on TV blinking too fast, it's because I'm suppressing the urge to torch the curtain."

Then she was gone. Upstairs. Into her next costume change.

The remaining taco was cold now. The seniors had finished stretching. The net art drifted lazily above. An alert on his phone brought him back to earth. A breaking Observer article opened with a flourish only scandal could summon: "Playhouse Suspends Season Amid Embezzlement Probe—Prescott Brooks Named in Criminal Investigation." Keith read it three times, each pass worse than the last. The production of Who's Afraid of Virginia Woolf? was canceled "indefinitely," though the word did more concealing than clarifying. The board had issued a statement—thin, stiff, vaguely remorseful. There was a photo of the marquee, letters mid-removal, a ladder leaning against it like an exhausted truth.

The article quoted anonymous sources—technicians, former stage managers, one "longtime patron" who claimed she had "always felt something was off with that man." Prescott had not been reached for comment. Allison had not been named, though the paragraph describing the "recently installed interim director" made Keith wince. She was collateral now. Public-facing. Tangled in someone else's reckoning, and maybe her own.

The bench beneath him had grown harder, or maybe he'd run out of postures to disguise discomfort. He closed the article, set the phone on his thigh, and let his eyes drift past the tree line. A lawn crew in matching polos clipped ornamental shrubs to a uniform height. Above the path, the sculpture swayed again—soft geometry, all form, no obligation.

Two days earlier, his daughter had told him everything without knowing. They'd been in the kitchen—he slicing strawberries, she pretending not to read ahead in her math workbook.

"Daddy?"

"Yeah?"

"Do you know Drew?"

Keith didn't look up. "Which Drew?"

"The one from Mom's work. He does the microphones. He wears bracelets."

That narrowed it.

"She says he has the ears of a god," she added, chewing the last syllable like it was candy.

Keith's knife paused mid-stroke. "She said that?"

"Mhm. And she talks to him all the time. Sometimes even when she's picking me up from ballet. I can hear her through the car."

He resumed slicing. "What does she talk to him about?"

"I dunno. Sometimes she laughs. Sometimes she's quiet. Once she said, 'If I had met you ten years ago, everything would be different.'"

His hand stopped. He placed the knife down carefully, like it might detonate.

"Did she know you were listening?"

"I don't think so. She thought I was playing with my photo app."

Keith offered a smile, half-believable. "Let's not tell your mother we heard that, okay?"

"Okay. Can I have whipped cream?"

He gave her whipped cream. He gave her the largest dollop possible. Then he stood at the sink while she ate and watched her reflection in the window. The photo app chimed from her tablet. Her head bobbed. She had no idea what she'd said. No idea what she'd named.

Now, back on the park bench, the conversation with Allison unspooled in his mind, the way it would go if she ever admitted it, which she wouldn't.

"You want to talk about Drew?" he'd ask.

She'd sigh, not defensive yet, but already tired. "Not really."

"You've been talking to him a lot."

"I've been managing a crisis. The whole place is on fire."

"And he's what—your fire extinguisher?"

"He listens. That's more than I can say for—"

She'd stop herself. Maybe. Keith knew the script. Knew the tone she'd use, that blend of weariness and studied righteousness that women in midlife acquire like a second skin. She would say she deserved tenderness. That she didn't do anything. That Drew saw her, which Keith had always found to be one of the more treacherous verbs in the English language.

He imagined saying, "You could have told me."

And her reply: "Would it have made a difference?"

It wouldn't. That was the problem. He wouldn't yell. He wouldn't leave. He would nod and swallow the ache and load the dishwasher while she cried into a dish towel. He knew his part, too. He looked at his phone again. A fresh comment on the article: "Theatre kids grow up to become theatre criminals. Sad!" Fifty-seven likes.

A man in athletic gear jogged past, talking into earbuds about Q4 projections. Keith pocketed the phone. The taco tray sat discarded beside him. He would go home tonight and act surprised. He would ask if she was okay, if the story was accurate, if she needed anything. She would answer in abstractions. They would not touch. Not then. Maybe not ever again. Their marriage was a production—still running, still lit—but the crew had already gone home. He stood, joints stiff, stomach sour. Across the green, the net sculpture sighed in the breeze, a tensile hymn to civic optimism.

And behind it, the buildings that funded the art. Clean glass. Polished concrete. Offices built on deferred maintenance and grant laundering. He knew the smell. Knew the taste. It was the aftertaste of every deal he'd ever analyzed: confidence masking deceit. He walked back to the sidewalk, phone still warm in his pocket. Someone nearby laughed—bright, braying. A sound tech's laugh, maybe. A director's. A donor's. Keith didn't look back. He already knew the scene.

The walk back up Greene Street was only seven minutes, but Keith stretched it to ten, pausing at crosswalks even when the signal changed, as if the few extra seconds granted him time to reorganize himself. The sun had come out in full, warming the tops of the hybrid cars idling at the curb, the glass lobby awnings gleaming like someone had just wiped them down for a new quarter's worth of investor optimism. He watched a man in blue slacks scan a badge at the entrance to a branded coworking space where even the plants were leased.

He felt the folder again—not physically, not in his hands, but in the shame that had followed him since getting the ZIP to Alan two weeks ago. A package of contracts, communications, and transaction histories so cleanly damning that even the legal team's jargon couldn't disguise intent. Parcel 524-B. The red sand. The recommendation to work it into the "pre-regulatory remediation" framework. He'd sent it in silence. No reply had come. That was fine. He hadn't done it for Alan. He'd done it because he thought it would make him clean.

He thought handing over the files would transform him. He imagined it as an exorcism. A single moral act, disinfecting years of feigned neutrality. He had convinced himself that one act of witness would clarify everything else: the creeping dread in his marriage, the daily indignity of knowing things he did nothing about, the small cowardices he fed like stray cats. It was supposed to be enough. It was supposed to be a hinge.

But this morning, Allison hadn't spoken to him. She left her coffee on the counter and her phone in her purse. She hadn't smiled. She hadn't looked up when their daughter spilled cereal on the floor. He knew she had read the articles. Knew she was waiting for him to say something about Drew, about the theatre, about what any of it meant. And he couldn't. He couldn't do a thing but wipe the milk with a paper towel and nod like it was all manageable.

As he approached the glass base of the tower, he saw them: two men in identical navy suits, collar seams sharp, shoes with too much shine for actual work. One stood slightly ahead of the door, the other with his arms crossed in discretionary authority. They weren't talking. They weren't checking phones. They weren't waiting for a ride. They were watching the entrance.

Keith didn't slow his pace, but his pulse caught in the back of his throat like it had somewhere else to be. They weren't police. They didn't need to be. Security at this level had mastered the art of implication. They weren't there to stop anyone. They were there to be seen. He reached for his keycard in the side pocket of his bag. It was there. It always was. He kept walking, steps even, the tower rising above him, its windows reflecting only the parts of the city polished enough to warrant concern. Sweat gathered at the back of his neck.

He had thought doing the right thing would simplify the rest. He had believed, stupidly, in internal balance. One truth counteracting years of compliance. One risk unspooling a tangle. He reached the revolving door. Neither man moved. One of them looked at him—only briefly, not even recognition, just a glance to confirm whether Keith saw them too.

"Sir," one of the men said, the taller one, his voice pitched to carry. "Can I see your ID badge, please?"

Keith froze just inside the vestibule. The elevator light hadn't yet arrived—just a dull, unchanging glow overhead and the thrum of some unseen mechanical system that always seemed to be fixing itself.

"I work here," he said, pulling the badge from his lanyard anyway. His voice cracked at the edge, confusion gilded with civility.

The man took the badge but didn't even look at it. "Thank you, sir. If you could come with us, HR would like a word."

"HR?" Keith asked. "About what?"

The second man joined them now, flanking just enough to form shape but not threat. "They'll explain everything upstairs."

Keith glanced toward the reception desk, but the woman there had her eyes locked on her screen, mouse hand moving in slow arcs like she was solving a problem and could not afford to look up.

"I haven't done anything," he said, hearing how wrong that sounded the moment it left his mouth.

"No one's saying you have, sir," the first man replied, still unbothered. "We're just here to escort."

Keith took a step back. "I have a meeting in—"

"They're aware."

He looked at the badge still held in the man's hand, like it had changed owners, become an instrument of permission that no longer belonged to him.

"Is this about a security protocol or—" he started, then stopped. He'd always believed in the soft middle ground, where a question could slow things down, where doubt could stall authority. But this wasn't doubt. This was choreography. They had done this before. Probably that week. Probably that morning. He followed.

In the elevator, no one spoke. The ride up was glacial, nineteen floors, no music. Just the ding of the floor counter. The two men stood like partitions. A third body in a system designed to function whether he was in it or not. Keith stared at his own reflection in the elevator wall. The lighting was direct, the angles cruel. His shirt had wrinkled near the waist. A small stain from the taco clung near the hem. It looked like something spilled in retreat.

He ran the calculus: He hadn't used his company email. He hadn't logged the documents from his work computer. The ZIP file had been assembled at home. Sent through a burner Gmail address, tethered to his phone's hotspot. There was no direct trail. No signature. Alan wouldn't have exposed him—not deliberately. Alan wasn't the type to hand over a source. Not after everything they used to believe.

Unless there had been surveillance on Parcel 524-B. Internal audit. System flagging for any access to the Midland Legacy Trust records. Maybe it hadn't been Alan. Maybe it had been the act itself—the download, the cross-referencing, the quiet tracing of shell companies that weren't meant to be touched. Maybe it had nothing to do with morality. He worked in analytics. He knew how fast systems learned the shape of deviation. The elevator dinged. Floor nineteen. Executive wing. Glass walls and opaque speech. The doors opened to a carpeted silence.

"We'll walk you in," the man said. It wasn't a request.

Keith stepped out, heart suddenly heavy in his chest. He had imagined it differently. He had imagined a confrontation. A moment. Something righteous. But this was just procedure. Just the quiet, well-dressed machinery of removal. Somewhere beyond the next door was a woman from HR who would smile tightly and speak in clauses designed by legal. Someone who would call it a conversation, a clarification, a misunderstanding. Until the document appeared and the pen followed and the badge no longer unlocked anything. Keith adjusted his collar and kept walking.

The conference room had been named after a tree—The Sycamore—though there was no wood in sight. Only glass, steel, and a soft-gray carpet that muffled all human sound. The windows framed the city like a concept. Clean edges, gleaming angles, the illusion of scale. Keith entered behind the men, who peeled off without a word, their presence superfluous now that the door had shut behind him with a final hydraulic sigh.

Three people waited at the far end of the long, unloved table. Two wore navy blazers with department-issued smiles. HR, almost certainly—Jocelyn from Employee Experience, and the other one, Susan. The third was a man Keith didn't recognize, his lanyard marked with a red security stripe that meant something sharp. No one stood. They didn't shake his hand. The room had already decided what it thought of him.

"Keith," Jocelyn said, bright as always. "Thanks for making time."

"I didn't," he replied. His voice sounded steadier than expected.

Susan gestured to the chair across from them, a low-backed swivel thing upholstered in a synthetic leather that stuck slightly in humidity.

"Please. Let's sit," the man in the red-striped lanyard said. "We'll try to keep this brief."

Keith remained standing for a breath, then sat.

"We just wanted to clarify a few things," Jocelyn said, clasping her hands like she was about to start a mediation workshop.

"We've had a system-level flag on our network activity logs from last week," Red Lanyard said. "Which, in and of itself, isn't uncommon. But the escalation path led us here."

Keith blinked. "What kind of flag?"

The man opened a folder with corporate theater. Printed paper, though they had the file onscreen. The performance mattered.

"A search query originating from your workstation last Thursday," the man continued. "It involved internal audit trails related to a defunct redevelopment initiative. That item is not part of your current portfolio." He looked up, polite but dull-eyed. "Can you walk us through that?"

Keith kept his hands in his lap. "I was reviewing old contracts. Historical funding structures."

"For what purpose?"

"I was curious."

"Curiosity isn't typically logged at that access level." This from Susan. She wasn't smiling either now.

"You think I breached something?" Keith said, half a laugh under the words. "I didn't move any documents off the server. I didn't email anything. I didn't download—"

"We know," the man said. "That's part of what makes this unusual. There's no outbound activity. No access through sanctioned channels. But we did log an unsanctioned device pairing near your workstation that same day. Something broadcast through a mobile tether, bypassing internal controls."

Keith's throat pulsed. "You're saying someone was in my office?"

"We're saying someone used your credentials and proximity badge to trigger access to non-current archives via mobile bridge. You were the only individual on-site at the time. The mobile tether ID corresponds to a personal phone registered to your benefits account."

Jocelyn broke in gently, like a counselor in a scripted intervention. "Keith, we're not here to assume intent. We're here because of behavior that appears inconsistent with our acceptable use policies. This is a conversation. Not an accusation."

He laughed once, quietly. "That's what we call it when the walls close in?"

Silence. Not offended. Just indifferent.

Keith leaned forward, elbows just touching the table's edge. "So what happens now? You make me sign something? A memo full of soft language and a bullet point list of noncompliance? You walk me out with a cardboard box and tell the staff it's restructuring?"

Jocelyn opened her mouth, but it was the man from IT security who spoke first.

"We're not there yet," he said flatly. "Right now, we're gathering context. Unless there's something you'd like to share."

Keith stared at them. All three. A triad of procedural calm. They didn't want truth. They wanted containment.

"I did it," he said finally, voice calm. "I pulled the records. I copied them. I sent them outside the company. You already knew that. You just wanted me to confirm it."

The room didn't react.

"Who did you send them to?" the man asked.

"I'd like to speak to legal," Keith said.

Another silence. Longer this time.

Then Jocelyn nodded, as if the conversation had ended the moment it began.

"We'll make that arrangement."

And just like that, it wasn't a meeting. It was a process.

The walk from the conference room to his office was done without eye contact. A junior HR associate led the way like a docent on a silent tour. Behind him, the IT security man followed. They moved past the glass partitions of departments that had names like "People Strategy" and "Capital Narrative," past coworkers who raised their eyes but quickly lowered them again. This was not a parade. It was a ritual. And they had seen it before.

Keith's nameplate was already missing from the wall outside his door. Inside, his monitor had gone dark, mouse cord unplugged, chair rotated precisely toward the window like it was expecting someone else. The desk across from his had a new bag on it—a pale green tote with a branded podcast logo. Someone new had started today. Someone clean.

"You have ten minutes to gather personal belongings," the HR associate said, gently, as if announcing rain.

He stared at her. "You could just say I'm fired."

She tilted her head, but didn't answer.

There wasn't much to collect. A notepad with diagrams no one understood but him. A black pen he liked because it didn't smear on his left hand. A framed photo of the children from two summers ago at Topsail, hair plastered by salt air. No picture of Allison. That one had come down months ago, quietly, during a Friday cleanup. The cardboard box they'd given him said Sustainably Made on the side. A sticker sealed the flap with a circular arrow chasing its own tail.

The termination letter was waiting at reception. Two pages, one signature line, one paragraph that used the phrase "internal restructuring" and another that stated no material breach had been determined, but that the company reserved the right to reinterpret findings at a later date. The non-disclosure language was exact. Broad enough to gag, narrow enough to hold up in arbitration. He signed. His hand trembled. Not from fear—his fear had already calcified—but from something duller: the understanding that no one would fight for him. Not even Allison.

The escort walked him through the lobby. The woman at the front desk did not look up. Outside, the revolving door spun him back into air that smelled like construction dust and lavender from the sidewalk planter. He stood there, the box in his arms, the sky suddenly uncooperative. The kind of sun that made a lie out of endings.

He thought of Allison. She wouldn't be home yet. Rehearsal probably canceled. Maybe she was with Drew. Maybe they were debriefing the crisis, unwinding into each other. He wondered if she would ask about the job. If she would feign concern, or let relief flicker behind her disappointment. He thought of their bedroom. How she had started facing the wall even before she was asleep. The job had been the last shared structure. She never liked what he did, but she liked that he did it. It gave shape. Respectability. A lever to pull when her own stage sagged. Now he was just a man in the city, holding a box full of unnecessary items. He walked toward the parking deck, unsure what lane his pass would still open.

The Volkswagen didn't belong in his driveway. It was dull red, speckled with pollen, and parked slightly crooked on the left side of the driveway, as if whoever had pulled in didn't expect to be seen. The windows were rolled up tight. Keith sat with the engine idling, watching it from behind the wheel. The car was older—mid-2000s, maybe earlier. The kind people still drove when they were waiting for a break that wouldn't come.

It was 2:36 p.m. Allison shouldn't be home until four. Her calendar had rehearsal blocked until then, though everything about this week now felt like an improvisation. The neighborhood was quiet—trash cans tucked back beside garages, UPS trucks lumbering past with logistical purpose. The street had been repaved last month and still smelled of tar when the sun hit it right. He parked beside the Volkswagen, pulled the handbrake, and sat for a beat. The engine ticked as it cooled. The air inside the car grew close, recycled. He opened the door and stepped out, every joint loud in his body.

Keith walked to the Volkswagen and leaned slightly, eyes scanning the interior. In the front seat, an empty coffee cup, logo faded to anonymity. The glove compartment sat ajar, a theatre parking pass wedged into the windshield's corner. In the back: two stacked cases of audio equipment, a spool of cable, a pair of over-ear headphones looped around a gear bag.

He stepped back. Looked at the house. All the curtains were drawn. The side door, the one off the garage, was closed but not fully latched. A breeze had moved the hanging basil plant above the railing. Up the driveway now, slow. His shadow crossed the mulch bed where the rosemary had gone dry. His shoes crunched over stray pine needles the last storm had dropped. He touched the handle of the side door. Listened. A car passed on the main road, bass thudding. From inside the house, nothing.

They had bought this house ten years ago. Too much square footage, not enough back yard. The kind of house that looked good at dusk but felt empty by nine. Allison had painted the mudroom herself, music blaring, hair pulled back. There was still a streak of dried blue on the baseboard. Keith opened the door. The sound that reached him first was not movement but absence. No footsteps, no TV, no distant music. Allison's purse was on the kitchen island, slouched open, her keys resting half out of the pocket like she'd dropped them in a rush. The lipstick cap was missing. One of the straps was twisted.

He stepped forward. In the living room, the light had been dimmed. Not off, just lowered, as if intimacy required calibration. Two pairs of shoes by the ottoman—her low brown flats and a pair of black Vans, laces looped loosely, worn at the heel. The couch cushions were out of order, some on the floor, one pushed under the coffee table, which had been nudged an inch off its rug alignment. A man's jacket—denim, worn, arms tucked as if tossed and not moved since—lay across the center cushion. The house held a strange silence, not empty, but layered with things not meant to be overheard. Then the sound came—muffled, fast, undeniable. Aggressive in cadence, low and rhythmic, like a fist to a wall not meant to be heard.

Keith moved through the living room, across the grain of the wood floor, shoes catching on the finish. The hallway was darker. His pulse moved without pace, throat tight but not restrictive. Down the hall. Another sound now—something sharper in it, a gasp muted into fabric, bodies trying to stay quiet and failing. He reached the doorway. One hand lifted, not to knock. Just to touch the frame. To anchor. He stood there. Listening. Breathing. Nothing else.

He stood at the door to the spare bedroom. The sounds were no longer vague. The rhythm was unmistakable—flesh meeting flesh in deliberate, repeating contact, a cadence without hesitation. Breathless laughter broke through, then a murmur that froze him: Allison's voice, low, coaxing, full of a kind of pleasure she hadn't expressed in years. He stared at the doorknob. His hand hovered over it, fingers flexed without purpose. The sound continued. Her voice again—he couldn't make out the words, but he recognized the tone. Intimate and unguarded. He pulled his hand back and walked away.

The floor creaked once beneath him, and still, no interruption behind the door. Back in the living room, the evidence remained: jacket, shoes, the air itself different now, warmer with the residue of movement. He sat in the armchair across from the couch, where one of the cushions had slid onto the floor. His hands rested on his knees, elbows out. His back straightened without thinking. He waited.

The house moved around him. Upstairs, a faint creak of settling wood. A bird outside the window flicked its wings, tapping the sill once before lifting off. A car passed. He sat, listening to the last part of something break.

Twenty minutes passed after the last sound from the bedroom, the last gasp drawn out too long to be anything else. Keith sat in the chair and waited, legs uncrossed, hands resting on his thighs, every muscle quiet but alert. The silence was too real. Eventually, the toilet flushed. From the hallway, she emerged. The robe was white and short at the hem, one of the ones she used to wear after fundraisers, after garden parties, after performing her beauty all day. Her hair clung to one side of her neck, cheeks red from friction or shame or neither. The moment she saw him, the color dropped from her face so fast he could feel it.

"What are you doing here?" she asked, her voice bright in the wrong way. Not defensive yet, but desperate for normal.

He looked past her. To the hallway, to the closed door behind which a man now dressed, silently, trying to reduce the sound of zippers and belt buckles into something untraceable. The robe's sash hung loose on one side. Her toenails were painted. She had curled her hair, he noticed. Not recently. But with intention.

"I thought you were—working late," she said, eyes flicking to his shoes, then his face, then the house keys in his hand like they didn't belong to him anymore.

"I got fired," Keith said. "Forty five minutes ago."

Allison blinked. Her jaw twitched. "What?"

"They called it restructuring." He didn't shift his weight. "There was a document. I signed it."

Something in her posture released. Her arms dropped from their half-crossed shape. Her hand brushed the frame of the hallway as if she'd forgotten it was there.

"I didn't—Keith, I didn't know."

He nodded once, not to reassure her. Just to confirm receipt of the sentence. The room felt like an office after-hours. Staged but emptied of function. He stepped aside, toward the den. The jacket still lay where it had landed, half over the armrest. A sock—black, thin, not his—rested near the floor vent. He smelled something now, not cologne. Sweat and the trace of lust evaporating.

"You should tell him to go out the back," Keith said. "It'll be easier."

Her breath caught as she took the items. But she didn't argue. Didn't ask what he meant. He walked to the sink. Turned on the faucet. Cold water ran fast, shallow in the basin. It always took a moment to warm. The window above the sink hadn't been opened in weeks. He stared through it anyway, watched a squirrel vault from the fencepost into the branches of the pine.

"I didn't want it to be like this," she said behind him finally. Like a line from a play they'd rehearsed too many times.

"I know," he said. He turned the tap off. Dried his hands on the dish towel. They stood like that, in the dead middle of something too long delayed. The moment didn't swell. It simply lasted.

Then the back door opened. The sound of a man's shoes crossing the deck, quick but careful, each step calibrated for plausible silence. Keith didn't look. He had no interest in Drew, in the angle of his jaw or the posture of retreat. The man had been handed something that didn't belong to him, and he'd taken it without flinching. That wasn't the crime. That was just the moment. Allison still hadn't moved. Keith stepped past her, reached for his jacket from the coat rack by the stairs. His hands were steady now. Whatever trembled before had gone.

At the door, he paused before turning the knob. "You'll need to tell the kids something," he said, eyes forward.

Allison didn't reply.

He opened the door and stepped outside. The sun had softened. Somewhere down the block, a dog barked, insistent and small. Keith walked down the drive, past the empty rectangle where the Volkswagen had been, past the oil stain that never quite lifted, past the rosemary bush now brittle with neglect. He reached the car. He didn't start the engine. In front of him, the house stood unchanged. White siding, dented gutter, blinds still drawn in the guest room. Keith didn't cry. He just reached for the wheel like it might give him some direction.

19

The city began buzzing before it stirred. Before eggs cracked into pans, before joggers tugged compression sleeves over their calves, before the trash trucks wheezed and lifted their mechanical arms into the still-shadowed streets—before all that, the news was already moving.

Across fiber optic cables strung beneath sidewalks and office towers, through server stacks in IT closets alive with the early strain of algorithmic warm up, across cell towers disguised as pine trees, the article flew. It was Alan Ransome's name above the fold, digital and print, and the city knew what that meant. The latest op-ed, long and searing and sourced like a legal brief, posted at 5:07 a.m. and by 5:22 was the top read on three local aggregators, had two dozen reposts on the regional subreddit, and one heated thread on Nextdoor where a man named Wayne accused the university of "funding Marxism under the guise of soil science."

By six, screens were glowing in breakfast nooks from South Elm-Eugene Street to Lake Brandt Road. The digital edition of the Greensboro Observer opened with a photo of red-streaked soil, a close-up from Alan's article: the soil seepage at the new playground. Beneath it, the headline stretched clean and brutal: "THE LAND STILL REMEMBERS: How a Development Deal Buried Poison and Truth Beneath Downtown's Growth." A subhead named the parcel. Parcel 524-B. Another mentioned the chemical. Chromium VI. The kinds of names that usually didn't stick in the public mind. This time, they would.

The city's machinery woke next. Printers in office supply closets coughed out the ink version. Lobbyists clipped the PDF and forwarded it to contacts with the subject line "Need eyes on this today." The city manager, up before his dog had even stirred, skimmed it on his treadmill and muttered "Goddammit" four minutes in. His wife called through the door. "You're swearing again, honey." He didn't respond.

By 7:05, Goldie Hayes had read it twice.

Her neighbor Tamara texted her the link at 6:38 with a string of fire emojis and a single word: Finally. But Goldie was already on her second cup of coffee and had marked the margins in red. Alan had gotten the names right. The parcels. The flow of money from the hospital to the shell firm to the city's acquiescence. She paused at the line where he quoted Walter Horn, the sanitation worker: "They dumped it like it didn't matter. And for a long time, it didn't." She read that one aloud to the room.

North across town, in New Irving Park, the mayor was having toast with avocado mash and crushed red pepper, her daily indulgence, when the link arrived from her communications director, who included no salutation. Just a sad face. The mayor read the piece on her iPad with a growing ache in her temples. She skimmed quickly at first, as if that would make it less real, then slowed at the block-quoted section from the internal memo, the one referencing "pre-regulatory contaminants" and "narrative repositioning." Her husband—a real estate attorney who believed in the corrective power of philanthropy—said without looking up from his phone: "Is it about that park again?"

"It's worse," she replied. "It's all of it."

The local NPR affiliate had the piece printed out in the hands of the morning news editor by 7:18. She circled key phrases and handed it to the intern tasked with writing copy for the 8 a.m. top-of-hour summary. "Start here," she said. "And don't say 'alleged.' Say 'documented.'"

On the country club patio, three men whose names routinely appeared in planning board minutes passed a single phone between them, reading silently as one muttered, "This is going to wreck the timeline for Phase Three." They all agreed that it was unfortunate, that Alan had talent, that they should have looped him in earlier, that someone had mishandled community relations.

At the university, a teaching assistant texted Alan at 7:42: You're going to need to stay off campus today. Or bring a megaphone. A second message followed: They're losing it in the faculty Slack. Alan hadn't responded. He was still in bed, the light not yet on, the glow of his phone casting his profile in relief against the wall. The notification bar filled, cleared, filled again.

In a high-rise downtown, an executive vice president of Guilford Health System was already on a call with a legal consultant out of Charlotte, his tone measured, his tie still not on. "We'll say we acted on best available data. We'll invoke the pre-regulatory aspect. They knew about the red sand—we reported that last year, in the appendix." Pause. "No one reads appendices."

In a group chat titled SouthSide Moms, the link was pasted without comment. By the fifth message, someone had mentioned their son's asthma. By the eighth, the conversation had turned to whether they should test the soil around the bus stop. No one yet had said the word "lawsuit," but the tension in the chat moved like a cold front.

Talk radio picked it up at 8:10. "A local professor with nothing to lose, apparently," the host quipped, "has just published what some are calling a bombshell. Others are calling it a left-wing hit job." His co-host read the headline aloud while the audio played behind him—wind chimes and children laughing, Alan's words in voiceover, quietly devastating.

And above all this, somewhere inside the cloud, the data kept moving. Clicks registered. Engagement tracked. The numbers updated in real time, vertical and precise. It was trending statewide by 9:00. But it wasn't viral. It was heavier than that. It didn't flash. It spread. Parcel 524-B was no longer a term used in planning meetings or internal memos. It had entered the city's bloodstream.

The envelopes dropped into the mailbox with a clean, satisfying weight—four in total, each addressed to a nonprofit board on which Paula had served with cultivated grace and deliberate distance. The Guilford Wellness Alliance, the Historic Preservation Commission, the Community Foundation, and, of course, the Health Equity Arts Partnership—a name she had once praised for "sounding like it's trying to help without ever saying how."

Now they were gone. Each envelope contained a single page: handwritten, restrained, free of explanation. Thank you for the opportunity. I've decided to step away from public service for the foreseeable future. She turned from the mailbox and began walking up the long stone path toward the house, her slippers slapping across the patterned concrete David had insisted on after seeing it at a resort in Arizona. The air was damp with late spring, magnolia-heavy. Across the street, a landscaping crew edged the McKellens' lawn with machine-like competence. She noticed, not for the first time, that David had forgotten to schedule the mulch delivery.

Inside the house, it had started with the click of the espresso machine, the hiss of steam not quite masking his tone. He'd called her name from the kitchen in a voice that was still calm but arranged for impact.

"Paula."

She walked in slowly, tucking her phone into the pocket of her robe, already bracing.

He was at the counter, laptop open, still in a performance-fabric shirt, though it was unzipped slightly at the collar, a detail he wouldn't have allowed if he'd known she'd see him like this. He pointed to the screen without turning it toward her.

"You've read it?"

She hesitated just long enough to calibrate. "The article?"

"Alan's little manifesto. Yes."

"I skimmed." She moved to the fridge, opened it, closed it again without taking anything. "I didn't realize it was causing this much of a reaction."

"It's not just causing a reaction, Paula. It's shaping one. I've gotten four texts and two voice mails since six. One from the hospital's donor liaison asking if I 'anticipated reputational implications.' Reputational implications. As if I were consulted on pre-regulatory brownfields in 2006." He snorted. "They think I'm mentioned. I'm not even named."

"No, you're not," she said, returning to the counter, arms crossed, head tilted in concern. "But people read implication faster than facts."

He shot her a look. "What does that mean?"

She kept her tone flat. "It means I understand how people think."

He tapped the trackpad hard enough that the coffee splashed in his mug. "524- B was flagged for review three years before I joined the Strategic Realignment Committee. Everyone knows that. And the remediation pivot came from city consultants, not the hospital board. The phrase 'pre-regulatory landfill' didn't even exist when I was chair."

"You should say that publicly," she offered. "If it's true."

"It is true," he snapped, and then softened immediately. "Sorry. I just... this is calculated. It doesn't accuse. It arranges. By the time you finish reading it, you've already formed your conclusion, and he hasn't said a damn thing that could get him sued."

She watched him. He looked tired, in a way that had nothing to do with sleep. He wore his panic like a well-cut suit. Structured, expensive, but unmistakable in its fit. The espresso hissed again behind him.

"Do you want me to reach out to the pastor's forum?" she asked. "To say something on your behalf?"

He stared at her. "God no. That'll just signal damage control. Right now, silence is strength."

"Unless silence is guilt," she said, almost too quietly.

He caught it. Of course he did. "Are you implying something?"

She met his eyes. "I'm saying I know you're not legally liable. But you have your fingerprints on enough committees, enough task forces, enough steering groups—"

"They were advisory, Paula."

"I'm just saying it's a lot of heat in a very small room."

He laughed. Dry. Bitter. "You think this is funny? You think I engineered this?"

"I think you built a wellness corridor over a brownfield and called it equity. And I think now someone's opened a window and the smell is coming through."

His face went slack for a second, then rebuilt itself. "You're really enjoying this."

"No," she said, evenly. "I'm just not going to pretend I don't understand it."

He looked back at the screen. "Alan's always wanted to burn something down. Now he finally found the timber."

"And you gave him the match," she said, brushing past him to pour herself water. She drank half the glass before turning back. "He didn't make the mess. He just pointed at it."

David stood there, jaw working slightly. "This isn't going away."

"No," she said. "It's not."

And she walked out, upstairs, each step deliberate.

Now, coming back inside from the mailbox, she felt that silence still hanging in the foyer, the espresso machine powered down but still warm. She opened the front door, stepped inside, and set her phone in the small lacquered bowl near the console table. In the hallway mirror, her face looked composed. Just the right amount of color in the cheeks. She didn't look like a woman whose husband was unraveling. But then, she'd never needed her face to match the facts.

Paula moved through the foyer. Upstairs, she could hear David moving. Closet doors opening with quiet violence, hangers scraped across the rod, the dull thud of a belt yanked from a drawer. He was dressing like the day could still be salvaged by panache.

The bedroom door stood half-open. She entered without a sound. His phone buzzed again—sharp, brief, insistent—on the dresser where he'd tossed it beside his cufflinks and watch. A matte black case, always face-up. The screen lit once more. The message previews scrolled by, one after another, their tone sharpening with each sender. She read them silently.

Angela R (Community Foundation): "Need to discuss Alan's piece before noon. Project fund exposure unclear."

Caleb (Council Liaison): "Press asking if you advised on corridor site selection. Need a position."

Diana (Legal): "Please confirm when you can be on Zoom. Timeline needs clarification ASAP."

Unknown number: "You knew about 524-B. We ALL did. Don't act surprised."

Andrew K (Hospital): "Board review imminent. We'll back you, but need talking points."

Megan (Communications): "Media watchlist added Ransome to flagged terms. No interviews until cleared."

Ellis (Investor): "Pulling out of Phase III if narrative control isn't restored by end of week."

Buzz. Buzz. Buzz. Each vibration brief but building. The screen dimmed, then came alive again.

Angela R: "Did you see the new soil report? That creek photo is everywhere. Alan's framing it as negligence. You're in the middle even if you're not in the piece."

She heard him in the bathroom now, running water, muttering low, rehearsing his jawline into a shape of confidence. She stood beside the dresser and watched the phone light up once more.

Caleb: "Pre-regulatory doesn't mean cover-up. We warned you."

The phone buzzed again. Then again.

She turned and walked out. There was nothing left to learn from it. Only things left to say.

The kitchen window above the sink was open an inch, and the morning air pushed in, just enough to lift the corner of a recipe card Paula had clipped to the fridge six years ago and never followed. Her daughter stood in sneakers on the tile, flipping through a wrinkled script, a half-buttered slice of sourdough clutched in her hand like a prop. The child's hair was still damp from the shower, moistening her collar. Her voice was high and trying for gravity.

"I'm not afraid of you, even if you want me to be," she read, chewing the line mid-sentence. "You don't control the truth."

Paula filled the coffee pot with water from the fridge spout. It chugged with the soft urgency of routine. Her daughter paced once around the island, reciting now in rhythm with her steps.

"You have to say it, even if it scares you."

Paula froze. The water overflowed by a fraction, arcing down the side of the carafe. Her hand trembled as she moved to the coffee machine. A drop spilled onto the edge of her wrist. The cold registered instantly. She watched the water absorb into her skin, watched her hand hold steady around the glass despite itself.

"You have to say it," the girl repeated. "Even if it scares you."

The line wasn't aimed at her, but it hit home.

"Darling," Paula said, voice measured. "That was... very good."

The girl looked up, beaming. "Ms. Haley said I have to project more. But I think it's better if it sounds like I mean it."

"You should always sound like you mean it," Paula said, almost without breath.

David entered the kitchen, jacket on, tie loose at the neck. The phone wasn't in his hand anymore, which meant the calls were scheduled now, crises moved from reaction to management. He touched his daughter's shoulder.

"Ready for carpool?"

"Almost." She took one last bite of toast and stuffed the script into her bag. "Mom, did you ever do plays in school?"

Paula smiled with effort. "Once. I was a tree."

The girl laughed. "Boring."

She darted out, sneakers squeaking against the floorboards. David followed, phone already vibrating again in his pocket. The door closed. Paula stood alone in the quiet kitchen. The coffeepot sputtered to life behind her. Outside, a bird called once and went unanswered. The girl's voice echoed: "You have to say it, even if it scares you."

Paula looked at the puddle on the counter, the line of water curling down the base. Everything she'd built—every gala, every public comment, every carefully balanced neutrality—had grown in silence. And now, her daughter, with her clean face and her honest little mouth, had spoken the thing Paula had never said out loud.

The rag was already damp when she reached for it, the edge wrinkled from yesterday's half-hearted wipe-down of the stovetop. Paula cleaned the spill in concentric strokes, first the puddle, then the drip along the carafe, then the smear along the lip of the warming plate where the burnt coffee had gathered. She replaced the carafe on the burner and smoothed the edge of her blouse. Her daughter's words had lodged somewhere behind the bone.

"You have to say it, even if it scares you."

Paula turned without instruction. Her hands dropped to her sides. She walked through the living room, past the framed diploma from Carolina that David had insisted they display despite its general irrelevance. Past the art that had been chosen by committee, not for meaning but for show. Past the sideboard where the crystal bowl from the healthcare gala sat empty, the engraved plaque turned toward the wall. She stopped at the entrance to David's study.

The room was immaculate by force. Leather chair centered to the desk. Shelves arranged with titles chosen for presence, not consumption: The Innovator's Dilemma, Equity in the Built Environment, Profiles in Negotiation. The carpet bore no signs of pacing. The lamp cord was coiled with deliberate neatness, tucked behind the end table. The only object out of place was a notepad on the desk, one corner turned as if he had written something and torn the page free.

She stood in the doorway. Her hand hovered on the trim. The house around her was still. The steady, airtight quiet of a home arranged to never betray its secrets. From this vantage, she could see all of it: the chair where he took his calls, the printer he used for drafts he didn't want on the cloud, the locked drawer to the right of the desk that she had long stopped wondering about.

She let the moment widen around her. Paula Moss, volunteer. Paula Moss, board chair. Paula Moss, silent wife in tailored blue, voice measured at luncheons, eyebrows lifted just so when uncomfortable questions were asked. Paula Moss, whose real position was firewall. She had not read Alan's article twice because she doubted it. She had read it because it knew things she had long suspected but had never dared assemble. And now the assembly had arrived. Alan hadn't drawn blood. He'd simply held up the map and said, look where we are.

She stood at the door of her husband's mind. If she crossed the threshold, it would not be for ceremony. Not for access. Not for tidying. She had one letter still unsent. Truths unnamed. A daughter rehearsing courage over toast. Paula took a single step forward, into the study.

The birds outside had gone quiet, as if the rhythms of suburban life were too regular to warrant their song. The sun, unencumbered by clouds, cast long, unforgiving lines across the study floor, through the transoms, across the bookcase. The home held its light. Her mouth was dry. Her thoughts moved not in sentences but fragments. "You have to say it..." The phrase felt like instruction.

The light struck the spines of white papers stacked along the far shelf. Regulatory filings, foundation audits, printed agendas for regional partnership retreats. She moved without hurry. Every step deliberate. This was a room designed for reverence. A confessional chapel of corporate ambition, lined not with icons but with strategies. No family photos. No paperweights from vacation. Two fountain pens in a bespoke holder, and the outline of where a laptop usually rested—he'd taken it with him, of course. He always did when something went wrong. She crossed to the shelf behind the desk. The bottom one, back corner, where the dust gathered and the books never changed. She reached beneath it with a surgeon's precision, fingertips grazing until she found the telltale edge of electrical tape, the little tab folded over. She peeled it back. The key came loose in her hand, warm already.

The drawer stuck slightly before giving way. Inside, she found what she had expected and what she had not. A navy folder. Thicker than she'd expected. Inside: Letters from the environmental consultants. Long, jargon-laced pages on regional soil metrics and chromium decay curves. The early letters flagged concern. The later ones hedged. One summary report had been annotated in David's handwriting, circled in bold at the bottom: "Disclaim without disclosure. Pre-regulatory!" Drafts of press releases. Paragraphs rewritten in pen. "Pre-regulatory brownfield cleanup" replaced with "landscape potential for civic space." One version crossed out the word toxic entirely. In the margins, a note: "Community won't absorb guilt—offer opportunity instead." Email printouts. Internal language stripped of tone, raw and exposed. Legal redlines everywhere.

"Mitigate language."
"Downplay residuals."
"Control optics."

Another read: "We own the first paragraph. After that, it's just cleanup."

Her hands did not shake. She gathered the folder, closed the drawer, and locked it behind her. She returned the key to the tape, pressed it back under the shelf. She looked around the room one last time. The blinds. The lamp. The untouched surface of the desk. The space where silence had held vigil for a decade. She left without closing the door behind her. Some things were better left ajar.

The car was already warm when she backed out of the driveway, the leather seats softened by sun, the steering wheel hot enough to make her fingers flinch and regrip. She didn't open the windows. The silence suited her now. Air moved through the vents in engineered currents, neither cold nor warm. A manufactured equilibrium. The folder sat on the passenger seat beside her, unbuckled, its cardboard edges blunt and heavy.

Outside, the city had come fully awake, and not gracefully. Horns jabbed in staccato from the intersection at Lawndale, where a delivery van had blocked the right-turn lane and a driver in an imported sedan honked as if the problem could be solved through force of insistence. On Friendly Avenue, a man with a Bluetooth earpiece screamed into the air while crossing against the light, gesturing with a rage that suggested disappointment. A woman in medical scrubs jaywalked with a smoothie and eyes halfway between shifts.

Paula merged into traffic without signaling. She drove slowly enough to not attract attention. She hadn't called. Hadn't emailed. She wasn't even entirely certain the address was current. A line in a Christmas card from one of Alan's colleagues—"He's still over by the university, near the bike shop"—had embedded itself in her mind, a pin on a mental map she'd never expected to consult. It was enough. It had to be.

The stoplight at Market Street caught her. She braked harder than intended. The folder moved slightly. She looked down. A corner of one memo had come loose from the clasp—Phase II Stormwater Oversight, Draft Response. She slid it back inside without reading. The light turned green.

The closer she came to campus, the less ornamental the city became. No manicured traffic island landscapes. No branded campaign banners. The strip malls here were still honest: tax prep, cell phone repair, cash for gold. Students on bikes wove between buses like they didn't care if they lived. The sun had climbed fully now, flattening shadows, waking even the parts of town that tried to sleep through crisis. The air had the texture of mid-May: humid but not cruel, pollen yellowing the edges of windshields, birds clustered on power lines like they'd seen this one before.

She took a left at the corner where a mural had faded into pastels, remembered the sharp turn near the public library. Somewhere here—she couldn't say precisely where—Alan lived. She would know it when she saw it. She didn't think too far ahead. Not what she would say. Not how he would look at her. Not what this meant for David, or the foundation, or the life that still waited in the master-planned quiet of New Irving Park. Those questions existed just beyond the windshield, waiting to be asked.

The apartment complex rose in plain red brick, the kind laid hurriedly in the early nineties and never reloved over time. A mismatched fence ran along the parking lot, half chain-link, half aluminum slats meant to suggest modernity.

Paula parked beneath a maple tree whose shade didn't quite reach her windshield. A campus shuttle passed behind her, low to the ground and wrapped in university branding, the side panel boasting "Sustainable Transit" in a font a bit too hopeful. She sat for a moment in the car, the engine off, the key still in her hand, the folder a weight beneath her elbow. She didn't know which apartment was his.

There were no directories, no callboxes. Just a row of beige doors. Nothing about the place declared itself, and that, too, seemed correct. Alan, even in his most righteous years, had never demanded aesthetic. She unlocked her phone. Googled "Alan Ransome Greensboro NC university." Her finger hovered. Then: "Alan Ransome home address." The algorithm, shamefully eager, offered an autofill. Property sites. Voter roll data. The petty bureaucracy of exposure.

She clicked. The address populated. Unit 3B. She got out of the car.

The heat met her face. Midday in North Carolina offered no indulgence. She walked across the asphalt, past a cracked curb where weeds forced their way through. The folder was tucked tight under her arm, and still, it felt exposed. She passed two young men carrying laundry baskets. One held a bag of fast food, the grease already spotting the bottom. Neither looked at her.

At the stoop, she stopped.

Three concrete steps. A faded rug with the word "Welcome" worn into ambiguity. To the left, a utility meter blinked green. A rusted mailbox, open, held nothing but junk and a coupon for flu shots. Her reflection flickered in the storm door's glass: hair pulled back, blouse creased with purpose, eyes unreadable.

Inside, someone's radio played noontime jazz. She stood there and didn't knock. The folder pressed against her chest. Regret rose without theater. It was elemental. The years, counted too slowly. The committees chaired for causes she didn't believe in. The fundraisers thrown with borrowed crystal and hollow morality. The nights with David, his voice low in strategy, her nods silent in collusion. She had not lied. She had endorsed. She had refined the truth until it passed inspection.

Twenty years of table settings and avoidance. Twenty years of not saying what scared her. She looked at the door again. Three steps up. One knock. The weight of choice settled not on her shoulders, but in her hands. What she carried now—what she would give him—was not confession. It was correction. It was, perhaps too late, the only act left untouched by rehearsal.

She raised her hand and knocked. A polite, measured tap against the aluminum-framed storm door, more hesitant than demanding. Alan muted the radio and rose from the kitchen table, bare feet brushing crumbs across the linoleum. When he opened the door, he froze.

Paula stood on the landing, framed by daylight, her blouse drawn tight across her collarbone. She held a folder against her like a ledger, her mouth flat, unreadable.

He blinked.

"Paula?"

She didn't smile. Didn't shift her weight or offer any of the hesitant courtesies she was known for. No polite touch at her collar, no gaze cast off to deflect discomfort.

"Don't speak," she said. Her voice clipped at the edges. "Just—listen."

She stepped forward—not in, but closer—her hand lifting the folder between them, offering it the way one might a wrapped gift. Her fingers found his as she passed it into his hands. She let them linger a moment.

"It's everything," she said. "The parcel. The falsified remediation studies. The redline drafts. The internal memos with language so boiled down it burns. His name's on most of them."

He didn't open it. He looked at her instead, at the face he'd once known too well to forget. There was still sharpness in her features, but the composure had cracked. Just slightly. Enough to let something real through.

"Why are you giving me this?" he asked.

She exhaled, as if the effort of holding it all had finally passed from her lungs into his hands.

"Because I'm done laundering the city's conscience," she said. "The city's wound is paved in my name."

Her voice was flat and accurate. "This is my tourniquet."

He stepped back, the door swinging wider now. Light spilled in behind her, flattening the colors on his threadbare rug, catching on the chipped veneer of the kitchen chairs. He opened the folder without sitting.

Consultant letters first—language threaded with legal restraint, hazard redefined as redevelopment. A map, Parcel 524-B outlined in neat red ink, the legend blurred where it had been scanned too many times. The press drafts followed—community reassurances stripped of truth, rewritten in softer language that cost nothing.

Then the emails.

He read the phrases as if reciting them: "Mitigate language. Downplay residuals. Control optics." His eyes moved fast, but his breath didn't.

He looked up.

"You're not protected anymore."

She didn't flinch. "Neither are they."

The silence held. Not awkward. Not uncertain. Simply long enough for the words to finish settling.

Alan closed the folder gently, the corners aligning in his hands. He nodded once. A movement that acknowledged history, not forgiveness. He did not thank her. There was no name for what she had done—not whistleblower, not ally. Something harder. Something more final.

She turned. Her heels clicked once against the concrete. Sharp. Singular. Then stopped.

"Paula—"

He said it softly, but the word reached her anyway. She paused with one foot already descending the stoop.

"You asked me once if I believed cities could be healed," she said without turning back. "I said yes."

Her voice caught. Just enough to count.

"I lied."

She stood there for a moment, still facing away, as if she'd forgotten something or remembered too much. Then she stepped off the stoop and walked to her car without looking back. Alan stood in the doorway, folder in hand, Greensboro finally broken open.

20

Alan shut the door with a quiet finality, the kind of silence not born of caution. Her scent still lingered in the doorway—a trace of orange blossom and rose, the same way it had clung to her scarves in winter, the same way she had once pressed it into his chest when they were young and wrong about everything.

He didn't go to the window. He didn't watch her leave. Instead, he returned to the kitchen table, pulled out the hard-backed chair and sat, the folder still in his hands. The jazz station, still quietly piping from the radio, struck a wrong note now. Trumpet over piano, improvisation trying and failing to soothe. He reached and flicked the knob.

His laptop pinged. Once, then again, then rapidly. Email alerts from editors, colleagues, a few congratulatory texts forwarding the article now running on the front page of the Observer. Some with attachments. One subject line: "Fallout begins." Another: "You're a marked man now, brother."

His phone buzzed on the table. He ignored them all. He stared at the folder. Still unopened. His fingers rested on the flap. He was not afraid of the content. He'd read enough municipal reports to understand the genre: euphemism, liability, abbreviation. But this—this came from her. Not the woman he'd once loved, not the face he had imagined too many times aging beside his, but from the Paula he had not known before. Paula the accomplice. Paula the perpetrator's wife. Paula the witness who had not spoken when it would have mattered most. And now: Paula the one who had, finally, said it even though it scared her.

He opened the folder. It wasn't a bomb. Not right away. It was too well-organized for that. The first sheet was a correspondence log—typed headers, dates, institutional letterhead from the Health Equity Development Trust. A name he'd once mocked aloud in a public panel.

He moved through the pages. Memos, internal. Revisions in tracked changes.

"Public concern re: contaminants exaggerated. Language must prioritize transformation, not remediation."

"Pre-regulatory brownfield is a narrative challenge—not a barrier. Suggest reframing as innovation zone."

He slowed. Maps. Parcel 524-B, a red oval of crime amid gray zoning blocks. Below it, layered scans from environmental consultants. Trace metals, groundwater flow, soft annotations in red ink—David's handwriting.

"Community input already captured. Further engagement unnecessary."

It went on.

A legal brief: phrasing that ducked, swerved, buried. Risk defined not by harm, but by press cycles.

He moved to the second stack. A letter with Paula's name at the bottom. "On behalf of the board…" it began. He read every word. She had signed it. She had sat at a table and lifted her pen. She had smiled as they photographed her in front of the new greenway that cut across land once soaked in refuse.

He turned the page. Then came the third stack.

Less polished. More desperate. Communications strategy memos marked DRAFT. One with a note: "If media asks about red sand, refer to community partnerships, not historical data." Another: "Avoid technical detail. Pivot to future potential."

Alan pressed his hands against the edge of the table.

This wasn't about David now. Not about corrupt ambition or strategic failure. This was about a machine built with toxic fingers. It was about the way people like Paula—people with grace and invitations and nothing so crude as greed—made it work. She had not just handed him documents. She'd handed him the blueprint of complicity. The social engine of civic erasure. And she had handed him her name. He closed the folder.

The phone buzzed again. His laptop lit up with another ping. He shut the screen. In his chest, something unfamiliar. Not triumph. Not rage. Responsibility. He could publish this tomorrow. He could end careers. Tank contracts. He could be remembered or reviled. But he could not unknow what she had chosen to do. Paula Moss had betrayed her husband. But more than that—more astonishing, more damning—she had betrayed herself.

Alan exhaled. His hands were shaking now from understanding.

He cleared the books from the living room floor, shoving them in uneven piles under the side table, displacing a mug ring on the wood that had never quite been scrubbed away. He knelt awkwardly—knees stiff, shoulder aching—and opened the folder for the second time, this time not as a reader but as an investigator. The documents came out in sections, layered like soil: policy memos, consultant briefs, email threads, maps annotated with color-coded overlays. He spread them out across the floor in rows, each paper building off the one before it. The early materials were technical, bloodless. Toxins renamed as "compounds of concern," groundwater tables redrawn with boundary lines that neatly avoided inconvenient truths. But even these carried fingerprints—David's marginalia, precise, impatient. "Too cautious—needs more vision." In another: "Get Paula to frame this as community uplift."

He found the drafts next. Public statements gutted of accountability, language scrubbed raw: "What was once a brownfield now brims with opportunity." And then, softer ink, smaller handwriting, looping at the edges—Paula's.

In one margin: "Add emotional pivot before stats." In another: her initials—PM, underlined once, as if to remind herself it had passed through her hands, if only briefly.

Alan sat back and took a breath. He had spent nights here arguing with himself, shouting aloud to no one, trying to thread cause from consequence in the city's sickness. And now it was laid bare on cheap laminate, in half-faded ink.

Alan pressed the heels of his palms into his eyes. Emotion flooded him—grief, recognition, something knotted deep. She loved David. And now she was burning it all down. He found himself laughing, bitter and sudden. She could've stayed quiet. She had everything—status, foundation ties, a place at every table that mattered. Her name opened doors. And she handed him all of it.

"She didn't come to confess." He thought it again, slower this time. "She came to destroy the structure."

This was not a plea for redemption. This was an act of refusal. A surgical cut against the tendons of the civic body she had spent two decades holding aloft. Paula wasn't making amends. She was declaring war.

The sorrow was thickest around that truth. Not that she had chosen action over silence—but that it had taken this long. That they had once imagined something real together, and now, at the end of everything, she had done what he always believed she was incapable of: "she told the truth."

He lifted a memo, reread a phrase he had already memorized: "Control optics. Preempt inquiry."

Not anymore.

He rose. The papers rustled on the floor behind him. This would end things. It would end careers. Friendships. Alliances that had stretched between boardrooms and council chambers. But maybe it would begin something, too.

He stood among the papers as if in a sanctuary of deceit. The pages sprawled around him, overlapping. His feet were bare, and he could feel the ghost of every motion beneath them. The way one draft had been replaced by another, the way truths had been reshaped and then neatly buried.

He moved to the sink. The glass was clean because he used it every day. He filled it with water and drank in slow swallows, the kind that steadied. In the hush of late morning, the city's noise had softened to the occasional low whine of traffic farther off. He pressed the cold of the glass to his forehead and looked out the window, not seeing. This was what he understood now: David hadn't needed to orchestrate every lie. He had simply arranged the symphony.

The soil report—initially cautious, marked with consultant hesitation—had been pulled apart until it said nothing at all. The early legal reviews, clear-eyed in their caution, were overwritten with redlines not to correct fact but to dull it. At every stage, someone else had done the final editing. David's brilliance had been in delegation. His genius wasn't in deception—it was in distance.

What Alan saw, finally and fully, was the machinery of plausible deniability. Parcel 524-B hadn't been hidden. It had been documented, debated, reframed, renamed, and then offered back to the city in language so sterile it couldn't be understood. This was the legacy David had managed: nothing direct. Just layers. Just enough distance between his name and the toxic soil.

Alan turned from the window and looked again at the floor. The scope of it was numbing.

Paula's annotations weren't dense, but they were deliberate. Her lines undercut the narrative structure, her questions scribbled in margins—"Why this phrasing? What happens if someone asks?" They weren't protests. They were records of hesitation. And now they were evidence. David hadn't told the city what to believe. He had made sure it wouldn't know what to ask.

Alan felt the certainty settle at the base of his spine. This wasn't carelessness. It was managed care. The city hadn't been betrayed by accident. It had been complicit. And now the documents spoke. Each one a tile in a mosaic of harm. Each memo another refraction. Alan set the glass down on the counter. He turned back to the papers, slower now, reverent. He would name it. All of it.

The conference room was technically reserved for a research colloquium on urban resilience, but no one was using it, and no one had wiped off the dry-erase marker from the last committee meeting: "Adaptive Systems Require Adaptive Governance." Alan unlocked the door with his faculty badge, which still scanned, and let the others file in. Ava first, dragging her laptop bag and her certainty, followed by Tanisha, who paused to check her phone before taking a seat with her back to the window. Gale Clarey arrived last, her reporter's notebook already open, pen poised above a page labeled "Parcel 524-B – Tuesday, 3:12pm."

Alan set the documents on the table. A banker's box opened like a wound. Folders unstacked. Maps spread flat. Memos in plastic sleeves, the kind used to protect legal artifacts from the smudge of human touch. He didn't launch right away. He let them look.

Ava leaned in first, flipping pages without reverence. She'd seen too much institutional cowardice to be impressed by headers or seals. Tanisha scanned the soil data, brows pinched, her expression unreadable. Gale read aloud under her breath—"Reframe red sand as pre-regulatory fill"—then underlined it in blue.

Alan waited. When the silence began to build with understanding, he said, "It's all real."

"No one doubted that," Ava said. "We just didn't expect it to be this organized."

"Or this obvious," Tanisha added, tapping a memo marked "STRATEGIC LANGUAGE COORDINATION."

Gale kept reading. "This one cites a cleanup that never happened."

Alan nodded. "There's more. The financial trail, David's committees. Deferred funds from the streetscape bond routed through community arts programs. 524-B reclassified as a wellness corridor without a single environmental impact review post-2006."

"No RFP?" Tanisha asked.

"Just a narrative briefing," he said. "Prepared in-house, never published."

They sat with that. The fan above them churned stale air into still corners. A hint of institutional carpet cleaner lingered, sterilizing the drama into something too real to be theatrical.

"There's risk," Tanisha said. "Lawsuits, retaliation. Not just from the city. From the hospital. From the university."

Gale looked up. "I'll print it. But I'll lose half our ad base by Friday."

"I can anonymize the source," Alan offered, though the words felt thin in his mouth.

"No," Ava said, looking at him, sharp and steady. "That's not what this is."

He looked down. The documents were now patterns. Not new information, but undeniable record. His fingerprints on them. Paula's handwriting. David's quiet shadow.

"You wanted proof," Ava said. "Now you have it. What are you going to do?"

He took a breath. Not a rhetorical pause. A full, cellular inhale.

"We go public," he said. "All of it. Before the next council meeting."

Silence again, but this time it held something electric. Movement inside stillness.

Ava opened her laptop. "Press release. Clear headline. Pull quotes from the documents."

Tanisha started a spreadsheet. "We need a timeline of decisions. From the zoning reclassification to the grant and bond disbursements."

"We'll need a digital drop," Ava added. "A full archive. Open-source. Hosted off-campus. Permanent. Screenshots, PDFs, scanned emails. Metadata embedded."

Alan nodded, more approvingly this time. "We lead with the land," he said. "Make them see what they've buried."

Gale underlined something in her notebook again. "You're not just reporting. You're detonating."

"No," Alan said. "I'm describing the crater. It's been there. We're just lowering the camera."

The room moved now with urgency. Laptops clicked. Pages were sorted. The whiteboard marker squeaked as Ava scrawled "TIMELINE" in quick block letters.

Outside the window, students passed without looking in. Another day on campus. Another building. Another sealed room where something had changed and no one had yet heard it. Alan leaned back in his chair, listening not to what they said, but to the way they said it. This wasn't protest. It was precision.

They would not win. He knew that. But they would not lie. And that, finally, would be enough.

By the time they scanned the final memo—Paula's handwriting trailing into the corner of the page like a smile she hadn't meant to leave—it was well past eight. They worked under the yellow warmth of a floor lamp, files stacked neatly beside the scanner, the documents fed one by one like offerings to a machine that couldn't possibly know the power of what it was processing.

Ava packed her laptop. She offered him a nod before disappearing down the hallway, a faint "Text me when it's done" trailing in her wake.

The PDF archive—three hundred and twelve pages—sat in a clean file on his desktop. He named it "Wellness Corridor Archive, v1", as if there would be more. There wouldn't. His back ached from hours hunched over the table, and his eyes burned from the glow of the screen. But his fingers didn't hesitate. He zipped the files. Uploaded them to the secure server he'd paid for months ago, before he ever knew what he'd do with it. A domain name he'd registered without telling anyone, a title that meant nothing until now: gsoremembers.org.

He watched the upload bar fill. Slow, indifferent. He rested his hand on the mouse and waited.

When it hit 100 percent, he hovered a moment over the "Publish" toggle. Then clicked. The page went live.

He copied the link. Sent it to the entire city council. Pasted it into emails to the Observer, News 2, Channel 12, Gale's alt-weekly, the national outlet that still ran long-form investigations when everyone else wanted lists. He sent it to the environmental law group in Raleigh. And then, finally, to himself. As if to confirm that it existed.

The messages weren't dramatic. Just the link. Just the truth. He leaned back in the dark. The laptop screen lit his face in a dim pulse. He closed his eyes. The silence rang. Then the phone buzzed on the table. Once. Then again. Then again.

Ava: "It's alive!"

Keith: "Jesus."

Unknown number: "You're making a mistake."

He stared at the screen. The words didn't blink. But the cursor did, back on the laptop, where the site now stood open to the world. Nothing viral yet. The facts, holding steady. Parcel 524-B. The maps. The emails. The handwritten memos. David's signature. Paula's initials. The wound, named.

The blinking cursor pulsed again. Alan didn't flinch. He watched it like a signal fire. Quiet. Fixed. Unafraid.

By dawn, Greensboro was already in motion, though its residents might have claimed otherwise—might have said it was just another Wednesday, that the sky was too bright for scandal, that the air smelled of mulch and honeysuckle and not of institutional toxicity rising to the surface. But the city was awake, and the story was everywhere, in the language of rupture, in the scroll of headlines and the sudden, collective tightening of the throat.

The leak had landed like a tidal wave. Planned, perhaps inevitable, but still staggering in its velocity. Gale Clarey's exposé dropped at 5:14 a.m., distributed across two platforms: the local alt-weekly paper, where her reporting had teeth but also neighbors, and the national watchdog site based out of Durham, where the science was denser and the stakes nationalized. She had led with the image: red sand in a child's cupped palm, filtered by early evening light, unvarnished, unmistakable. That photograph did more than words could.

Within an hour, the image had migrated to regional media, where it was cropped and reframed. A subheader in the Observer named David Moss without directly naming him: "Documents from High-Profile Advisor Reveal Coordinated Messaging on Environmental Risk." On social media, the discourse erupted predictably: indignation, deflection, tactical silence. Every local station had some version of the same line: "Sources close to the redevelopment commission express concern."

David, for his part, had gone dark. His assistant claimed he was "out of town for professional obligations." A reporter staked out the New Irving Park address and was offered a quote by a teenage neighbor: "He's in the mountains, I think. Or hiding."

In the story's second paragraph, Clarey quoted Goldie Hayes: "We were told it was nothing. It was everything." The line spread fast, clipped and shared in boldface, posted beside maps, screenshots, a cropped scan of the phrase "Control optics" circled in pen.

Later that afternoon, Gale posted a follow-up: isotope analysis from the state environmental lab. It matched the chromium found in Parcel 524-B to that of Bingham Park. Same decay profile. Same industrial signature. Two decades apart, two neighborhoods apart.

The city's response was predictable and clinical. A subcontractor, conveniently out of business, took the fall. Permits were reexamined but not revoked. A statement from the Office of Environmental Review cited "ongoing dialogue with stakeholders." The corridor remained funded. The playground construction was ahead of schedule.

Damage, it seemed, was quantifiable. Action was not.

But the story was not forgotten.

By evening, as the city returned to its rituals—drive-thrus humming, porch lights came on, televisions rewarming themselves with weather and sports. Alan walked east. Past the spot where Goldie sometimes met Ava for tea, past the shuttered post office whose renovation had been stalled since the 2008 economic collapse, down toward Bingham Park.

The sign still read "Temporarily Closed." Behind the fencing, the soil had been recovered, but nothing planted. The land lay exposed, patient. Children played along the edge anyway, tossing a tennis ball between them on the sidewalk. Behind them, windows lit one by one, golden rectangles suspended above cracked concrete.

Alan stood at the fence. He didn't take a photo. He didn't post. He just watched. A breeze picked up, carrying the scent of something earthy and faintly metallic. From a few streets over, the sound of car audio. Laughter. A bike chain skipping. The city did not yet know how to repair itself. But it was learning how to look.

The remote stuck slightly as he pressed the channel up, the rubber buttons worn smooth from use. He'd lost track of what night it was. The folder still lay open on the far end of the couch, its papers half-reordered after Gale's story broke. A few stray pages had slid to the floor, like they couldn't bear to be filed again.

The local news came on with the urgency of a high school play. That usual flattening of tragedy into bullet points: "Tonight, a political storm brewing over downtown redevelopment. Two city officials speak out."

Alan turned up the volume.

Councilman Dent's face filled the screen, his complexion fixed in that uncanny shade of bronzed sincerity favored by men who vacation on Hilton Head and mistake lighting for credibility. He was standing on a city sidewalk with a branded step-and-repeat behind him, wearing his navy windbreaker that Alan knew he reserved for controversy.

"The documents paint a troubling picture," Dent said, as if he'd just learned what documents were. "But we have no reason to believe there was intent to deceive. We're talking about decades of interdepartmental complexity, not criminal misconduct."

Alan exhaled, long and silent.

Dent smiled at something the reporter said off-camera, nodding as if preparing for reelection. "And let's be clear—this is a city that acts when it knows. We can't be expected to solve what was never brought to our attention officially."

The word "officially" stuck the landing, giving bounce to the lie.

Then Councilwoman Hoffman, the evening's designated conscience. She stood in front of a playground—the one on Parcel 524-B, of course—her earrings catching the glow of the parking lot floodlights.

"It's easy to cast blame when people are hurting," she said, voice dipped in that preemptive calm politicians learned at donor breakfasts. "But let's remember, we're building here. We're creating space for families, for joy. That matters, too."

Alan let out a laugh, sharp and involuntary.

"Joy," he repeated, to no one.

Hoffman gestured toward the play structures behind her. "I've spoken to moms in this neighborhood. They're proud of this place. And they're tired of having their community turned into someone else's crisis."

Back in the studio, the anchor nodded gravely.

Alan muted the TV in disgust. The kind that swelled under the skin like a sting. Dent's tone, Hoffman's phrasing. Deflection perfected. They didn't even need talking points. It was muscle memory. He looked down at the floor where one of Paula's memos lay half-folded, her handwriting delicate in the margin: "Reframe before they can react."

He sat in the quiet. The TV still flickered, silently showing b-roll of Parcel 524-B's art installation waving in the breeze. He didn't need to watch anymore. He'd seen it all before. And next week, there'd be a ribbon-cutting. A new splash pad. A student jazz trio playing under a pop-up tent.

Progress.

Always Goddamn progress.

21

The jet wobbled once as it descended, just enough for the man in 3D to clutch the armrest. David didn't react. He'd taken too many flights, ridden too many atmospheric seams between cities promising opportunity, to be impressed by turbulence. The window showed the waking edge of Washington, D.C.: monuments of marble, commuter bridges, the Potomac just visible beyond the runway, slick with early morning light. The seatbelt sign pinged its last warning.

He hadn't slept. Not in the mountains, where the stillness was too accusatory, where even the silence was structured. He'd left Ashe County around 1 a.m., winding down the switchbacks with one hand on the wheel and the other cycling through radio static until a station out of Winston-Salem offered him a full hour of jazz without commentary. Greensboro's west side had been dead when he passed through it, just past three, empty stretches of I-40 leading to the airport.

The mountain house hadn't helped. It never did. Meant as retreat, it had long ago been repurposed into staging ground: a place for drafts, for whiteboard diagrams, for language massaged into something polished. He'd gone there because there was no one to answer to and nothing to explain. But the quiet had a way of distorting everything. He'd stared too long at the trees and thought too hard about how everything that had built him was now being fed into the machine of public opinion.

Now, taxiing toward the terminal, the nation's capital bracing against the influx of another professional gathering, David felt the dread crawl up the back of his neck. He adjusted his collar. He straightened his jacket before standing. No one in the plane met his eyes. That was new.

The speech was scheduled for Thursday. "Urban Futures: Redevelopment and Responsibility." A panel, a keynote, a post-lunch breakout on "narrative pathways for legacy spaces." He was meant to open the conference with a ten-minute framing address, the kind that ended with applause timed to the last sentence. The irony made him want to laugh, though he couldn't quite locate the humor anymore.

He stepped into the jet bridge and blinked against the artificial dawn. The email from the D.C. hosts had been short and careful: "We're confident your remarks will bring the clarity this moment requires." Clarity. Not truth. Not defense. Just another calibrated fog.

He hadn't spoken to Paula. He hadn't needed to. He knew. The folder had been taken from the study drawer. She knew the key. Of course she did. He hadn't moved it in years. She could've burned the papers. She could've let the story pass like so many others. But she hadn't. What gnawed at him was not the leak. He could have weathered that. What gnawed was that she had done it not in anger, not to punish him, but because something inside her had eroded. He had seen it in the kitchen that morning when she stood by the coffee pot and didn't speak. That wasn't rage. That was resolve.

He moved through the terminal without checking his phone. No point now. Every message was a variation on the same theme: caution, silence, preparation. He passed a woman in a blazer reading the Post, and though he couldn't see the front page, he imagined the red sand photo was somewhere inside it, framed in columns, captioned with precision. He had built a career on distance. Not deception—he never directly lied—but the kind of eloquent ambiguity that passed for leadership in cities like Greensboro. He had never touched the soil. That was the point. He orchestrated, advised, refined. And somehow that was now the indictment.

The escalator dropped him into the arrivals hall with its perpetual fog of tired light and carbon fatigue. Families clustered near baggage claim, half-awake children slumped against rollaboards, lobbyists and consultants thumbing screens while pretending not to read headlines. He walked with his usual posture, shoulders squared, pace deliberate, never hurried, never idle. His carry-on trailed behind him in soft, disciplined thumps.

He spotted the newsstand before he reached Carousel 5. A rack of newspapers in a steel-framed grid, each one announcing the day's panic with proprietary fonts. But it was the Times—of course it was—that had claimed the above-the-fold corner: "Southern City Faces Scrutiny Over Contaminated Redevelopment Deal." The lead photo showed the red sand again, cropped tighter this time, turned grainy by overuse. But it wasn't the image that stopped him. It was the two photos beneath the headline.

Alan Ransome—slightly out of focus, jaw set, his faculty photo aged by entropy. Next to him, Goldie Hayes, mid-sentence, head tilted just enough to suggest gravitas. Together they formed a visual accusation. David stood there for a moment, his left hand still gripping the retractable handle of his suitcase. He didn't buy the paper.

He knew what the piece would say—an aggregation of known facts threaded through just enough fresh phrasing to pass editorial muster. It would hint at systemic negligence. It would nod at institutional harm. It would quote an ethics expert from Chapel Hill. It would reference the parcel, the isotopes, the community "activists." It would mention Moss only once, in the passive register: "Documents obtained by an anonymous source indicate involvement by advisory figures close to the project's narrative strategy." That phrasing had been workshopped. He knew because he'd once helped people like that write it.

He walked past the stand, through the automatic doors, into the press of D.C. morning.

He thought of the legal briefings from the week before. Three separate firms had weighed in—one from Charlotte, one with deep ties to the public-private sphere in Raleigh, and a third retained on speed if the federal angle gained oxygen. The consensus was the same: the documents weren't good, but they weren't fatal. The redlines weren't instructions, they were suggestions. No forged approvals, no unreported financial gain. Nothing prosecutable.

"Manage optics. Let the news cycle do its work," the Raleigh counsel had said, sipping espresso through an orthodontic retainer like the world couldn't touch him. His own role had been minimized. He hadn't signed off on the reclassification. He hadn't attended the Parcel 524-B roundtable. Paula had. That stung more than it should have. The plan was to weather it. Hold position. Wait.

Phase III was already permitted. The corridor would proceed. The grant from the wellness alliance had cleared its second disbursement. A new art piece had been commissioned—a light installation shaped like hands. The playground would open in two weeks. He'd seen the renderings. Laughing children under LED halos. A walking trail softened with native grasses connected to the city greenway. Interpretive signage that explained nothing and gestured toward everything.

He paused at the restroom, not to go in, but to see his face in the mirror. It was intact. Just older. Fatigue, creeping at the edges. Outside the terminal, the nation's capital rolled open in ribbons of concrete and tinted windows, early traffic darting between lanes. David squared his shoulders. He would give the speech. He would smile when they asked how Greensboro was handling the pressure. He would say "challenges" instead of failures, "disruption" instead of harm.

But somewhere deep—beyond his press statement, beyond his power tie, beyond the fabricated lightness of the lobby he would walk through in two hours—he knew what Paula had taken from him. She hadn't exposed him. She had finished him. Quietly. Precisely. He stepped into the morning, and no one stopped him.

The hotel room was aggressively neutral—taupe walls, ergonomic chair, a desk bolted to the floor, the kind of furnishings designed to accommodate conference men and their PowerPoint slides. David dropped his bag on the bench by the door and sat on the edge of the bed, still wearing his blazer. The burden of recent days clung to him.

He dialed Paula again. Fourth attempt in thirty-six hours. Straight to voicemail. He said nothing. Hung up before it connected. He sat back. Remote in hand. Turned the television on.

PBS. He hadn't meant to land there, but his thumb stopped on the channel when he recognized the banner: "Health Corridor Redevelopment Under Scrutiny." He dropped the remote without meaning to. It thudded lightly against the carpet. On screen, a map of Greensboro hovered next to the anchor's shoulder—bright overlays showing the corridor cutting north to south, Parcel 524-B glowing like a caution light. Then came the interview clips.

Goldie first, seated on her front porch in Cottage Grove, the screen door open behind her, her voice calm but knotted. "We were told this would heal the community. But how do you heal something you've never admitted you broke?"

Then Alan, standing outside Bingham Park, arms crossed—not in defiance, but in defense. "The public was fed a narrative instead of information. They were managed. That's not healing. That's deflection."

David clenched the hotel keycard in his hand until it bent.

Now the in-studio segment. Gale Clarey, seated beneath soft lighting, her expression composed but unflinching. The anchor offered questions with studied balance: "We're hearing conflicting reports about who knew what and when…"

Gale replied without blinking. "They all knew. The documents are dated. The memos were circulated. What's new isn't the knowledge—it's the clarity."

David stood and walked to the minibar. Opened it. Stared. Closed it again.

Back on screen, the anchor: "The city says the corridor moves forward. That the playground will open next week."

Gale: "The development will survive the truth. That's how this works. But the cost—"

David looked back at his phone. No missed calls. No message from Paula. He imagined her somewhere in the house, lights off, blinds drawn. Or not. Maybe she was out. Maybe she was already being rewritten as something else entirely.

He sat down on the bed again. He wondered how long it would last. This frenzy. This theater of outrage and pretense. He'd seen it before—public appetite moving quickly from shock to exhaustion to something resembling amnesia. They'd ride it out. They always did.

But still, he couldn't stop replaying her silence. Not the calls she didn't return. But what she had already said without words.

His phone lit up on the nightstand like it had been waiting to betray him. Paula. He answered before it could ring twice.

"Hey," he said, softening his voice. "You're up early."

"I couldn't sleep," she said. "How was the flight?"

"It was fine," he said. "Uneventful. Crowded."

A pause.

"D.C. still looks like D.C.," he added, smiling into the receiver though she couldn't see it. "Grey suits and better sidewalks."

She exhaled something close to a laugh. "Did you get the room you like?"

He looked around the hotel room, suddenly aware of its sameness. "Same carpet, different view. Yeah. It's fine."

Another pause. Not the awkward kind. The kind where both people are waiting to see if the conversation will become real or just drift politely into silence.

"How's—how's she?" he asked.

"She's fine. She's still memorizing her monologue. The one about telling the truth even when you're scared."

His stomach tightened. Not because he didn't expect it, but because she said it without malice.

"That line again," he said.

"She's been repeating it," Paula said. "All week."

He let it hang there. He wasn't going to be the one to change the subject first.

"I saw the segment," she said after a moment. "PBS. You looked like yourself. At least what's left of it."

"I wasn't on," he said.

"They had your corporate head shot," she said. "Close enough."

Another pause.

"Can we just—" he started, then paused. "Why?"

She was quiet. He thought maybe the call had dropped.

"Why what?" she asked finally.

"You know what I mean."

"I do."

He leaned forward, elbow on knee, the phone pressed close now, like proximity could repair anything.

"Then just tell me, Paula. After everything. After the appearances, the boards, the fundraisers, the panels. You torched the structure while we were still standing on it. Just—tell me why."

There was a rustle on her end. Probably her walking. He pictured her barefoot in the sun room.

"You've been talking about structures for twenty years," she said. "I finally realized I was the cornerstone. Holding everything up while pretending I didn't notice the pressure."

He didn't respond.

"I'm tired," she said. "I'm tired of the language. The precision. The correct phrasing. I'm tired of supporting things I'm not allowed to question. I'm tired of hearing you explain how it's not about you, but somehow it always is."

"You had to go to Alan?" he said, not accusing, but not hiding the edge.

"No," she said. "I had to go to the truth. He just happened to be standing there."

He moved the phone to his other ear, the leather of the hotel chair creaking beneath him.

"I would've told you," she added. "Eventually."

"Would it have mattered?"

She didn't answer.

He waited. Then: "So what now? We have the conversation where you say you need space and I pretend I'm okay with that until we both settle into the logistics of separation?"

"Yes," she said. "That one."

He laughed once. It didn't sound good.

"I think you should get a condo," she said. "Downtown. Something up high with a gym and a concierge. You've got friends with access."

"You think this is funny?"

"No," she said. "I think it's clean."

He leaned his head back against the wall. The drywall gave nothing.

"I need time," she said, and this time her voice wasn't angry. Just honest. "Time to remember who I am when I'm not planning your narrative."

He closed his eyes.

She said nothing more. Neither did he.

Eventually the line went quiet, though he didn't remember ending the call. Just the silence of the connection severed.

The Marriott conference level smelled of off-brand coffee and freshly printed handouts. A thousand ideas about civic progress floated in the air like mist: signage urging "Vision Through Infrastructure", "Wellness by Design", "Equity in Built Form." A man in a performance fleece with a clipboard jogged past a display table covered in branded canvas totes. Somewhere nearby, a microphone was being tested with the phrase "check one, check two, check equity."

David adjusted his collar and stepped from the elevator into the thunder of post-breakfast chatter. The name badge clipped to his lapel had been printed before the documents leaked. "DAVID

MOSS, Senior Vice-President, Guilford Health System (Greensboro). The parenthetical now read like a footnote to scandal.

A young staffer approached him, brisk and purposeful. She wore a bright pantsuit and had a poise that outpaced condescension too many times to flinch.

"Mr. Moss? I'm Mia. I'll walk you to the front."

He nodded, grateful for the escort. Every other face had already turned toward him. Not rudely, but with the intensity of recognition. A few conference-goers stood frozen mid-pastry, jaws tensed. Someone snapped a photo from near the coffee urns. The ones who'd read the exposé were easy to spot: eyes sharp, arms crossed, notetaking already in progress. Those who hadn't were reading the room and adjusting accordingly.

Mia leaned slightly as they walked. "If you'd like to address the current events before your remarks, we have a minute to cue the tech team."

"No," David said. "We won't be doing that."

"Understood," she said. No judgment in her voice.

They passed a table where a group of urban planners in recycled-fiber blazers leaned toward one another with discretion. One whispered, "That's him," and another responded, not softly, "He's the narrative guy, right?"

David kept walking. Mia kept pace.

A reporter he recognized from the Chronicle of Civic Design intercepted him near the stage stairs. "Mr. Moss—quickly, if I may—would you say the situation in Greensboro reflects a failure of public-private oversight, or a misalignment of community outcomes?"

David didn't break stride. "It reflects a failure of nuance," he said, and moved on.

The reporter nodded, typing before he'd even finished the sentence.

At the head table, a stack of folders sat untouched. Water bottles perspired under the stage lights. A woman from the organizing committee offered him a tight smile that didn't reach her eyes.

"We're honored to have you, David," she said, in the same tone you might use to welcome a priest who'd been caught skimming from the collection plate. "The room's a little... charged. But your experience matters."

"Good to know," he said.

He scanned the crowd. The room held two hundred, maybe more. Most pretending not to watch. A few trying to capture the moment discreetly, phones angled across tables. Someone had projected his name onto the screen beside the stage, where it loomed beneath the conference logo: "David Moss – Reimagining Infrastructure: The Long View."

He exhaled. Adjusted his tie.

This wasn't a reckoning. This was theater. And he'd written most of the script.

Mia returned, murmured something into the headset of a man behind the curtain. The moderator stepped to the podium. "Ladies and gentlemen, please welcome our keynote speaker, a national leader in sustainable infrastructure and civic equity—David Moss."

There was no applause. He stepped onto the stage, his pace measured, shoulders squared against the silence. He reached the podium. Looked down at his notes. Then up at the crowd.

David's voice came out strong, polished, with just enough downward tilt on the last word of each sentence to signal authority. The lights were low enough to obscure the crowd, and that helped. He could pretend they were leaning in, not recoiling.

Behind him, the massive screen lit up with the first slide: a rendering of the downtown wellness corridor in full conceptual bloom. Green canopy overlays, joggers smiling in slow-motion across a sculptural pedestrian bridge, a child frozen mid-laugh at the center of a splash pad that would never work as intended. The city, perfected in pixels.

"We're building healing environments," David said. "That's not just a phrase. That's a design mandate."

He moved the clicker. Another slide. A color-coded phasing map: Phase I complete, Phase II under construction, Phase III just permitted.

"The wellness corridor connects clinical care with everyday life," he said. "It's infrastructure that breathes. It's wellness embedded in the built form."

No one laughed. No one interrupted. He was flying.

What followed was the full narrative treatment. His best work. A looping video montage narrated in the baritone of a voice actor trained to sound credible at all volumes. Goldie was absent, of course. Bingham Park wasn't mentioned. The red sand did not appear.

Instead: drone footage over treetops. Renderings of "community-facing" meditation spaces. A shot of a young black couple walking hand-in-hand past a mural titled "Resilience, Reimagined", funded by the state arts trust and painted by an out-of-town collective who had never been south of Baltimore until that grant dropped.

David was in rhythm now. He'd hit his key turns, smoothed every pivot. He gestured precisely. Just enough to suggest passion under control.

"Public-private collaboration," he said, "is not just about resource sharing. It's about mutual authorship. We're not imposing.

We're co-creating." He said "co-creating" like he'd invented the word yesterday.

A few heads nodded. One woman near the front—badge from Seattle, notebook open—looked visibly relieved. She hadn't traveled across three time zones for moral ambiguity. She wanted innovation, delivered without friction.

Another slide. Health metrics. Smoothed curves and bar charts in colors that evoked trust.

David cleared his throat. Slowed the pace, softening to signal sincerity.

"Design is moral," he said. "That's our premise. That's our promise. When we shape space, we shape outcomes."

He paused. Looked out into the room with the expression he had cultivated over years of panels and luncheons. A blend of humility and foresight, like a man who had survived worse storms than this, and emerged better for it. Inside, a different sensation bloomed.

The guilt, if that's what it was, had been filed long ago. What remained was harder to name: a hollowness shaped like victory. Because this was, in a certain frame, a win. The project was alive. The funding intact. The controversy framed as noise in a broader narrative of long-term growth. And he had just given a perfect performance. Even now, he felt it. That exquisite sensation when the room begins to trust you again—not because you've earned it, but because you've made trusting you easier than resisting.

He clicked to the final slide: "A Model for the Future: Infrastructure as Remedy."

He stepped back. Applause followed, polite, sustained. Some rising from relief, some from obligation, a few from genuine assurance. David nodded once, humbly, as if he had not orchestrated the entire experience down to the millisecond. He returned to the head table, smile calibrated to charm. And for a moment, he believed it all over again.

A month passed and the city, as cities always do, resumed the task of forgetting. Not maliciously. With that peculiar civic rhythm known to bureaucrats and developers alike: the beat of the next thing. Attention shifted like the tide on the shoreline.

The morning Gale Clarey's follow-up article posted, the Observer led with a different story: a full-color photograph of the grim police chief standing beside a grieving widow, flanked by two city council members and a folding table stacked with canned Sprite and roses. The off-duty officer, shot two days earlier in a botched beer theft outside a corner store in East Market, had become the city's new narrative center. Talk of health equity and pre-regulatory contaminants could not compete with a widow in sunglasses.

And so the story of Parcel 524-B, the documents leak, the isotope matches to Bingham Park—those once-electrifying revelations had been pushed below the fold, then off the page altogether. Gale's latest dispatch ran online only, tucked beneath the local tab on the alt-weekly's increasingly sponsor-laden website. "The Plan Continues: Downtown Corridor Advances Despite Public Outcry." Few shared it. None of the council returned her calls.

It was not that the city refuted the evidence. The strategy was more elegant than denial. The documents, now indexed on a municipal file server behind password-protected layers, were classified under "Planning Considerations." The redlined phrases—"control optics", "downplay residuals", "community uplift framing"—were reinterpreted as early brainstorming, iterative thought. Nothing binding. Nothing criminal. Ideas, not policy. You can't prosecute a draft.

David Moss was back in Greensboro by then. The Washington conference had gone better than expected. There had been applause. Someone had quoted him in a LinkedIn post titled "Designing Trust in the Public Realm." He'd returned with a fresh haircut, more visible gray at the temples, and a small condo downtown—industrial chic, cement counters, concierge who called him "Mr. M". Paula had remained at the house. She'd asked for time, and so far, time was winning.

David didn't just survive the scandal. He metabolized it. Guilford Health System issued a quiet statement thanking him for his years of "unrivaled advisory excellence." The wellness corridor's community page scrubbed his name from the leadership bios, but internal emails still copied him when phrasing needed massaging. His number was still listed under "Priority Contacts". Everyone knew what that meant.

At City Hall, Phase III of the corridor passed with only Yvonne Hightower voting no. The same ribbon-cutting gestures. The same photo-ops with children. The signage still referenced "resilience" rather than "remediation." The term "cap and cover" entered the city's public vocabulary as casually as "stormwater management" had twenty years earlier. Capping and covering—that was the compromise. That was how cities healed: not by digging deep, but by sealing it in and building a story on top.

Bingham Park was next. The city announced its "Revive the Roots" campaign—public art, new mulch, an open-air amphitheater for spoken word events. A drone video was released, set to a lo-fi jazz loop, showing contractors in branded vests rolling synthetic turf over compacted red clay. The footage stopped before reaching the southern edge, where groundwater seeped up during heavy rain.

The contracts went to the usual firms. A familiar landscape designer. A PR firm based in Charlotte but "deeply invested in Greensboro's growth." People like David moved through this world without friction. Their crimes, if they existed, were below the surface. Invisible to the naked eye, but built into the foundation.

And Alan? His inbox, once volcanic, had gone quiet. The story had crested, then receded. The archive still existed, of course. Gale still wrote follow ups. Goldie still spoke at neighborhood meetings. But their voices now floated beneath the churn—ethical flotsam in a city that was scanning the horizon for its next federal grant.

Because the wheel never stops. The money flows where the renderings are glossy. And the public, conditioned like tired shoppers, prefers ribbon cuttings to reckoning.

22

The soil behind the church was stubborn. Dry in the top inch, too wet underneath, the kind of inconsistency that spoke to years of runoff and bad drainage and the silent fact that no one had ever hed enough money to grade it properly. Goldie knelt anyway, one knee pressed into the dirt, the other leg angled for balance as she dug the tip of her trowel into a pocket of resistance. The sun was already high enough to bake the concrete along the alley behind the old sanctuary, but here in the lot, ringed by chain-link and dusted with pollen, the light came in just right: filtered through the aged pecan tree and the side of the red brick church, slanted, warm, real.

"You don't want to crowd the roots," she told the girl beside her. "They'll tangle if you're not gentle. And then nothing grows but arguments."

The girl, maybe eight, maybe nine, looked at the small plastic pot in her hands like it held secrets. "Like when my brothers fight?"

"Exactly," Goldie said. "Same thing. Boys or flowers—you let 'em fight for space, you end up with bruises or stunted blooms."

The girl smiled and set the pot down beside a shallow hole already waiting.

A breeze passed, weak but welcome. From a nearby stoop, someone played a jazz ballad from WNAA on a Bluetooth speaker. It was Nina Simone's "Wild is the Wind":

Don't you know you're life itself
Like a leaf clings to a tree
Oh my darling, cling to me
For we're creatures of the wind
And wild is the wind
So wild is the wind

Goldie didn't look up. She pressed her hand into the earth, smoothed the lip of the hole, then reached for another starter plant.

The mural loomed behind them, just over the back wall, finished two days earlier and already tagged on local Instagrams by people who'd never set foot in the neighborhood before. A triangular prism in bold strokes, bursting outward in radiant bands of color. Each band carried names—some scrawled, some block printed. Names of asthma victims, stillbirths, and old men who'd died with no diagnosis but everyone knew anyway. Her name was there too. Between the red and the orange. Not a victim. Not a martyr. A witness.

The city had made its decision on Bingham Park. Twelve million to cap and cover. Thirty-five to clean. The choice had been framed as responsible stewardship of public funds. The mayor had used that exact phrase. Councilman Dent had called it "an opportunity to demonstrate practical compassion." Councilwoman Hoffman, face pulled taut with something that looked like fatigue but was probably calculation, had promised the new design would "honor the past while protecting the future."

Goldie had sat in the back of the council chamber and said nothing. She already knew how it would go. The math was always moral when the soil was bad and the voters were poor.

"You water the roots," she said now, handing the girl a dented tin can, "not the leaves. Don't waste it on what looks thirsty."

The girl nodded, eyes serious. Goldie sat back on her heels and looked at the row they'd planted—sunflowers, zinnias, a single row of marigolds along the back because they were cheap and hardy and looked like celebration if you didn't get too close.

Children ran between the rows with buckets and gloves too big for their hands. One boy tried to hold a shovel like a sword and got corrected by a teenager who'd shown up unprompted that morning, carrying a thermos of sweet tea and a folded tarp. Someone brought popsicles. Someone else brought more seedlings. No one mentioned the park. This was not the solution. She knew that. This was not the cleanup. This was not justice. But this was the work.

The dirt on her palms was real. The names on the wall were real. The children laughing through the chain-link were real. She pressed another starter into the soil, smoothed it, looked up.

"Good," she said. "That's it. Now keep going."

She saw him before the kids did—standing just beyond the garden's edge where the pavement met the grass, his hands in the pockets of a faded jacket, the kind of posture that said he wasn't sure if this counted as arriving or interrupting. Alan didn't wave. He nodded, the kind of gesture that existed somewhere between acknowledgment and apology.

"Professor!" one of the boys yelled, holding up a watering can like it was a trophy.

Alan smiled. "Just Alan," he called back, but the title stuck anyway. It always did.

Goldie rose slowly, brushing dirt from her knees. He met her halfway, stepping over a low stretch of chicken wire someone had looped around the flower bed. Up close, he looked tired in the way people look when the adrenaline has fully worn off but the world hasn't offered any reward for their trouble.

"Been a minute," she said.

"It has," he said. "You look well."

She looked down at her hands, still dusted with soil. "Health by dirt," she said. "The old medicine."

He laughed. "More effective than policy."

They stood in the heat for a moment, watching the kids resume their tasks, half-wild and barefoot and just right for the space they occupied. Someone had started dragging a hose from the church's side spigot and it was already knotting itself into chaos.

Alan turned toward the wall, where the prism mural burned against the cinderblock like stained glass. They stood side by side, the breeze finally arriving from the southwest, just enough to lift the hem of Goldie's shirt and scatter pollen over the mulch.

"It's striking," he said.

She nodded. "They gave it light without permission."

He narrowed his eyes at the prism. "Did you come up with it?"

"No, I gave them the names," she said. "The children gave it the shape."

The mural was vibrant in color but quiet in composition—bands that moved from violet to red to orange to a kind of wound-open gold, each shade carrying hand-painted names, each letter vibrating with the knowledge that someone had remembered on purpose.

"Some of them died slow," she said. "Some never got a diagnosis. Just disappeared into the data."

He didn't answer.

She kept going. "We didn't build this for permanence. Paint fades. The sun will eat it. Rain will wear it. Maybe that's the point."

"I tried to make it permanent," Alan said, softer. "The archive. The documents. I thought... if we just showed enough proof..."

"I know," she said.

They stood again in silence. The mural seemed to grow brighter, the heat pushing its pigments forward like something living.

"It's not a monument," she said finally. "It's a mirror. You look at it and remember what's already under you."

He turned to her then, brow furrowed. "Do you think it mattered?"

She tilted her head. "To them?" She nodded toward the kids, who were now spraying each other with the hose, ignoring every instruction. "Yes."

"To the city," he said.

"No," she said. "But cities don't remember. People do."

He looked down at the dirt on her hands. "You still believe in this."

"In what?"

"This," he said, gesturing toward the rows, the hose, the mural. "Work that doesn't scale."

Goldie smiled, not kindly but honestly. "Work that doesn't scale is the only kind that matters."

Behind them, the mural kept burning. Not with fire. With names. With color.

The church had once been a place of small voices and hand-fanned air, the kind of brick-and-board sanctuary that smelled of furniture polish and the past. But now, stepping through the side entrance, Alan felt something. The stale pull of doctrine had been replaced with movement, with breath. Light came in through old windows scrubbed clean, catching dust motes that danced like intention. The air was different here. It held memory without smothering it.

"This way," Goldie said, her voice quieter now, as if raised volume might startle something into flight.

They moved past the fellowship hall, past the folding chairs and the water cooler and the table where toddlers once colored while sermons were happening. Into the sanctuary proper, where the pews had been cleared, the pulpit dismantled, the altar left bare. What remained was space—open, full, pulsing with presence. And art. Everywhere, art.

The exhibit was called "Cottage Grove Remembers."

At the center of the space stood the prism—repeating wooden frames joined at angles, each surface strung with hundreds of colored beads, bottles hung from thread, bent wire encasing leadlight. When the sun drifted through the windows above, the prism shattered into spectrum, tossing ribbons of color across the floor, the walls, the faces of anyone who stood too near. Children had woven small charms into the strands: initials, beads painted with thumbprints, plastic rings from gumball machines repurposed into signifiers of something lasting.

Alan stood still, arrested not by the form but by the weight of attention it demanded. The light refracted not just in color, but in time.

To the left, a series of mixed-media portraits hung from pulleys. Each one told the story of a person gone or damaged—canvas embedded with fabric swatches, soil, printed photographs sewn into linen. A man who'd died of lung cancer at fifty-two, painted in blues and greys, his eyes replaced with mirrored shards. A teenage girl who miscarried at fifteen. Her portrait had no face, only her hands cupped in offering, the paint layered so thick in places it cracked like a dry field.

To the right, a sound installation. Headphones hung from carved hooks. A boy's voice counted out calendar days. A woman whispered stories in Gullah, too fast to follow, too beautiful to interrupt. Footsteps on gravel. Rain on metal. One track featured nothing but breath—long inhalations, followed by silence.

Above the doors, they had mounted three video loops on flatscreens. Footage from city council meetings, overdubbed with static and low thunder. Parcel maps slowly fading into body outlines. At regular intervals, the screens blinked white and then flared into deep red, as if the system had momentarily failed to contain itself. Goldie moved beside him, her palms open at her sides.

"The kids call it the spectrum room," she said. "Said the light looks like it's arguing with itself."

Alan turned in place, letting the light hit his eyes, color fraying against his vision.

They stopped in front of a sculpture made of hospital gowns and PVC piping, shaped like a tree split down the middle. One side pristine white. The other scorched black, the hem burned to a curl. On a small plaque: "For the ones who were told it was genetic."

"The science didn't change them," she said. "The knowing did."

He looked at her.

"Meaning's a form of survival," she added. "You give people something to hold and they start remembering forward."

"Do you think it'll last?" he asked.

"No," she said. "But it's the truth."

Alan looked again at the prism. How it fractured the sun, how it made the room feel full just by holding and scattering light. Outside, children played in the sun. Names clung to walls. Colors shifted. They stood there, in that old, re-formed space, where no shepherd watched but something holy pulsed all the same. Light moved through fabric, through pigmented glass, through air, and became something more than its parts.

Jeff Sykes is a native of Forsyth County, N.C. He graduated from WCU and became a newspaper reporter and editor, winning press awards in North Carolina and Virginia. As a child, Jeff wrote poems and lyrics and pursued songwriting as a young adult. Since 2014, he's focused on fiction writing, publishing the novella, Another Form of Prayer, and the short story collection Touch Your Defenses.

Follow Jeff on social media via **@byjeffsykes** on multiple platforms. Visit www.jeffsykes.com to sign up for his website and mailing list.

www.ingramcontent.com/pod-product-compliance
Lightning Source LLC
LaVergne TN
LVHW041739060526
838201LV00046B/860